KATERINA DIAMOND bur

with her debut novel *The Teacher*, which became a *Sunday Times* bestseller and a number 1 Kindle bestseller. It was longlisted for the CWA John Creasey Debut Dagger Award and the Hotel Chocolat Award for 'darkest moment'. Her second novel, *The Secret*, became a number 1 Kindle bestseller too and received widespread acclaim. Having lived in various glamorous locations such as Weston-super-Mare, Thessaloniki, Larnaca, Exeter, Derby and Forest Gate, Katerina now resides in East Kent with her husband and children. She was born on Friday 13th.

By the same author:

The Teacher
The Secret

The Angel

KATERINA DIAMOND

avon.

AVON

A division of HarperCollins*Publishers*
1 London Bridge Street,
London SE1 9GF

www.harpercollins.co.uk

A Paperback Original 2017

5

A catalogue record for this book is available from the British Library

ISBN-13: 978-0-00-820913-1
ISBN TPB: 978-0-00-824811-6

Typeset in Sabon LT Std by Palimpsest Book Production Ltd, Falkirk, Stirlingshire

Printed and bound in Great Britain by
CPI Group (UK) Ltd, Croydon CR0 4YY

MIX
Paper from responsible sources
FSC® C007454

FSC™ is a non-profit international organisation established to promote the responsible management of the world's forests. Products carrying the FSC label are independently certified to assure consumers that they come from forests that are managed to meet the social, economic and ecological needs of present and future generations, and other controlled sources.

Find out more about HarperCollins and the environment at
www.harpercollins.co.uk/green

To Oliver,
Work hard and stay out of prison. Love Mum x

Prologue

1986

The snow had clogged the driveway and most of the village too. Since the morning, it had been relentless even though the news had only predicted a mild flurry. Martina looked outside at the road; it was thick with it, crisp and untouched; an idyllic prison. The neighbour's Christmas tree was abandoned by the bins. The binmen had refused to take it week after week, but belligerent old Murray left it there as a point of protest. Even the rubbish looked pretty when it was covered in snow.

She wondered how long she had before the baby woke up. He would be hungry when he did and she was out of formula. Her husband was trapped at work and she couldn't be without the formula when Jamie woke up. There would be no going to the shops; she doubted most of them were even open.

Martina threw another log on the fire; even though it wasn't cold inside the house, she loved the feeling of security the flames gave her. The fire kept her company when she was alone, when the baby was asleep. Her husband had been stuck at work more times than she could remember; since she had had the baby she was almost certain he was having an affair. She was always aware that she was a trophy wife in the first place and she had lost her sparkle in the last year or so; pregnancy had almost destroyed her and post-partum depression was finishing the job. She just hadn't expected it to be this hard, this lonely. She picked up the red Bakelite phone she'd got for Christmas and dialled the neighbours.

Charlie and Sophia had been their next-door-but-one neighbours for the last three years and in that time they had become close. Martina and Sophie had gone through their pregnancies together.

Charlie answered the phone.

'Hi Charlie.'

'Martina? Is everything all right?' His voice was a whisper.

'Sorry, did I disturb you?'

'No, it's just Soph has the flu, she's asleep and I don't want to wake her up.'

'Oh, I was just wondering if you had any formula I could borrow, I'm all out and when bub wakes up I'm going to be in trouble.'

'Yeah we have an extra tin . . . I'll bring some over . . . hang on.' His voice tailed off.

'What's wrong?'

'Just thinking I should probably bring the little 'un with me, Soph's in no condition to deal with him.'

'Have you eaten?' Martina asked. 'I'll do you a trade – grown-up food for baby food?'

'That sounds brilliant, are you sure?'

'It's just me and the baby here, you'll be doing me a huge favour so it's the least I can do.'

'OK, give me half an hour to sort some soup out for Soph and feed the baby, then I'll be over.'

'See you then.'

Martina poured the Badedas into the water and watched as it bubbled. Why was she having a bath? She was excited at the prospect of Charlie coming over on his own, but she felt guilty for it. This was probably the first time she had thought of Charlie as a man, usually he was just Sophie's husband, the neighbour, but the idea of seeing him without Sophie had separated him somehow: now he was just Charlie.

She put some rollers in her hair, she'd only washed it yesterday, so hopefully it would hold the style better. She was making herself pretty for a man who wasn't her husband. It was his own fault; he had made her feel ugly, both during the pregnancy and since the baby had been born. She knew she wasn't ugly and so maybe this flirtation would be enough to boost her confidence, encourage her to start making an effort again. She sprayed herself with Opium and opted for a green chiffon dress; the red was maybe a little too daring but the green made her brown eyes look like creamy dark chocolate. She looked at herself in the mirror and reached for the lipstick that was the right colour for her; she had read in *Cosmo* that you should wear a lipstick the same colour as your nipples if you wanted to attract someone – as if they would even know, but the user surveys assured her it worked.

The doorbell rang and Martina answered it, her heart beating fast. It was still glowing outside even though the sun had gone down, the snow reflecting the street lamps. Satisfaction crept over Martina as she saw a flicker in Charlie's eye, a recognition that she was a beautiful woman. She hadn't seen that look for a while, least of all from her husband. He handed her the baby formula. She looked at the tin in her hand, confused for a moment, almost forgetting why she had invited him over. Smiling, she walked inside, leaving the door open and without even asking the question. She put the formula next to the sink and turned to see Charlie standing behind her, a little too close. She could see him concentrating on making sure his eyes stayed fixed on her face; no glancing down.

'Would you like some wine?'

'Yes please, that sounds perfect. Can I put the baby down somewhere? He's just nodded off.'

'Sure, put him in the cot with Jamie.'

Charlie disappeared upstairs and Martina adjusted her breasts, undoing one more button on her dress. She took the roasted chicken she had made in the afternoon out of the oven and placed it on the table, then set the table for two and took a bottle of white wine out of the fridge.

Charlie appeared again and smoothed down his

trousers nervously before sitting at the table. Martina served him some salad and a leg of chicken while he poured the wine for them both. She cleared her throat. This felt like a date, which hadn't really been her intention. Or had it?

She tried to think about Sophie laid up in bed, or her husband stuck at work, kept away by the snow. The smaller villages outside the city were never really a priority for the salt that the council sometimes provided to keep the roads clear.

They ate together, making small talk while the babies remained asleep. Martina opened a second bottle of wine, aware that she was feeling tipsy, a welcome warmth in her belly that only came when she was drunk. It had been so long since she had relaxed, it hadn't even occurred to her before how tense she felt usually. Being in a conversation with a different man awakened her to how bad the conversations she had with her husband were, with him always making her feel stupid or shutting her down before she had even started.

His obsession with their son had taken over their lives; she had become someone who only existed to make sure the baby got everything he needed. She didn't begrudge Jamie, but she did begrudge the change he had made in her husband – who was now only ever interested in the world as it affected his son. It was as though it were the first time he was feeling love, and the intensity of that had driven him slightly insane. She wondered what he had felt for her, if his professions of love were more to do with lust and the fact that she was desired by others.

She needed to shake this feeling; she needed Charlie to leave. It was closing in on eight o'clock and somehow this had become something real, something dangerous. As they finished the second bottle of wine she caught Charlie looking at her; within half an hour she had seen his eyes rest on her knee, her breasts, her eyes and now her mouth. Slowly, he leaned forward to kiss her, she leaned in too and they met halfway. The line had been crossed, now there was nothing to stop them as they moved in clumsily, crashing into each other, standing and pawing at the buttons and zips, frantically searching for a way to an intimate connection.

As Martina's dress dropped to the ground she felt the wetness of Charlie's lips on her breasts; unfamiliar, not her husband's, not better or worse, just different. She couldn't pretend she was the faithful one anymore, though she was aware that her husband wasn't innocent. Maybe he was snuggled in front of a different fire with some other woman right now. She refused to feel bad. He showed her no affection and so this was his fault. That's what she would keep telling herself anyway.

Charlie moved with her and against her; this was the first time she'd had intercourse since the baby, it had been months and it felt good. She was an attractive woman, a mantra she told herself every time her husband grunted at a new outfit she wore, a new haircut, new lingerie. She had ceased to exist for him, it was just the baby and whoever else he was seeing behind her back. He would never know about this though. This would be her little secret.

She wouldn't do it again, she told herself. She would

knock this on the head straight away. If her husband ever found out about Charlie she would be in big trouble and he would probably kill him. She had seen him do things that had shocked and repulsed her, his assurances that they were unusual instances rang less and less true each time. She pushed thoughts of her husband aside and dragged Charlie towards the sofa, sitting down while he climbed on top. The way his hands grabbed at her, the way he pushed her back and moved her legs so he could climb between them, it was all different.

Charlie was frantic now, her nails dug into his back and he buried his mouth in her neck as he moved faster. She had never been with another man before and she was surprised at how good it felt. They crashed together until finally he let out a groan. Almost simultaneously, the baby started crying. Charlie collapsed onto her and they both laughed. For her it was a nervous laugh, it was the acknowledgment that they were back in the present and they had done something unforgivable. After a minute or two, Charlie climbed off her and pulled his trousers on properly, surveying the floor for his shirt. She could tell he was shocked; he hadn't come over here with this in mind. Now it had happened there was no reversing it.

'That's yours,' she said.

'Excuse me?' he answered, his face flushed, the full weight of his guilt now evident.

'That's not Jamie's cry.'

'Oh . . . OK.' Grateful, she assumed, for the distraction, he pulled his boots on and rushed upstairs. She took the opportunity to search for her own clothes, buttoning her chiffon dress up quickly.

'Martina! Oh, my God, Martina!' Charlie's voice rang out over his baby's cries.

'What?' She ran up the stairs and into the baby's room. Charlie was holding his child, staring into the cot in horror. The look on his face told her everything she needed to know. Before she even looked inside, she was holding her breath. Jamie, her little boy, the child she and her husband had so desperately wanted, was blue. Her heart stopped.

'What do I do?'

Charlie handed her his own son and took Jamie out of the cot, rushing to the bathroom. 'Call an ambulance,' he shouted. She ran upstairs with the phone in time to see Charlie run warm water into the bath. He lay Jamie in the tub and scooped warm water over him until he warmed up, then pulled his little body out of the bath and wrapped a towel around him, massaging his chest. Within moments, Jamie was crying again. It wasn't his usual cry though. It was a soft, tentative cry. She felt so helpless.

It wasn't long before they heard the sirens; nothing got the ambulance moving faster than a baby in distress and not even snow could stop them, there were chains on the tyres. Charlie was covered in water and Martina just stood there helplessly, watching as two paramedics wrapped her child in blankets and hurried him out to the ambulance.

'Is he OK? Is my baby OK?' she said frantically.

'We need to get him assessed properly, it depends

how long he was without oxygen. There may be permanent brain damage, but it's impossible to know at this point.' One of the paramedics made eye contact with her, the other wouldn't meet her gaze.

Charlie grabbed his son and followed as Martina hastily did the rest of her dress buttons up and grabbed her coat. That's when she saw her husband's car, pulling into the drive just as the paramedics got in the back of the ambulance. One of them offered her a hand to bring her inside too. She saw her husband get out of the car and approach them, saw his confused gaze as his eyes wandered over her dress. She looked down and saw she had buttoned it wrong – he then looked at Charlie, his trousers hanging from his hips, shirt half untucked, no ambiguity about what had been going on.

'Martina? What the fuck is going on?'

'I'm so sorry, it's Jamie, he stopped breathing!'

'Are you coming with us, ma'am? We really need to get going. He was without oxygen for at least a couple of minutes, he needs to see one of the doctors ASAP,' the paramedic's voice was urgent. Martina saw panic flood her husband's face.

'No, I'll come,' he said, stepping in front of Martina as though she wasn't even there.

'I'm sorry! I didn't mean for this to happen!' she cried, tears streaming down her face, knowing full well that he knew what she had done.

'Mate . . .' Charlie looked at his feet.

'I'll deal with both of you later!' He clambered up into the ambulance and pulled the door shut.

Martina watched as the ambulance pulled away. Just

at that moment Charlie's son started to cry, a normal cry, a baby out in the snow cry. She couldn't look at him. She ran back inside, slamming the door. She couldn't let Charlie back in the house, not now.

The phone rang and Martina answered. It was her husband.

'Is he OK?'

'I want you out of the house by the time we get home. I never want to see your face again.'

'But . . . it was an accident.'

'I know what happened. I know what you did. It was obvious from the state of you both.'

'I was lonely. I know it's no excuse but since Jamie was born you have made me feel worthless. I just wanted to feel special for one night. I didn't mean for that to happen, you must know I didn't!'

'And that makes it OK?'

'No, of course it doesn't.'

'He's in intensive care at the moment. I want you to know if he doesn't pull through, your life won't be worth living.'

'Please . . .'

'Both of you will wish you were dead.' He put the phone down.

She knew that he wasn't one to make idle threats, she had seen him do things that other women would have run a mile from. She knew a dark side of him that most people didn't see. It had excited her at the beginning; the way some people would look when he walked into a pub or a club, the way people backed away from him and feared him. The time he had shoved a broken bottle into the face of a man in the street who was rude to Martina had been the moment she knew he was the one. No one had ever defended her like that before. He wouldn't let this go.

She grabbed her Valium from the bathroom cabinet and a bottle of gin from the kitchen. She couldn't live without her son, she couldn't live knowing she hadn't been there when he needed her the most, knowing that while her son lay almost lifeless in the room upstairs she was having a meaningless encounter with a man she wasn't even particularly attracted to. Her husband had made it clear that she wouldn't be a part of Jamie's life anymore and so she took the pills one by one with a swig of gin. She was already fairly drunk from the wine at dinner, and it was an easy decision to make; barely a decision at all. She drifted away on her terms, wanting her husband to feel the pain of her loss. She wanted him to feel bad for speaking to her that way, she wanted him to feel as though he should have come home in time to wake her. She wanted him to feel like this was his fault. This time, she would have the last word.

Chapter 1

2017

Gabriel Webb was a killer. He didn't know it yet, but before the day was out he would know what it felt like to take someone's life. He turned the music up in his bedroom to drown out the sound of his parents arguing about him. Apparently, he was 'out of control' and 'needed to be taken in hand'. His mother had suggested sending him to live with an aunt in Cheltenham. His father had suggested forcing him to join the army, which 'might show him how good he had it at home'. All this because Gabriel had shoulder-length hair and occasionally wore eyeliner.

He pulled on his red tartan punk trousers and leather New Rock boots, feeding the laces through the chrome shin panels on the front. Searching through his tops, he tried to decide which one to wear today, which one would be best for what they had planned. His phone beeped and he looked at the screen. An array of emojis all signifying excitement from his girlfriend Emma, listed in his phone as Proserpina, Roman Goddess and Queen of the underworld. He was in her phone as Pluto, the God of Death. Embracing darkness was part of the fun of being a goth. Tonight, they were going to see Apocalyptica, a nu-metal band, in a local club, a rare occurrence in Exeter now that the artisan hipster gin bars had all but taken over the city.

Gabriel pulled on his black wet-look cycling top; it hugged his lean muscular frame and he loved the way Emma looked at him when he was in it. He would catch her eyes resting on his chest as she swallowed hard, suppressing whatever desire his body aroused in her until they were alone. He grabbed the black buckled leather cincher out of his wardrobe and put it on, despite his parents' voices echoing in his head. *A man in a corset? Ridiculous*. It wasn't like it pulled his waist in or anything, it was just a fashion statement – not a nod to his sexuality. He couldn't worry about what his parents thought though. His clothes were an expression of himself, for himself. It wasn't about shocking anyone or even about rebelling. It was about feeling good in his skin, and this outfit made Gabriel feel good. He wrapped black electrical tape around his wrists and hands, then picked up the black eyeliner and drew a star on his left cheek. He was ready.

On entering the kitchen, his mother took a deep breath and turned her attention to the kitchen sink. Avoiding being a part of the conversation that was about to happen.

'What the hell are you wearing?' Michael Webb, Gabriel's father, had an expression like thunder, but that wasn't unusual, it was the standard greeting these days.

'Clothes.' Gabriel grabbed an apple and started to eat it. He had a foot on his father, but he was still uneasy. He wouldn't say what he wanted to say, he never did. It was always better just to let his father rant and then leave anyway.

'You're a bloody man – when are you going to start acting like one?' his father sniped. 'Who's going to employ you looking like that? You're nineteen years old for God's sake. Isn't it time to grow up?'

'A job like yours, you mean?' Gabriel said. 'I should be a drone?'

'My drone job pays for those god-awful trousers you are wearing! I mean what the hell are all those straps and chain things hanging down? What kind of message do you think you're putting across with those?' His father tugged hard at the cord that linked the trousers together, ripping it. He looked at Gabriel with a sneer.

Gabriel smiled back with a pinched mouth. He was contemplating punching his father in the face – and not for the first time.

'Anything else?' He leaned down closer to his father, locking eyes with him – making sure he didn't look away first.

The anger in his father's eyes faltered for a moment.

'Don't even get me started on your face. Men don't wear make-up, and what's with the star? You look like a fucking communist.'

'Michael! Language!' Gabriel's mother Penny said.

'I'm off to meet some friends, I'll probably stay out tonight.' Gabriel walked out, shaking his head, his father's insults getting fainter as he got further from the house. It was the most disrespectful he had ever been but he couldn't tolerate this nonsense today. He was in a good mood and he wasn't going to let his father ruin it. He was going to see Emma; he had texted her before he left, so she should be waiting outside. She lived three streets over. He had first seen her working in his local supermarket sometimes at the weekends, she'd always stood a little straighter when he walked past and so he knew she had seen him too. One day he just asked her out; she had said yes immediately and the rest was history.

Emma was standing outside her house with her new friend, Leanne. He saw Emma's eyes light up as she saw him approaching, sucking in her breath in a way that turned him on. He knew what she was thinking about as she glanced at his body for a split second. He was thinking about it too. There had always been a certain electricity between them, he felt an involuntary breathlessness around her that only abated when they were locked together. He was always anticipating the next kiss.

'You changed your hair again.' He pointed to her roots which were a neon red, the rest a trailing black tangle down her back. She chewed on the back of her labret lip piercing and smiled at Gabriel. Leanne was obviously clueless about personal boundaries as she hung onto Emma's arm. Emma's eyes said *later* and he found himself excited at being forced to wait.

'We're going to go meet Leanne's mates, they're coming too.'

Gabriel didn't know Leanne well but she had attached herself to Emma lately. They worked together at Tesco on Saturdays. Together, the three of them walked up through Heavitree and past the bus station. They kept walking, past the town, up towards the prison and beyond that, to the fencing that separated the railway tracks from the road, keeping local kids and cats from sliding down the bank and wandering into the path of an oncoming train.

It had started to spit. As they approached the fence, Gabriel saw two guys in their late teens standing waiting for them, hoods pulled up against the rain. Leanne yanked up some of the chicken wire fencing and disappeared behind it. Gabriel and Emma followed. The disused signal box near Exeter Central station was a known hangout for some of the less savoury characters that Leanne was friends with. As they made their way down, Gabriel heard a commotion and the sound of glass smashing; he was kind of excited at the rebelliousness of it all. In Gabriel's eyes, the only thing worse than being bored was listening to his parents either fighting or fucking. Tonight was going to be far from boring, he would make sure of it.

Gabriel had seen the boys by the tracks in town before; they were Laners. Laners were the scum of the city as far as most people were concerned. Burnthouse Lane had a reputation for being home to some of the more violent members of local society. Between the ASBOs and the muggings there was little love left for the Laners. The kids were left to fend for themselves and the adults just did what they wanted. There was no community feel to the Lane, except among the teens. Several of the boys claimed to be the offspring of the Sly crew, the firm of football thugs that supported Exeter FC and made a name for themselves in the eighties. The Sly crew were not only well known for their random acts of violence, but also their almost myth-like status. None of the teens were sure if they had ever actually existed or not, which somehow made them even more terrifying to boys like Gabriel growing up. Everyone from the Lane had a story about the Sly crew, usually exaggerated to the point where they had witnessed a murder or were owed a massive favour that they could call in at any time.

Inside, the signal box was set up like an office, with all the levers chained to the wall, although most likely no longer connected to the tracks. There were three large chairs facing the centre and various wrappers, bottles, needles and other rubbish lying around the place. Gabriel stayed standing, aware that they may need to start running at any moment if anyone figured out they were in there. Emma wrapped her arms around herself, rubbing her arms as though she was cold and huddling up on a chair, crossing her legs to stay warmer.

'This is Trey and this is Chris.' Leanne pointed at her friends, who took the other two chairs. 'Fucking hell, it's freezing in here!'

Gabriel didn't like the way the boys were looking at Emma, as though she were somehow there for their entertainment. He hated the idea that just because she wore a short skirt and fishnets that somehow that was for anyone other than herself. It was a mindset that people who weren't part of the alternative scene didn't appreciate. You dress for yourself. It would never occur to Gabriel to tell Emma what to wear and yet she had the same problem with her parents that he had with his. Today, she was wearing a very short black denim miniskirt with a bustle, fishnet tights and knee-high boots. He could see what these boys were thinking. They were making assumptions about the kind of things Emma would or would not do just because she wore black leather and studs. Gabriel hated people sometimes.

Emma shifted uncomfortably in her chair. Gabriel wished he had a coat he could take off and give to her.

One of the boys pulled out a crack pipe and Gabriel clenched his teeth. Why the hell were they here? This was a little more rebellion than he liked to engage in. Gabriel had smoked weed a few times, he had even had some skunk, but this stuff? No, this was not his place at all. People often assumed Gabriel was on something because he was so slim and he had long hair, and because he sometimes wore make-up; it was just the way people operated. They made assumptions. But this really wasn't Gabriel's idea of fun.

Emma looked up at Gabriel with an apologetic face. She knew how much he hated these kinds of people.

The Laners grunted and looked Gabriel up and down.

'Want some?' One of them held the black, stained pipe out towards Gabriel.

'No thanks,' he replied.

'Are you going to be a problem?' the other man said.

Gabriel looked at him more closely; the name Trey was tattooed on his neck. Gabriel shook his head slightly and watched as Trey twirled the glass pipe in between his fingers, a smile on his face.

'It's fucking Baltic in here,' the one who Gabriel now supposed must be Chris said, rubbing his hands together.

Trey dropped a few rocks of crack into the pipe and sucked in a couple of deep breaths as though he were about to dive into the sea before putting his lips to the edge of the pipe. He held the lighter under the glass bowl and gently rolled the glass stem in his fingers as he slowly drew the milky smoke into his lungs. His expression changed and he sat back in his chair. Chris took the pipe from him. Gabriel noticed that Leanne was watching Emma the whole time, obviously trying to gauge her reaction to this, to see if she was open to it. He saw her shiver again.

'We should go. It's freezing in here,' Gabriel said, stepping closer to his girlfriend. The sun was going down and he didn't fancy crossing the tracks in the dark, plus he really didn't want to be here with these people any longer.

'Killjoy.' Leanne grinned, her face like a viper.

'It's OK. We'll go in a bit.' Emma smiled at Gabriel. He noticed how people were different with each other; Emma behaved differently when they were alone, she behaved differently with her family too and she was definitely behaving differently here with Leanne. This behaviour didn't feel like her, it was a side he hadn't seen before. A tapping sound echoed against the window as the rain began.

'It's starting to chuck it down,' Gabriel said, looking

at Emma hopefully, trying to impart to her his strong desire to leave. She just shifted her gaze away.

'Why don't you see if you can warm it up in here?' Leanne asked him, it was a challenge, a threat maybe; there was something about her that made Gabriel really uneasy and it seemed amplified in here.

Gabriel went to the corner and grabbed the metal waste paper bin that had been left in the signal box. He didn't want to cause a fuss; maybe his argument with his father earlier had made him extra defensive, maybe he wasn't thinking straight. He collected some of the rubbish from the floor and piled it in before picking up one of Trey's lighters from the table and snapping the head off.

'What the hell are you doing?' Trey said.

Gabriel tipped the fluid from the lighter into the bin and then picked another lighter from the table. He found himself trying to prove something to Leanne; she had a way about her that made him feel impotent, it explained why Emma was the way she was around her.

'Don't break them all!' Chris said, holding the crack pipe in his hands, menace in his voice.

Gabriel lit the edge of a piece of card and threw it into the bin. It ignited immediately. He concentrated on the flames, hoping this part of the evening would be over soon enough. He felt strangely vulnerable. Something terrible was going to happen.

Chapter 2

DS Adrian Miles held his hand out to his partner DS Imogen Grey to help her over the railway sleeper, his other hand lighting up the wet ground with the torch app on his mobile phone. Imogen tutted and stepped over the sleeper without assistance, trudging off ahead. They walked along the side of the tracks until they got to the burnt-out signal box which was illuminated by the lights on the fire truck. There was no more smoke now; it was a dripping carcass of a building.

'You look nice, Grey,' Adrian said as his torch beam hit Imogen's face. He instinctively stepped out of her reach as he complimented her. She had her hair up and lipstick on; tonight must have been a special occasion. He by contrast had been lying on his sofa watching old episodes of *Star Trek* when they got the call.

'I was out to dinner.'

'Wow, that sounds so grown-up.'

'Shut up, Miley.'

The fact was, it was good to see Imogen like this. Her mother had not long woken from a coma and, within a few weeks, had left to go on a 'restful' holiday, leaving Imogen with only guilt that she hadn't protected her, that the attack on her towards the end of their last police case was somehow Imogen's fault. She was often distracted by it at work, but Adrian knew better than to mention it, he had to trust that she would know she could confide in him if she needed to.

'Is Dean all right? Behaving himself?' Adrian asked, checking there were no uniformed officers listening in. Despite all of Adrian's predictions to the contrary, Imogen and Dean were still together. Even with Dean's sketchy history, something he'd apparently assured Imogen was in the past, they had managed to make it work. It wasn't illegal to date an ex-con but it certainly wasn't looked on favourably. At some point, they would have to declare it, which would mean even more scrutiny from the higher-ups, something Adrian could do without.

'He's good.' She looked down and smiled. 'It's his birthday, so we went out for a curry.'

'Wise not to subject him to too much of your cooking if you want to keep him around.'

'It's not my fault that mushroom risotto got burned,' she protested.

'I was impressed, I didn't know you could burn anything in a microwave, let alone soggy rice.'

A firefighter walked over to them, cutting through the darkness of the night.

'Looks pretty serious,' Adrian said. The firefighter nodded.

The train station manager was approaching down from the platform with a quickened pace; he had probably been dragged in from home as well.

'Officers,' he said, nodding at them both.

'Follow me,' the firefighter said, beckoning them towards the ruined signal box. They got to the foot of the building; the wooden staircase was completely gone, as was the entire top floor.

'Deliberate?' Adrian asked, pulling out his notebook.

'We've had a lot of trouble with kids and homeless people breaking into this one in the past,' the station manager offered. 'Until the investigation is complete we can't say for sure, but it definitely looks that way. Even though this is old wood it's a rainy night, and from the calls we got, it escalated to disproportionate levels for what we would expect from a building like this. There does seem to be some evidence of accelerant.'

'Do you think it's arson then?' Adrian asked him.

'I'm leaning that way. The point of origin seems to be a waste paper bin, but we'll need to check that out further.'

'Do you have any CCTV footage?' Imogen turned to the station manager.

'We do. My colleague is just retrieving it for you now. It's a poorly lit area and with the terrible weather the visibility will be even crappier, not to mention the fact that it was actually night when whoever it was came out. It's possible that when the arsonist was leaving some of the station lights or the lights on the bridge illuminated the area a little better though.'

'Did they not tell you the main reason you're here?' the firefighter asked, looking between them curiously.

'What do you mean?' Adrian asked.

'We found a body.'

Imogen and Adrian looked at each other.

'You probably should have led with that,' Imogen said crossly.

'The fire started in the upstairs part of the building but the body was in the room with the mechanics on the ground floor. Probably male, possibly homeless, but that's really a wild guess as the body is so badly damaged. It's most likely he snuck in here for a kip or something. They come into the bottom of the building because there are no windows. It happens all the time. We'll know more when the investigators have done a proper search and you get your pathologist down to the site to have a look before the body is moved.'

They made their way forwards, the firefighter handed them hard hats although it seemed unnecessary as there was nothing above them anymore, the ceiling and roof had been completely burnt through. Adrian started picking through the rubble of the structure. The floor was burned, the machinery charred black and as their eyes adjusted, they could make out a human-being-shaped pile of debris. The firefighter shone a light at the ground.

The station manager gagged and crumpled forwards at the sight of the body. Imogen looked at Adrian who gave a nod.

'Show me the CCTV,' Imogen said to the station manager before following him back out towards the platform, leaving Adrian to deal with the body.

Adrian bent down and looked at the ground. The body was contorted, almost in a foetal position, crisp and delicate, with obvious fracture points where the entire floor had caved in on top of it, smashing the skull to smithereens. What was previously the floor now lay around the body in charred splinters, the wood had been so dry it had almost entirely burnt away. He shone his torch upwards to see the smouldering hole where the fire had torn through the roof and exposed the inky sky overhead. Back on the ground he noticed debris, rat droppings, chunks of wet, singed wood. It was like staring at a black and white TV, everything in monochrome, various shades of grey. Dark wet ash, light dry ash, everything covered in some variant of grey dust. Even the red-brick walls were blackened with soot.

The crime scene technicians approached and Adrian took a couple of markers, the bright yellow practically glowing against the dirge of this tiny burnt-out structure. He focussed on the shape of the body, the hands shrivelled into claws. Adrian shuddered at the thought of the man, hiding in here from the cold when the fire broke out.

'How long does it take for a body to get like that?' Adrian asked the crime scene technician once he'd checked that Imogen had taken the station manager a safe distance away.

'It really depends on how hot it got in here. It's a small space and fairly well insulated despite the broken glass upstairs. There's a lot of metal in here too, which would have added to the intensity of the heat. I spoke to one of the firefighters and he said it was at least forty-five minutes before they made it down here onto the tracks safely. It's out of view, and although there aren't many trains at this time of night, a lot of calls had to be made before they could access the building. It's a tricky spot to get to as well. And who knows how long it was burning before anyone noticed, the CCTV footage should be able to tell you more.'

'Will we be able to get DNA from the body?' Adrian had taken out his notebook and was scribbling as the technician talked.

'I can't say at this stage, I'm sorry. It really depends on a variety of factors. We'll know more when we get the remains back to the lab.'

'Thank you.' Adrian closed his notebook and walked back to find Imogen. He felt strange walking alongside the tracks, remembering his mother's old obsession with the fact that this was probably how he would die. Growing up, their house had backed onto the lines at Exeter St Thomas station, and every time he left the house she would warn him not to play about on the tracks. The trains had been delayed tonight, so he knew he was safe. Still, this felt like an act of betrayal.

Adrian stepped into the railway office and saw Imogen sitting with the station manager, going through the CCTV footage of that night. He went over to them and sat down, wanting a closer look at the screen. They were rewinding back from the fire. Five figures came out of the signal box, two wearing hoodies. They looked like males, probably teenagers. The rain was coming down. Adrian could see a girl with a baseball cap on, but there was no clear shot of her face, and another girl who was wearing a short skirt and had a newspaper covering her head. There was a young man with her, holding her hand and helping her down the stairs. He was tall, with shoulder-length dark hair obscuring his face and clearly alternative clothing.

'We'll never get an ID from that picture.'

Imogen spun around on her chair to face him. 'There's not many places for the alternative crowd to go around here, Miley. I think I know where we can start looking.'

Chapter 3

Imogen showed the girl on the door of the nightclub her police ID and was waved forward into the club. She felt a rush of adrenaline as they entered; this was her thing, this was who she used to be. It was hard to rebel against her flighty mother when Imogen was a teen. Irene Grey would waft around wearing bright, multi-layered skirts and cardigans, smoking pot and occasionally flashing the neighbours as an act of protest. When Imogen was small her mother had insisted on dressing her in much the same way. As soon as Imogen could, she'd started wearing a pair of baggy black skater pants and a hoodie, partly to fade into the background, but also to make sure everyone knew that she was nothing like her mother. She would go to the local goth clubs, and her mother became increasingly concerned that she was exhibiting the same mental health issues that she had. The opposite was the truth; Imogen was just trying to pull away from Irene, to become an individual in her own right.

She tugged now at the clip in her hair and let it fall onto her shoulders. For the first time in a long time she felt like a traitor, slightly uncomfortable being here on duty. Here to disrupt the enjoyment rather than take part in it. The goths she had known were all quite anti-authority. She tousled her hair a little and clocked Adrian staring at her curiously. She doubted he had ever set foot in a place like this in his life. Girls in short skirts, corsets, excessive theatrical make-up. Men in motorcycle masks, tight-fitting clothing and eyeliner. There were a few people who didn't fit into either category at a cursory glance.

'How did you know about this?' Adrian shouted to her above the music.

'I know lots of things. Besides, I was going to come anyway, the band they have on tonight are pretty decent.'

'You like this?'

'Oh yeah, I like this.'

Adrian nodded to the bar; Imogen looked over and saw a tall man waiting to order drinks. He had shoulder-length hair, and was dressed in the same way as the man they had seen on the CCTV footage. He had the same red tartan punk trousers on, also known as bondage trousers, with straps that crossed and clipped to the opposing legs, expensive and distinctive. His hair was tucked behind his ears. Imogen looked him up and down. He looked the right height and build for the man in the video. He turned toward them and met Imogen's gaze, she flushed a little. She composed herself before walking over to him and flashing her ID.

'Can we have a word?' she asked.

The man looked at the ID, he seemed a little confused but not alarmed. He necked his drink and followed them both into the lobby.

'I'm DS Imogen Grey and this is my partner, DS Adrian Miles.'

'Gabriel Webb.' He held his hand out, Imogen took it and shook it. He was very direct and seemed both polite and unfazed by this interaction.

'Can I ask where you were this evening?'

'With some mates. Around.'

'We have CCTV of you leaving a signal box.'

'Right, yeah, I was there.' He brushed his hair out of his eyes.

'Who were you with?' Adrian asked.

'Why?' Gabriel Webb narrowed his eyes. He didn't seem like someone with something to hide.

'Did you perhaps start a fire inside the signal box?' Imogen asked, hoping to God he said no. Perhaps he had no idea at all about the man in the room below in the signal box. The repercussions of this were bigger than anyone his age should have to deal with. Despite his height, he had a young face; he couldn't have been much older than eighteen. She wanted to send him home, before his world got turned upside down. It was always hardest with the young ones.

'In the bin, yeah, but it burnt out before we left. Who told you that?'

'Where are your friends now? Are they here?'

'There's something you're not telling me, isn't there?' Gabriel's pale face looked even more ghostly than before as the gravity of the situation started to dawn on him.

'I'm not implicating anyone else until I know what's going on.'

'We're going to need you to come to the station with us,' Adrian said gravely. He made eye contact with Imogen, and she knew what he was thinking. They were potentially about to ruin this kid's life.

'I'm going to have to call some officers to come and interview the people here if you won't tell me who was with you,' Imogen said, knowing that the girls in the video's heads were obscured and their clothes generic; if they were here the chance of identifying them was quite small.

'I can't tell you who I was with, I'll come with you but I'm not saying anything about anyone else.'

Imogen felt a weight in her stomach as Gabriel went to tell the girl on the front door where he was going; she was clearly a friend of his. Imogen watched him as he spoke. She didn't want to tell this kid the truth. Yeah, he was a tall guy, but underneath the black eyeliner and sinister-looking clothing he was probably quite insecure. She had known guys like this when she was a teenager herself; it was war paint, a mask, a way to be a part of a world you don't feel like you fit into.

Gabriel Webb sat in the interrogation room facing Adrian. He looked a little less confident than he had before, but he clearly still had no idea what had happened.

'We're not sure if you know this,' Adrian began, 'but earlier tonight, Friday the twenty-sixth of June, after you left the signal box, a fire broke out. It took the firefighters a long time to put it out.'

'Oh, my God!' he said, shifting nervously in his seat.

Adrian tried to read Gabriel; he didn't seem to be hiding anything, but then sometimes the people they had in these rooms were just very good at lying. Adrian wondered if he could trust his own instincts about this young man; was he reading him right or was he being manipulated?

Imogen walked into the room with a glass of water and put it in front of Gabriel before sitting down next to Adrian.

'For the record, DS Grey has re-entered the room,' Adrian said into the tape recorder that was positioned on the table in front of him.

'Tell us what happened, Gabriel,' Imogen said.

Adrian sat back and let his partner take the helm for a moment; she seemed to have a better rapport with the man and that might help them get more honest answers out of him.

'I was out with some friends and we ended up at the signal box.'

'Have you been there before?'

'No, never.'

'Which friends were you with?'

'Does it matter? I already told you I started the fire. No point in anyone else getting in trouble.'

'Why did you start the fire?' Imogen asked.

'It was cold. The rain was pelting down; I didn't know it was going to rain so I wasn't wearing a coat.' He paused, obviously trying to think of how to word his answers. 'One of the girls was cold. It was a metal bin and the fire didn't even last very long.'

'Go on.'

'That was it. We left and went to the club to see the band.'

Adrian looked briefly at Imogen, who looked every bit as sombre as he felt.

'Unfortunately, arson is a pretty big deal, Gabriel,' Adrian said.

'Arson? No, it wasn't that. I wouldn't do that.'

'That's for the judge to decide.'

'Judge? What do you mean? Are you charging me with arson? It was an accident.'

Imogen sighed audibly, exhaling and then holding her breath again.

'There's something else, I'm afraid,' she said.

'If you call my parents they can pay for the damage.'

'I'm afraid it's more complicated than that.' Adrian paused and looked at Imogen. 'There was a body found in the signal box,' he said.

The force of Adrian's words knocked the colour out of Gabriel's face. 'What?'

'There was someone in the room below when the building caught fire. There's every likelihood it was a homeless man, but we don't know for sure at this point until there's been a thorough examination of both the site and the body.'

'No . . . it was just us,' he said faintly, his chest heaving.

'Are you all right?' Imogen asked. Gabriel was shaking; he looked as though he was going to throw up.

'It might help your case if you tell us who you were with; they can corroborate your story about the fire.'

'Can you call my parents? I think I need a lawyer or something, I don't think I should say anything else.' His breathing was shallow and laboured. He started to wheeze, fighting to inhale.

'Gabriel, do you have asthma?' Imogen asked him urgently.

He nodded as he struggled with the leather buckled corset around his waist. He looked like he couldn't get enough air.

'Interview suspended at 00:15,' Adrian said as he stopped the recording.

'Help me get him on the floor,' Imogen said.

Adrian helped his partner lower Gabriel onto the ground; he was cumbersome, but they needed him to calm down. He arched his back and stretched his neck, rasping for air.

'Can I help you take that off, Gabriel?' Imogen asked, gesturing to the corset as the teenager nodded, tears falling from his eyes and trickling down the side of his face.

'Do you have any medication on you? An inhaler or something?' Imogen said.

He shook his head.

'What do I do?' Adrian asked.

Imogen pulled at the buckles on Gabriel's cincher until it was undone and yanked it off; he breathed in air greedily and Adrian watched as Imogen stroked his forehead. His breathing seemed to normalise a little.

'You'd better get some help.' Imogen turned to Adrian who tried to hide his surprise at her tenderness; there was something maternal about the way she was handling

Gabriel Webb. He went to the door and called to one of the constables, instructing him to get a doctor.

'I'm OK,' Gabriel wheezed. 'I'm fine, it just happens sometimes.'

'We'll get someone to sit with you until you can be checked out by the duty doctor. OK?'

Gabriel started to get up slowly, still breathing in short bursts but much calmer than a few moments previously. Adrian held out a hand to him and helped him stand up. He remembered only too well the feeling of being nineteen; you're a man but you're not, he thought. You're not a child, you're kind of nowhere. It was a horrible age.

'What happens now?' Gabriel sat back down, his eyes glassy and full.

'Depends on the outcome from the scene of the fire.'

'Do you understand that if we don't get to speak to your friends, the people with you at the signal station, then in all likelihood you're going to go down for this?' Imogen interjected.

'What do you mean?'

'Gabriel, if they determine its arson, then we're going to have to charge you with manslaughter.'

Adrian stood by his car and lit a cigarette; he had given up on giving up and he felt much better for it. Imogen walked out of the station, pulling her hair back into an updo. She was shaking her head.

'God, I hate this job sometimes.' She took the cigarette out of Adrian's hand and sucked on it before giving it back to him.

'You believed him then?'

'Absolutely. Shame it doesn't matter what I think.'

'It will matter to him. He liked you, I can tell.'

'What about his parents? Did Denise get hold of them?'

'Yeah. They said they'll come tomorrow. They think a night in a holding cell will do him good.'

'He seems like a nice kid, though. I feel so bad for him.' Imogen couldn't help but feel a pull towards Gabriel, maybe it was just her self-preservation in action because he reminded her so much of herself at that age, before she decided to become a police officer.

'I'm sure those big sad blue eyes and that cute little cleft in his chin have nothing to do with that.'

'OK, he is good-looking, but that kind of makes it even worse. I hope he's strong enough to handle it on remand.'

'First Dean Kinkaid and now this kid. I think I know what your type is, Grey. Convict.'

'Piss off, it's not like that. Don't be gross. If I was ten years younger, then yeah – he would have been the kind of guy I looked at, but not now. I don't know,' she paused, 'I think he reminds me of me.'

They both stood contemplating for a moment as they shared the remainder of Adrian's cigarette. Two minutes of silence as they processed what had just happened, and what was most likely about to happen. It didn't seem as though Gabriel had any intention of saying who the other people were, and there was no way to ID them from the video. Hoodies and miniskirts were standard clothing for anyone under twenty and that was a significant proportion of the population, it would be like looking for the proverbial needle in a haystack.

'Anyway, tonight sucked. Are you hungry?' Adrian finally spoke as he put the cigarette out.

'No, not really. I can't help worrying about what's going to happen to him. That kid's going to be eaten alive in prison.'

'What can we do?'

'We can start with identifying that body.'

'Let's get going then. My weekend has been screwed over yet again by Dominic and Andrea, they've taken Tom to London to see a show or something.'

'Again?'

'He'll be sixteen next year, then he can spend his weekends where he wants.'

'And you're sure they're safe?'

'Dominic wants me to know he's got my family, it's not about hurting them, it's about winding me up. I think they're safest where they are for now, until I get some concrete evidence on him. Gary's working on it for me.'

'I'm not sure I could be so calm about it.'

'I'm not sure if calm is the right word. I like to keep busy to keep my mind off it.'

Adrian had been investigating his son's stepfather for around four months now, since Tom had come to him with a suspicion that Dominic was cheating on his mother. While Adrian had managed to disprove the cheating, he'd found out some things he couldn't ignore. Financial irregularities of large sums of money, money that couldn't be explained legally. Until he had proof though he was powerless to act and he couldn't open an official investigation. He had no evidence. Every time he got the chance he would look into Dominic, with the help of Gary Tunney, the forensic computer technician at the police station, who also loved to solve puzzles in his free time. But Dominic was good; so far they hadn't found anything that would stick. A little over two months ago, Dominic had somehow found out that Adrian had been snooping around in his affairs. They would have to be more careful in the future but Adrian wasn't going to give up, he was confident that Gary would get to the bottom of it. The fact that Dominic had threatened Adrian and made it clear to him that he should stop, or his life would get more difficult, was just more incentive to get his family out of there. If not now, then soon. Dominic was going to pay; Adrian just had to make sure he didn't take his whole family down with him.

'I'll call Dean and tell him not to wait up then.'

They walked back into the station for what would undoubtedly be a night of scintillating closed-circuit TV viewing. With any luck, they might be able to get a better angle on Gabriel and his friends, see if they could work out who he was with.

Chapter 4

Gabriel couldn't move his arms. They were pinned down by his sides, his broad shoulders each touching the side of the metal box he was in. He had anticipated a five-minute journey but an accident on Magdalen Street meant that they were stuck for a little while, at least until the cars were moved out of the way. He wanted to stand up, he wanted to go for a walk to stretch his legs. More than that, he wanted to scream.

The windows of the Serco prison transport van – or sweatbox as it was more affectionately known – were blacked out from the outside, but from the inside he could see the people on the streets going about their business. He saw a skater flipping off a hotel step and instantly wished he had his deck, just to feel that freedom. Freedom; something he had never fully appreciated until he was sat in this box. He was being put on remand until his hearing. He tried to focus on his breathing, unwilling to let his asthma get the better of him in here of all places. He didn't even know if they would open the door if he had an attack. If they would even hear him? If they would even bother to help? Instead, he just counted inside his head to make the rising panic go away. He couldn't think about what he had done to get into this situation; the fact was that he was here and he was guilty. Of arson. Of manslaughter.

He had never meant to kill anyone. The words went round and around his head. He was a killer; he had ended someone's life. He couldn't allow himself to cry. He couldn't be seen to be entering the prison with tears in his eyes. He had a few friends who had done time in Exeter prison, and by all accounts it was grim. Understaffed and overpopulated, the Victorian building that was barely fit for purpose – not in this day and age – still housed well over five hundred prisoners both on remand and serving shorter sentences. And he was about to join them.

At least the police had seemed to believe that he hadn't intended to start the fire; hopefully the judge would too. Every time he closed his eyes, Gabriel imagined what it must feel like to burn alive. Why hadn't they checked the place was empty? Why had he allowed himself to be pushed into something so bloody stupid? He longed for the sound of his parents screaming at each other when they thought he was out of earshot. Anything but this.

The van started moving and Gabriel allowed himself to breathe. He looked outside, wondering if he would ever walk on a street again. He was afraid that he wouldn't even last a week in jail; either the asthma or something worse would get to him. The invisible strap around his chest tightened. One, two, three, four, five. He soaked in as much of the city as the route would allow. The bus station, the pub he went into with Emma sometimes. As they pulled into the prison, Gabriel held his breath again. He had very little idea of what to expect, but he was going to keep his head down, speak when spoken to and keep himself to himself. He was grateful at least for his six foot two inches of height, hoping that might deter any unprovoked attacks.

The first thing that hit Gabriel was the smell. It was a musty kind of clean. The kind of clean that was masking a multitude of sins. Industrial cleaner that has an unpleasant bite. He tried not to think about it as he stood with the prison officer at the end of a long room that was more like a giant corridor. B-wing. Doors with cross-hatched, reinforced windows in them. A hatch and a big bolt on the outside. *Breathe.*

The wing itself was light and airy, empty at the moment apart from the two men with mops and buckets at either side of the long room. Instinctively he wondered what they did to get put inside when they looked so harmless. Most of the doors that lined the walls of the gallery were open. He wondered what was behind the doors that were closed. There was a vaulted ceiling with skylights, fenced off by a metal barrier, and they were on the second level, a gallery looking down onto a communal area with ping-pong tables and sofas. Above everything was a steel net, presumably to stop people from throwing themselves – or others – over the railings.

'All right, son?' The prison officer smiled and touched Gabriel on the shoulder to indicate that he should move forward. Gabriel noted the look of sympathy on the officer's face and realised he must look terrified. He opened his mouth, stretching his jaw; it had been clenched for so long that it had started to hurt. He settled his face into a more stoic expression, feeling his jaw tightening all over again. He pouted his lips to at least make his anxiety seem like confidence, looking down his nose as he walked forward with a strong, assertive stride. He couldn't let them see his fear, he couldn't show any weakness. They were about two thirds of the way into the room when the officer stopped.

'Your stuff's already in there. When you hear roll call, make sure you come and stand here again and answer when they call your name. If in doubt, just copy everyone else.'

You'll soon get the hang of it. Just stay calm.

Gabriel considered the room. It was very innocuous with its cream walls and bunk beds. There was a desk and a cupboard each for belongings, and two comfortable chairs against the far wall.

'Thanks,' Gabriel managed to squeeze out. *Thanks for locking me up. Thanks for facilitating my incarceration. Thanks for saving me from myself.*

'Your pad-mate will be back off work duty soon.' The prison officer put his hand on Gabriel's shoulder, giving him a gentle pat, or a nudge maybe. Maybe it meant something else altogether.

That was Gabriel's cue to move from the doorway, to leave the long light corridor of the wing and enter the small space he would occupy for the foreseeable future. At least until he had to appear in court for sentencing – until they decided how much of a risk to society he was. The guard left without closing the door. The idea that anyone could walk in at any moment was not something Gabriel had considered. He had prepared himself to be locked in, but not for this.

He grabbed his bag from on top of the cupboard. He couldn't tell which bunk was his and so he sat in one of the chairs and waited for his cellmate. He was nervous about conversation. Worried he might say the wrong thing to the wrong person. Upset someone without meaning to. Hopefully his cellmate wouldn't ignore him. He had been counting the words that had come out of his mouth since he had been charged, aware that he had only spoken when he had to, when he was spoken to first. He wasn't sure if it made him feel more or less lonely. He had said fifty-five so far, most of them answering the nurse or counsellor in the screening as they processed him to enter the prison.

Gabriel looked through the bag of clothing his mother had sent in to see that his favourite T-shirt was missing. The Slipknot tour T-shirt that Emma used to sleep in. He hadn't even washed it – he wanted it to smell of her. The rest of his stuff seemed to be there.

'I'm Jason Cole. Who are you?' A man entered the room, bounding straight towards Gabriel with his hand held out. Gabriel stood up awkwardly.

'I'm Gabriel.'

'Well it's good to meet you, Gabriel!'

'Thanks.'

'You been inside before? I'm guessing by the look on your face the answer is no.' Jason sat down on the edge of the bed.

Gabriel stuffed his things back into his bag and put them in the empty cupboard. He could sort it all out later.

'Roll call!' A booming voice came from outside the cell.

Jason nodded Gabriel towards the door and they both stood up. Gabriel was a good few inches taller than Jason, who had on a red shirt and blue jeans. Gabriel was once again feeling out of place in his fully black attire. Jason went outside and stood to the left of the door, and Gabriel followed, trying to remember what they had told him at the induction. So far so good though. Jason didn't seem to be violent, at least.

As he stepped out of the cell, he looked up and down the wing without moving his head and without making eye contact. He stood to the right of the door as Jason stood to the left. That seemed to be what everyone else was doing.

Another prison officer stood in the centre of the floor below, calling out names from a sheet. His voice carried through the whole of the wing, reverberating off the walls and silencing most of the murmuring inmates. He had some lungs all right. There was no whispering or messing around as the guard reeled off the names and the men responded. Gabriel noted how strange it was that these men, these law-breakers, were all so obedient. He could feel eyes on him but didn't want to know who was looking at him. He kept his face straight ahead.

'Webb?' The guard called finally. There was no hiding anymore. His presence had been announced.

'Present,' Gabriel responded. *Fifty-nine words.* He heard a couple of murmurs and wondered why his voice had elicited such a reaction. He didn't want paranoia to get the better of him, but he felt so alone. He took a cursory glance around before stepping back inside his cell, confirming that he had been noticed.

'Half an hour bang-up then it opens up for a few hours so we can get dinner and kick back,' Jason said. He looked at Gabriel. 'What you in for?'

'I killed someone,' Gabriel responded quietly, not wanting to shock Jason, whose demeanour changed immediately. His casual stance disappeared. His back straightened and Gabriel heard him suck in a breath before smiling and looking down to avoid eye contact with Gabriel. To avoid eye contact with a killer.

Gabriel was big, but he knew he had a young face. Younger than his nineteen years at least. Angelic was how everyone had described him when he was a baby, and that's how he was named. Angel Gabriel. It could have been worse.

Jason grabbed a puzzle book from the top of his cupboard and slid into the lower bunk, facing away from Gabriel. The conversation was over. At least now Gabriel knew which bunk was his.

The officer that had initially shown him to his cell stuck his head around the door. Gabriel looked at his name tag: Barratt.

'Everything all right?'

'Yes thanks,' Gabriel said, getting used to speaking again.

It felt good not to be completely isolated. It's one thing to be deliberately moody and a bit reclusive when you can do what you want, he thought. When you have no other options, it gets old, fast.

For the first time since Gabriel had entered the cell, the door closed completely. The cell still felt like a room by all accounts; it was kind of how Gabriel imagined university halls to be – a place he'd never had much interest in, much to his parents' disgust. Barratt pulled the latch across and Gabriel heard the thunk of the bolt as it slotted into place. He felt his throat closing. He pulled himself onto the top bunk and tried to concentrate on his breathing again. He didn't want to rely on his medicine in here; he didn't know when he wasn't going to have access to it. Claustrophobia was not something Gabriel had ever experienced before but here it was, the walls closing in on him. There was no way out. The knot in his stomach grew tighter and he tried to distract himself for the twenty-five minutes that remained until the doors unlocked again.

Gabriel opened his eyes to find the door was open. He jumped off the bed and saw Jason was gone from the lower bunk; he assumed he was getting his dinner, at least he hoped he hadn't scared him away on their first day together. He could hear chatter outside the cell and saw people walking past, milling around as though this were all perfectly acceptable. He wished he'd brought a book with him; somehow, it didn't seem like a good idea to touch any of Jason's things. He smoothed down his hair and shook his head a little so that it fell in front of his eyes before reluctantly walking towards the door.

'Hey.' A man with a mop of thick black curls was standing in his doorway. He was about as tall as Gabriel but he was bulkier; not fat, but not shredded either.

'Hi.' Gabriel folded his arms and stood by the door, just inside as though some invisible force-field would protect him if something bad should happen.

'I'm Solomon Banks, I'm two cells down.' The man pointed to the left of him. 'Everyone calls me Sol.'

'I'm Gabriel.'

'Hi Gabe.' A big smile spread across Sol's face. It was warm and friendly-looking, but Gabriel had already been warned that in prison everyone is out to get you. The police had told him, the duty solicitor, the nurse. They had all told him to watch himself, whether to scare him or give him a heads-up he didn't know. *Everyone is just looking out for themselves*. 'If you grab your bowl and stuff I'll take you down to the servery,' Sol continued. 'The food's not great but it's not too bad either.'

'Thanks.' Gabriel was hungry. Maybe he needed to take a chance with this Solomon guy. Surely it was better than walking into the unknown by himself. He hoped his instinct about Sol was right because he genuinely seemed OK. He wondered what he was in for; he imagined he'd be wondering the same thing about everyone he was going to meet in the foreseeable future.

The duty solicitor had explained to him that a remand prison was a mixed bag with a lot of traffic. Some of the sentences were much harsher than others, from petty theft to manslaughter. Some of the inmates were just waiting to be sentenced and moved on.

Gabriel grabbed his things and stepped onto the wing, crossing the threshold from his sanctuary into the fray. It was different to when he had arrived just a short while earlier. Again, he noticed the smell. The powerful odour of the cleaner had been replaced with the smell of men. The taste of sweat, both old and new, hit the back of Gabriel's throat. He could smell that horrible tar soap he remembered his grandad using.

There were men everywhere. Booming laughter and heated discussions. Mumbled conversations, profanities and platitudes. A cacophony that reminded him of the changing rooms at secondary school, another place where he'd been at the bottom of the food chain, at least until he'd grown to well over six feet tall. He kept his head down as he followed Sol to the servery. They passed some big white men with shaven heads on the way down the narrow metal stairs onto the lower level. They walked past the ping-pong tables, Sol calling out hello to several of the players.

Then came the showers. Gabriel was horrified when he noticed that you could see inside; there were four men in there, showering completely naked and no one was batting an eye. There was a small wall that came to about hip-height on Gabriel, just to allow for a little modesty. Although forsaking his freedom was something that Gabriel had resigned himself to, he hadn't considered the complete lack of privacy. Nothing was his anymore. He was part of this organism, part of this system that he had to adjust to. The realisations about his new life were coming thick and fast for Gabriel as he walked over to the long queue for dinner. He stood behind Sol. One thing he had also noted on his walk was the authority Sol seemed to command, or if not authority then maybe just respect. Not fear though, definitely not fear.

'You're in with Jason?'

'Yeah,' Gabriel said, still struggling to find his voice.

'If I were you, I'd stay out of his way.'

'Is he dangerous?' Gabriel tried to sound calm, knowing full well that tonight he would be locked in a room with Jason for a very long time.

'No, but he is stupid,' Sol whispered as he nodded hello to one of the other inmates, a young man with a ginger beard and a crew cut. Gabriel watched as the man's eyes travelled up his body. He shivered involuntarily.

'Stupid?'

'Never borrow and never lend. Rule one. Especially if you don't have permission. When all you have in the world is twenty things, suddenly those twenty things take on a whole new importance. Jason took something of importance to someone. He's going to get a kicking and you probably shouldn't be there when it happens.'

'Shouldn't you tell the guards?'

'Rule two: don't tell the guards anything. Not many people in here get treated worse than a grass.'

'Gotcha.'

'If you see something happening then leave, that's my advice,' Sol said. 'It's hard but in here you have to look out for yourself. That's what everyone else is doing.'

Gabriel stared into the cottage pie on his tray. The mashed potato was white and shiny, with beads of liquid on the surface as though it had been sweating. It was watery and soft. There was an orange tinge to the mince that looked both unnatural and unappetising. He scooped some of the mixture onto his spoon; it was mushy but also unwilling to separate as he pulled the spoon away. The mashed potato hung like mucus as he moved it towards his lips. He was so hungry, he put the food in his mouth; it was warm but not hot. He tried to imagine each mouthful as though it were something else entirely, which got more difficult as it got colder. It sank to the bottom of his stomach like sand. Without warning, Gabriel gagged and the horrible potato decided to come back out; he rushed to the bin in the corner of the servery and threw up. He heard laughter and looked up to see the men on the table opposite were watching him. One of them was the young ginger man. His eyes were burning into Gabriel. Suddenly, he wasn't hungry anymore.

Roll call.

Gabriel walked back to his cell and stood in position outside the door. Jason was nowhere to be seen.

'Cole!' the prison officer said for the fourth time, this time looking up in Gabriel's direction. Gabriel's discomfort was magnified as three other screws walked briskly towards him. Everyone was looking. Gabriel felt the colour draining from his face. He tried to look tall, not vulnerable. He tilted his chin back and stood up straight, shoulders back. It was the kind of stance he would have used in a club as he surveyed the room, everyone trying to look more badass than anyone else.

Gabriel looked at the names of the officers. Marcus Hyde, Kyle Johnson and Steve Barratt.

'Where's Jason?' Barratt asked.

'I don't know.' Gabriel answered. *Eighty-two words.*

'You don't know? When was the last time you saw him?' Hyde barked at him, just inches away from Gabriel's face. Gabriel was taller and it felt strange having this smaller man shouting at him. He hated having to ignore it, to take the anger. It went against everything he was. He wasn't violent, but he was proud. Although he had no reason to be proud anymore.

'In the cell. Before dinner.'

'We're going to need a little more information than that,' Hyde pushed.

'When I woke up I went to dinner, he wasn't there when I left or when I came back.'

'Is that true?' Barratt stepped in, clearly playing good cop to Hyde's aggression.

'I swear.'

'Lockdown!' Hyde shouted, his voice reverberating through the wing. The prisoners groaned and moved back into their cells. From what Gabriel could tell, this seemed like something that happened quite often.

Hyde left the room and Barratt seemed to be waiting until he was out of earshot before he spoke to Gabriel again.

'If you had nothing to do with this I suggest you keep your nose out of it,' Barratt whispered.

'What do you mean?'

'I mean Jason upset the wrong people and those people are not going to get caught.'

'Why are you telling me this?'

'Because you're new. We see a lot of the same faces in here over and over again. I've never seen you before so I guess that means maybe you aren't such a bad guy. Keep your nose clean and your time in here will go a lot faster.'

'Keep my nose clean how?'

'Just don't get mixed up with the wrong people. Keep yourself to yourself. Use your nous.'

'What's happened to Jason?'

'We'll probably find him pretty soon, beaten up if we're lucky, dead if we're not.'

'If you're lucky?'

'You cannot imagine the bureaucratic nightmare of finding a dead inmate.' He walked to the door and pulled it closed with a final warning before he locked it. 'Keep your head down.'

Barratt left. Gabriel walked over to the door and looked out of the strip of vertical glass to see what was going on. There was a distinct lack of panic on the wing. Everything was routine. Everyone sat patiently in their rooms, the prison officers checking each cell individually before closing it and locking the occupants in. It was barely 7 p.m. and they were done for the night.

Gabriel was torn between relief that he was alone and a concern that something terrible had happened to his cellmate. He watched as two officers ran past his door; they had obviously found something. He saw nothing except the faces of his fellow inmates, pressed up against the glass of their own doors, also trying to find out what was going on. Resignedly, Gabriel took a book from on top of Jason's cupboard. He had a feeling his cellmate wouldn't be needing it tonight.

Chapter 5

Adrian was watching DI Fraser speaking to their new DCI. Jonathan Fraser seemed visibly relieved at the fact that he was no longer acting DCI, as he was better suited to taking orders than giving them, and everyone knew it, himself included. DCI Mira Kapoor was a completely new face, brought in to battle the ongoing allegations of corruption within Exeter Police. She was a PR wet dream for the district with her exemplary record and connections in the press. Fraser signalled for Adrian to come over.

'DI Fraser speaks very highly of you,' DCI Kapoor said as she shook Adrian's hand.

'Ma'am.'

'Looking forward to working with you, DS Miles,' she said as she let go of his hand.

'Thank you.'

'DS Miles is investigating the fire down at the signal box four nights ago,' Fraser said. 'They're trying to identify the body.'

'Any luck?'

'No missing persons, we asked around the homeless community.' Adrian sighed. 'If someone *is* missing, no one has noticed yet. As you can imagine, it's proving very difficult.'

'What do the forensics say?'

'No DNA, it seems the floor collapsed onto the burning body and the damage sustained to both the skull and the rest of the body means we can't get a match on dental records either. We really don't have much to go on.'

'Well, keep going. We're being watched.' She bowed slightly and nodded towards the desk sergeant, Denise Ferguson, who was standing next to Adrian's desk, pointing him out to a young woman with a pea-green satchel who was standing next to her. 'Excuse me.'

Both Adrian and Fraser watched DCI Kapoor walk away. Adrian couldn't help wondering if she was on the level; he had learned the hard way that power and corruption go hand in hand. She was from outside the county which was a promising start. He was at least a little hopeful that she wasn't being controlled by Dominic, who seemed to have his hands on everybody's strings.

'She seems nice?' Fraser said, his voice getting higher at the end. A hint of optimism in the form of a question, as though it were more of a request than a statement. At least Adrian wasn't the only one who was concerned.

Adrian rolled his eyes and headed back towards his desk. He knew better than to be optimistic, anything could happen and he wasn't about to put his trust in anyone just yet. Not after everything they had been through; he would be an idiot if he did.

Denise Ferguson smiled as he approached, as did the woman with the green bag. But hers wasn't a friendly smile, it was a knowing smile and it immediately made him suspicious.

'The DCI has asked that you take care of this young lady, Adrian. She's a freelance journalist doing a piece on the dangers posed to the escalating numbers of homeless people in Exeter. Wants to know about the identification of the man in the fire.'

'What?' Adrian looked back and the DCI smiled at him; he was missing having Fraser as his boss already.

'Play nice.' Denise smiled before tottering off back to her desk.

'DS Miles, nice to meet you.' He held out his hand to the young woman. She stared at him for a few seconds too long. He hated journalists but he knew the department had a lot of damage to repair, damage which he felt at least partially responsible for. He would play along for now, until he figured her out.

'Lucy Hannigan. Nice to meet you too.' She ignored the gesture and sat down. Adrian detected a tone to her voice that was bordering on sarcasm. He dismissed it as paranoia and his general mistrust of the press. 'I wasn't even sure anyone would be investigating this man's death,' she continued. 'Presumably it was a man.'

Adrian pulled out the pictures of the fire and placed them on the desk in front of her.

'That's about all we know for sure at this point. The building having collapsed on him hasn't helped at all.'

'Is it just you working on this?'

'Me and my partner, DS Grey.'

'I think I read that she got shot last year. Is that right?'

'It is. Good memory.' He wasn't about to elaborate if that's what she wanted, he wasn't going to give her any more fuel for her fire; this was about containment and nothing else.

'Oh yeah. I have a great memory.' There was that tone again.

'Well, when my partner arrives we'll be heading down to the food bank to see if they have any knowledge of anyone that might be missing. So far, it's a bit of a mystery. We're not even sure if it's a homeless person, but it seems like the most likely scenario at this point.'

'Good job you're a detective then, isn't it?' She was definitely being weird with him.

'Sorry, have we met before? You seem to have some kind of issue with me?'

'No wonder they gave you a badge.' She smiled.

Adrian could tell that he looked puzzled. She seemed to be amused by his confusion. He was racking his brain but he couldn't place her. Which could only mean one thing. He concentrated for a second on her lips, curled ever so slightly into a smirk. There was something familiar about her . . . something intimate.

'Did we . . .?' He tailed off awkwardly.

'Ironic really that I should get stuck with you now. I have to be honest, if you don't even recognise me that casts some serious doubts over your ability to do your job.'

He saw her again in his mind, a fragment of a memory, her lying beneath him, his hands on her body, his mouth on her skin. It was still a little hazy.

'What did I miss?' Imogen slammed her bag on the table and bursting the tension.

'Miss Hannigan is a freelance reporter,' Adrian said, flushing red, grateful for Imogen's interruption. 'We've been asked to brief her on the body in the signal box.'

'It'll be a short briefing to be honest. We're kind of stuck at the moment.'

'So I hear.' Lucy Hannigan reached into her bag and pulled out a business card. 'This lady does a lot of charitable work with the homeless in the area, she might be able to help you out. I've written my number on the other side, in case you don't have it already.' She looked pointedly at Adrian. What was he missing?

She put the card on the table and stood up.

'Thank you, we'll check that out right away.' Adrian picked the card up, looking at it to see if it sparked anything. He still couldn't remember the exact circumstances under which he'd met Lucy; he knew it was a couple of years ago, and she looked completely different now. He hoped it came back to him before he bumped into her again.

'I'll be in touch. I'd like to follow the investigation. I don't suppose there's any chance I can get a copy of those pictures, is there?'

'I'll see what I can do. I'll have to clear it with the DCI.' Adrian said.

'Thank you. Good *seeing* you again, Adrian.' She was being sarcastic. Adrian's face felt hot.

Adrian and Imogen watched her leave.

'Do you know her?' Imogen turned to him and asked, her eyebrows knotted in confusion.

'I think I probably do.' Adrian cringed. He changed the subject before she pushed any further. 'Where have you been? You're normally here first.'

'I was talking to my mother. They're in Crete at the moment.'

'Is she well enough for that?' Adrian sounded concerned.

Imogen sighed. 'The doctor says rest is what she needs, it's probably good that she's in a different setting, having people wait on her hand and foot.'

'Did you speak to Elias? Did he say how your mother was doing?'

Her parents were together in Crete; it was a strange thought. She had never known her father and suddenly almost thirty years later they were back together, a man whose name she hadn't even known growing up. Her mother had always kept him a secret and she had accepted it, but because of his apparent involvement in a case she was working on, it had all come out earlier this year and now here he was. She hadn't gotten used to the idea of having a father yet. Imogen had asked him if they could get to know each other slowly, but the truth was she didn't want any part of it. She had managed this long without him. Her mother was finally reunited with the man she'd lost, but as far as Imogen was concerned, he was a stranger. Finally learning his identity had been a huge shock that she just wasn't prepared for.

'He's making sure she's taking all her medicine, their cabin is top of the line so she's really comfortable.' She paused and took a deep breath before speaking again. 'When he comes back he wants me to meet his children, and grandchildren. They don't know about me yet, he said he wanted to talk to me about it first but he doesn't want any more secrets.'

'Are you going to meet them?'

'I've been an only child to a single parent my whole life, I've never known anything different. To go from that to having three younger brothers and a bunch of nieces and nephews . . . I don't know if I'm ready for all that just yet.'

'Then tell him to wait.'

She shook off some imaginary burden, jingled her car keys and started towards the exit. 'Enough about my crap anyway, Miley. We should go see if there are any more cameras around the nightclub after we speak to this charity lady, see if we can work out who Gabriel Webb was with that night. The only camera they had in the club was pointed at the till and he always went to the bar alone.'

'I don't know why he just won't tell us. Who is he protecting?'

'A girlfriend of course.'

'You sound very sure about that. Did his parents say anything? Do they know who he was going out with?'

'No, they don't really seem to know much about him at all. They don't seem to care either,' she said as she opened the door for Adrian. She had spoken to his father on the phone and his reaction to the arrest was almost a gloat, followed by a comment on how it might make him grow up eventually.

'Well I know how that goes. My dad was only ever interested in drink and women. At least for the first half of my life, before he got into the harder stuff.'

'I don't think that's Mr Webb's problem.'

'It's all the same though, isn't it? Selfishness. Since having Tom I can't imagine it, I can't imagine putting myself or my pride before him, ever. I don't understand it.'

'How does that poem go? "They fuck you up, your mum and dad . . ."'

'Poetry was never really my thing.'

'You surprise me.' She raised her eyebrows before getting in the car. She thought about her own parents in relation to the poem, how all of their choices had impacted her life, made her who she was. Another line sprang to mind: *Man hands on misery to man.* Never a truer word was spoken.

Chapter 6

Imogen rang the doorbell to the STREETWIZE charity HQ, a disused clothing shop in Exeter's Sidwell Street, next to a kebab shop Adrian had visited many times before after a drink in town. Adrian walked around the building and found a side door. He banged on it. They heard some movement, followed by the sight of a woman in a dressing gown opening the door. Her face was flushed red and her eyes were swollen and puffy. She coughed uncontrollably the moment she started to speak.

'Hi, I'm DS Grey and this is DS Miles. Are you the lady that runs the STREETWIZE charity?' Imogen asked when the woman had stopped.

'I am. My name is Claire Morgan. Sorry, I'm just getting over the flu. Come in, but I'd keep my distance if I were you.'

They went inside, to a small living room with a two-seater sofa and a coffee table strewn with little balls of screwed-up tissues. There was a palpable taste of eucalyptus in the air where copious amounts of Vicks had obviously been applied. Imogen was hit by the sheer heat of the room. The lady pulled her dressing gown around her tighter, oblivious to the heat.

'We're investigating the fire in the signal box up at Central Station,' Adrian said.

'I saw that on the news. What's it got to do with me?'

'Well I don't know if you saw, but we found the remains of a male in the room; we think he was seeking shelter from the rain in there. It seems quite probable that he was homeless,' Imogen said.

Claire Morgan's hand went up to her mouth and Imogen saw the clear look of distress in her eyes.

'Do you know how many homeless there are in the city?' Adrian asked.

'I used to but the numbers are always growing. It's getting a lot less . . . personal.'

'Is anyone missing, to your knowledge?'

'It's hard to know when someone is missing,' Claire said. 'Sometimes people just want to be alone. Sometimes people move on, sometimes they get moved on. There can be a variety of factors why they wouldn't be around anymore. Over the last few months I would say there's a couple of people I haven't seen in a long time. But there are new faces too. As you can imagine, it's a very transient community.'

'Do you keep records of the people who pass through your charity?' Imogen asked.

'No, I don't. Some people are homeless by choice,

and I think it's only fair to respect that choice and respect their privacy.'

'And what is it you do here exactly?'

'People donate money and the money buys supplies for the homeless. So, if you wanted to donate thirty pounds, I would put together a pack of a sleeping bag, a thermal blanket and some protein bars or something like that. Then when people come in and ask for help, I can give that to them. It's not much, but it's all I can do.'

'It's a lot more than most people do.' Imogen smiled at her, feeling guilty that she didn't do more.

'I was homeless myself once,' Claire said. 'Not through choice. I was lucky that people helped me and eventually I got myself back on track. Most people genuinely try not to think about it. It's as if they think about it, it might happen to them – as if it's somehow contagious. So they actively choose to ignore it.'

Imogen pulled out a card and handed it to the woman. 'Please call us if you hear anything.'

'I will.' She smiled and paused as though she was thinking for a moment. 'It's good to see you're taking it seriously.'

'One more thing, if you don't mind.' Adrian stepped in. 'Do you know of anyone who used to sleep in that signal box? Or have you heard of anyone who maybe hung out there?'

'The only one I can think of is a man called Bricks,' Claire said slowly. 'But the last I heard he had been arrested and put in prison. He had some mental health issues – he tried to rob the post office last year. He's spent his whole life in an out of the system in one way or another.'

'You don't happen to have a picture of him, do you?'

Claire frowned and shook her head. 'No, I'm sorry, I don't.'

'OK, Claire, thank you for your time. We'll see ourselves out,' Imogen said, not wanting to make the poor woman stand up again.

'Feel better,' Miles said as they pulled the door closed.

Imogen was glad to be outside again, out of Claire Morgan's house which seemed to be an incubator of sorts, the air so hot and thick you could feel yourself getting sicker with every passing moment. She breathed in heartily, ignoring the myriad of smells coming from the industrial wheelie bins in the alley adjacent to the charity.

'Never thought I would be grateful for the smell of old kebabs.'

'Come on, a nice doner with a big salad and chilli tomato sauce is one of your five a day!'

'You disgust me.' She smiled and walked on ahead.

Chapter 7

The prison bed wasn't comfortable. The blanket was itchy and the pillow may as well not have been there at all. At least there was a mattress – something that hadn't been in the police holding cell. Gabriel's eyes were closed as he tried hard to block out his surroundings. He thought of Emma and her white skin. She wore talcum powder instead of foundation to make it even whiter and when they would kiss he could taste it on the edge of her lips. He imagined her lips on his and realised he was holding his breath. He couldn't ask her to wait for him. It would possibly be weeks until he got a trial date and the sentence he was likely to receive would mean that it would be foolish to hope that she could put her life on hold. They had been apart for nine days now and already he found himself giving up on the idea that he would be with her again. Without that hope he didn't know what else he had to hold onto. He'd had relationships before, but this was different. She was the one. They just fit together. He couldn't imagine never seeing Emma again; his stomach hurt at the thought of it.

He found his mind returning to that day. Why had he not checked the building before starting the fire? Why had he even gone there in the first place? He deserved this punishment. He had taken someone's life.

He was grateful for the darkness. His eyes were so sore from the air in here; it was noxious, unclean and unfiltered. He sucked in a breath hard as he tried to fill his body with clean air. Any air. He gulped to try and stop the tears that refused to stay beneath the surface any longer. Ready to burst from his bloodshot eyes.

Surely this was all a big mistake? Prison? He couldn't be here. This couldn't be real. Just over a week ago, he and Emma had been making plans for the summer. Everything they had talked about was now gone. No going back to college or work or holidays. No more hope. No future. Or at the very least, a future he hadn't accounted for and most certainly didn't want. This would never go away. It couldn't. Someone had died because of him. Someone had lost their father, brother, son – all because of Gabriel's stupidity.

He couldn't feel sorry for himself, but he could feel anger. The numbness inside had gone. He had spent so long focussing on how to behave and making sure he didn't upset anyone that he hadn't allowed himself to feel anything. His eyes no longer stung and he realised he was crying. Thank God he was alone.

Gabriel turned on his side and drew his knees up to

his chest. The release of pressure was immense; he could feel himself letting go and breathing for what seemed like the first time in a week. Tears coming until there were no more. The short burst of emotion had calmed him down. His breathing normalising, he drifted into thoughts of Emma, wishing he had that T-shirt so he could at least inhale her scent.

That's when he noticed the light. A break in the darkness. His heart stopped as he heard the sound of metal against metal. The bolt sliding across and his door opening, followed by shuffling and quiet footsteps. Should he hold his breath or pretend to be asleep? Should he turn and look? He balled his hand into a fist, ready to punch anyone who touched him. No one had said anything to him when he was arrested, but he knew what they had all been thinking. It had been his first thought when he'd been told he was going to prison. Prison rape was a joke to most people. *Don't drop the soap*. It had stopped being funny the second the prison gates opened and the van pulled inside.

Gabriel heard whispering in the room now, but the sound of his exaggerated heartbeat in his ears made it impossible to discern the words. This was the most vulnerable he had ever felt in his life. This was worse than the strip search, which at least had taken place in the daylight. This was worse than using the servery for the first time, shoulder to shoulder with the unknown, eyes all over him. He didn't recognise the whispered voices but there were more than one. It was becoming clear that they weren't here for him though. They were going through Jason's things. Taking them away. He heard them toss the mattress aside and check underneath it. What had Jason done? What had happened to him? Whatever it was, Gabriel hadn't heard Jason's name spoken among the other inmates in the nine days since he had gone. He didn't want to get himself in trouble by bringing it up, but he found it very odd how quickly the disappearance was accepted. Why wasn't anyone else curious? The lack of curiosity was more upsetting to Gabriel than Jason's unexplained departure.

When Gabriel was sure he was alone, he opened his eyes. The room was dark again, silent once more. He allowed his sight to adjust before turning over in his bed. He wanted to see what had been taken. He moved as though he were still asleep, eyes open a sliver. Everything belonging to Jason was gone, the cupboard empty, door open. The books and pictures on the wall had vanished. It was though he had never been there.

Chapter 8

Imogen knocked on the door of the church and pushed lightly against it. It swung wide open. The building inside looked empty. She had never been a religious person but she found the church quite calming in itself; the well-worn wooden seats, the dancing light from the stained-glass windows, the smell of incense and burning candles. It reminded her of her childhood; her mother was always burning incense and leaving candles lit through the night. It was a miracle there had never been an accident. She thought of her mother, painting by candlelight and she knew that was why she liked churches: they reminded her of her mum, the peaceful mother that would quietly paint in the half-light and not the manic mother that would continually forget to collect her from school.

'Hello?' she called out tentatively.

Adrian had no such compunction and walked down the aisle and up towards the altar.

'Hello?' His voice echoed hers. Seconds later a door opened to the side of the altar and a priest emerged.

'I'm Father Berkeley. How can I help you?'

Imogen joined Adrian as the priest approached, they both pulled out their IDs and the priest's smile got a little tighter.

'We're conducting an investigation. We heard that you have a lot of homeless people in and out of here. We just wondered if you had noticed anyone missing recently?' Imogen said, as Adrian wandered off towards the candle bank, the tiny shine of the tea lights burning away even when no one was there.

'It doesn't really work like that,' Father Berkeley told them politely, clearly already eager for them to leave. 'People come and people go.'

'Do you know a man called Bricks?' Imogen asked him.

'Yes, Bricks came here sometimes. He was a strange one. I occasionally invite people to eat with me. He came and had dinner a couple of times but I didn't invite him back a third time.'

'Why was that?'

'He was quite unpleasant and made me feel uncomfortable. You know when someone has a darkness about them? I imagine you get something similar in your line of work, like an instinct about people.'

'When was that, sorry?' Imogen ignored the priest's extraneous comments, unwilling to engage in a conversation with him about the similarities between their line of work.

'Probably around a month ago. He had a bit of money on him. I had to ask him to leave because he was quite rude to one of my parishioners, used the "c" word.' The priest shook his head. 'I threatened to call the police and he went off. I haven't seen him since then.'

'A month ago?' Adrian looked at Imogen and pulled out his phone. This was news to them.

'Do you have any idea who he hung out with? Do you have a photo of him?' Imogen said to the priest.

'No I don't, he was always a bit antisocial, never came to any of the church gatherings for the homeless. I don't think he liked me. You can't like everyone though, can you?'

'Indeed,' Imogen said. 'Thank you.'

The priest nodded and went into a back room. Imogen turned to see Adrian putting money into the collection box; as she watched him, he picked up a candle and lit it, placing it in the tiered metal candle holder. She thought he might even be praying for a moment before he turned to look at her.

'Anything?'

'Nope. But he obviously wasn't in prison a month ago. We need to get Gary on the case. What are you doing?'

'What does it look like?'

'I didn't think you were into all that.'

'I'm just lighting a candle, Grey, calm down.'

'I think we've known each other long enough for you to know that telling me to calm down is a bad idea.'

'Why don't you light one?'

'Why would I do that? I'm not Catholic.'

'You just do it for yourself, to remind yourself of the people you care about,' Adrian said. 'It just feels good.'

'Who would I do it for?' she said. Her mind immediately went to Dean, followed by a quick burst of shame for not thinking of her mother first.

'You could do it for your mum; you're already thinking about her.'

'That's not going to help her though, is it?' Imogen's mother Irene had never gone for more than a week without her. Now she was away with a man Imogen didn't even know, in another country.

'No, but it might help you.'

'Fine.' Imogen wasn't sure who she was more concerned for. Irene for being with a strange man, or her newly found father Elias, who might disappear altogether again after spending so much time with Irene. After realising how unstable she was.

Adrian pulled out another pound coin and put it in the collection box. Imogen lit a candle and placed it next to Adrian's, while she desperately tried to stay focussed on thinking about her mother. That was how it worked, wasn't it? Bizarrely, she did feel better.

'Who did you light yours for?' she asked him.

'You.'

'Me? What's wrong with me?'

'The age-old question, eh?'

'Seriously – why?'

'Because you've got a lot going on right now, Grey.' His expression was kind. 'Plus, I'm not actually allowed to say anything nice to you for fear of you knocking my block off.' They stared at each other for a moment.

'Let's go, Miley. We've got work to do, we need to find out who the body in the signal box belonged to, and how long Bricks has been out of prison,' she said, conceding that it was nice to have someone in her corner that she trusted. She knew she gave Adrian a hard time, but she got the impression he liked it that way.

Chapter 9

Gabriel sat in the waiting room outside the mental health nurse's office. He was disturbed by the fact that he was actually looking forward to it, looking forward to speaking to someone in private without the fear of something terrible happening. Apart from mealtimes, Gabriel didn't see much of anyone else, especially now that Jason was gone, forgotten, and it didn't seem like he would be coming back. Sol would walk past every now and then and knock but that was as much human contact as he'd had since being inside. So far, he had witnessed three fights break out, all minor, but still with an intensity that threatened to spread among the other inmates and cause a much bigger problem.

Gabriel had carefully studied the prison officers to see which ones he needed to be on guard with. The officer who had escorted him here, Hyde, seemed to be the most volatile of the bunch. His bloodshot eyes were disengaged, he always looked tired and was constantly rubbing his eyes with the backs of his hands. How long before you got burnt out in a job like this? Gabriel wondered how many years he had worked here. He thought about all the men he must have seen come and go and then come back again. Who was really in prison here? Most of the prisoners here would do three years at most and then they got to go home, wherever that was, and forget. The unlucky ones like Gabriel would get moved to a different prison after sentencing. Not everyone came back, not everyone reoffended. Hyde, however, had been here longer than most of the other guards, he seemed to be the one that they turned to when things went south. He stared at these same walls as the prisoners every day, locked in the same buildings, leaving only to go home and sleep in his bed at night before returning again in the morning.

'Come in,' the nurse called from inside. Natalie Barnes was the mental health nurse provided to various facilities in the area. She visited this prison twice a week but this was Gabriel's first visit with her; he was nervous, but looking forward to spending time with a female. The complete absence of women in the prison was something nobody had prepared him for and he hadn't really considered it until he'd been faced with it.

Gabriel stood up and went in, sitting himself down in the chair next to her desk. She nodded to Hyde to leave them alone and he closed the door.

'How are you doing, Gabriel? Just want to check and see how things are.'

'OK.'

'This is your first offence?'

'It is.'

'How do you think you're adjusting to the routine?'

'OK.'

'Have you made any friends yet?'

'Not really.'

'Time goes a lot slower when you're on your own, you know. It's important you make a connection in here if you can. It can help with the day to day.'

'I'll keep that in mind,' he said reluctantly, not comfortable with conversation yet.

'What are you missing most about the outside world?'

'Everything?' He half-laughed at the stupidity of the question. Freedom, freedom is what he missed the most.

'I mean one thing. What one thing do you miss the most? Your parents? Your girlfriend? Your dog?'

'I don't have a dog; my parents have washed their hands of me and I don't think my girlfriend is my girlfriend anymore.'

'There must be something.'

'To be perfectly honest with you, I miss walking. Just going outside and walking wherever I want. It's that simple. And music I guess, I miss listening to music. I've never really been one to watch TV.'

'Did they not tell you that you can buy a radio through the canteen?'

'No?'

'It will only be a basic thing, but maybe that will help.'

'Thank you.' Gabriel was excited for the first time in a week; the concept of a radio giving him an unexpected burst of hope.

'OK, well I'll check on you again next week. Please – do think about what I've said and try to make some friends.'

Gabriel stood up and Hyde opened the door. Back to the cell. He was surprised at how quick the meeting had been. Was it because he had said all the right things? If he had said he needed help, would they have listened? The whole thing felt like an exercise in box ticking, no one really cared if he was coping or not.

Bang-up again, thirty minutes in the cell to think about his meeting with the nurse, to think about what she'd said and how he should be making friends. He was lonely, and left alone with his thoughts he knew it wouldn't be long before he slipped into a rut of despair; he needed to trust someone, he needed to at least try.

Gabriel was working out in his cell at every opportunity he could get. The outside facility had been closed due to constant outbreaks among the inmates and the fact that on two occasions a drone had dropped suspect packages into the exercise yard. The prison was in the process of appealing for funds to stop this kind of thing. In the thirty minutes 'bang-up' time, Gabriel had worked his way to over a hundred press-ups in less than a week, marginal gains, adding an extra five onto every other set he did. When he'd arrived in jail, he'd barely been able to do a quarter of that without the asthma niggling at him. He figured his breathing was like any other muscle that needed to be stretched, and so he did ten rounds of twenty press-ups a day, pausing for breath in between.

He was just finishing up when the doors unlocked.

Roll call.

He noticed less and less people looking at him during roll call, which was a blessing. He was no longer the new guy, no longer unpredictable and unknown, he hadn't done anything rash or exciting and so now he was no more interesting than anyone else. He sometimes wondered if they even knew he was there. Beside his brief interactions with Sol, everyone else stayed away from him. He would slip out and then back in without anyone so much as batting an eyelid. Just the way he wanted it. Roll call was over and he went back inside his cell.

'Webb?' Barratt said from the doorway.

Gabriel stood up immediately.

'Yes?'

'I believe you wanted one of these?' Barratt held out a box with a brand-new radio in it. For the first time in a week, Gabriel smiled.

Chapter 10

Adrian walked along his road, past Uncle Mac's corner shop. The orange and grey tones of dusk were settling into daylight. He hadn't been in the shop for a long time, not since they had connected it to a human-trafficking operation four months ago, an operation that was still under investigation. The place had been stripped and new management had taken over, but he still couldn't bring himself to go inside. He thought about his old friend Eva, the girl who had worked in the shop, and wondered if he would ever see her again. The thought of it filled him with anxiety; seeing her again would force him to confront the guilt he felt. When he thought of all the time they spent talking, she could have told him what had happened to her, that she had been trafficked, that she was there against her will. He wanted to blame her for not saying anything but the truth was he should have known something was very wrong. These days, he walked to the nearest supermarket on the main road for his necessaries. He counted the extra fifteen-minute walk as part of his punishment, it did nothing to alleviate his conscience though.

Adrian's phone beeped in his pocket, it was a text from Tom. Adrian had made Tom promise to check in every morning since the menacing visit a couple of months ago from Tom's stepfather, Dominic. He asked Tom to come and live with him on a weekly basis but Tom insisted he needed to stay home and look after his mother, Adrian's ex Andrea. The text was a timely reminder for Adrian to check in with Gary for progress on their own little investigation into Dominic. He replied to Tom and then sent Gary a message before putting his phone away.

As he reached his front door, Adrian felt in his pocket and realised he didn't have his house keys. Again. Brilliant. He walked around to the side of the house and down the alley that the terraces backed onto. He hoped to God he had left his back door open; the lock was dodgy and sometimes he left it open because he was prone to forgetting his keys. He slung the carrier bag with the bread and milk over the wall, hoping the milk had made it intact; it usually did. He scaled the brick wall that backed onto his property, noticing that it was much harder to do than the last time he'd tried it. Clearly, he was out of shape.

'Breaking and entering?'

He turned his head to look behind him back into the alley and saw Lucy Hannigan with her phone pointed at him, taking a photograph as he straddled the wall.

'I forgot my key.' He swung his leg over the side and she disappeared from view.

The back door to his house was open; he walked in

and through to the front door. He could see the outline of Lucy in the glass just as the doorbell rang.

'Fancy seeing you here.' He smiled and opened the door.

'I'm not staying.' She stood steadfast in the doorway, hands in her jacket pockets.

He shrugged. 'Fair enough. How did you get my address?' Had he brought her back here last time? His brain hurt every time he tried to remember their previous encounter.

She pointed at her chest. 'Investigative journalist – remember?'

'Right.'

'I googled you. After all that business with the news-agents near your house, it wasn't hard to find. I just hung around a while until you turned up. To be honest I didn't expect you to be up this early.'

'I see. And what can I do for you?'

'I found out the name of your missing man.'

'You did?'

'The homeless man that usually sleeps in the signal box, the one they call Bricks.'

'How did you find out – no wait, don't tell me . . . did you google him?' Adrian smiled at her sarcastically.

'No, although sometimes that does work. I have a few connections on the street, they know homelessness is an issue close to my heart, which means people that wouldn't speak to you might speak to me. I've spent a few months working with these people in order to write this exposé, and they're grateful that someone gives a shit, I guess. I spoke to Claire Johnson, the lady whose number I gave you, and she told me who you were looking for. I asked around and there were a few people who knew your guy, so I got his real name. Thought it might help you out.'

'So, what's his name then?'

'His name is Theodore Ramsey – or Teddy Ramsey – or, you know – Bricks.'

Adrian nodded, making a mental note of the name. 'Well, thank you for letting me know. Are you sure you don't want a drink or anything?' He was hoping she would say yes, there was something about her. He didn't understand why he couldn't remember her properly; she had rich brown hair that tumbled from her head, haphazard but perfect at the same time. Her eyes were so bright, especially with the thick black liner she wore deliberately smudged around the rims. She seemed impossible to forget. Yet somehow he had.

'No thanks, I have a blog post to write.' She winked as she backed away.

'Sounds important. Am I in it?'

'Not until you do something interesting . . .' she called behind her.

He watched her until she disappeared around the corner. She seemed to be quite dismissive of him on purpose, which meant she had the measure of him. There wasn't much that turned Adrian on more than an attractive woman with no interest in him whatsoever. What had he done to piss her off so much the first time they met?

Adrian closed the door with a big smile on his face. He walked back into the house and as he passed the threshold of the lounge door his skin prickled. Without looking in, he knew someone else was there.

'Don't worry, I've just come for a chat.'

Adrian pushed open the lounge door to see Dominic sitting on his sofa, smack in the middle, arms either side of him as though he had sat there a million times and this was perfectly normal.

Anger surged through him. 'You can't just let yourself in here whenever you want.'

'Obviously I can.' He shrugged. The fact that Adrian was a police officer obviously didn't scare Dominic, and that scared Adrian.

'What do you want, Dominic?'

'Just checking in, seeing what you were up to.'

Adrian glanced over to the dining table; the bag of paperwork he and Gary had been working from was tucked safely to the side of it, undisturbed. It was in a reusable carrier bag so he guessed it probably didn't look all that important.

'Why?'

'I just wanted to make sure you were behaving yourself.'

'Get out before I call for back-up.'

'Come off it Adrian, you don't frighten me and you know it.' He smiled. 'Actually, this visit is about Tom.'

'What about Tom?' Adrian felt sick whenever Dominic said his son's name.

'He's not been very cooperative at home lately, I think maybe he needs a little stability at the moment, so you won't be seeing him for a while.'

'You can't do that.'

‘According to the court, we need your signature to take Tom out of the country. He’s had a tough year, I think you’ll agree, and he needs a treat.’

‘What are you talking about? Take him where?’

‘Undecided at present, but he’s going to be missing some weekends with you, I’m afraid. I have discussed it with Andrea and we both agree that these visits with you are unsettling for him.’

‘I have a custody agreement.’

‘Of course, this is a courtesy. I am asking nicely.’

‘Well, I’m saying no nicely.’

‘You know, I could make sure you never see either of them again. I can make them disappear.’

There was a pause. Adrian wasn’t sure exactly what he was saying. Was he threatening to kill them? Knowing that he had contacts in human-trafficking added a certain gravitas to Dominic’s threats, it had to be said. Adrian didn’t have anything now, no concrete evidence to pull Dominic in. His instinct was telling him to kill him, but that wouldn’t help anyone.

‘Why are you doing this? Why are you fucking with me?’

‘I don’t like you.’

‘I’ve made it clear that I’m not interested in Andrea anymore, so what threat am I to you exactly?’

‘No threat at all.’ Dominic stood up and dusted his coat as though he had just fallen in mud. ‘But, Adrian?’

‘What?’

‘If I find out you have been sticking your nose where you shouldn’t, you’ll be sorry. You’ll never see your son again.’

Adrian tried to ignore the sound of his own heart pounding in anger; he mustn't submit to it even though all he wanted to do was drive his fist through Dominic's expensive porcelain smile. Instead he stood to the side, waiting for Dominic to pass. Dominic didn't move for a few moments, just stared at Adrian. A cold stare, a stare that turned Adrian's stomach, like the dead black eyes of a shark. The beginning of a smile adorned his face as he passed Adrian and walked to the front door. Adrian followed behind him, making sure he stepped onto the pavement. He didn't turn to look back at all, just started walking away. Adrian closed the door behind him. He wanted to look out of the window and watch him leave properly, make sure he was gone, but that felt too much like succumbing to fear and he'd promised himself a long time ago that he wouldn't be bullied. Instead he walked straight out of the lounge and into the hallway, punching the wall to release the fury that had built inside him.

How dare he? How dare he come into his house, how dare he mess with his family? Adrian felt powerless against this man, but he needed to find out more before he took any action. If he behaved rashly, he might put his son in danger and that wasn't something he was prepared to do. Patience was not something that Adrian had an abundance of, but he needed to be smart here. He needed to play the long game to win rather than employing his usual reactionary tactics of hit first, ask questions later. He rubbed his throbbing knuckles and tried to calm down. He couldn't let Dominic push his buttons, couldn't let him win this time.

Chapter 11

No one had mentioned Jason to Gabriel since the first night he had been in. He had had his cell to himself and, although it was unbearably lonely, it felt safer. He hadn't slept well since he'd arrived, even worse since someone had come into his cell at night. He was afraid that it would happen again but it never did.

Solomon Banks had started to knock for Gabriel at mealtimes, and they usually walked to the servery together. He could feel himself adjusting to the routine. Roll call took place several times a day, breaking up the hours spent alone in his cell because he hadn't been granted his labour order yet. He had to stay on his own while the rest of the wing went to their jobs, which mainly consisted of working in the servery or the laundry. There was also no shortage of cleaning gigs around the prison. The most sought-after employment was in the library, it was clean, quiet and quite civilised. It didn't involve you getting wet or dirty. Gabriel wasn't allowed to enrol on any courses yet either, not until he had been sentenced and he hadn't even been given a court date yet.

The uneasiness he had originally felt in the prison had become a part of his day now; he didn't really notice that he was scared anymore, he just got on with things. Being afraid was the new normal. He followed the rules and spoke when he was spoken to. He hadn't made any friends, but he hadn't upset anyone either. Gabriel knew there were cliques in the wing for sure; he just had to figure out which ones were the most dangerous and stay the hell away from them.

He needed to hold on like this for a while longer. He longed to laugh, to really engage in a conversation, but he felt himself disappearing slowly with every single day. It was no more than he deserved.

The door was opened for lunch and Gabriel stepped outside to find Sol there as usual, this time accompanied by two other men. The fear that Gabriel thought he had adjusted to reared its head with a vengeance. It hit him like a bolt of lightning and his stomach tensed so hard that it started to cramp.

'Relax, Gabe, this is Kenzie and this is Sparks, they bunk together in the cell next to mine.' Sol grinned at him.

'Hi,' Gabriel managed a smile, noting that both men were shorter than him. There were a lot of short men in prison.

'This is Gabe.'

Kenzie shook Gabriel's hand firmly. He must have

been of a similar age to him, but he still had a teenage frame, awkward and angular.

Sparks nodded and started to walk towards the servery. 'Let's get there early so it's not stone cold today. I hate cold sausages – all the fat gets clogged up in them and then I get the shits.'

As they headed towards the metal stairwell, Sol held his hand out to the side as though he were a mother trying to stop a child venturing into the road. Gabriel followed the direction of Sol's eyes and saw a group of men walking towards the stairs as a man came up them.

'We should disappear,' Sol said in a low voice, more serious than Gabriel had seen him before.

'What's going on?' Gabriel asked.

'Someone's about to get a kicking,' Kenzie said excitedly.

'For fuck's sake,' Sparks said. 'I'm starving.'

They walked away from the commotion and Gabriel saw one of the group of men grab the guy on the staircase. Then the three of them laid into him, punching him in the face in quick succession. The guards hadn't noticed yet. Sol grabbed Gabriel by the arm and pulled him into the cell across the way from him. The ginger man with the beard that Gabriel had seen on his first day was sitting in one of the cell chairs, reading. He looked up and smiled as he saw them. Gabriel had noticed the way he looked at him before, his eyes travelling over his frame at a snail's pace, resting on his neck, shoulders, torso, hips. He was doing it again and it made him uneasy.

'What the hell do you reprobates want?' the ginger

man said, putting down his magazine and shifting his gaze to Sol briefly.

'It's kicking off out there,' Sol said, 'we're just hiding out.'

They could hear shouting and people shuffling about out on the wing.

'I'd better get some fucking dinner,' Sparks exclaimed in a huff.

'Who's your new friend?'

'This is Gabe. Gabe, this is Asher.'

'Gabe.' He said the word with a twinkle in his eye. He held his hand out and Gabriel nodded acknowledgment but didn't take the hand.

Asher smiled. 'Suit yourself.'

'Hi,' Gabriel said, reluctantly.

'Who is it?' Asher asked Sol, leaning over his shoulder to look through the door of the cell.

'Andy Welsh. They got him on the staircase. It doesn't look good,' Sol said.

'Maybe they tried his cooking,' Sparks offered.

'Isn't Welsh in with you?' Asher said to Sol. 'You burn through cellmates faster than anyone else in here.'

'I was going to ask for a cell transfer anyway, Welsh is a twat,' Sol said.

Sparks stuck his head around the door quickly, presumably to see what was going on outside the cell.

'Lockdown!' Gabriel heard Barratt call out.

'Do we go back to our cells?'

'Nah, stay here. They just want the wing cleared to sort the mess out,' Asher said.

'Do you think he's dead?' Sparks asked.

'You're such a fucking gossip,' Sol said to Sparks.

'Shall I look?' Kenzie asked.

'Just relax. He's obviously not or it would be going mental out there,' Sol said, as ever the voice of reason.

'Sausage and mash is literally the highlight of my bloody week,' Sparks grumbled.

'Will you stop going on about food, man!' Kenzie barked, wrapping his arms around his stomach. 'At least with Welsh gone we might get something edible next dinner time.'

Gabriel wasn't a big eater, he had already lost weight since being inside, but the truth was, the meals were only just filling enough to get you through to the next one and so any kind of delay felt like unnecessary cruelty and a stark reminder of their circumstances. You could almost pretend once you had settled into the routine that everything was OK and that this wouldn't be forever. But, in reality, you were usually just counting meals – or whatever else your crutch in prison was. He had seen some people obviously on drugs on the inside, but he had no idea how they were being distributed. He didn't want to know either. His brief had warned him to just keep his head down until the hearing came.

'OK boys, go get your food.' A dishevelled Barratt knocked on the door.

Gabriel noticed that Barratt always looked a mess, and he didn't smell great either. There was just something worn about him, something that wasn't quite up to standard. Maybe he'd recently separated, maybe he was living alone for the first time in years – it was as though it was all new to him. His shoes were scuffed, all his seams frayed and there were lots of stains on his uniform, the kind that probably would wash out if you just tried. It was almost as if Barratt had given up on himself. Maybe this kind of apathy came with the job.

They all walked out on the wing, Asher following a few feet behind them. One of the inmates Gabriel didn't know was mopping blood from the foot of the staircase. He felt sick again but no one else was even paying attention, stepping over the blood as though it were a spilled drink. They all headed to the servery and continued the conversations about the food on offer. Gabriel couldn't even think about food, his appetite had all but disappeared.

'Have you had a shower yet?' Sparks asked.

'Not really, not properly.'

'I thought as much, you're a bit whiffy, mate.'

'It's very rare for bad shit to happen in the showers. It's not like the movies, you know,' Sol chipped in, as though sensing Gabriel's worry.

'The screws are opposite anyway. It's pretty heavily monitored; it was a condition of the last inspection,' Sparks added.

'I'll get round to it,' Gabriel said, trying not to be as evasive as he felt.

'Listen Gabe, you need to relax a little, find your groove,' Sol said. 'Everyone in here is mostly trying to keep their head down, do their time and then get out. Don't let stuff scare you. If you're thinking about your cellmate Jason, he was just an idiot, that's all. If you're that worried you should request to stay with me.' It seemed Sol had already written off his own cellmate, who was probably being carried off to the infirmary as they spoke.

Gabriel sighed. 'What happened to Jason anyway? Will someone tell me now?'

'He's in the infirmary and then he'll be moved to D-wing. If he recovers,' Sol said. He always seemed to know what was going on around the prison. People spoke to him.

'You probably shouldn't mention him again. If the screws catch you, they will be pissed off,' Sparks said.

'Why?' Gabriel asked.

'Because he's just a reminder of how little control they have in here. If we all decided to kick off at the same time, they would be fucked,' Sparks whispered.

'Look, Gabe, the fact is, I'm surprised you've been alone this long and I don't particularly want you to be in the pad-mate lottery,' Sol said. 'They won't let you stay alone forever and you never know who you're gonna get. If people know you're my cellie they will leave you alone.'

'Yeah, just like Welsh back there.' Sparks winked at Kenzie and they both laughed.

'But I'm on remand and you've already been sentenced.' Gabriel ignored them and continued talking to Sol.

'If you request it, they'll consider it. Unless they think we're a couple or something,' Sol said.

'Does that happen?'

'If you're lucky.' Kenzie laughed and winked.

'Sorry, I didn't mean anything by that.' Gabriel could feel himself blushing.

'Don't worry, mate, you aren't my type.'

'Kenz likes a sugar daddy.' Sparks laughed and Kenzie thumped him in the arm.

'Oy!' Prison officer Hyde shouted across to them across the servery. 'Pack it in!'

'Just messing about, sir,' they said in unison. Gabriel instinctively turned to look at Asher, he didn't know why but at that moment he felt like he should. Asher was just staring at him again, a look on his face that made Gabriel a little more than uncomfortable. It made him scared.

Chapter 12

Imogen pulled up outside Adrian's house and honked the horn. He stepped out with a piece of toast between his teeth just moments later and jumped in the car.

'Don't get crumbs in my car, Miley.' She pushed on the accelerator before he had a chance to properly close the door.

'I found out Bricks' real name, it's Theodore Ramsey. And good morning to you too.'

'Do we know if he went to prison for certain? If so, do we know if he got released and if there's any chance of him being the person in the signal box?' Imogen swung the steering wheel to the left, firing questions at him as they rounded the bend at the end of Adrian's road.

'We don't know anything past his name at this point. I texted Gary to see if he could find out for us.'

'Why aren't we doing that?'

'He called me; I said we would be in soon and he asked if I needed anything,' Adrian protested.

'I think he's got a bit of a man crush on you.'

'What's a man crush?'

'It's a crush on someone you can't have – and realistically don't want. It's like admiration, I suppose. I don't know, I'm not good with words.'

Adrian's phone beeped and he looked at the screen. Gary had looked Ramsey up; he had gone to prison, but he wasn't there anymore. He was in the system, though, and Gary had managed to find a picture from an earlier arrest.

'Ah, Gary. Always comes up with the goods. I think I might have a man crush on him, too.'

'Because he does all the hard work for you?' Imogen teased.

'Hush. Anyway, he says he's got a picture of Mr Ramsey, he took a dump in a public fountain a few years ago, and we got his mugshot.'

'He sounds nice. Who told you his name anyway?'

'Lucy Hannigan, she dropped by my house early this morning.'

Imogen raised an eyebrow at him. 'Did she now?'

'Yes. She said she had some information and she thought she should share it with me.'

'It couldn't wait a few hours?'

'Are you jealous?'

'Um, no Miley, you're far too . . .'

'Good? Moral? Respectable? Does my clean record make me undesirable to you?'

'Yeah, that's it. Kill someone and we can talk.' Her face darkened a little as she remembered that her boyfriend *had* killed someone, at least one someone, probably more.

'How is Dean?'

'Really? That's the segue you choose?'

'Sorry!' He laughed, even though Imogen's face was anything but amused. 'But seriously, how is he?'

'Fine, he's fine. We're still taking things slowly.' She didn't like talking about Dean at length. She had met him on a previous case and their relationship felt inevitable from the very first meeting, she couldn't explain it if she tried but she was drawn to him, even though he had a criminal record and more than a few secrets. She didn't think Adrian could understand that kind of relationship; for as long as she had known him he had only ever had one-night stands after splitting with his ex Andrea, Tom's mother.

'Sure you are.' He raised his eyebrows as he shoved the last piece of toast in his mouth.

She slammed her foot on the brake and they jolted forwards, causing Adrian to almost hit his head on the dashboard. He started to choke on his toast.

'Sorry, my foot slipped.' She pulled into the station car park and stopped the car properly.

Inside the station, Gary was waiting patiently next to Adrian's desk. Imogen had always thought he had a bit of a thing for her, but seeing the way he was with Adrian maybe she'd got that wrong, maybe he was just a loyal friend and a good copper. He was one of the few people she trusted. Adrian being one of the others along with Dean. As usual when she was at work, she pushed Dean out of her mind in case the thought police could see into her mind and figure out what she had been doing. Having someone like Dean for a boyfriend would put Imogen under an undue amount of scrutiny. It wasn't like she didn't know that, but for some reason she just couldn't stop herself. After the shit show that was her brief affair with her former boss, Dean was not only a welcome distraction but someone she could depend on, no matter what.

Gary handed Adrian the file, who in turn put it on the desk and opened it.

'Although this Bricks character has been picked up a few times by the police, he's only been properly charged once, for that attempted robbery at the post office last year,' Gary said. 'He spent a few months in prison on remand, but the trial fell apart and he got out a few months back. There is no official psychiatric evaluation as he refused them all. So, whatever his mental health problems are, they aren't documented anywhere as far as I can see.'

'Anything else?' Adrian asked.

'His name pops up a few times in relation to other crimes, but he's managed to stay out of prison for the most part.'

'And this is all we have on him?'

'Yep.'

'He's definitely not in prison now then?' Imogen asked as Adrian continued to read through the police report.

'He is not,' Gary said.

Imogen picked up the man's photo, he had a full beard and a few large, matted dreadlocks. He looked stoned in the picture, not remotely concerned that he had been picked up by the police. Possibly even a little defiant.

'When was this picture taken?'

'Last year, it's the only one I can find.'

'What about Gabriel Webb's phone? Did you get anything from it?'

'Nothing. There's significant contact with this Proserpina, his girlfriend, though I think we can assume that's not her real name. There are no photos of her on there, no indication of where she lives, what her real name is or even where she works.'

'You can't trace the phone then? What about the phone company?'

'It's pay as you go, sim card probably bought in a pound shop or something, there wouldn't be any need to register the name.'

'Isn't that pretty unusual?'

'Actually, not really; lots of kids use second phones.'

'Why?'

'If they want to keep secrets from their parents and they don't have the right credentials to get a contract. Usually the parents pay for a contracted phone but they can then access the bills and stuff. Also, there are a lot of family tracker software apps out there now; there's a chance it's to do with that.'

'He's not a kid though, he's nineteen.'

'Yeah, but he lives with his parents.'

Adrian thumbed through all the paperwork that Gary had collated for them, including the photo of Ramsey, it was more than they'd had to go on half an hour ago.

'Thanks for all this Gary, you're a legend,' Adrian piped up. 'I'll buy you a beer after work one of these days.'

Gary smiled and left them alone to go through the file. As far as Imogen could tell, this Bricks guy was more annoying than anything else. No violent crimes on his report at least, aside from the post office robbery – he was usually just pulled up for mouthing off at people and occasionally getting thrown in the drunk tank. But he had been moved out of the signal box at least twice in the past.

'What do you think?' Imogen asked.

'I don't know. How do we even confirm whether our dead body is Bricks?'

'I guess we keep considering it. There is no way to get DNA from the body. Do we tell the DCI it was Bricks or what?'

'I don't think we can do that just yet, let's keep hold of his file for a while.'

'Oh, keep hold of it for a while? When have you ever done that before? This has nothing to do with Lucy Hannigan, a certain doe-eyed journalist doing a piece on the homeless?'

Adrian smiled and closed the file.

'Nothing at all . . .'

Chapter 13

'Hello?'

'Hi Lucy, this is Detective Miles.' He could feel her smiling on the other end of the phone. He wondered how it was that you could hear smiles; it was strange. 'I wondered if you were doing anything tonight.' There was a pause. He pushed on. 'Are you out with friends? Maybe I could buy you a drink. I've got some information you might be interested in; we could go through it together and see if we can figure out anything new.'

'I'm afraid I'm all tucked up in bed, Detective,' she said. 'I've got an early start tomorrow morning. Is there something else you wanted?'

Of course, Adrian's mind immediately hit the ground running, imagining her lying there. All women slept naked, didn't they? He took his coat off and unbuttoned his shirt with one hand while walking upstairs and climbing onto his own bed.

'Just had a rough week in all honesty. Maybe I just need someone to give me a hard time.' He stared up at the ceiling, he couldn't remember the last time he had lain down properly. Recently he had been sleeping on the sofa, nodding off with a drink in his hand.

'Well, that's not fair. It's harder for me to hate you if you hate yourself.'

'You hate me, do you? That's a strong word.'

'It's a strong emotion. Tell me, do you even remember me yet? Be honest.'

'No, I honestly don't. Give me a clue.'

'Ouch.' She laughed. There was a fair pause before she continued. 'We met on the Cathedral Green, one lunchtime, I was sitting with some friends and you were sitting on the wall chucking your sandwich at the pigeons. You seemed to have bonded with one of them because you came over and asked for our leftovers so you could continue.'

'And you said I shouldn't feed them because they were vermin.' He remembered her then, leaning back on her elbows in the grass.

'That's right.'

'And you wouldn't give them over, so I had to bribe you. Your friends left and we went for a drink together.'

'Ah, see, now you remember me.'

'Your hair was different, it was black and short. Plus we had quite a few drinks. I blame those.'

'OK show-off, I believe you.'

'It was a good day, except I remember you beating me at pool a lot.'

'I won every game.' She yawned.

'I'll let you go, I wouldn't want to make you late for your thing tomorrow.' He was embarrassed that he had forgotten her, they'd had a good time together. In his defence, she did look completely different now, but he felt that excuse wasn't good enough.

'Well thank you for calling, Detective, it's only a year or so too late.'

'Goodnight, Lucy.' He smiled down the phone.

Adrian hung up the phone and unbuckled his belt, ripping it from the loopholes and throwing it into the corner. He started to unbutton his jeans, slipping his hand inside his boxers. The phone rang; he looked at the screen and smiled. It was Lucy. He picked it up. There was a few moments' silence, with just the sound of faint breathing in the background.

'Suddenly I'm not that tired,' Lucy finally said.

His half-open jeans got a little more uncomfortable as she spoke; she sounded different to a few moments ago. The smile had most definitely gone.

'Is it a cliché if I ask you what you're wearing?'

'T-shirt and pants, nothing glamorous, I'm afraid. What about you, where are you?'

'I'm on my bed, fully clothed.'

'Yes, but where are your hands?'

'Well, one of them is holding the phone.'

There was a pause. 'Do you remember my body, Detective?'

'Yes, you have a tattoo.'

'Who doesn't these days?'

'Yours was a black rose on your shoulder blade, with a big thorny stem.'

'Do you remember anything else about me?'

'I remember everything.'

Chapter 14

Patty Wallis pulled the net curtains of her living room window back for the fifth time that evening; the kids on the road had been setting off bangers for the last hour or so and her dog, Pickles, was going crazy. It wouldn't be long before the kids descended into something a little more destructive; last time, they had stolen her hanging basket and thrown it over the wall of St Leonard's church.

She listened to the sound of Alf's gentle snoring in the moments when the television presenter paused for breath. She had to turn the volume up even more as her husband's slumber intensified. Pickles moaned and buried his head under Patty's feet as the noise outside got even closer to the house just before stopping altogether. The dog grumbled as he skulked off to the back of the house; she heard the flap go as he ventured outside into the garden to do his business. It was a cat flap really, Pickles was barely big enough to call a dog, but he was better company than Alf, more coherent at least. His ears pricked and head tilted from side to side whenever she spoke to him, unlike Alf who was almost completely deaf.

Patty sighed. On the television screen, the conundrum appeared and she guessed it straight away, annoyed that no one was present to witness her sharpness of mind. She had always been good at puzzles and word games. It wouldn't be long until *Deal or No Deal* was on, which meant it was almost time for dinner. Tonight they would be having a pasty and mash, packet mash, she didn't quite have the strength to mash her potatoes to the desired creaminess. She had lost interest in cooking a long time ago, if she was honest. It wasn't like Alf really cared what they ate anyway.

She looked outside the window again. The kids seemed to have gone, but she saw Pickles on the pavement outside the house, peeing on the lamp post. He must have slid under the side fence and pushed past the wheelie bins. He was so tiny that he could do it if he wanted to. Thankfully, he never wandered far. He came to the front gate and started wagging his tail. She pulled herself out of the armchair and went to find her outdoor slippers, the ones she wore for the garden, not that she went out there much anymore. She couldn't stand the cold and really didn't care for the sun, it played havoc with her skin. Her hanging basket was about as much of a garden as she could manage these days. As she slipped her misshapen feet into the soft rubbery shoes, there was a knock at the door. All the neighbours knew Pickles and this wasn't the first time he had escaped. She saw the silhouette of someone holding him behind the frosted glass, and opened the door with a grateful smile on her face.

As the lock clicked open and the light from outside began to seep inside, Patty was propelled backwards, the heavy white PVC of the door crashing into her cheekbone and her face simultaneously exploding with pain. Within seconds she was on the floor, her full weight jarring through her buttocks, hips and ribs. She looked up and saw two faces, unmoving. It took a few moments for her to realise she was looking at masks, one with a wide, contorted, thin-lipped grin, bulbous white cheeks and a furrowed brow, the other an exaggerated sad face. Not quite like the comedy and tragedy masks from the theatre but similar. Horror pulsed through her.

The two figures rushed past her, dressed from head to toe in black. One of them had Pickles under his arm. They trampled on her hand as they went past. She tried to sit up, but her body hurt, her legs felt more brittle than ever as she tried to shift the weight onto her knees, to get on all fours. It might take her some time, but she had to do something. They were in the front room now; Patty heard the sound of Alf crying out and various things smashing against the walls. Alf's cries became more frantic as she finally managed to pull herself up. She was dizzy, the physical exertion had caused her head to spin, her face throbbed and she could feel the blood filling up in her eye as well as the taste of it on her lips.

'We haven't got any money!' she called out, her voice

high and shrill, alien to her. Making her way to the door of the living room was a massive effort, she leaned against the wall as she walked, every step causing her pain. She watched as they hurled her son's wedding photo at the wall, before picking up another picture and swinging it – a picture of their son as a baby. Alf continued to scream as they drove what looked like a hockey stick into the TV, Pickles cowering under his feet for protection, whimpering. There was a thud and Patty was pushed forward, she felt a sharp pain as she landed on her hands; another man had come up behind her. He had a mask similar to the other two but with a different expression, probably much like the one on her face at the moment – the painted expression of fear. The high-pitched sound of laughter coming from behind the mask bounced around in Patty's head. The front door must still have been open. Why wasn't anyone coming to help? The third figure was now holding a phone, keeping it trained on Alf's increasingly demented screams. The smiling figure brought down his stick and Patty heard the anguished whimper as it collided with Pickles – he brought it down again and again until the only remaining sound was a dull wet thud and Alf's protracted moans. Pickles was dead. For a brief moment the fear inside her was overtaken by anger, then sadness but then she thought of Alf and how she couldn't protect him and the fear came creeping back.

She tried to see if the figure had any distinguishing features, but all three were wearing gloves and black shoes, everything was just black. The only thing Patty knew for sure was that there were three of them and they were young. There was a bounce in their step that only comes with youth. The smiling masked man put his gloved hand into Pickles' blood. Patty assumed that he was a male – the clothes he wore were loose and misshapen – but she felt it was a boy. Why was he doing this? Why were they doing this?

His gloved hands were now covered in Pickles' blood. Violently, the man grabbed a fistful of the dog's sopping wet fur and tore it out. She cried out in anguish, she wanted to scream louder, to alert someone but she was afraid they would turn their attention to her. He started to draw on the wall with the clump of bloody matted hair, from her position on the floor Patty could see that it was a symbol of some kind. It looked Irish, but she wasn't really up on those things. Her vision was blurry. Her head pounded.

When he had finished drawing the symbol, the man turned to Patty. She kept her eyes on Pickles' blood as it dripped down the wall, knowing full well that she would be dying soon. The other two masked figures pulled Alf from the armchair and started to kick him; Patty tried to block out the noise. It didn't last long; Alf was fragile and they weren't gentle. She hoped it would be as quick for her as the third figure grabbed her by the hair and pulled her into the centre of the room next to the mangled remains of Pickles. She wasn't one for prayers but she figured now was as good a time as any. In her mind, Patty recited the only prayer she remembered until she couldn't anymore.

Chapter 15

Gabriel couldn't sleep again. It was warm tonight and he felt so unclean. The prison was unusually noisy. One of the new inmates was screaming across the way and banging on the door. Gabriel jumped out of bed, grateful that they hadn't put the screamer in the same room as him even though he had a spare bed. He knew it wouldn't be long before that space was filled even though this was technically a one-person cell. He had put in a request to share a cell but was refused, he didn't know on what grounds and they didn't have to give him a reason. He walked to the door and stood to the side, trying to watch through the glass without making himself visible. The new man was smashing his face against the window, blood smeared and dripping down the glass. He looked distraught and Gabriel felt his pain, almost admired him for the courage he had in going with his own emotions. Releasing the frustration and anger instead of squashing it down and swallowing it. Gabriel thought back to his own first night and remembered the feeling of wanting to abandon himself, of wanting to do anything to make the pain stop. He could admit to himself now that he had blocked his mind from thinking about suicide, because to think about it now would make it an option. He knew there was only a small step between contemplating suicide and going through with it. Stopping himself from thinking about it altogether was the key.

Gabriel couldn't see which guards came, but within moments he heard the new inmate's screaming increase as they opened the cell door and then dissipate as they dragged him off, presumably to the infirmary. He wouldn't be coming back to this wing at any point soon, most likely he would be moved to D-wing for the more vulnerable prisoners. He'd be thrown in amongst the ones that were a danger to themselves, and those who were in danger from other prisoners. The child molesters, rapists and wife-beaters.

Gabriel got on the ground and started to do press-ups, knowing it would be a while until breakfast or even association, the allocated time out from the cells to associate with other inmates. He had become accustomed to being alone in the dark. He had hardened his heart to his own loneliness.

On his third set of twenty, Gabriel noted his breath was controlled, not the ragged pant it had been when he'd first started his new regime. He could feel the distant pull of his asthma creeping up in the background but he kept going. He felt a burst of pride at changing something he had always been too lazy to correct before.

Even though he was slim and toned, it was largely down to a lucky metabolism and possibly the fact that he walked everywhere. While he'd been in prison though, he had done more exercise than he'd done all year and he felt good for it.

He stood up and looked out onto the wing again, a little more tired now, ready to claim an hour's sleep before he was awoken and sucked back into the daily routines. He saw prison officer Johnson open Asher's door and go inside. He watched and waited for over ten minutes before he reappeared. Gabriel could see that as Johnson said goodbye and left the cell, Asher had a funny smile on his face. Relations between the guards and the inmates hadn't even occurred to Gabriel and he found himself shocked at his own surprise. He had to let go of his naiveté before it got him hurt, or worse, killed.

He lay down, mind racing, until the cells were finally unlocked and breakfast was announced. As soon as the doors opened, Asher walked over to Gabriel's cell. Gabriel braced himself as Asher put his hands on either side of the doorway, leaning in, blocking Gabriel's only way out.

'I saw you watching us.'

'I don't know what you're talking about.'

'You don't have to sneak a look, darlin'. All you need to do is ask if you're curious.'

'I'm not . . . I've got a girlfriend.'

'So have I.' He winked playfully and backed away from the door. Seconds later, Sol appeared.

'We're going to the showers now, before breakfast is

better than after. You might get the shit food but at least you usually get some privacy. You can't keep washing in your cacks.'

'OK,' Gabriel said nervously as he picked up his spare clothes and towel. He didn't want to be alone in his cell after his brush with Asher.

Gabriel was acutely aware of his form as he stood in the shower. He didn't know how to stand. He positioned his naked body as close to the taps as he could and concentrated on stopping himself from shaking. He didn't want to look around. There were three other men in there, besides himself, Sol and Kenzie. Just wash and leave, he told himself. He pressed on the tap and lukewarm water dribbled out. It lasted just shy of a minute before he had to press it again. He had read an article once on the internet, just one of those throwaway health advice segments that get tossed around: how to effectively shower in four minutes, the Australian way apparently. You get your body wet, cover yourself in soap then rinse. It sounded obvious to Gabriel, but he usually took a lot longer. This would be the quickest shower he ever had. He quickly grabbed the shampoo and rubbed it in before hitting the button again and rinsing it out. He couldn't see behind him; he didn't want to. It took five presses of the button to get him close to clean. He made sure he washed the top of his thighs where sweat and friction had caused an angry red rash to appear on his skin.

On the way to the showers, prison officer Hyde had told him he had a visitor coming later that day. As far as Gabriel could remember, he had sent visiting orders to both his parents and to Emma at her request. He was sure it wouldn't be his parents coming. He allowed a smile to cross his face as he wrung the excess water from his hair. He grabbed his towel, proud that he had made it through, a glimmer of hope that maybe he could survive in here.

This was the cleanest Gabriel had been since he'd arrived in prison and he found himself with the unfamiliar feeling of anticipation. He was excited to see Emma. He hadn't seen her since the night he'd walked out of the club with the detectives. He missed her, and not even just her if he was honest with himself; he missed the look and smell of a woman. Surrounded by men all day in this environment was not something he'd prepared for. It was doubly bad when he knew every single man around him was a criminal, almost everyone had done something bad. The feeling of constantly being on his guard was new to Gabriel, although thinking about it, it was just a slightly more intense version of how he felt around his father.

Chapter 16

Imogen sidestepped the crime scene markers that had all been photographed already. There was blood spattered everywhere. The Wallis house had an overwhelming smell of lily of the valley, detergent Imogen supposed, or maybe some kind of air freshener. It was a smell she remembered from the one time she'd ever visited her maternal grandmother's home; the woman had had a habit of using old sheets of soap from folded cardboard packets to clean her hands. She pulled herself back into the present.

The residence was a Victorian terrace, like most houses in this part of town, dated but well-kept inside. Imogen glanced around the lounge; this couple didn't seem to have much of any value to anyone other than themselves. Holiday souvenirs and lots of ceramic ornaments smashed into tiny pieces littered the floor. One solitary clown on a bench remained unscathed on the top of the dresser; he was resting his chin on his hand

and looking down with an expression of emptiness, of horrifying loss, at the mosaic of carnage on the mint-green carpet.

She turned to Adrian who was standing in the centre of the room, looking down at the matted, bloody mess on the floor. The corners of his mouth were turned down as the photographer placed the ruler next to it and took a photograph. With horror, Imogen realised it was a dog. She averted her eyes so as not to capture any more detail than that – she would have to build up to that one.

On the sofa was a slumped and bloodied body. It was a man, elderly and obviously quite frail. Imogen's discomfort at her surroundings turned into anger. In a way she was grateful; anger made crime scenes easier. Who would do this? There was no money here, the TV was old and had been smashed, there was nothing worth stealing. The senselessness and cruelty of the crime struck Imogen. She was aware that no one was speaking. She assumed, like her, that her colleagues felt the scene spoke for itself, there was no need to point out the horror of it and it was far too heinous to make jokes. Murders were always horrible, but when it was someone so helpless it seemed even more unnecessary, even more cruel.

Adrian looked up at her. As he negotiated his way around the crime scene markers, he almost tripped on the leg of the armchair but managed to stop himself just in time. Everyone looked up, the disturbance pulling them out of their own thoughts. The spell was broken; it was OK to speak now.

'There's another body in the kitchen. The wife by the

looks of it. Seems like she's been dragged there, judging by the blood trail. Whoever did this . . .' Adrian said, his voice trailing off. 'Just when I think I have seen the worst of humanity . . . I still get surprised now and again.'

'Well, what do we think then?' she asked him, trying to stay matter-of-fact.

'Who knows? It seems completely nuts, destructive.'

'What is that?' Imogen pointed; she had only just noticed a large symbol painted in blood on the wall, not because it was small or unnoticeable in any way, but because there were other, more horrible things that kept catching the eye.

'No idea, it's a pretty common symbol though, so it could mean anything.'

'Is there anything missing?'

'Fraser had a quick look; the wife is still wearing her wedding ring and a gold chain so it's unlikely this was a robbery. They also found a jar with cash in the kitchen, it was hidden but not to someone who was looking for money.'

'What's the motive then?'

'It's got to be personal, hasn't it?

'Personal? Against these folks? No, I don't see how. Look at them!' She pointed at a family photo that remained on the wall, tilted and with a damaged frame. It was the elderly couple, with presumably their grandkids.

'This has to be more than one person,' Adrian said, frowning. 'What stopped one of the occupants from calling the police? Why didn't they scream or try and make a run for it?'

'I'd better go and look in the kitchen.' Imogen trudged

reluctantly towards the back of the house, she had been in the shower when she'd got the call so had arrived after Adrian. She heard multiple clicks of the camera and took a deep breath before entering the room, following the trail of blood. The wife lay on the ground, the extent of her injuries far worse than her husband's. She didn't seem as frail as him, from looking at her frame. There was a knife sticking out of her arm, but no blood directly around the wound, so it was post-mortem, which was a relief to Imogen; at least Mrs Wallis wouldn't have felt that particular attack, even if she had felt the others. She noticed a gold chain around the woman's neck, the word *Nan* formed in the centre, the letters now embedded in Patty Wallis' clavicle. Imogen pulled her eyes away from the body and stood up to look around. The kitchen was equally as smashed as the lounge. Adrian had a point; with this much destruction there had to be more than one perpetrator, which led to a load more questions, not least, how do two people decide to commit a violent and horrific murder together? Maybe it was drug related.

'It's not druggies,' Adrian said, as though he had read Imogen's thoughts.

'How do we know?'

'The wife is on some serious pain medication, there is no way junkies would leave all of that there.' Adrian pointed over to a shelf above the kettle. 'That stuff has decent street value as well.'

'We need to find out as much as we can about them. Has anyone notified next of kin?'

'Not yet, I was waiting for you. Let's go.'

Chapter 17

There was an optimistic buzz around the wing, with an undercurrent of sadness. Optimism from the men who would most likely be visited, contrasting with the crushing loneliness of some of the others who would not. Gabriel had felt that desperate heartache just the week before, so he had a little empathy for the other men. Men like Sol who had no one on the outside, no one to come and visit, no letters and no life beyond the prison walls. It was one of the main reasons for reoffending. No support system, more friends inside than out. For the first time since he had arrived, Gabriel felt lucky.

Hyde opened the door to the visitors' lounge and there she was. Emma was sitting at a table in the centre of the room. She looked scared. The other visitors didn't have the same look about them, obviously used to this ritual. The others could have been sitting in a pub waiting for their friends. Not Emma though, her wide eyes didn't know where to look. Her hair was different yet again, she had pinks and purples running through it this time, and the roots had grown out even longer in the couple of weeks since he had seen her. She wore a T-shirt slashed through the neck so that her breasts were in full view, rounded and swollen, bursting their way out of her neon lace bra. He saw her mouth turn up at the sight of him losing his shit over her. She hadn't come to break up with him. She stood up and he saw the short denim skirt. He looked at Hyde who nodded for him to go over; once there, he glanced across again and Hyde nodded once more. Gabriel assumed that meant he was all right to touch her. He breathed in her smell as he leant down to kiss her; she only came up to his armpits. His eyes hovered on her lips for a moment then he kissed her hard, and she slipped her tongue inside his mouth. For that moment, he could taste tropical fruit juice mixed with a hint of Doublemint, the faint smell of the patchouli oil that was always stronger just behind her ears. He heard a baton tapping on a table and knew instinctively that it was directed at him. Reluctantly he pulled away and saw Hyde giving him a disapproving look. He sat down opposite Emma and just looked at her for a few moments, trying to commit the image of her right now to memory. She was different to how he had remembered her. Or maybe it was that he was a different person now to the man who had looked at her all those days ago.

'I've never been in a prison before,' she finally said.

'Me neither.' Gabriel shrugged.

They both laughed.

'I'm so sorry. I can't believe this has happened. I can't believe there was someone in there,' she blurted out.

'Don't.'

'It's my fault. I should never have invited Leanne and I should have worn a bloody coat.'

'You can't think like that. You didn't know it was going to go down the way it did.' He paused. 'You OK?'

'I'm fine . . . Christ . . . What are you going to do?'

'What is there to do? I just have to wait for my sentencing.'

'If I spoke to the police . . .'

'You don't have to do that, you're in the clear. They haven't identified you.'

'No, but they still could.'

'Girl in a short black dress in a goth club? Good luck to them.'

'Let me come forward, let me tell them what actually happened. I can't stand the thought of you in here.'

'No, you can't. If you get arrested too then I'll never forgive myself. I've already told them it was an accident. I have to do this.' Gabriel didn't want to incriminate Emma; if that meant protecting the identities of the others then so be it.

'Why won't you let me help you? You weren't the only one there.'

'Look, I told them what happened, I just left you all out of it.'

'Please. Let me come forward . . .'

'No, don't. Best to leave it the way it is. No point

both of us being banged up.' He looked away from her briefly. 'I understand, you know, if you want to break up.'

'I don't – are you kidding?' She smiled at him. 'Having a boyfriend in prison is winning me major cool points. Everyone thinks you're this big thug who goes around . . .'

'Killing people?' he challenged, clenching his teeth to curb the spurt of shame inside him.

'I wasn't going to say that.'

'It's OK. I appreciate you coming here today. I don't suppose you know anything about my parents?'

'I don't. I'm guessing they don't know about me or the police would have come round already.'

'We don't really "share" much. In fact, they haven't even been to see me.'

Emma looked down at the table. 'I don't know when I can visit again. It took ages for this visit to come through. But I'll put a request in for another one straight away. It was horrible coming though, they had to search me and check my hair and stuff.'

'Welcome to my world.'

'I miss you,' she said softly. 'You look good.'

'You look . . .' He smiled and looked down. 'Like a sight for sore eyes.'

A loud buzzer sounded through the room and people started to pull away from their huddles instinctively. Knowing it was time to go, Emma stood up and Gabriel studied her once more, trying to keep this picture in his head, something to dream about tonight. He stood up and they kissed again. He didn't want to pull away, it was harder than anything he had done before, harder even than walking into this place.

'I'll see you soon. Hang in there.'

He watched as she left before being escorted out himself.

It took every ounce of Gabriel's energy not to cry as he was walked back to the wing; he had half an hour bang-up to get himself together before the doors opened again and the other men wandered past ready for lunch. He got on the floor and started pressing, pushing past his normal twenty, pushing as far as he could until his breathing was laboured. The lump in his throat propelled him to push harder, work harder. He had pressed fifty before he noticed the wet spot on the ground in front of him; tears were dripping from his nose onto the floor. He kept going, his asthma still under control. By the time he reached seventy press-ups he had slowed considerably, his arms juddering as he pushed himself and lowered, then pushed again. The tears were now replaced with a sweat he could taste on his lips. At ninety-one press-ups, he finally collapsed on the floor.

He lay there for a moment, staring up at the strip light and forcing back the tears. Seeing Emma had broken the toughened exterior he had worked so hard to achieve. He was afraid again. He could smell Emma on him, patchouli and Doublemint. He looked at the clock and stood up. Climbing up onto his bed and turning towards the wall, he was overcome with the urge to touch himself while he could still smell her, while the feeling of closeness to her was here. It would be gone soon, he would feel alone again before he knew it and so he had to take it now. He had to. Maybe it was the feeling of being clean as well, but he was aroused. It didn't take much to stir him to erection, he just remembered the bra, the boots, the legs, the smile. The way she bit her bottom lip slowly when she looked at him from beneath her eyebrows. Within moments he had forgotten where he was and was lost in thoughts of Emma, free from anxiety, just a man in a room with a hand and a cock. He held his breath and stroked himself gently and then harder, trying to remember the way Emma would do it, even though he could do it better – he wanted to feel like she was here with him, touching him. He relaxed into the moment and let himself go. Not wanting to dirty either his bed or his clothes he lay on his back to come. Once it was done, he remembered where he was and jumped off the bed to clean himself before the doors opened and someone came in. He was hit with a thought in that moment. This could be it, for the next ten years or however much he got. Just him and his hand. The idea of no intimacy was terrifying to him. Not only sex, but the other things that came with a relationship, like sharing a drink or a bed or a bath.

He had to put it out of his mind for now; he couldn't allow himself to slip into depression. Once it got a grip on him he wouldn't be able to get out from under it. It wasn't always as simple as mind over matter but there was an element of choice in it for Gabriel. Sometimes he grabbed hold of the depression with both hands and let it take him where it needed him to go. Most of the time he suppressed and repressed. Pushing it down, squashing it. If he ever got out of this shithole he would give himself the luxury of depression. Right now, he needed to keep it together.

Roll call. As with every lunch or association time, Gabriel tried not to look at Asher. He noticed that every time he did so, Asher was looking straight back at him. Even when he wasn't looking, he knew where Asher was; the man had a presence. He was always in the corner of Gabriel's eye, always watching him. He had one of those faces, the face of a person who knows stuff, personal stuff, intimate stuff. Gabriel felt like Asher could tell what he was thinking about just from looking at him: what he'd done, what drove him, what he desired. He made Gabriel uneasy, there was something sinister at the very heart of him.

Sol and Sparks hadn't turned up but Gabriel was hungry so he went down to lunch.

Asher appeared in front of him by the lunch queue and smiled, looking down at Gabriel's crotch and then back up at his face with a knowing smile.

'I hear your girlfriend is hot.'

'She is.' Asher's pad-mate appeared at his side with a goofy smile on his face. 'I saw her in the visiting room. She's fucking nasty-looking.'

'Hey, shut up,' Gabriel said, not angry, not yet – but still. He didn't like them talking about Emma – or even thinking about her.

'Is she nasty, Gabe? Does she do nasty things with her mouth?'

'Shut the fuck up.'

'I bet you had a fumble didn't you, when you got back to your pad, all on your own, thinking about her dirty mouth. Did you bang one out, Gabe?'

Before Gabriel even had a chance to think about what he was doing, he had his hands around Asher's throat – he pushed him against the wall, his thumbs on his Adam's apple. Asher was a little shorter than Gabriel, probably around six feet tall and he was muscular, his pale freckled skin showed a network of distended veins in his arm. Asher pouted his lips and kissed at Gabriel, which sent him over the edge. He drove his elbow into Asher's face, it glanced off his nose and the blood erupted immediately. The release of anger brought a rush of emotion to the surface and Gabriel found himself hitting Asher again and again. Asher looked scared but somehow excited. The blood had coated his teeth, deep red outlining each one. A pool had collected in his bottom lip and trickled down his chin and neck onto Gabriel's hand. This was what he wanted. He wanted to push Gabriel over the edge. Gabriel felt a thwack on the back of his knees and his legs crumpled, before another smack landed on his shoulders. He let go of Asher immediately.

'Both of you back to your pads,' Johnson said.

'It's all right – there's no problem here.' Asher rubbed his neck and spat blood onto the ground, his face already swelling but the grin remaining.

'Just get in your fucking pads!' Johnson screamed.

'Yes sir,' Asher said with a smile, but Johnson's frown was fixed.

Maybe Gabriel had been wrong about what he

thought he'd seen. He had assumed that their meeting had been sexual, Asher had obviously wanted him to think that. There didn't seem to be anything between Asher and Johnson – at least not on Johnson's side.

'Move!' Johnson shouted as Gabriel got to his feet. He manhandled him down the corridor, away from the servery, then shoved him into his cell and shut the door.

Gabriel was angry, his heart was thumping in his ears – he looked at the blood on his hand and pulled his T-shirt off to scrub it; it made him feel dirty and disgusting. He grabbed a fresh T-shirt and put it on. He would shower in the morning.

The door opened again and Barratt was there with Hyde. They grabbed Gabriel by either arm and pulled him out of the cell.

'What's going on?' Gabriel went with them but they still pulled on his arms as though he were somehow resisting.

'You're going to Seg.'

Chapter 18

Imogen knocked on the door of Richard Wallis' house. There were balloons and a happy birthday banner attached to the frame. Great timing as usual. She stood side by side with Adrian as they waited for it to be answered. Inside the house, they could hear children running and playing. The door opened and a petite woman with a perfectly formed black bob stood before them, cake batter in her hair and some kind of orange liquid splashed on her skirt.

'Hello?' she said with an ever so slightly manic tone to her voice. 'Can I help you?'

'Is this the Wallis residence? Is Mr Wallis at home?'

'Richard!' she called out, looking back into the house. Richard Wallis appeared at the door, holding on his hip a three-foot Spider-Man with a birthday boy badge on.

'Hello?' he said, immediate concern showing on his face.

Imogen and Adrian both held up their warrant cards.

'Mr Wallis,' Imogen said.

He tried to hand the child over to his wife but the little spider-man was having none of it, clinging to Richard's neck until his mother gave him a sharp tug, his arms still reaching out as she took him away. The screams trailed off as she closed the kitchen door.

'He's five today so we invited a few friends over for his first party. Turns out he hates parties.' Richard grinned wryly at them.

Imogen smiled tightly. 'Sorry to interrupt but we need to speak to you about something if we could come inside?'

'Of course, of course. You can come into the lounge, just mind the puddle in the corner, we've had to quarantine them to the kitchen after one of his friends threw up all over Renee, my wife. Too much pop.'

'That's not a problem.'

They followed him and sat down. He seemed a little embarrassed by the state of the house; it wasn't exactly messy but it was obvious that it was usually much tidier. Imogen could hear the kids screaming from the kitchen and she felt a little pang of sympathy for Renee Wallis.

Imogen looked at the artwork on the walls, she recognised one of the pictures as being by an acclaimed local artist her mother had admired, in fact she remembered they had a print of that exact picture on the landing in her childhood home. This was no print though; this was the real thing. It was a nice place; they obviously had taste.

'I'm afraid we've got some bad news for you, Mr Wallis,' Adrian started.

'What is it?'

'Your parents. Perhaps you'd like to sit down?'

'What's happened?' His eyes furrowed as though he were struggling to comprehend what they were saying.

'We are still investigating what exactly happened, but I am really sorry to inform you that they are both deceased.'

Richard Wallis ran his fingers through his hair, eyes bulging as wide as they could, and then buried his face in his hands. Standing up, he walked to the window and looked out.

There was a pause. 'Both of them?'

'Yes, I'm afraid so.'

'What about Pickles?'

Imogen was confused as to what he was referring.

'Is that the dog?' Adrian asked.

'Yes, has he been taken to the pound?'

'I'm afraid not, no. The dog is also deceased.'

'What?' Richard Wallis said with even more surprise than he had shown at his parents' death. 'What happened to the dog?'

'I'm afraid we can't discuss the particulars with you right now.'

'Do I need to come and identify the bodies?'

'No, not yet, we will contact you if and when that happens,' Imogen said, knowing full well that the bodies were in no condition to be viewed by a family member just yet.

'What happens now?'

'Our liaison officer will be in touch with you very

soon to tell you what happens next but for now we will leave you with your family.'

'Was it quick? Did they suffer?'

Imogen didn't know how to answer that honestly without lying. 'We'll be in touch when we know more.'

Outside, they got back in the car and sat in silence for a few moments.

'Thoughts?' Adrian said.

'I don't know. That's never easy.'

'No. Never.'

'Did that feel a little easier than it should have or am I being paranoid?' Imogen asked.

'Just because you're paranoid doesn't mean you're wrong.'

Chapter 19

Adrian drove along the tree-lined Southernhay Street, what remained of the sun peeking through the leaves and bouncing off the seemingly infinite small window-panes in the tall Georgian houses. It was important to soak these moments in when you spent the rest of your time wading through crap. His window was open and the breeze tickled his ear, there was silence in this part of town as it was after normal office hours. People were at home eating dinner, deciding whether to venture back out for a cold drink on this warm summer evening. Lucy Hannigan was waiting to cross the road further up ahead, she hadn't spotted Adrian yet so he took the opportunity to really look at her, without her scrutiny making him look away. He had forgotten that the newspaper office was in this part of town. She shook her hair back out of her face, her mop of unruly brown curls misbehaving as usual. She closed her eyes as though enjoying the breeze. Adrian glanced away; he hated to interrupt but he had to. He pulled up alongside her and wound down the window. Her eyes were still closed, lost in some idea or thought.

'Do you need a lift anywhere?'

'No. I have a car, I decided to walk for a reason. You should try it some time, it's nice.' She didn't even open her eyes. Had she seen him already then?

'I walk sometimes.'

'You can't park here.'

'I can park over there though. I'll walk with you . . . if you don't mind.'

'Fine.' She smiled and opened one eye, looking down on him with a wink.

When he turned the engine off she was standing by the car, swinging her satchel playfully, a knowing smirk on her face.

'Did you just finish work?' he asked, but she ignored the question.

'Take me to dinner, I'm hungry.' She crossed the road, and he followed obediently.

They settled into a booth in a Chinese restaurant minutes later. The red lighting accentuated Lucy's cheekbones and made her blue eyes purple. He struggled not to stare at her.

'Have you been busy today?' Adrian asked.

'We're past this, aren't we? I mean we already slept together and had phone sex, so can we skip past the small talk? I loathe it.'

'What do you want to talk about then?'

'Why did you become a cop?'

'If I see any of this in an article . . .'

'Please . . .' She waved her hand dismissively.

'The honest answer is that I wanted to be good, and do something good for society. I know that sounds cheesy,' he said. Another honest answer was that he was a teenage father and wanted to do the right thing, earn money and be there for his now ex, Andrea, and his son, Tom. He wanted to be better than was expected of him. The police seemed like an obvious way to do that.

'It's cute. Why did you want to do that?'

'Because I didn't want to be dictated to by the path that was laid out in front of me, I wanted to be my own person. My father was a drug addict and he did a lot of bad things, a lot of things that made me ashamed of him, of my family in general.'

'I didn't know that about you. I didn't think that would be the answer.'

'Why did you think I became a cop, then?'

'I don't know, I think maybe you just thought it was cool.'

'Not many people think the police are cool.'

'True.'

'Why did you become a journalist?'

'I love puzzles and I love to write, it seemed like a logical step. Plus, I believe people have the right to know what's going on in the world.'

'A regular Lois Lane.'

'Does that make you Clark Kent?'

'No I think I'm more of a Jim Gordon . . . but realistically I'm probably Harvey Dent.' He acquiesced, pausing for a second. 'I'm so embarrassed that I didn't remember you, I'm really sorry. You must think I'm a complete dick.'

'I'm not usually one for second chances but you seem quite different to how you were before.'

'Different how?'

'More grown-up, I guess. Don't get me wrong though, I knew what was happening the first time we were together, I wasn't hanging by the phone waiting for you to call me or anything. You just seem calmer, there was an edge to you before.'

'I was in a bad place, a case I was working on. I'm sorry anyway, it's no excuse. I don't do that stuff anymore.'

'Well I hope that's not true. I didn't really come here because I was hungry.' She shot him a look that made him draw his breath. She was different to how he remembered her, too. More confident? Harder?

He blushed, thankful for the red glow of the restaurant to hide his embarrassment. The waitress brought over the duck they had ordered and they started to eat. They ate in near-silence, but with glances that hurried them along. He watched her fingers as she placed the folded pancake in her mouth, moments later sucking off the excess sauce that had dribbled onto them. After three or four pancakes she put her hand up and the waiter came over.

'Can I have the bill?' Adrian asked, still watching her. She smiled.

'Is there something wrong?' The waiter looked at their plates.

'No, it's really lovely, can we have the rest put in a doggy bag to take away?' Lucy said diplomatically.

Being out of breath when you are with someone new was one of the most exciting feelings Adrian knew. It wasn't something he had felt many times in his life, but when he did, he noticed it. He relished it. He tried to commit this moment to memory, the moment when there was still a mystery to be solved. Before they found out that the things that excited them the most would almost always turn out to be the things that annoyed them the most in the end. Of course, this might not even get that far, he knew that, but it was nice to think that it was possible. Adrian remembered the moment with his ex, Andrea; he had always loved the way she carried herself, as though she were royalty, untouchable, out of his league – and then finally that was one of the things that tore them apart. Just like she had been attracted to his roguish charm but cited it so often in the list of reasons why he couldn't spend time with his son.

Lucy commanded that sense of interest and mystery, of confusion and unpredictability. Never quite knowing what someone was going to say or do next was hot, but only if you were already attracted to the person. Being surprised by someone kicked up the level of intrigue and the need to get to know them better. Adrian had always been the most interested in the women he couldn't figure out within a few sentences. Lucy was one of those women and he could feel himself being drawn in; he hadn't been pulled towards someone like this for years and it was a welcome break from questioning himself. There was no decision to be made here, it was all being done on a level that Adrian had no control over. He had missed this.

They left the restaurant quickly and walked back to Adrian's car, an unspoken promise between them, words unnecessary at this point. At the car, he stopped at the passenger door and grabbed the handle to open it for her. She put her hand on his and pushed the door shut, leaning up and kissing him on the lips.

'Just so we're clear, we're going back to your place now, right?' she said as she leaned her whole body against him. He fell back against the car door and pulled her to him, kissing her again then pushing her away. If they stayed here much longer he would struggle not to throw her on the bonnet of the car, which was covered in bird shit. So, for everyone's sake he bundled her in and jumped in the driver's seat, getting home before the blood had left his head altogether.

Chapter 20

Although the segregation block was cleaner in many ways than his regular cell, it was entirely bleaker and made Gabriel realise how much more he had to lose. He missed Sol, Kenzie and even Sparks. Left alone with the thoughts that reverberated in his mind, he couldn't block out the things he had done, all he could think about was the man that had burned alive because of him, all he could smell was burning flesh, like a barbecue. He wanted to sleep, he wanted to shut the noise off, the noise of his memories, the sound of his father's disapproval and what he imagined to be his victory over Gabriel, the fact that he had been right about him all along. The fact that Gabriel had been a bad penny – that he had fulfilled the prophecies his father had spat in his face from the day he was born. The relentless disapproval. There was something wrong with him, there was something bad inside – and he was right. A man was dead and it was all Gabriel's fault.

He had learned the hard way after kicking the bedpost that everything was bolted down; he was pretty sure his toes were broken.

Alone, the question the nurse had asked him played over and over in his mind. What did he miss the most about being outside the prison? The answer wasn't freedom, not really, now that he had thought about it some more. The answer was in fact possibility. Possibility is such an intangible thing, he thought, such an inconsequential thing that you don't appreciate until you don't have it anymore. A life without possibility was a bleak outlook indeed. This room, this room that he was in for every hour of every day, was in fact the beginning and the end of possibility for him. He had to do what he was told, he had no choice but to colour inside the lines. No choice – no possibility – for anything different until someone else said, until someone else gave that to him. This must be growing up. This must be what it felt like to realise that all actions have consequences – he knew that from now on he would consider the consequences of everything he did.

Three times a day, the slot in his door slid open and food appeared. Every day, Gabriel hoped he would sleep, but sleep was more elusive that ever. He lay on the bed and closed his eyes but his head swam more than it had on the wing. The silence had become deafening and he couldn't remember the thoughts he had gone through over and over to conclusion a thousand times already. He yearned for the wing again, he even missed the feeling of threat, the feeling of anything but loneliness. Being alone with himself was harder than he had expected, especially knowing that this was just the beginning of his time in segregation. Knowing that he could be out in a week if they felt like it, or a month if they didn't. None of it was within his control. He'd thought being alone like this would come as a relief but it hadn't. It was anything but. He couldn't imagine anything more soul-sucking. He had lost himself, without other people around him to show him who he was. Everything he admired in other people, everything he hated about them, were all just reflections of his feelings about himself. Without others he didn't know who he was anymore.

Why had he let Asher push his buttons like that? He had no one to blame but himself again. He would do better; if he ever got out of Seg he would be the model prisoner, and if he ever got out of prison he would be the model citizen.

What if they forgot about him? What if no one came to feed him? He was completely at the mercy of the officers on this block. This room was his world now, and every hour felt like an eternity. He looked at the anti-suicide blanket and thought for the hundredth time of chewing at the stitching until he was able to tear a strip from the thick synthetic cloth and tie it around his neck, wrapping it two or three times so that even if he clawed at it he wouldn't be able to pull it off. For the hundredth time, he talked himself out of it and consigned himself to the never-ending cycle of thoughts that started over again, from the top.

Chapter 21

Like everyone else in the country, Imogen and Dean saw the viral video of the Wallis attack online. It had been shared thousands of times and the counter was clocking up at a rate that was unstoppable. Adrian had sent Imogen the link just moments before with a message that he would be picking her up first thing in the morning; they had to get in work early. She and Dean sat together on the couch and watched it on her mobile phone.

'Is this your case?' Dean asked as the video began. Eight minutes to go.

'Yep, it's going to get a lot worse, I've seen how it ends. Are you sure you want to . . .?'

He raised an eyebrow at her. 'I can handle it.'

They watched in silence for a minute.

'Those poor people,' Imogen said. 'What the hell is up with the world?'

'Any idea of a motive?'

'No. They were just a couple of pensioners, all they left behind was a son and three grandchildren. They had no money to speak of, nothing of value seemed to be taken from the house so this was seemingly all just for kicks.'

'What about the attackers?'

'Kids, I guess – or young, anyway. No fingerprints, no audio. There's nothing much to go on in that way. Our tech is probably trying to find out how and when this video was uploaded. Kids are clever though. This lot must have an agenda; they seem to be going to a lot of trouble – surely it's not just to be violent.'

'Turn it off, it's obviously upsetting you. You won't sleep.' He nuzzled into her.

'There's only a minute left, I may as well watch it,' she said. 'That's all I'll be doing in work anyway.'

She saw one of the perpetrators rip a clump of dog fur from the now dead dog and start to draw on the wall. Whoever was holding the camera split his time between him and the other guy who was mercilessly beating the old man. The camera swung slowly from one act of senseless violence to the almost primal drawing on the wall of the living room. The video had been put through some kind of software that made it look vintage, sepia-toned and crackling. She didn't recognise the music playing over the video either but she could probably find out in seconds with one of her phone apps. Dean was right though, she should turn it off; this felt too much like bringing work home, even though everyone in the world could see it if they wanted to. She watched the counter climb as people clicked to watch those poor people, she couldn't understand why that would be something you would want to watch. She looked at Dean who had fallen silent, an unnatural silence, his breathing had slowed as though he were trying to control it somehow. She looked back at the screen and saw the black figure putting the finishing touches to the symbol and then the screen froze.

She felt for the couple who were most likely dead by the time the video ended, the dignity of their final moments taken away from them. Posting it online somehow added to the violence of it, the total disregard for another person's privacy as they were so vulnerable and helpless. She thought of the times that she had felt that way, and the idea of it being on the internet made her feel physically sick. Imogen shook her head and tried to dislodge what she had just seen.

'How can anyone do that?' she said, wondering if Dean had ever done anything that brutal. She had seen his violent side before, as an enforcer for her father. The one who got his hands dirty when someone needed shaking up or intimidating. This, however, didn't strike her as something he would stoop to. She looked at him as he stared at the screen, his eyes fixed on the bloody symbol. Maybe she was just making excuses for him. What did she really know about him anyway? Did she know what he was capable of? She pushed the thoughts out of her mind, as she had been doing for months now. One day they would need to be addressed. 'I wonder what that symbol means,' she said instead. 'Is it some sort of pagan or Satanist thing?'

'It's a triquetra,' Dean said, his voice catching slightly.

'A what?'

'A Celtic symbol; it means love, honour and protect, or at least that's what some people say it means.'

'How do you know that?'

'I know things.' He smiled and stood up. 'I could use a drink. Do you want one?'

'Not really.' The image of the glistening blood, even in monochrome was enough to turn her stomach.

'Then what?' He turned to face her, pulling his shirt over his head.

They didn't spend every night together; she had made that a rule of the relationship – if you could call it that. So much between them that hadn't been labelled, because to give it a name meant that she would have to deal with it in the real world and she wasn't ready for that. But when they were alone together it always ended the same way. Bad day at work? Argument with family? Money problems? Headache? Whatever the problem, the antidote was always sex.

Tonight, it was the antidote to mortality, it was how they could combat the shit in the world, by being alive and not afraid. By caring for one another, by not succumbing to depression or fear. Lust was useful that way.

Dean seemed different somehow tonight in bed, focussed and intense, almost like the first time they'd slept together. He wasn't just making love to her, he was consuming her. It felt desperate and somehow final. When they were done, he pulled her towards him, her back against his chest. She lay with his arms around her, her body safely coiled inside his, his hand stroking her shoulder. She felt his heart thumping just behind hers, except his was faster. They were out of time.

Chapter 22

The wing felt different after being in Seg – it felt like home, somehow. Gabriel found himself almost pleased to see some of the faces that he hadn't realised he knew.

Johnson walked him back to his cell, Gabriel tried to avoid looking at Johnson who had stitches above his right eyebrow and a bruise on his chin, he didn't have to think too hard about who he got those from. When he got back to the cell there was another man in there. He had a new pad-mate.

'I'm Bailey.' The man held out his hand. He was smiley and enthusiastic; clearly, this wasn't his first time in prison.

'Gabe,' Gabriel said, shaking the man's hand. He wanted to get a reading on this guy early on.

'Keep your nose clean and you might get a labour pass soon,' Johnson said as he stepped out of the room. Gabriel wasn't sure which one of the men he was talking to.

'Seg, eh?' Bailey said. 'What did you do?'

'I punched one of the twats opposite in the face.' Gabriel jumped up onto his bunk and relished the feeling of the mattress under his sore back. The mattress in Seg was a piece of foam no thicker than a sheet when a body was lying on it. Gabriel closed his eyes, but his pad-mate kept talking. Clearly, Bailey wasn't in the least bit intimidated by Gabriel, or even wary in any way. It occurred to Gabriel after a few minutes of constant talking that maybe Bailey wasn't particularly socially advanced. A verbal stream of consciousness was pouring from him with no sign of let-up. In a way, Gabriel was grateful for the noise, after the silence of where he had just been.

'Do you know this Bailey guy then?' Gabe asked Sol in the queue for food later that day.

'Yeah, he's been in here a couple of times before. He can be quite intense, but he's not a bad guy.'

'Intense how?'

'Just a talker, once he runs out of subjects he starts asking questions. People don't like questions in here. He usually gets moved to a Cat C – but he's habitual, we've seen him before and no doubt we will see him again. Harmless though.'

Gabriel saw Bailey approaching and looked for somewhere to hide. Noise was good, but constant, unnecessary noise was quite annoying. There was – of course – nowhere to hide.

'What's on the menu today then?' Bailey said enthusiastically.

'Spaghetti,' Sol answered.

'Who's in the kitchen?'

'No one you know, but he's good.'

'What happened to Welsh? Why isn't he doing it? Is he still your pad-mate?' Bailey was jostling in next to them in the dinner queue.

'Nah, he's been moved to D-wing.'

'Ouch, but yeah – good, he was crap.'

'I wouldn't jump the queue, mate, things are pretty tense in here right now,' Sol said.

'Fair enough.' Bailey moved away and to the back of the line.

Gabe turned to Sol. 'Things are tense?'

'Gabe, you missed a lot of excitement while you were in Seg, although it's probably for the best that you did.'

'What kind of excitement?'

'Asher's pad-mate got really sick, chucking his ring up, blood and everything. Asher went fucking ballistic, demanded a new cell. Got into a bit of a scuffle with Johnson.'

'Johnson?'

'Yeah . . .' Sol said, looking at Gabriel suspiciously. 'Why?'

'Who won?'

'Asher's in the infirmary and Johnson is up on possible disciplinary. Depends on whether Asher presses charges. He's been in there almost as long as you've been in Seg.'

'What happens then?'

'Then the police get involved. Only assaults on guards

get dealt with in-house. I doubt Asher will do anything though. Him and Johnson have fallen out before.'

'Is there something going on with those two?'

'Like what?' Sol said innocently.

'I don't know, I just notice things sometimes.' Gabriel said, not quite believing that he was the only one who noticed.

'Well, do yourself a favour and try to stop noticing things.'

They got to the front of the queue. Gabriel allowed himself a brief look around the canteen – there were faces he didn't recognise. It occurred to him that he wasn't the newbie anymore. He wasn't scrambling around for advice on how to behave or feeling so completely out of place that he wanted to scream. He was adjusting. He recalled that first day, when he'd wondered whether he'd ever adapt to life on the inside. He had decided in Seg that he was going to ask the counsellor about getting onto one of the education programmes in here as soon as he had been sentenced. He needed something to focus on, something to make himself better. There was no way he could carry on this ride without distraction, something to pour his energy and attention into. He could be in here for ten years, they had told him that was the best-case scenario as there was a new hard line on arson, and the fact that someone had died in his case meant that he would be made an example of. He would get a degree, or whatever he could, and just work. He couldn't waste his life anymore. He hated that it took the death of an innocent man, his incarceration and loss of freedom for him to realise how precious this time was, how much he had been given in life and how much he had thrown away.

The next day, Gabriel kept his eyes closed through the thirty-minute bang-up period before dinner. Bailey had not stopped speaking for the entirety of the time they'd spent alone in the cell together. Gabriel would have to find out about getting some headphones in the very near future. He wasn't a violent man, but Bailey was grating on his nerves to the point where his fists naturally closed into a tight ball every so often. When Gabriel thought about the possible alternatives for a pad-mate he supposed he felt quite lucky – even if it didn't feel that way for the majority of the time – but considering the amount of time he had been out of Seg, it was worrying to him how quickly he had become fatigued with Bailey.

'Hey. I asked if you have any brothers?' Bailey's voice piped up.

'What? I'm trying to sleep.'

'Sorry. I don't like the quiet.'

'I noticed.'

'Am I annoying you?' Bailey asked, somewhat crestfallen. 'I'm sorry, I know I'm a bit annoying, everyone tells me I am. I find it very hard to relax, especially in here.'

Gabriel felt bad for being annoyed at Bailey. All things considered he was probably OK. 'No, I'm just readjusting to being out of Seg, that's all.'

'I have three brothers,' Bailey informed him. 'They're always telling me how annoying I am.'

'What do your brothers do?' Gabriel swung his legs over the side of the bunk and jumped off, giving up on the idea of any sleep.

'One of them's inside up in Nottingham and another is in Dartmoor. My oldest brother moved to Australia about ten years ago, and doesn't really have any contact with the family at all.'

'Wow. I don't have any brothers – or sisters. Just me, to my parents' disappointment. Especially now.' Gabriel tried to shake off the image of his mother at the sink, as she always was. Always with her back to whatever situation was going on, her back to the world, buried in housework so she didn't have to deal with the fact that her family was broken, that she'd married the wrong man and probably shouldn't have had a child.

'I don't have any parents anymore. They died a long time ago. As soon as I hit eighteen my oldest brother who was looking after us all just scarpered for Oz. I was left with the other two and one of them went inside soon after, he's on his third sentence now.'

Gabriel sighed. 'Bailey, has anyone ever told you that you talk too much?'

'Once or twice. Like I said, I don't like the quiet.'

'I kind of do like the quiet, so we need to figure out a way for us both to be happy.' Gabriel rubbed his temples, pre-emptively soothing the headache that was already emerging.

'I'm sorry, I'll be quiet.'

'Well no, you can talk. But how about you don't talk when I have my eyes closed? Do you think we can stick to that one for a start?'

'I was in the car when my dad rolled it,' Bailey said suddenly. 'I was in intensive care for a while before I got out, and since then I've always had this habit of being a nervous talker or something, or maybe something happened to my brain. They aren't quite sure.'

'Well that's fine, I'm just not used to sharing in here.'

'I'm really sorry.'

'Stop apologising, Bailey, its fine.' Now he felt bad.

'Silence just makes me really uncomfortable and a bit stir-crazy.'

'I get that, maybe put the radio on?'

'I don't like radios.'

'Oh.' Gabriel stopped for a moment, realising he hadn't asked the obvious question. 'How old are you?'

'I'm thirty-seven.'

'You seem a lot younger,' Gabriel said; at certain points in their conversation, it had felt like he was talking to a child.

There was a pause. 'You're a lot nicer than the last guy I was in here with. He would tie a T-shirt around my face to keep me quiet.'

'Jesus. I'm not going to be doing that.'

'I didn't like that.'

'Well no, I don't suppose you did. You could try reading a book or something?'

'I don't really read well. I can read, I just start thinking too much when I'm reading, like someone else's ideas make my own ideas seem bigger and then suddenly I think about too many big things and it makes me feel crazy.'

'OK, don't do that either then.'

Roll call.

Association.

Gabriel left the cell as soon as possible, hoping Bailey wouldn't see where he went. He liked Bailey enough really, but if they were going to live together, he'd need a little space from him outside the cell. He went into Sol's pad and sat in the chair. Sol was laying in the bed.

'Had enough of Bailey yet?' Sol asked.

'Just about. I just needed a break.'

Sol looked up at him. 'What are you going to do when you get out of here?'

'You mean when I get remanded to another prison?'

'No. No, I mean when you finish your whole term? This term.'

'I have no idea. I don't know where I'm even going to be next year – and if I get ten years . . .'

'You won't get ten years. First time offender.'

'Someone died.'

'People die, Gabe, you didn't murder him.'

'But he's dead because of me.'

'Maybe. Maybe it was his time.'

'Please – don't start with the destiny crap. What are you gonna do?'

'I've got some things lined up,' Sol said. 'Might try and reconnect with my daughter. If she'll ever speak to me again that is. Going to get a little flat, maybe overlooking the river if I can afford it, and I'm going to try to start my own business. Gardening or window cleaning or something where I don't need a CV or references. Tried that last time and it didn't go so well.'

Sparks appeared at the door, Kenzie not far behind him.

'Your boyfriend's back.' Sparks smiled at Gabriel.

'Asher's out of infirmary and he's got a fuck-off scar over his eye. He looks pretty badass,' Kenzie said, wide-eyed.

'Pissed off, too. He won't have forgotten what you did to him.' Sparks nodded.

'That's just what I need.' Gabriel sank even further back into the chair.

Chapter 23

Imogen awoke before the alarm, way before. It was around 5 a.m.; she stretched and turned to find that Dean was gone and his side of the bed was cold. She climbed out of bed reluctantly and threw on a robe before walking through her place. She could feel the emptiness before she had even checked all the rooms. It wasn't unlike Dean to wake up early and leave, but this was more than early. She doubted he had even gone to sleep, just waited for her to drift off. It was essentially still night-time. She decided to run herself a bath while she looked at the information for the case; she would be ready before Adrian got there to pick her up for work. The bath wouldn't take long to fill.

After a little while, she turned the hot water off. She could see the steam rising and became impatient to get in, but part of her ritual was to let it cool on its own for about fifteen minutes.

She went to her bag to get the file of the Wallis

break-in – she had made some copies and brought them home, just some financials of the family and the photos of the crime scene. If she didn't work at home sometimes, she wouldn't get anything done, particularly not much thinking. Sometimes you just needed to get away from the office, stare at a photo for a really long time and absorb every aspect of it; like one of those magic eye posters, suddenly a clearer picture appears after a while.

She dug inside her bag for the paperwork and pulled out the file. It was light, strangely so. Opening it, Imogen found that it was empty apart from a single post-it note in Dean's handwriting. *Sorry. x.*

Imogen's breath caught in her throat. Dean had taken her case notes. What interest could Dean possibly have in the case? He hadn't shown much interest before today, in fact it wasn't until he saw the video . . . had he seen something that she hadn't? Whatever it was, she had a feeling it was another one of those big, complicated messes of his that she would struggle to decipher. If she knew Dean at all, she knew he would rather stay away than lie to her face, when questioned directly at least. She picked up her phone and called him, knowing full well that he wouldn't answer, but he needed to know that she knew, and that she wasn't happy. He wouldn't answer his phone until he was ready. She just hoped he didn't do anything stupid before she got a chance to ask him what the hell was going on. At the very least she hoped he didn't get caught with her paperwork. This kind of thing was exactly what she had been afraid of, she just hoped he wouldn't push her so far that she might have to arrest him. She groaned audibly at the prospect.

Going back to the bathroom, Imogen sank into her bath and tried to imagine all the ways her boyfriend, or even her father, could be tied to this case. It was strange to her that they were so close, that they had no secrets between them – Dean knew Elias, her father, far better than she ever could, he had practically been raised by him. According to Dean he had saved his life when he was a kid, stopped him from being transferred into an adult prison from the Young Offender Institution he was in. She thought about the things Dean had said before they went to bed, his reactions to the video, anything he might have done that was out of the ordinary. The truth was she didn't know him well enough to know what was out of the ordinary. In fact, there was nothing ordinary about Dean. There was something about their lovemaking last night though; it had almost felt like a goodbye.

Imogen sighed. This situation exactly was why things between her and Dean were never going to work. Being with him was just delaying the inevitable and making her care for someone she really couldn't have. The thought of not seeing him again made her stomach tense. She wasn't entirely sure if she would arrest him if it came down to it, if he did something really bad. She had to believe she would even though it didn't feel that way at the moment. It was almost as though he was pushing and pushing to see how much he could get away with. Was he testing her to see if she really loved him? Or was it far simpler than that – did his needs come first, and her career, her life – did they come second? Maybe he couldn't change. Maybe this was who he was. All she was sure of was that he wouldn't put her in danger. She trusted him that far, at least.

Chapter 24

Gabriel was three minutes into his shower when Asher walked in with his pad-mate, who had obviously fully recovered. The man had never been formally introduced to Gabriel, but whenever he saw him he was always just a few steps behind Asher, the Igor to his Dracula. Next to him, Bailey was gargling with the shower water which seemed to shut him up so Gabriel didn't try and stop him. Asher planted himself on Gabriel's other side, turning the shower on as his pad-mate hung back at the doorway, watching for the guards. Gabriel turned slightly, shielding himself from Asher's smirk and gaze. Asher stripped down confidently and started to lather himself. Gabriel rinsed the rest of the soap off, grabbed his towel and wrapped it around him as casually as he could, ignoring his trembling fingers.

'Bailey, hurry up.'

Bailey's hair was full of foam and looked as though it would be for a good while; he must have emptied half the bottle into it. But Gabriel couldn't leave Bailey in there alone with Asher; God only knows what he would do.

Gabriel pulled his pants on, the fabric clinging to his wet legs and dragging on the hair; he needed to be dressed though, he needed to be ready to fight. He could tell that Asher was up to something, he didn't know why or how but he was in his head. This was what Asher wanted, he wanted to play on Gabriel's mind, he wanted to make him second-guess himself. Gabriel could feel that this was all a game to him. He sensed Asher watching him as he soaped his body; he wasn't turned against the wall and guarded like most people in the showers, he was facing outward and stroking himself. Gabriel wasn't looking at him directly as he rubbed his torso down with the towel but he could see in his peripheral vision that Asher was making himself hard.

'Bailey, hurry up,' he said again, frustrated.

Asher was stroking himself even harder now, his eyes were travelling over Gabriel's body, he could feel it.

'Just turn a little more so I can see your cute backside, will you, Gabriel?' Asher said breathlessly.

Gabriel pulled his shirt over his head quickly and put his trousers back on, trying not to look panicked.

'Bailey? Come on!'

Finally, Asher let out a gasp as he ejaculated onto the wet tiles.

He laughed. 'Thank you!' he called out to Gabriel as he kicked his semen into the drain.

Bailey's shower shut off and he grabbed his clothes.

'Get dressed, we need to go,' Gabriel urged.

'OK, jeez. Go if you want, I can catch you up!'

'Yeah you go, we'll look after your friend here.' Asher grinned as he walked towards them, still naked.

'Fuck off, Asher.'

'Now that's no way to speak to me, I'm just being nice, aren't I, Bailey?'

'Gabriel told me to be careful of you.' Bailey said, a childish frown on his face.

'Well, did he? Why is that, Gabriel? You worried your handsome friend here is going to turn my head?'

'Shut up, Asher, and put some fucking clothes on!' Gabriel's fear manifested in anger, he didn't want to play Asher's game because he was always a step ahead of him, Gabriel's reactions always seemed to play into Asher's plans for him.

'Just trying to be friendly. There's no need for bad language.' Asher stroked Bailey's hair. Bailey pushed his hand away and Gabriel grabbed Asher by the wrist.

'Asher, come near me or Bailey again and I will fuck you up, that's a promise.' He released him.

Asher brought his face close to Gabriel's. 'I can get you put in Seg any time I want, just remember that. Any fucking time. Then who is going to look after your special little friend?'

'What do you want from me?'

'I would have thought that was obvious.'

'Obvious?'

'I want you.'

Gabriel felt sick. 'Never going to happen.'

'Well, history tells me otherwise. I've met boys like you before, the ones who think they're straight but really, underneath it all, they just want to feel a cock inside them.'

'Never – like – ever. It won't happen.'

'I'll break you and then you will beg me for it. I would put money on that. Everyone has a breaking point; I'll figure out what yours is.'

'I'll leave you to your delusions. Come on, Bailey.'

Gabriel had to get out of there fast, he handed Bailey his clothes and he put them on quickly. The pair of them walked back to their cell.

'Stay away from him, Bailey,' Gabriel said.

'I will, I don't like him. What he says and the way he makes you feel are like opposites. He's always smiling but he's being mean. He's bad, I can tell.'

'He is bad.'

Gabriel jumped on the top bunk and closed his eyes for a bit; the run-in with Asher had been more stressful than he wanted to admit. Asher's words rang out in his mind. Could he do that? Could he make Gabriel do what he wanted just by wearing him down? Why had he protected Bailey, why hadn't he just left the room? He barely knew Bailey and already Asher was using him to control Gabriel. He couldn't let this happen. Gabriel had to look after himself before he looked after anyone else, he had to.

Chapter 25

When Imogen and Adrian arrived at the station, they had one of the rooms set up with the 55-inch TV, which was showing the Wallis video repeatedly. Gary Tunney sat nearby with a laptop, capturing the moments DCI Mira Kapoor instructed him to; she was standing close to the screen, watching intently. Imogen dumped her bag in her chair and walked into the room to see what – if anything – they had discovered. They paused the video as they walked in.

'Don't stop on my account,' she said as she slumped into one of the chairs. Adrian sat next to her. She saw the noticeboard to the left of the TV with some of the images already printed off and pinned up. The two faces – tragedy and comedy – and a foot – a Converse shoe, most likely belonging to the person holding the camera or phone.

'We're working on getting it taken down but the host site is in the Czech Republic, plus it's been ripped God knows how many times already. It's popped up on several other sites. There's no way of un-exploding this bomb – it's probably staying out there for good,' Gary said.

'Any leads?' Imogen asked.

'Standard shoes, which doesn't help; Converse are available all over the place. Standard black clothes, no logos or labels visible – nothing really that is in any way distinguishable.'

'What about the masks?' Adrian asked.

'I think they're home-made or at the very least hand-made, can't find any like them that are commercially available.' Gary frowned. 'It's possible they're modified from a simpler mask. You can buy stuff quite easily to do something like this. I can't really tell what these are made of, but judging by the size of them and the composition I don't think they're clay or anything. Maybe moulded plastic – but they're originals, one of a kind anyway,' Gary said. 'I found a twelve-step "how to" guide online, looks pretty close – it could be something like wonderflex, or a more complex product where you need a heat gun to mould the plastic.'

'How easy is it to get hold of stuff like that?' the DCI asked, frowning.

'Really easy is the short answer.'

'Looks kind of specialist?'

'Well you would think so, but the fact is Cosplay is massive these days, so you can get this stuff easily online. The thing is, without knowing exactly what it's made from there's no way to know where they got it from,' Gary said.

'So, we need to get a hold of one of those masks?' Adrian asked.

'Well yeah . . . that's the ideal. But what we can tell is that whoever made them had some skills, we can consider locals with that kind of ability, see if there's anyone that sticks out,' Gary said.

'What's Cosplay?' Imogen asked.

'It's where adults dress like superheroes – in a nutshell,' Adrian said.

'Don't knock it till you've tried it!' Gary said to Imogen.

'Who says I haven't?' Imogen smiled.

'Please make Grey go undercover as Catwoman to a local convention, do we have budget for that?' Gary pleaded.

'As much as I would like to see Grey in a black catsuit, I think we probably don't need to do that just yet.' Adrian smiled.

'Just . . . keep it in mind,' Gary said.

DCI Kapoor coughed and raised her eyebrow, a subtle indicator that they should focus.

'Anyway, Cosplay is not only popular, its mainstream now – not even that niche,' Adrian said.

'You think these guys are Cosplayers then?' Imogen said.

'I think one of them may be, or might be linked to that world somehow. We shouldn't rule it out. But it's possible they just wanted something unique and googled it online.'

'But you don't think so?' Adrian said.

'I think they look polished, professional. So, I think

the person who made them had practice, or at least some skills with the tools.'

'What do we know about the faces that were chosen?' the DCI interjected. 'Do they mean anything aside from the obvious tragedy and comedy thing?'

'I'll look into it,' Adrian offered.

'And the symbol at the end?'

'It's not linked to any known groups as far as we know,' Adrian said.

'So where does it come from?'

'It could be personal to them, let's hope so. It might be an avenue to explore.'

'It's a Celtic symbol called a triquetra,' Imogen offered.

Adrian furrowed his brow at her. 'How did you know that?'

'I have this really useful thing called the internet,' she said sarcastically, rolling her eyes at Adrian. She would tell him about Dean when they were alone together, there was no point confusing things. She didn't need the new DCI scrutinising her relationship, she wasn't even sure if she knew about it and Imogen thought shifting any focus away from the investigation at this point could only be detrimental to the case. At least this was how she was justifying things in her mind.

'What about the music?'

'Recent-ish, mainstream again. Not sure if it's significant or not,' Gary said.

'Let's just assume it is for now. DS Miles, can you look into it?'

'Shame it wasn't a Madonna track, you know it

would be taken down immediately,' Imogen said cynically. Murder was fine but copyright theft was serious business when it came to video-hosting websites.

'Put it on again! There must be something we are missing, keep watching it. People are going to want answers and so far we don't have a thing. We need a lead!' Mira Kapoor said as she exited the room leaving just Gary, Imogen and Adrian there. Everyone let out a deep breath.

'Spit it out,' Adrian said to Imogen, knowing she would talk freely now that the DCI had gone.

'What?'

'Something's bothering you, what is it?'

Imogen sighed. 'I took some stuff on the case home, copies of pictures, bio on the family, crime scene report – things like that . . .'

'And?'

Gary started up the video again.

'I think Dean took them.'

'You think?' Adrian asked.

'Dean took them.'

'Why?'

'I don't know, he's not answering his phone.'

'The DCI had better not find out about this.'

'Tell me about it,' Imogen said.

'Do you think Dean knows something about this case?'

'He's the one who told me about the triquetra, it means love, honour and protect.'

'Maybe he's just trying to help.'

'Let's hope so,' Gary offered, his eyebrows raised so high they had virtually disappeared into his hairline.

'Gary, can you get the CCTV footage of the signal box fire up for me?' Adrian asked.

'Shouldn't we focus on this? If the DCI comes in again . . .'

'We are, just get it up for me please. Split screen if you can.'

Gary tapped away on his keyboard for a few moments and then both videos were running at the same time. 'Like this?'

'Right yeah, now go to the bit where Gabriel Webb leaves the signal box.'

'OK.' Gary found the bit of the video just before Gabriel Webb opened the door and came down the steps.

'So now, go to the bit of the Wallis video just before the attackers enter the house. Then run them together.'

The videos started playing, and suddenly, Imogen saw what Adrian had seen. Behind Gabriel were the two girls, and behind them were the two other men in hoodies. One of the men grabbed the man in front's shoulders and shook him a little, almost as if he were excited about something and wanted to share it with his friend. They'd seen this all before, but when it ran alongside the video of the Wallis attack, they could clearly see the exact same movement take place between the two men on camera in the other video. This could not be a coincidence; it was definitely the same men.

'We need to speak to Gabriel Webb again,' Imogen said urgently.

'Oh God, I hate filling out those stupid forms,' Adrian complained.

Chapter 26

True to his word, Bailey didn't say a thing while Gabriel slept. However, when he woke, their eyes met and Gabriel could see how desperate the man was to speak. He felt like the owner of a dog who had to spell out the word park letter by letter, so the animal wouldn't get overexcited. Slowly sitting up in the bunk, Gabriel was suddenly hit with a horrible smell.

'What the hell is that?'

Gabriel jumped off the bed, immediately feeling the wetness under his feet and guessing what had happened.

'Jesus, Bailey, did you piss all over the floor?'

'No, mate, I swear I didn't.'

'Then what the fuck happened?'

'It was that Asher guy and his friend, they both came in here and pissed on me while you were sleeping.'

'What?'

'They came in here and did it on me. I think most

of it went on the floor though, I was waiting for you to get up because I didn't know what to do.'

'Why would they do that?'

'Asher said that it would only get worse and the decision was yours. What decision?'

'Why the hell didn't you shout so I could have stopped him?'

'You told me not to wake you up!'

'Did you tell a guard?'

'No, not supposed to do that.'

'OK, well it's OK to wake me up in emergencies. Don't let people piss on you, mate.'

'Sorry.'

Gabriel sighed. 'Let's get you back in the shower.' This was happening to Bailey because of him. As much as he wanted to look out for himself only, his conscience wouldn't let him; Bailey was vulnerable and Asher would use him to get to Gabriel. The stakes were rising, and he had a horrible feeling that this was only the beginning.

The cell was finally clean after Sol had one of the other prisoners working on cleaning duty come by and mop the floor. The idea that there were any traces of Asher's urine on the floor meant that Gabriel wouldn't be going barefoot for the foreseeable future. The thought made his stomach turn.

The next few days passed without any more physical run-ins with Asher, just the occasional glance. Asher's laugh always seemed to sound out above all the others in the wing, and whenever Gabriel turned around he was looking at him – always looking at him. It was as if the world didn't exist outside of the two of them, and Asher was right about one thing: it was wearing Gabriel down. He couldn't understand why he was letting Asher get to him. But why had he singled Gabriel out above everyone else? It made Gabriel feel weak. He wasn't a fighter, but he knew bullies – he knew that they just kept pushing and pushing and pushing. He also knew that it was never about their victims, it was about them and the feeling of power that those people got from the weaknesses of others. He needed to find a way to be the kind of man that people didn't fuck with. He needed to stop Asher.

Chapter 27

Imogen walked into the corridor of the police station and was confronted with the sight of Dean, who was reading some interior design magazine from the pile on the small table beside him. She could see the file lying next to him on a chair. He stopped reading and put the magazine down, sensing her there. She stared at him, and slowly, he picked up the file and handed it to her.

'Dean, what is going on with you?'

'I'm not sure.'

'You're going to have to do a little better than that after stealing my shit.'

He paused. 'I thought the files might help me remember something.'

'Remember what?'

'It's so strange – it's on the tip of my tongue.' He stared off past her, behind her, his voice more detached than usual. 'Did you ever have a memory like that?'

'You can't take my files, Dean – if anyone ever found

out I would lose my job!' she ignored his words, she couldn't let him derail her again. She had to stay angry with him or where would it end?

'I'm sorry.' He looked her in the eyes.

'Well – did you find anything?'

'No, I'm sorry, not really anything to find. The Wallis couple seem like decent people.'

'What were you looking for exactly?'

'I'm not entirely sure, I'll know when I find it.'

'Are you even telling me the truth?'

Dean looked wounded at the suggestion that he was being anything other than honest.

'Always,' he said finally. 'Ask me anything and I'll be completely honest with you, if you want me to.'

'We both know it's not that simple.'

'Let's talk then. I promise I will answer what I can,' he sighed.

'I haven't got time for mind games.' She started towards the exit, but Dean followed and grabbed her arm. Imogen turned and looked at his hand; he let go immediately.

'I'm going to keep looking into this. I feel as though I'm close to something, but I'll stay out of your way. Call me if you want to see me, I'm not staying here to fight with you.' He walked out. Just like that.

What the hell did he mean? It wasn't like Dean to be cryptic, if anything his directness was what put their relationship at the most risk, but it was also what drew her to him. She wanted to believe him, but there would always be the knowledge that he was a criminal. Could she really be with a man she had witnessed cut off someone else's body part? As long as she didn't think about it she could. Maybe because of what they had been through together, there was a bond there that Imogen couldn't sever. They were stuck together, for now at least. Her mind wasn't strong enough to overrule her heart at this point. She just hoped she wouldn't destroy her whole life, everything she'd worked for, in the process of loving this man. Because that was one thing she felt like she had no control over. She felt weak; worse than that, she felt like her mother. For years Imogen's mother Irene had put both herself and Imogen second to Imogen's father. Imogen had never understood the kind of emotion that led women to behave in that way. Irrational, self-destructive, illogical. But here she was. She had no intention of letting Dean go right now. No matter what he did. That's what she was most afraid of, that he would do something so bad, so completely unforgivable – and she would still forgive him anyway.

Chapter 28

The sky was a mottled blue, and thin white clouds stretched across the surface of the pale, cold expanse. Gabriel sucked in the fresh air as though it were a narcotic, his lungs itching at the pollen – but even that was a welcome feeling. Deep, calm, controlled breaths; he could control this, he would control it. He looked around him at the other men; no longer under the warm fluorescent lights on the ward, they all looked various shades of unhealthy grey.

Kenzie and Sparks walked over to Gabriel, both wearing an unfamiliar squint, their pale skin highlighted even more by the sun, both with a complete lack of melatonin. Sol was in his weekly check-up with the nurse. Sparks lit a cigarette.

'How long has Asher been in here?' Gabriel asked them suddenly, the words spilling out of his mouth.

'This time? Only a few weeks before you got here, but our paths have crossed before,' Sparks said.

‘Is he always like this?’

‘A massive twat? Yes,’ Kenzie offered.

‘Not your type then?’

‘Absolutely not. He’s jail bent, straight on the outside. I like someone a little less confused about what they want. Plus, for him it’s a power thing, I don’t find that particularly sexy.’

‘Speak of the devil,’ Gabriel said, straightening up as Asher sauntered towards them.

Asher took the cigarette out of Sparks’ hand and took a long drag. Sparks shrank back a little. Gabriel noted that both of his friends were afraid of Asher – and that Asher knew it.

‘Can I join your boyband, too?’

‘Why are you such a fucking dick?’ Gabriel found it impossible to hide his irritation anymore.

‘Now that’s not a nice way to greet a friend, is it?’ Asher stepped forward, swaying slightly; like a flirtatious teenager, he traced his finger along the pattern on Gabriel’s T-shirt. Gabriel just watched him. Asher wanted him to move, to flinch, but he refused.

‘We’re not friends, Asher, but you know that.’

‘What are we then? What am I to you?’ Asher moved in closer, almost whispering.

‘You are absolutely nothing.’ He stared him straight in the eye. Gabriel noticed Asher hold his breath in the same way Emma did when she wanted him; was all of this just playing into his hands? Was Gabriel behaving exactly the way Asher wanted him to, had Asher accounted for these reactions? Were they part of his plan?

‘Maybe you should go talk to someone who actually

wants you around? Or you know, get in the shade with that complexion before you lobster out,' Kenzie laughed nervously.

'Is your girlfriend fighting your battles for you?' Asher sneered.

Gabriel put his arm around Kenzie's shoulder and pulled him in. Asher's expression changed yet again to mild bemusement.

'You know, on the outside, Asher, I wouldn't even look twice at you, our paths would never have crossed. We wouldn't even move in the same circles because you are that fucking far beneath me.' Gabriel's fists were clenched. He forced himself to take deep breaths.

'We're all the same in here though,' Asher said.

'Are you sure about that? Because all I see is a pathetic little rodent who is trying desperately to get noticed.'

'We should call you Roland Rat from now on,' Kenzie laughed.

Asher stared into Kenzie's eyes with a look Gabriel hadn't seen before, much less playful, a warning.

'I'll you see boys later.' He shrugged and walked off, cutting his losses, for now.

Chapter 29

Emma smelled of macadamia oil shampoo this time; he knew what it was as he remembered the bottle on the side of her bath tub. He recalled lying in there with her between his legs, her back resting against his bare stomach and chest, her long black hair stuck to his arms and the bathwater tinted whatever colour she had dyed her natural blonde roots. Gabriel breathed her in and tried to hold that smell in his mind, as much as you can hold onto the memory of a smell. He wondered how your mind could even remember something you couldn't see or hear; why did smells trigger such vivid memories? He made a note to himself to look in the library for more information on memory. Depending on the length of his stay in prison he was going to learn psychology, maybe even get a degree if he had time. The future was starting to feel real again, something he could work with.

'It's good to see you, babe.' She smiled, her eyes shifting from side to side.

Something was wrong.

'What's happened?'

'Why do you ask me that?'

'I can see it, I can see it on your face.'

Emma sighed. 'You know Julie who works in the club?'

'What about her?'

'She said the police have been round again, asking about the night you were arrested.'

'Again?'

'Yeah, apparently. They said it's really important they find out who you were with.'

Gabriel couldn't understand why they were still bothered about who he had been with, he had already confessed to starting the fire. Surely they were just wasting their own time?

'Did Julie tell them?'

'No, the next day one of those guys came round to my place, you remember Chris from that night?'

'How could I forget those charmers?' he said, wishing he could have grassed them up without implicating Emma.

'Well, Chris told me to make sure you don't tell the cops they were with you.'

'He did what?'

'He said if you told the cops that he would hurt me.'

Gabriel tried to suppress the rising anger in him. He felt so powerless again, just when he was starting to feel a spark of optimism for the future, that he might be able to get through this.

'He also said you're inside with his brother.'

'Did he tell you the name of his brother?' Gabriel felt his chest tightening; she didn't even need to say the name. He already knew.

'Ash or something.'

'What did Chris do to you?' Gabriel asked quietly, dreading the answer. If Asher was his brother, what sort of man might Chris be?

'Do? He didn't do anything. But he told me you were in trouble.'

'What kind of trouble?'

She leaned in a little, keeping her voice down so no one could listen in. 'All he said was that he could make it go away. He said if I slept with him he would tell his brother to look after you.'

Gabriel shuddered involuntarily at her words. 'And what did you say?'

'I said no, of course. Was he telling the truth? Is someone in here trying to hurt you?'

Gabriel thought for a minute. This was a threat, but not to him, no. Ash had found his Achilles heel. They were threatening Emma. He knew what the payment was. They were telling Gabriel it was him or her, one of them would have to give it up. Inside or outside, they had him by the balls. He had to think. He couldn't let them do this.

Their time was up, people started to leave and Emma stood up. Gabriel could see she was worried, he didn't want her to have to worry about him and he didn't want her to do what Chris wanted. There was only one solution he could think of.

'Look. It's all sorted, you don't need to worry about

me. But I want you to call the police – you need to find a detective called Imogen Grey and tell her I need to speak to her, it's urgent. I'll put her on my visitors list. Don't tell her your name or anything, don't implicate yourself, but call her, please. I trust her.'

Chapter 30

Gabriel drifted in and out of sleep, thinking about Emma, his thoughts mutating into dreams of a time when he might be out again, or when they might be together. There had been a couple of unusually hot days that were now brewing into a storm, the humidity magnified inside the prison. He thought about his visit with Emma; it was worrying, but something told him she wasn't in immediate danger. For some reason, this was all about him.

As he shifted his weight from one shoulder blade onto the other, the itchy blanket rubbed against his warm and clammy skin. He longed for a hot bath and a bed covered in cold white sheets. He thought back to the start of the summer, when he and Emma would lie on the grass in the cemetery by the catacombs, her hands behind her head, midriff showing through her black mesh top. Her skin was a milky white, even after hours in the sun. She would move in slow motion on days like that and it was as though the whole world ceased to exist aside from them. He imagined lying there with her again as sleep came over him like a warm blanket. This time he was lying on his back and she was propped up on one arm, whispering into his ear, telling him her plans for his body later on as he tried to remain calm. He felt her hot sweet breath as she spoke and his body stirred. Her fingers, covered in silver and onyx rings, were brushing against his forehead, across his temples and down to his lips, moving across them gently. The dream began to erode but the sensation was still there. And so was the whisper.

Gabriel's body tensed; he wasn't asleep anymore. Someone was standing by his bed, someone was whispering in his ear, touching his face, touching his mouth. He didn't want to open his eyes, he didn't want to confirm his suspicion.

'Wake up, sleepyhead.'

Gabriel opened his eyes, it took a few moments before they adjusted but when they did he saw Asher standing by his bed. Jerking upwards, Gabriel grabbed him by the throat, his heart thumping. He wanted to throw up. The door was wide open. How had he got in? Someone must have unlocked the door and let him in.

'Get out or I'll hurt you.' He squeezed tightly for a moment then released him.

'Relax, cupcake,' Asher said. 'I've come to invite you to a party.'

Gabriel jumped off the bed. Bailey was fast asleep, his mouth open with a trail of saliva running from his lips to the pillow. Bailey never had trouble sleeping.

'What are you talking about?'

‘Follow me,’ Asher whispered.

‘I’m not following you anywhere.’ Gabriel whispered back, unsure why. Surely if he just shouted someone would come, wouldn’t they?

‘Follow me or I’ll make you.’ Asher reached forward, putting his finger in the centre of Gabriel’s chest and slowly pulling it downwards; as his reached his naval Gabriel smacked his hand out of the way.

Gabriel could put his hands around his throat right now, he knew he was physically stronger than him but he had to think about Emma and what might happen to her if he hurt Asher. For now he had to bide his time and go with Asher. He put a sweatshirt on over his T-shirt. He wasn’t cold but he wanted more layers between him and Asher.

He followed Asher out onto the wing. It was strange being out at night like this, alone with Asher. Gabriel looked to the end of the gallery to see who was on duty but the guards weren’t there. The only other door open was Kenzie and Sparks’ cell door. As they came into the light, Gabriel glanced at Asher’s hands; there was blood on them.

Inside the cell, it was dark but Gabriel could see someone else standing there. At first he thought it was Kenzie or Sparks but then he registered that it was Johnson, stood next to the bed. His arms were crossed and as his face came into focus, Gabriel could see that he was anything but calm; he looked white and clammy, nervous and scared.

‘Why the fuck did you bring him here?’ Johnson sounded panicked.

'Relax. He won't say anything. Will you?' Asher turned to look at Gabriel.

'You'd better be right,' Johnson said.

Gabriel looked at the bed. Kenzie was on the top bunk. At first Gabriel thought he was asleep, but there was something not quite right about the way he was lying. Gabriel rushed over and felt for Kenzie's pulse.

'He'll be fine in a little while,' Asher said.

'What did you do to him?'

'A bit of pressure to the windpipe and he passed out. Couldn't have him interfering while I was working on his friend.'

'Working?' Gabriel spun around. 'What are you talking about?'

Sparks was on the bottom bunk, turned to the wall, his blanket wrapped around him. What Gabriel had first thought was snoring now sounded more like a pained wheeze. Gabriel dropped to his knees and pulled the cover back. Sparks was covered in blood.

'Sparks! Wake up!'

'Keep your voice down!' Johnson said urgently.

'Sparks got into a fight with Kenzie here, Johnson's just about to find him on the floor of the cell. Nasty business.' Asher was smirking, enjoying the lie.

'What did you do to him?' Gabriel asked again.

'No need to be jealous, I didn't do anything kinky, I'm saving myself for you.' He paused for a moment, staring at Gabriel's lips before taking a deep breath and stepping back. 'Did you know if you wrap a toothbrush head in cling film and then burn it, it becomes rock hard? Then you just rub the sides of the head on the ground at an angle until you get a razor-thin blade like this.'

Asher held up a sharpened toothbrush that was covered in blood. Sparks' blood.

'Where's the blood coming from?' Gabriel checked Sparks' neck but it wasn't cut. That was a good thing.

'Kenzie just kind of went crazy and slashed him up. Punched him a few times as well. Lovers' quarrel, I reckon.' Asher paused. 'At least that's what the screws will think.'

'Sparks isn't even gay.'

Asher shrugged. 'Well then, maybe he refused his advances. It can be pretty hard to keep taking rejection. Can make you do something crazy.'

'Is this about what Kenzie said in the yard?' Gabriel began to understand how Asher worked, he was punishing Kenzie by hurting Sparks, which meant he wouldn't hesitate to punish him by hurting Emma.

Asher shrugged. 'He was a bit rude, you all were. I thought this was as good a way as any to demonstrate to you how shit works in here. All of you.'

'You won't get away with this!'

Asher looked over at Johnson and nodded him towards the door. Gabriel hated the look on Asher's face; he clearly wanted a moment alone with him. He still had the bloody toothbrush in his hand. Johnson acquiesced reluctantly, what else could Asher make him do?

'Behave yourself for fuck's sake. There's only so much I can explain away convincingly,' Johnson said.

'Don't worry about him,' Asher said to Johnson as he was leaving. 'He certainly isn't going to grass me up.'

Sparks started to moan in pain, the sound turning into a tiny sob.

'What do you want?' Gabriel said.

'If this is what I can do in here, with all of the guards keeping an eye on me, just imagine what my brother can do to your girlfriend on the outside where no one is even looking,' Asher said quietly. 'Maybe take her to a party, get her jacked up on drugs, pass her around his mates.'

Ignoring him, Gabriel pulled the cover back over Sparks; he was shivering now. 'It's all right mate, you're going to be all right.'

'While you're down there . . .' Asher said with a tease in his voice.

'You're scum, Asher, you know that?'

'Stop, you're turning me on.' Asher grinned.

Gabriel stood up and moved in closer to him. Using his physical presence, the only thing he really had, he leaned forward until Asher backed away a little, intimidated but excited by Gabriel. He could feel the tension in Asher as he looked up at him, head tilted back, breathless in anticipation of Gabriel's next move. As much as Gabriel wanted to hit him he had to be smart. He had to figure out another way out of this. He had to stop giving Asher everything he wanted.

'You're not going to win,' Gabriel finally said before walking out. The sooner he was out and back in his cell, the sooner Johnson would help his friends.

Gabriel resigned himself to the fact that he wasn't going to get any more sleep tonight. He couldn't do anything about Kenzie or Sparks right now, but maybe he could talk to Barratt about it in the morning. He couldn't believe Asher would get away with this. He hated feeling this powerless.

Now that he was locked safely back in his cell, he dropped to the ground and started on his sets of twenty, trying to put the sight of Sparks' blood out of his mind. Halfway through a press-up, he heard a commotion outside in the hall. Crawling over to the door, he looked out of the glass; the sliver of light he could see was illuminating the door to Kenzie and Sparks' cell. It was a few minutes before Johnson re-emerged, dragging a limp and bloody Sparks and holding onto the parapet for support. None of the other guards appeared. Asher followed them, and turned towards Gabriel, as though he knew he were watching. He kissed the air in Gabriel's direction and got back in his cell before Johnson sounded the alarm.

Chapter 31

Every time he closed his eyes Gabriel saw Sparks' broken body being dragged to the staircase and Kenzie, confused and handcuffed, being removed and presumably taken to D-wing. He looked outside of the cell again. There were guards going in and out of Sparks and Kenzie's room now. This was a warning. A warning to him, he was sure of it. He thought about their altercation with Asher in the yard and how he had looked at them before he left. He must have a phone in his cell, he must have convinced Johnson somehow to let him go at Kenzie and Sparks. Gabriel had never once considered giving Asher what he wanted, but things were getting real now, people were getting hurt. The threat against Emma suddenly seemed like a distinct possibility.

There must be another way; the idea of Asher's hands on him was as repugnant as any feeling he could imagine. He felt secure in the knowledge that what Asher wanted was his permission; that was the game but he couldn't, he couldn't do it, he couldn't offer himself up. He had to think of something else, he had to think of a way to keep Asher at bay until DS Grey had a chance to investigate. If anything happened to Emma, Gabriel would never forgive himself. She didn't deserve this. He had held onto her selfishly and now she was in danger, he knew that even if he finished with her it wouldn't protect her. Asher was too clever to fall for that – he'd know that Gabriel still cared. What could he do? How could he stop him?

Gabriel ignored the emptiness inside him, it was now a few hours past the usual breakfast time and the cells were still not open. He felt bad for feeling hungry while there was something like this going on. Miraculously Bailey was still asleep. The slot in the door opened and a tray was placed on the shelf with some bread and fruit and a few biscuits. Gabriel rushed over and grabbed Barratt's hand before he had a chance to walk away. Swearing, Barratt opened the door.

'Now is not the time.' Barratt looked up and down the wing.

'I just want to know what's going on. Is Sparks OK?' Gabriel's voice was urgent.

'No, he's not,' the guard said. 'He and his paddy got in a fight and matey boy Kenzie stabbed him.'

'What about Asher?'

'I'm sorry?'

'I saw Asher in there, in the cell.'

'You must be mistaken,' he said unconvincingly.

'I'm telling you, I saw him, he had blood on him. Kenzie would never hurt Sparks.'

'Look, unless you want to be in lockdown for the rest of the month I suggest you forget what you saw,' Barratt whispered. 'What you're suggesting would turn this place upside down.'

'How so?'

'The only way Asher could be in that cell is if a guard let him in, and if that was the case and then Asher stabbed Sparks, we would all be in the shit.'

He made as if to move away and Gabriel reached out, grabbing his arm. 'Is that what happened to Jason?'

There was a pause. 'Ash has a lot of sway in here. Being on his bad side is not a good place to be.' Barratt tried to pull his arm away.

Gabriel gripped tighter. 'What about Sparks? Is he dead?'

'He's in a bad way. They are looking after him though.'

'Will you make sure he's all right?'

Barratt nodded almost imperceptibly. 'Trust me, boy, you don't want to get involved in whatever that was all about.'

'It was about me!' Gabriel whispered loudly, exasperated.

'Look, if Asher finds out you spoke to me then you will be in the shit and so will I,' Barratt said. 'I'll keep an eye on your friend but you absolutely shouldn't talk to any of the other guards about this, he's got more than one of them in his pocket. Now let go of my arm.'

'Thank you.' Gabriel took the tray of food and Barratt closed the door.

Gabriel grabbed a cheese roll and put the tray on

the cupboard. Bailey stirred in his bed, then sat up when he saw Gabriel pacing the room.

'Where'd you get that roll?'

'There's more on the tray.'

'What's going on? Why are you pacing like that?' Bailey shot up, reached across to the tray and stuffed a bread roll in his mouth before Gabriel had a chance to respond.

'There was a fight. Sparks got hurt.'

Bailey was chewing quickly. 'I like Sparks, he's always really nice to me.'

'I like him too. He's in the hospital now.'

'Who hurt him?' Bailey looked worried.

'They said it was Kenzie.'

'No way! Kenzie is a good person, he wouldn't get in a fight with anyone!'

'I know, mate.'

'We have to help him, they might move him to a different place. They'll probably put him on the bad wing.'

'I don't know how to help him; I wish I did, but I think he might be in the hospital too.'

'Asher must have done this, Gabriel. He's the only one that could get away with it!'

'You're probably right. Leave it to me though.' Gabriel was reluctant for Bailey to get too involved.

The roll was enough to dispel the gurgling cramp in Gabriel's stomach. He went back over to the door and looked out onto the wing. One of the cleaners was coming out of Sparks and Kenzie's cell, wheeling his cart, a bloody sheet peeking out of the black sack.

That's when he felt it: the eyes. He did everything he could to keep his own eyes trained on the goings-on in the cell a little further down from him but he knew Asher was looking at him. *Pretend you haven't noticed.* He could almost feel the smile, and the temptation to look up and check he was right was huge, but instead he just kept his eyes fixed on Barratt, who was standing by the door supervising the stripping of the room. Gabriel pulled away without looking at the cell opposite him, knowing that he had won the small battle, but the war was yet to come.

Chapter 32

Imogen walked through the prison gates and into the visitors' entrance. She was going in as a civilian, it seemed as though that was the way Gabriel Webb had wanted it. The phone call she'd had had been strange – from a girl called Sarah, instructing her that she needed to go see Gabriel. Before Imogen had had a chance to ask questions, the caller had hung up and she'd been unable to trace the call.

The prison felt cold. She thought about Dean and how she had never been to visit him when he was inside. They had met before he went inside when she was working on a case and then went through something terrible together. He was arrested and put inside, and she couldn't bring herself to visit him. She wondered whether that would always be a sore point between them. He hadn't said as much, but it was still something she felt guilty about, abandoning him in that way.

Imogen was processed and searched as she entered

the prison. They asked her to open her mouth and lift up her tongue while a female guard ran her hands over Imogen's body and through her hair. Even though she had been through this before it still felt somehow degrading. She had deliberately left her police ID in the car. No point in taking any chances until she had spoken to Gabriel and there was no legal requirement for her to state her profession. She did feel slightly guilty for not telling Adrian but there was no point, he would just worry. Once she'd been searched, she was led into the visiting lounge. She looked around the room, nervous for some reason, worried that either one of the other visitors or one of the other inmates would recognise her, even though it was highly unlikely.

After what seemed like an eternity, the doors opened and Gabriel Webb walked out; he was bigger than she remembered, his arms more defined. He had obviously been working out. His hair swung as he walked towards the table. His jaw was clenched and he surveyed the room before he sat down.

'Gabriel.'

'Officer.' He responded quietly, making sure no one overheard him. She noted his trepidation.

'You should call me Imogen, to be on the safe side,' she offered.

'Thank you for coming.'

'What did you want to see me about?'

'There's something weird going on here and I think I'm in danger.'

'Weird how?'

'The night I got here, my pad-mate went missing,

never to be mentioned again. My mate told me he'd been in the infirmary but he never came back. None of the staff ever really explained it to me.'

'Maybe he was transferred?'

Gabriel shook his head. 'I'm telling you, it was weird. He went missing in the middle of the day, and in the night, they came and removed all of his stuff as though he had never been there at all.'

'What do you think happened to him?' she asked, unsure whether paranoia had set in. Imogen knew that prison was an unforgiving place that did little or nothing to encourage trust. Paranoia among prisoners was not uncommon, they had far too much time alone to think.

'I was told he was hospitalised and then moved to D-wing. But now something else has happened.'

'What?'

'Someone I was friends with in here got fucked up really badly by another inmate, and the guards just let it happen.'

'Who?'

'His name is Sparks, I think he said his first name was Daniel.' Gabriel checked to see no one was watching him, everyone seemed to be engrossed in their own conversations but he leaned in a little more just in case.

'What happened to him?' Imogen whispered. Aware that to an outsider this would look like an intimate conversation, close and intense. Both focussing on the other's mouth.

'They say his cellmate stabbed him but that's bullshit. It was another inmate, guy called Asher. He and one of the guards concocted a story to cover their tracks.

I'm sure of it but no one else will say anything. It's like they're all scared.'

'Scared of what?'

'I don't know, but I don't feel safe. I feel like something really bad is going to happen.'

Imogen frowned. 'To you? Have you been threatened?'

'Maybe. My girlfriend said someone came to see her, said his brother was friends with me in here.'

'Proserpina?' Imogen said.

Gabriel was taken aback. 'How did you know?'

'We looked through your phone. I'm guessing that's not her real name.'

Gabriel's expression changed with the knowledge that Imogen had been reading all his private texts with his girlfriend; he seemed embarrassed.

'No, no it's not.'

'Is it Sarah? I had a call from a girl telling me to visit you. Was she with you that night in the signal box, Gabriel? You should tell us who she is. Obstruction can bring some pretty serious charges.'

'More serious than manslaughter?'

He had a point.

'And this guy who threatened your girlfriend said you know his brother,' Imogen continued. 'Do you?'

'Yeah – Asher, the same guy I was telling you about. He's a nasty piece of work. He's been inside a bunch of times by all accounts. I can't help wondering if he isn't running this whole place. He does what he wants, the guards don't seem to care. I think he stabbed Sparks, and I think he did it as a message to me. He's been threatening people around me – trying to get me to . . .' He trailed off.

'Trying to get you to what?'

'To fuck him,' Gabriel whispered just quietly enough for Imogen to hear him.

'Has he . . . done anything . . .' Imogen didn't want to finish the sentence; she hoped her eyes were conveying the message she needed to get across.

'He hasn't – he said he doesn't want it that way . . . he wants me to give it to him. He's basically threatened my girlfriend, I believe he'll hurt her if I don't do it.'

'You should tell me who she is so I can protect her.'

'I'm sorry, I can't do that.'

'How can I help her if you won't even tell me who she is?'

Gabriel frowned. 'Maybe you can find Asher's brother, the one who threatened her.'

'And what good will that do?'

'I'm telling you, something is going on in here, Asher Locke is something to do with it, and maybe his brother knows more. You need to look into it.'

He seemed to be trying to tell her something else, that's all she could assume by the way he kept repeating the point. Did this have something to do with that night in the signal box?

'I have less and less options,' Gabriel continued. 'Either I have to do things I don't want to or this guy's brother is going to make my girlfriend do something she doesn't want to do. I think in all honesty, I would rather die than go near Asher. But then what happens to Emma?' Gabriel's eyes glassed over, she could see him struggling not to let the tears fall. His hands were shaking and his teeth whined under the pressure as he clenched and unclenched his jaw.

'I promise I will look into it for you.' She placed her hand on his balled fist, it was cold and there was a faint tremor that dissipated after she had stroked his hand with her thumb for a little while. In his distress, Gabriel hadn't realised that he'd inadvertently given her Emma's real name. Not Sarah after all, then.

'Thank you. I really don't know who to trust anymore.'

There was a silence between them now, as though they'd reached a crossroads, neither ready to give in. After a moment, Imogen sighed.

'How are you feeling about your hearing?'

'I'll be glad of it now, this limbo is unbearable. I feel like I'm nothing. I think the only reason I'm alive is because I don't want to abandon anyone.'

'Is there a counsellor in here you can speak to?' Imogen asked. He seemed so young and vulnerable to her, barely a man really, caught up in something no one should have to deal with.

'I don't like my thoughts and feelings being written down. I've seen the counsellor but as long as she's part of this system it's impossible to trust her.'

'I understand.' She did understand, when she had been put in court-mandated therapy with a police therapist it had worried her that if she said what was really on her mind, she would lose her job.

People started shuffling around and getting up to leave. Imogen and Gabriel stood up; she instinctively put her arms around him and squeezed. She felt his tense body loosen slightly in her arms, and then he put his arms around her and hugged her back before Barratt coughed to separate them.

'Thank you for coming.'

'I'll come back soon, please, just try and hold on a little longer. You'll be sentenced and probably moved to another place soon. If you stay out of trouble they may even move you to a Cat C prison.'

'I'll try.'

He stepped away and back out through the doors. She felt so helpless as she watched him leave. She couldn't imagine the stress he was feeling right now. He was one of the people she had helped put inside and she regretted it before she had even read him his rights. He wasn't a bad person, anyone could see that. When they had first put him inside she was concerned for his safety, almost sure it wouldn't be long before they heard that he had committed suicide. He was stronger than she thought, but everyone had their breaking point and it seemed as though Gabriel was about to reach his. She had learned something that might help him though, she'd learned the name of his girlfriend, Emma. It wasn't much to go on, but it was a start. She would have to find her.

Chapter 33

Imogen stepped back into the station and took her coat off. Adrian wasn't at his desk. She looked around and saw him in one of the private glass-fronted rooms with the journalist Lucy Hannigan, they were hunkered over the table staring at some photos. She laughed inwardly at how obvious he was; the expression on his face as he looked at Lucy gave his feelings away. The girl was clever with her reverse psychology, knowing full well that by making Miles feel like he was unwelcome and unworthy, he would develop a kind of Stockholm syndrome, desperate for her approval, attention, anything. Clearly, it had worked so far. Imogen couldn't help but admire Lucy a little.

She walked over and knocked on the door. The pair of them jumped and looked at her as though she had caught them planning her surprise birthday party. Adrian waved her in. On the desk were the photos of the signal box, now familiar in Imogen's mind.

'Hello. Have I disturbed your secret tree house meeting?'

'Close the door would you, Grey?' said Adrian, all business.

'What's happened?'

'I've been going over the fire, to see if I can find any clues as to the identity of the homeless person. Something isn't quite sitting right with me about it. The fact that Bricks seems to have disappeared off the face of the earth isn't proof of anything. Not without DNA,' Adrian said.

'Right,' Imogen said hopefully.

'And now that you suspect it may be linked with this other case, the Wallis couple, I thought I might try and see if I could get more information about the fire, look at it from a different angle as it were.' He paused. 'What if the fire wasn't started in the bin at all?'

'You mean what if Gabriel Webb didn't start the fire?'

'You know what, I don't think he did. Someone must have seen them in there though because it must have been started moments after.'

'Why would someone want to set Gabriel Webb up for this?'

'I don't think this is about him,' Lucy chipped in.

'What's it about then?' Imogen stared at them both.

Lucy pulled out some more photographs and put them on the table, spreading them out next to the ones of the signal box. Imogen recognised the scene as another case of arson from a year earlier. Lucy pointed at the little pellets on the ground in both sets of photos; they looked identical.

'That's just rat shit though, isn't it?' Imogen said.

'Maybe. Maybe not,' Lucy said. 'I think it's worth looking into. It all looks too uniform to me, like synthetic somehow. I have a few connections I could ask for a second opinion.'

'How long have you known about this other fire?' Adrian snapped.

'Not long, I just needed to be sure.'

'What if this was all about hiding a dead body, making it look like an accident? What if we aren't looking at a homeless man at all? What if we're looking at a murder victim?' Adrian said.

'Well, you can't know that. The victim might have started the fire to get warm?' Imogen suggested.

'I just don't think so. Yes, his face could have been smashed in by the beams but it also could have been the way he was murdered, an extreme facial beating sustained during a brutal attack,' Lucy said.

'Are we sure we aren't just looking for monsters where there are none?' Imogen said. Adrian looked at Imogen, she knew what he was thinking – he was paranoid that they were forever destined to look for corruption, and worse than that – he was worried they would keep finding it.

'It's got to be worth looking though, hasn't it?' Lucy implored.

'Where does this leave Gabriel Webb? Is this enough to get him out of prison?' Imogen asked.

'Not yet, not even close, but surely that makes it all the more vital that we consider this thoroughly?' Adrian said.

Imogen couldn't tell if Adrian was just indulging Lucy or whether he believed all of this was a possibility. The notion that she could help get Gabriel out of prison was satisfying though. And to get his charges overturned completely? That would be great. Putting him in prison had never felt as though it were to protect society, but an extreme punishment for a moment's mistake. Yes, someone had died, but it had been completely and utterly unintentional – but more than that – it just felt like another injustice.

Imogen noticed that Lucy had lost her sarcastic facade around Adrian; she was watching the saga of their budding relationship unfold right before her eyes and she couldn't help but wonder where it would end. She thought momentarily about those first flashes of attraction she had had with Dean, and all the things that had changed since then. Reality getting in the way of romance. Another impossible love story.

Chapter 34

Dean sat opposite his probation officer, waiting as she read through the paperwork on her desk. There was a request he needed to get signed off. He was appealing to a different office, closer to Plymouth, and he had to ask nicely for it to be considered. He thumbed the resin ball on his pendant as he waited.

His phone vibrated in his pocket. He hoped it wasn't Imogen, he hated to ignore her calls. Probably still looking for an explanation for his recent behaviour, things he wasn't ready to talk about. The truth was he wasn't sure why he felt compelled to pursue this yet, but he knew when he saw the triquetra that he'd seen that symbol before. A coldness had come over him, as though his skin was moving of its own accord, crawling. He'd seen the symbol somewhere else, but it couldn't have anything to do with this – could it?

His probation officer looked up. 'This is highly irregular, Mr Kinkaid.'

‘I told you, I have a job that requires me to be in Plymouth.’

‘It might not be that easy to arrange. We’ll see what we can do.’ The probation officer didn’t like Dean, which was why things weren’t that easy. He had to try though. The more time he was spending with Imogen, the more difficult it was getting; he didn’t want to let her down and yet he couldn’t change who he was. If they had some distance between them then maybe it could work. Maybe if he didn’t feel like a lying piece of shit every time they were together, they might stand a chance. He’d never really considered the possibility that he could actually fall for someone. What was worse was that he had fallen for Imogen, Elias’ daughter and a police officer to boot. She was the one woman who could ruin his life, the one who could ruin his relationship with the only family he had ever known. He knew that when it came down to it, he didn’t come first with her and neither did he feel as though he deserved to – her job was her life and he had to respect that. Above everything, he had to try and be better. He had to keep reminding himself of what was at stake.

As the probation officer showed him out, Dean’s fingers stroked his pendant again. The wheels were in motion. At the very least, if he was going to do this, he had to cover his tracks better than he had ever done before.

Chapter 35

'Thanks for doing this for me,' Imogen said to Adrian as they pulled up outside Emma's house. Gary had found her through social media. One of the goth clubs in town had a photo gallery online, after finding several pictures of Gabriel with her, it was only a matter of running through the tagged people in the photo and looking at all of their friends. Easy to find her after that.

'It's my job, too. I don't want an innocent man in prison any more than you do, especially not after what you told me he was dealing with in there.'

They knocked on the door, it took a few moments but eventually a young woman answered. She was petite, with turquoise flashes in her long black hair.

'Can I help you?'

'Are you Emma?' Imogen showed her her warrant card.

Emma looked up and down the street before ushering

them in, she was clearly worried about someone seeing them. She took them into the lounge and they all sat down. She obviously lived with her parents, but then everyone did until about the age of thirty these days. It was a nice house, wallpapered with big flowers in beige and duck egg blue. Everything was coordinated in subdued and sandy tones. Emma looked out of place in this room with her low-cut black mesh top, a bright pink bra showing through the fabric, knee-high black patent doc martens and ripped tights. It was definitely the same girl they had seen in the CCTV video outside the station.

'Is this about Gabriel? Are you Imogen Grey?'

'Yes. You're the girl who contacted me about him? You said your name was Sarah.'

'Sorry, I didn't mean to lie, I was just scared.'

'Gabriel tells me you've been threatened?'

'I was, they said they want me to pay to protect Gabriel on the inside.'

'Were you there the night Gabriel was arrested?' Imogen asked.

Emma broke down and started to cry. 'You must think I'm a terrible person.'

'No one thinks that.'

'Why didn't you come forward?' Adrian asked.

'Gabriel made me promise not to. It wasn't that easy anyway, if it had been just me then I would have – but the people we were with, I don't know them that well and they aren't exactly good people.' She shifted uncomfortably in her seat.

'Who are they?'

'They told me Gabriel would get hurt if he told the police.'

'We can protect Gabriel, I've already had a word with the warden, let her know that Gabriel is helping us with an investigation and there will be hell to pay if anything happens to him. He's not in any danger for now,' Imogen lied, she hadn't spoken to the warden; the truth was she didn't know how deep the corruption went, so for now, the less people who knew about it, the better. She just had her fingers crossed no one got to Gabriel before they could get him out of there. 'So who else was there that night, Emma?'

'A girl I know from my Saturday job and a couple of her mates.' Emma started to bite her nails.

'Why are you worried about implicating them?' Adrian said.

'They're Laners, I don't really want to get into any shit with those people, they look out for each other.'

'You needn't worry about the kids from Burnthouse Lane,' Adrian interjected. 'They can be pretty feral but largely their reputation is disproportionately exaggerated.'

'Can you tell us the names of the people that were with you that night? It could really help Gabriel,' Imogen said softly.

'The girl is Leanne Bridges, like I said, I work with her. The boys were called Trey and Chris, that's all I know. Chris is the one who threatened me.' She looked uncomfortable for a moment, glanced away.

'What is it, Emma?' Imogen said gently.

'That was the first time I had met them, Gabriel too,

the whole mess is their fault. They insisted we go there. I think he did it just to shut them up, they were smoking rock and he didn't want anything to do with them.' She pulled her sleeve over her hand and wiped her eyes and nose, trying to compose herself.

'What do you know about this guy who came and threatened you? What did he do exactly?'

'He came up to me just outside, somehow he knew where I lived. I guess Leanne must have told him.'

'What does he look like?'

'He had a shaved head but I could see that he was ginger, he had like a ginger goatee and freckles. He was a bit older than me I think, about six foot tall, I reckon.'

'And what did he say to you, this Chris?'

'He just said that Gabe was in trouble in prison and that I had to do a job for him. That if I did it, I'd help keep Gabriel safe.'

'Did he say what the job was?'

Emma's face flushed. 'He made it pretty clear he wanted me to have sex with him.'

'What did Gabriel say to you when you visited him in jail?' Imogen asked.

'He told me to contact you and that he would sort it. Is this all about that night?'

Imogen paused. 'Partly, yes. But we may need to speak to the individual who threatened you about another matter, too.'

'Is he dangerous?'

'He could be. Here's my card,' Imogen said, handing it to her. 'If you see that Chris guy again, or if you are worried about anything, then just give me a call. Straight away.'

'Thank you,' Emma said.

'Now, do you know where can we find Leanne Bridges?' Adrian asked.

'She lives in the light blue house on Holly Road,' Emma said as Imogen and Adrian stood up. 'I can't remember the house number, I'm sorry.'

'You've been a great help Emma, thanks.' Imogen smiled as reassuringly as she could.

They left the house and stood outside waiting for Emma to close the door behind them.

'What are you thinking, Miley? Your face looks pained.'

'What is it about middle class goths?'

'Excuse me?'

'Goths are always middle class, have you never noticed that?'

'That's not true!' Imogen bumped him on the arm.

'Is it a way to rebel without actually rebelling?'

'I was kind of a goth, back in the day.'

'Yeah? Grey the goth. And what were you trying to achieve?'

'I wasn't trying to achieve anything, I just liked the clothes.'

'OK, maybe you're an exception to the rule. In my experience, though . . .'

'Your limited experience.'

'Let me finish.'

Imogen smiled. 'OK, go on.'

'In my experience as a police officer we don't arrest

a lot of goths, so this whole demonic Satan shit is a bit of a farce.'

'Maybe you shouldn't judge people on the way they look?'

'You're misunderstanding me. These kids all seem to come from nice backgrounds and have nice shit.'

'Well I don't know what to tell you, Miley, coming from a nice house doesn't mean your life is all that great. Look at Gabriel, his parents have pretty much disowned him. I called his house after I had visited and they weren't remotely interested.'

'Because of the way he dresses.'

'It's a fashion thing, and a statement against what is considered normal I guess. Maybe these kids have just figured out that there is no such thing as normal and want to express that through their lifestyle rather than conforming to what everyone else thinks they should be.'

'I see I hit a nerve.'

'Oh, you'll know when you hit a nerve.'

As they approached the car, Imogen spotted a man turn off onto the road perpendicular to Emma's. He was about six foot tall, with a black hoodie and what seemed to be a ginger beard.

'Did you see that?' Adrian said quietly.

'Yes.'

'He matches the description Emma gave us of Chris Locke.'

She groaned, remembering that she was wearing new shoes, not suited to running at all, still at the breaking-in phase. Oh well. She watched Adrian take off before taking a deep breath and starting after him. Even on a bad day with crippling shoes on she could outrun Adrian in both speed and distance.

She heard Adrian call out to the man as he turned the corner just before her.

'Where did he go?' she asked as she caught up to Adrian. There was no sign of the hooded man anywhere.

'He went left!'

Imogen picked up the speed, ignoring her shoes and the tightness across the bridge of her feet. Mind over matter was easy when you knew how. She heard the sound of Adrian's feet thumping grow more distant as she turned the corner just in time to see the suspect vanish around the next corner which led to the bus station. He could easily disappear in there, with the amount of entry and exit points, as well as the crowds of people and the chaos of buses pulling in and out.

She surveyed the bus station but couldn't see him. Moments later Adrian arrived at her side, slumped over and grabbing onto his knees for support.

'Do you think that was him?' Adrian finally wheezed.

'He sure as hell seemed to be running for a reason.'

'Well if he really is that Asher guy's brother, he might have a record, too.'

'So let's find him then.' She took one look at Adrian, whose chest was heaving, and rolled her eyes. 'Stay here, I'll bring the car round.'

Chapter 36

Adrian and Imogen drove down Holly Road looking for Leanne's house and managed to find it quickly; it was the only blue one in the street. As they walked up to the terrace, Adrian glanced through the window. There was a teenage couple in there, kissing on the sofa; the boy's hand up what was presumably Leanne's skirt. There was no net on the window and the curtains were open, bold as brass. Adrian opened his warrant card and pushed it against the window, knocking at the same time. The boy pulled back and started rolling a cigarette as if nothing had happened, while the girl got up off the sofa and disappeared. The door opened.

'Yeah?'

'Are you Leanne Bridges?' Adrian asked.

Her face was confrontational. 'Did I do something wrong?'

'No, we just need to ask you a few questions. Are your parents here?'

'What do you think?' She left the door open and walked back into the lounge.

'I'm DS Adrian Miles and this is my colleague, DS Imogen Grey.'

They sat on the sofa opposite Leanne and her boyfriend, although he seemed a fair bit older than her. He had a tattoo on his neck and ink all down his arms. He was leaning back with a strange smile on his face; clearly, this wasn't his first encounter with the police. The room was nothing like Emma's house, the ashtray was full to bursting on a table that was scattered with Rizlas, there was a grubby-looking throw on the sofa and a TV bigger than the sofa was mounted on the wall opposite. The fitting that the naked light-bulb hung from was barely attached.

'What is it you want?' Leanne finally broke the silence.

'We heard you were at the disused signal box at Central Station just before the fire broke out there a few weeks back?'

'What's disused mean?' Leanne's nose wrinkled in confusion.

'Not used, out of commission, no longer working,' Adrian said with a sigh, unsure of whether it was a genuine question or whether she was being evasive.

'Yeah, I was there, didn't start the fire though. That guy's already been arrested.'

'Right yeah, Gabriel Webb,' Adrian said.

'Who told you about me?' Leanne asked.

'There was some security footage, we had it cleaned up and showed your picture around,' Adrian lied. Until they knew who was threatening Emma, they didn't want to drop her in it any more than was necessary. Besides,

Adrian was getting a really bad vibe from the boyfriend. Was he the other guy in the signal box? Was he in the Wallis house? Adrian looked him up and down, but aside from the way his clothes hung on him, loose and baggy, there was no way to tell.

'Who are you?' he asked him.

'Trey Wilson,' the boy said.

'You were there too, weren't you?'

'So what? I didn't start nothing.'

So he was there; now they had all the players maybe they could start to get a full picture of what actually happened that night.

'Trey Wilson? I recognise that name.'

'Dunno, mate.' He smiled, showing his perfectly formed teeth, discoloured from nicotine.

'Is your dad Carl Wilson?'

'He is, don't have nothing to do wiv 'im though.'

Carl was a particularly rough guy, always in and out of trouble. Adrian had put him in the tank more than once back in his uniform days. Usually a drunk and disorderly, a few minor violent incidents until a couple of years ago, when he brutally assaulted another man with a cider bottle in a pub over his song choice on a jukebox. Adrian had always wondered what song choice could lead a man to commit murder, it was never listed in the report and no one at the scene could remember. He was in prison serving a life sentence over that song. Adrian couldn't imagine giving up his freedom over a song, except maybe "Tubthumping", but that's why he was a police officer and people like Carl were criminals.

'How old are you, Leanne?' Imogen said.

'Just turned fifteen.'

'And you, Trey?' Imogen asked.

'I'm eighteen.'

'You do know the age of consent in this country is sixteen, right?'

'Everyone knows that,' Leanne snipped.

'I'm not boning her.' Trey smiled again; Adrian saw Imogen wince at the expression.

'Any sexual activity is illegal under the age of sixteen,' Adrian said to Trey, who was far too self-assured for Adrian's liking.

'So I can go to prison for like murder or something but I can't say I want to have sex, that's mental!' Leanne snorted.

'And yet, it's the law.' Adrian tried his hardest not to sound too fatherly or disapproving, it wasn't Leanne he had the issue with in this scenario. He glared at Trey, who was the one in the wrong here. As the father of a teenager himself he found it hard not to look at these things from the stance of an overprotective parent. He made a mental note to talk to his son Tom about girls and the age of consent again; even though he knew Tom was more interested in the Xbox at this point, sooner or later his switch would flip.

'We're just very good friends.' Trey smiled again.

'On the twenty-sixth of June, the night of the fire, did you or any of the people you were with venture into the downstairs area of the signal box?' Imogen asked.

'No, we did not,' Leanne said.

'Did you hear anything coming from that room?' Imogen said.

'Nope, we went in and had a smoke, that Manson-looking fucker lit a fire, he was proper snobby, looking down his nose at us. Who's laughing now, eh?' Leanne said.

'I don't think he's laughing much to be honest with you,' Imogen said.

'Well, whatever, I didn't do nothing wrong, like I said before.' Trey stubbed his cigarette out before standing up. 'I need a slash.'

He left the room and Adrian heard him thumping up the stairs.

'Has anyone contacted you about Gabriel or Emma or that night?' Adrian said to Leanne.

'No one, even Emma doesn't want to hang out with me anymore.'

'Have you had any contact with Chris Locke lately?'

'I've seen him about. Not really.'

They heard a key in the lock of the front door and a few moments later a man walked into the room.

'What the fuck is going on here?'

'Your daughter was just helping us with our investigation.' Adrian stood up.

'Stepdaughter,' Leanne corrected him.

'You can't come in here without a warrant,' the man boomed. A man who seemed to know the law for all the wrong reasons.

'We had reason to believe a crime was being committed on the premises,' Imogen said, as Trey appeared behind Leanne's stepfather. Leanne's eyes widened and Adrian saw her catch her breath.

'The front door was left open.' Adrian jumped in

with the lie before Imogen mentioned what they had seen through the window, he didn't want to get Leanne in any more trouble.

'I've told you about that before, you idiot,' he snapped at Leanne. Adrian recognised the almost imperceptible flinch from Leanne as his hand instinctively moved then stopped itself. How many times a day did Leanne get a wallop around the side of her head?

Adrian took a step forward, then felt Imogen's hand grab his arm and hold him back. He wasn't planning on hitting the man. He glanced over at Leanne, who was still holding her breath. The tension in the room was palpable. Adrian pulled away, walked past the stepfather and Trey and left, Imogen right behind him.

'What the hell, Miley?' Imogen whispered outside.

'Tell me you didn't see that?'

'I saw you ready to knock his block off without provocation.'

'What chance do these kids have? I remember that Trey kid when he was about nine or ten, wide-eyed and dirty all the time, his dad was always getting pulled in and his mum was a drunk, too. How could he ever become anything other than this?'

'From what I understand you had a pretty shit father and you did all right.'

'I had people looking out for me, I had Andrea.'

'Bullshit. We all make choices, some of us are stronger than others.' Imogen's phone beeped and she looked at the screen.

'Was that a compliment?'

'No. Now let's see what Gary's got for us on the Wallis case, the one we're actually supposed to be working on.' She put the phone back in her pocket.

The pieces were starting to come together. Adrian didn't believe for a second that these kids had no idea what was going on. What he didn't understand was why.

Adrian sighed. 'I'm beginning to think we should just cut out the middle man and ask Dominic what's going on here.'

'You think he's connected to this? Why would he bother with these teen wannabes? Why would he kill a homeless man or a couple of old people? I think organised crime is more his bag.'

'Why not?'

'You're paranoid.'

'I may be paranoid. Doesn't change the fact that he's one step ahead of the curve all the time. I feel like he's behind every crime we investigate, or at least profiting from it in some way.'

'I'll concede that he is a smarmy git, I'm not entirely sure what Andrea sees in him. The fact is, though, there is zero indication that he has anything to do with this.'

'You didn't see him, Grey. You didn't see the look on his face when he was gloating to me. He's a very powerful man.'

'Are you afraid of him?' she said incredulously.

'I'm afraid of what he can do to Tom, to Andrea even.'

'Why don't you tell her?'

'Without evidence? She would apply for full custody and get some kind of restraining order. She's done it before. I don't think he will do anything until he's pushed though.'

'Is that why you're sneaking around with Gary?'

'You noticed?'

'I suspect half the station thinks you two are having an affair the way you're always whispering into each other's ears and huddling in dark corners.'

'I can't risk anyone knowing I'm checking up on Dominic. I'm not joking about this case either. I've got a really strong feeling he's connected to it.'

'OK, well we'd better get to the bottom of it then.'

Chapter 37

Gary Tunney threw the paperwork on the table and it landed with a thud in front of Imogen and Adrian. It was all the files relating to the Wallis murder. The victims' financials and some other public domain information Gary had found out about their son. Adrian was always so impressed with Gary, a part of him felt like he should be running the place. If Gary didn't understand something he worked on it until he did, then he moved on to the next thing, it was like he collected information. If Adrian ever went on a quiz show Gary would be his phone-a-friend; he knew everything.

'What's all this?' Adrian asked.

'Right, this pile is all about the Wallis couple.'

'OK, great.'

'And this pile is all about the Wallis son and his business interests.'

'And did you find anything?'

'I think so.'

Adrian grinned. 'Are you going to tell us?'

'So, first of all, looking at the victims themselves, they have no apparent material wealth but they do own their own home and have life insurance.'

'All of which goes to the son if they die?' Adrian said.

'Exactly. The house itself is fully paid for and worth over three hundred grand. Life insurance is for a hundred thou each, so that's half a million quid.'

'That's a pretty good motive,' Imogen said. 'What else did you find out about the son?'

'Public domain information and a quick internet search shows that his business is not doing well at all. It's a bit of a miracle that he's managed to stay afloat this long.'

'Motive just got a lot stronger.' Imogen folded her arms.

'If you can get me his detailed financials then I can work my magic on them.'

'Sounds good,' Adrian said.

'I better get on then. Just send them over when you've got them,' Gary said before leaving the room.

When Adrian was sure that Gary was completely out of earshot he turned to Imogen.

'He's going to tell us to sod off pretty soon.'

'Don't feel bad, Miley, he loves solving these puzzles. He gets full-on depression if he doesn't have loads to do. We're doing him a favour.'

'Really? Because I feel like I'm taking the piss.'

'I've seen Gary in a depression and, trust me, you don't want to see that. He will tell us if he doesn't want to help.' Imogen sighed loudly and Adrian looked across at her. There were dark circles underneath her eyes, and something sad about her expression.

'How are you holding up?' he asked her as he picked up the information Gary had given and stuffed it under his arm.

'Fine. Why do you ask?'

'You know you can talk to me? You've got a lot on your plate, it's written all over your face.'

She shot a look up at him. 'How do you do that, Miley?'

'Do what?'

'You make me want to tell you things; you know I don't like talking!'

'Sometimes talking about things is good.' Adrian could tell when Imogen was thinking about Dean.

'You never talk about anything,' she retorted. 'What about Lucy Hannigan, our intrepid reporter?'

'What about her?' he smirked.

'Do you think that will work? You need to keep our cases private, do you really want some investigative journalist going through your phone? Looking for a lead on a case so she can boost her career?'

'Says the woman who is practically living with a convicted criminal. You are full of it, Grey!'

'Yeah well, that is proving to be every bit as challenging as it sounds.' She paused and let out a heavy sigh. 'I'm just worried about you.'

'It's not that serious,' he said.

'Oh really?'

'I do like her; a lot more than I've liked anyone in a long time.'

'I can see that. I've never seen you like this; and she likes you too, I can tell.'

'So why the concern?'

'Maybe I'm just projecting, but watch yourself.'

'You've got enough going on without worrying about me as well, Grey. You need to learn how to get things off your chest, stop internalising everything.'

'When did you get so wise?'

Adrian took a deep breath. 'When my father was still here, I did it, I spoke to him, got some things off my chest, told him I loved him but I couldn't be around him anymore unless he cleaned himself up, but that was a joke in itself really; I knew he was never coming back from where he was. His whole life was over and he had nothing to come back to. He chose the drugs over our family so I was done with him, I didn't want him anywhere near Tom when he came along so . . .'

'That must have been hard.'

'I felt guilty about it for a while, then he died and I knew that it was all OK. I know that sounds weird, but I knew that he knew I loved him, and I knew he agreed with me about Tom.'

'I bet he would be proud of you now.'

'I wouldn't go that far.'

Chapter 38

DCI Mira Kapoor was out of the office, which was just as well. Even though they'd been looking over the case all day, they had nothing new on the Wallis murders. Those were still the priority, but for some reason Imogen was drawn to Gabriel's case, as though everything would become clear when she'd found out what happened that night. Maybe she was kidding herself, maybe Adrian was right and she did just have a thing for bad boys. Maybe this was about Dean, and her inability to help him, his unwillingness to let her. She had to feel like she was helping someone, she had to feel like she wasn't letting someone else rot in prison.

'Gary's just emailed some info over,' Adrian said.

'So, what do we know?' Imogen asked Adrian.

'The prisoner is called Asher Locke, his brother's name is Chris Locke. They haven't had a great time of it, their dad's been in prison for most of their lives and they got put in care for neglect a couple of times too. Their mother wasn't feeding them right, but it was ruled as depression-related because she fought hard to get them back when they were gone.'

'Have you got the address for him?'

'Already texted it to you.'

'These residential care homes they were in – I don't suppose we have the names of any of them?'

'Gary's already working on that. He said he'll send it over as soon as he can.'

'Let's get to Chris Locke's place then.'

Chris Locke lived just one street away from Holly Road, the streets even met at the end. If there was one thing that Adrian didn't believe in it was coincidences. Chris Locke himself didn't appear to be at home; the place seemed deserted. Adrian was parked around a hundred feet from the front door so they could see the direction he was most likely to come from. Imogen was checking her phone for what seemed like the hundredth time since they had got in the car together.

'Trouble in paradise?' Adrian asked, knowing that Imogen had the 'Dean' look on her face.

She sighed. 'It's just Dean. I mean, I get it, I had a difficult childhood too. It was pretty normal to me, I didn't know any different. It's only when I got older I realised it was so different to other people's.'

'But Dean had worse?'

'I know. I know it's not a competition, but if it was, he would be winning. I had a dysfunctional family but at least they were my family. My mum made a home, it was chaotic and messed up but it was home – he didn't have anything like that.'

'The way I see it everyone's got a story, and you can't compare them, because you can only know who you are in respect to the life you have had, so yes, you can look at Dean's life and think it was worse than yours, but how do you know how you would have dealt with his life? It's unquantifiable.'

'That's a good word.'

Adrian grinned. 'Thank you.'

'I just wish I could help him. I wish I knew what to do. I wish he wasn't shutting me out.'

'Maybe it's because you can't handle it, maybe because he's worried you will affect the way he normally deals with things?'

'What does that mean?'

'It means you know who Dean is, if he tells you his plans you might try and stop him, you might have to. He either doesn't want to hear it or doesn't want to put you in that position. You can't change people.'

'But people can change.'

'If they want to. Not because you want them to.'

Imogen took a deep breath to say something when Adrian held his hand up to stop her. Chris Locke turned the corner and headed towards his house. He looked around and behind him as though he were expecting to be followed. Maybe it was just because he was used to being in trouble. Adrian noted that Chris was dressed from head to toe in black. Black trainers, black hoodie and black jogging bottoms. Not that this was an uncommon way to dress at all but it made Adrian think of the viral video. It was a fleeting thought but it came back to Adrian's feelings on coincidences. Suddenly this man was very much on their radar. Maybe watching him was a better idea than confronting him at this point.

'What do you think?' Imogen said.

'Look at how he's dressed.'

'What about it?'

'Doesn't remind you of anything?' Adrian said.

'I dunno, about twenty other people we saw today?'

'And the gang that killed the Wallis couple?'

'Based on black clothes? We'd have to look at half the city.'

'Black clothes, the fact that he's the brother of a convicted criminal, us being here – now.'

'But what about the threats he's made against Emma?'

'I think these things must be connected. Gabriel Webb and the Wallis murder. I don't know how or why,' Adrian said hesitantly. 'We still haven't identified that body, but if we can link the two cases then the DCI should give us some more time on that.'

'Are you busy tonight?' Imogen asked.

'I was meeting Lucy, why?'

'How do you feel about hanging out with me here instead? If Chris Locke is anything to do with the Wallis murder, that immediately raises my suspicions about Leanne and her friends, and why they dragged Gabriel to that signal box. If we stay here we can see if anyone visits him or if he goes anywhere.'

'Unofficial, unpaid overtime? How benevolent of you,' Adrian said.

'Just for a few hours. Please? I feel like we are close to getting ahead of this thing.'

'Fine. Seeing as you asked so nicely.' Adrian folded his arms.

Chapter 39

Imogen chucked her coat on the sofa and slumped next to it. She still hadn't got used to the place being empty when she got home. It had been a week since Imogen and Dean had watched the viral video together. A week since they had made love, a little less since she had seen him or spoken to him and she felt awful. Homesick. She stared at her phone, knowing he wouldn't call, knowing he was stronger than her. He had left the ball in her court. What if he didn't answer? What if his phone was off? If she didn't call him she was in control. He couldn't ignore her if she hadn't tried. There was something about his behaviour the last time she had seen him that played heavily on her mind. She hadn't known many situations where Dean went a whole conversation without making a joke or cracking a smile. It was his way of reassuring her. Even when things were so bad it seemed completely inappropriate he still did it. During their last conversation, he hadn't smiled once though, if anything he'd looked confused, confounded. Maybe he was waiting for her to call, maybe this was a test. Maybe he needed her.

'Fuck it.' She resentfully picked up the phone and clicked on his name.

'Hello?' Dean's voice was quiet.

'Are you OK?'

'I am,' he said with a sigh.

'I don't think you are.'

'I won't lie, I've been better, but I'm OK.'

'Will you come over?'

'Do you want me to?'

'I do.'

The line went dead and she threw her phone at the other end of the sofa in frustration. She grabbed a cushion and put it over her face before screaming as loud as she could. That felt good. She looked through the films and put on an old movie, a black and white suspense she had watched with her mother on a Sunday afternoon. The old movies they used to watch together were a large part of the reason she became a police officer; she'd always watched them in awe. She wanted to try and relax before Dean arrived.

Half an hour later, Imogen awoke to the sound of gentle tapping on the door. The movie was still playing but she'd fallen asleep in spite of it. The knocking continued. Getting to her feet, she went to open the door.

Outside, Dean was staring at his feet. He was showered but she could see a fresh cut just above his eyebrow and a quick glance at his hand showed that his knuckles had split open recently.

'What happened?' She pulled him inside and dragged him into the kitchen, running the tap until the water was warm and then gently moving his knuckles under it. He stood and watched the water as it ran over his hand. She looked up at him; he was transfixed by the motion of the water as it cascaded down his wrist over his busted knuckles and through his fingertips.

'I'm glad you called,' Dean finally said.

'I was worried about you,' she lied; a white lie, she'd called because she was worried she would have to live without him, that he would never come back.

'Sorry I took your files.'

'Don't worry about that. No one found out. Just talk to me.' He sniffed and she noticed a tear had made its way down his cheek. 'What is it?'

They sat across from each other at the dining table. Imogen had never seen a more sombre expression than the one on Dean's face right now. She wanted to ask how he had hurt his hand but she had so many other questions that it would have to wait.

'You know I was in a Young Offender Institution from age thirteen, right?' He clenched and unclenched his fist; the wounds started to weep again. How had he got them?

'I did know that.' He hadn't told her, but she'd looked into him back when they'd first met. They had never spoken about it.

'Well, I went there for killing someone. You know that?'

'Yes,' she said. A part of her felt guilty that she was willing to overlook that fact.

He went to the fridge and pulled out a beer. Imogen followed him and wrapped a tea towel around his hand. Pulling away from her, he headed into the lounge. When she walked in, he was hunched over on the sofa, leaning on his knees and gazing at the floor. From his evasive behaviour she could tell that he was wrestling with something, some memory he had decided to tell her. She wasn't sure if she was ready to hear it, but he was here and he was ready to talk. She sat next to him, switching off the TV, but couldn't get him to look at her. She took his other hand in hers anyway, intertwining their fingers; he squeezed to show his appreciation.

'I was in care for most of my childhood, pretty much until I went to kiddie prison. Foster care is a strange thing. It's not permanent; the feelings you have are fleeting. You learn early not to get too attached to anyone because no one in your life is forever. I've had the full range of emotions from those places until there are no more emotions left to have.'

She didn't quite understand what he was saying but it was so unusual for him to talk about himself that she couldn't interrupt with anything more than a platitude.

'OK.'

'I know you have your own demons, we all do. But my demons were actually demons.'

'Go on.'

'I saw some fucked up stuff in foster care – and you had two choices – you were either with them or against them. They can make your life hell, if they really want to. No one gives a shit. I hope it's better now, but twenty-five years ago, there just wasn't the same level of sharing of information, there was virtually no media scrutiny. Some of those places were a law unto themselves. A little world on their own – outside of what's acceptable, of what's human. Kids used to go missing all the time. If you got hurt, the only place to go was your case worker and sometimes you didn't see them for months on end, and even when you did, you were never sure they were on your side. Sometimes the people looking after us would just bung the social workers some cash to look the other way. You learn to trust only yourself.' He pulled his hand out of hers. 'There was a place we would go to. They would take us there sometimes.'

'What kind of place?' She shifted uncomfortably in her seat, the tone in his voice was distant. She didn't like the direction this was going but she knew she had to stay strong for Dean, it was hurting him to tell her and so all she could do was listen.

'A house, we would have to entertain the guests.'

'Entertain how?'

'Well, they would make us fight each other, like dogs, sometimes with weapons, they would place bets on us . . . and then there was the other stuff . . . you know . . . don't make me spell it out.'

'Jesus. Is that why you killed that man? Did he . . . touch you?'

'It was more complicated than that.'

'So, what's this got to do with that video?' She shifted the focus of the conversation, trying to pull Dean back, putting the focus back on why this had all surfaced for him again.

'The house they took us to had a tiled hall when you walked in; it was a big house, I don't think anyone lived there. It was more of a private members' club. On the hall floor was a big Celtic pattern. In the centre was a triquetra.'

'Do you think the kids in that video had something to do with the place that you went to as a kid?'

'I don't know. It would make sense, I guess. I looked into the elderly couple who died though. They were decent people by all accounts.'

'We know, we already checked them out.'

'No offence, but I can find things out that you can't.' He clutched at his pendant, the tiny shell trapped in a ball of resin. Imogen glanced at it.

'Is that where you got the pendant from?' she asked. 'Someone you were in care with?'

'A girl I was in care with. We were together for a few years. I used to look out for her; she was the closest thing to a sister that I ever had, almost like family, really.'

'And what happened to her?'

Dean sank back into the sofa and pulled Imogen towards him, wrapping his arm around her. It was good to be so close to him again.

'The man I killed, he wouldn't leave her alone. He wasn't a good man. She was always afraid and I couldn't always protect her even though I tried. It wasn't long after I met Elias – someone who was good to me, maybe the first person who really seemed to have no hidden agenda. Elias wanted to take me out of care but I didn't want to leave because of her. I couldn't leave her with

. . . him. I spoke to my social worker about him and she did nothing, I don't think she could, then she left social services to have her own children. It wasn't until after I had killed him that I confided in Elias about the things that happened in that place. He got me a good lawyer and managed to keep me from getting transferred to adult prison after I had served my term at the Young Offenders Institute. In exchange for me not saying anything on the record about the foster home, the judge let me out at eighteen.'

He stroked her hair as he spoke with a calm clarity, his heartbeat back to normal.

'You think the kids in that video went to that place? The place they took you to?'

'I would guess at least one of those kids has come out of care. I've watched the video a hundred times and the one with the tragedy mask is the leader. I think he's older than the others. I would bet that he had been to that house. I hadn't thought about that place for a long time but seeing that brought it all home that maybe it was still there. I just couldn't help wondering how many kids went through that house? How long was it going on?'

'Do you remember where the house was?'

'No.'

'Is there any way of finding out?'

'What do you think I've been trying to do?' He held up his bandaged hand before clutching at the resin ball on his necklace. Imogen watched his fingers tighten around it, wondering.

'What was her name? The girl you were in care with?'

'Jess. She killed herself because I couldn't look after her.'

'You were a kid, Dean, and you protected her as best you could.'

'Suicide isn't uncommon, kids from a care environment are more at risk than most. If I didn't have Elias I would have felt completely disconnected from this world. I can't imagine I would have had a reason for sticking around.'

'Don't say that.' She couldn't help feeling some affection for Elias whenever Dean spoke about him, he hadn't been a father to her but what he had done for Dean made her feel some warmth towards him. It did nothing but help her opinion of the father who had only just come into her life.

'It's the truth.'

'I'm glad you stuck around.' She sat up and looked at him, his green eyes glistening.

'I don't think about any of it much anymore, it was so long ago. There's no point. Seeing that symbol brought back the memory of that place though.' The vacant look in his eyes returned.

'Would you come in and make a statement?'

'Really? At this point in time I'm not sure it's even connected,' he said, his reluctance evident. 'I might be completely wrong and this has nothing to do with it.'

'Was there anything else that made you think it might be connected? Besides the symbol, I mean . . .'

'The dog. The way they killed the dog. I've seen things like that before.'

'In that place?'

Dean nodded 'It was weird. I was only there twice.'

'What kind of people were there?'

'Different people, usually men, but not always; sometimes there were couples there, couples with money. Sometimes the kids would come back covered in bruises and all bloody, broken ribs, black eyes. Before I went there myself I couldn't even imagine what would cause that kind of injury. Until I saw for myself. No one ever talked about what happened there. Sometimes they would make the kids fight each other, presumably from other homes.'

'It sounds awful.' Her words sounded so unsuitable, not even close to capturing the horror those children must have experienced.

'Pretty much. The fear of what would happen if you didn't do what they wanted was greater than the fear of taking part.'

'Did you speak to your case worker about it?'

'No, but Jess did. They did nothing except speak to Clive, one of our carers, about it. He beat the shit out of her – which she preferred to the alternative. He locked her in a dark room for a long time. When they opened the door, she was hanging from the central ceiling joist. She had been dead for over a day and no one had noticed.'

'I'm so sorry.'

'I got lucky when I got put in a secure facility for killing Clive, it was like a holiday compared to that place.'

'Did you ever go back to the care home?'

'To that place? No.'

'What are you going to do now? Are you going to stay here?'

'What do you want me to do? I'll understand if you don't want me around.'

She looked at him. Despite everything he'd just told her, could she trust him to be completely honest with her? With this information she couldn't just cut him loose; he needed her. She had abandoned him once before and for all his faults he had never done anything but stand by her, even if she didn't agree with his methods.

'Promise you won't interfere with the investigation?'

'I don't know if I can do that.' He stood up.

'Is it revenge you're after?'

'No, there is no more revenge as far as I'm concerned.'

'What then?'

'I don't know. Answers maybe? I need to find that house. I need to go back and speak to people from my past.'

'Sometimes the answer is that people are fucked up – and sometimes other people get caught up in their bullshit.'

'I know that.'

'I know you do and I know there's nothing I can say either, I wasn't there. I hope you know that I want to help you as much as I can, Dean, but my job is important to me. I chose it because I believe in it. I can't just ignore the rules because of you.'

'I know you can't.'

'But me and you? We've been through things together. I know exactly who you are. You aren't a bad person.'

'There are things about me that you don't know.'

'And I probably don't ever want to know, because I love you, Dean.'

He half-smiled, a shrug within a smile, reluctant and instinctive. 'You shouldn't.'

'That's my decision though.' She was lying; it wasn't really a decision at all.

'The truth is, if I really loved you I would leave you alone; being with me is probably a huge mistake for you.'

'But it's my mistake to make.'

'I'm too selfish to let you go.'

'Good, because I wouldn't forgive you if you left me "for my own good". I don't need you to make those decisions for me.' She was lying again; maybe she did, maybe that was exactly what she needed.

'I won't.'

She stood up and kissed him gently on the cheek before taking him by the hand and leading him into the bedroom. They could lie together without the pressure of conversation, pretending for at least a little while that the outside didn't exist. She would reassure him that he belonged to her and then he would go and do what it was he did. The things she couldn't bear to think about.

Chapter 40

Imogen left Dean sleeping and went into work early. The plan was to trawl through child abuse and foster care case files all day. No one wanted to do that. She would start by looking up all the kids in the same places as Dean and then spiral outward. At least Dean made a lot more sense as a person now. His fierce protectiveness over people that mattered to him, the way he cared for them over himself. He had built his entire adult life around looking after Elias, because of loyalty not obligation. Whenever Elias needed someone to be persuaded, or warned off, Dean would step in. He did it because he needed to. When it came to looking after others he was selfless. She had no doubts he would gladly die protecting her, or Elias. But she hoped it would never come to that. Knowing what kind of things he had had to deal with growing up, she couldn't be angry at him for being who he was. She was also pretty sure she couldn't change him, which really was a terrifying thought because she knew his loyalty would be his downfall.

'How are your cases going, DS Grey?' DCI Kapoor asked.

'Still nothing on the homeless guy. It's on the back-burner for now because of this other mess. As for the old couple – we will be checking out possible motives but also looking at youths in the area, see if there's anything we can find on groups of kids, or the mask thing. Maybe look at any links within the YOI or care homes in the area. Check out any unusual activity at all on the thirteenth of July.' She slipped this last bit in; maybe she wouldn't have to tell anyone about Dean's involvement.

'Good thinking.' DCI Kapoor smiled approvingly.

She would keep Dean's secret as long as she could, as yet it was nothing more than wild speculation, it may have absolutely nothing to do with what they were investigating. Something was niggling at her though, and it was most likely guilt. She wasn't even sure if she could tell Adrian about Dean's past. She would have to play that one by ear. It added to the idea that Chris Locke was somehow involved in both cases, although she wasn't sure how. She didn't want to tell Kapoor just yet in case she tried to squash it. She hated this feeling of not being able to trust her boss but she had made the mistake of trusting people too easily before and wasn't likely to do it again.

'How far have you got?' Adrian asked as he put a coffee next to her on the desk before sitting on the edge.

'I got a list of residential children's care homes in the area, some have only opened in the last five years so we can rule them out for now, come back to them later. Still having trouble finding out which ones Chris Locke went to though.'

'How about known associates of his?'

'His brother, but he's inside as we know. A couple of others some time ago, none of whom are in the area anymore. Neither Leanne nor that Trey Wilson kid spent any time in care so apart from the night of the twenty-sixth, when the fire happened, there doesn't seem to be any connection.'

'You think Trey Wilson is part of the gang that killed that couple?' Adrian asked.

'His name is on our radar; that's enough to make me suspicious.'

'Anything else?'

'There are two homes we need to check out first. I don't know if you want to take a punt at one of those?' She had narrowed it down to two homes that were old enough for Dean to have also gone there.

'Fine, but you'll have to drive. I'm waiting on a new set of car keys. I can't find mine anywhere.'

'You are useless, Miley.'

Chapter 41

Dean watched the front of the townhouse. He remembered the door, it was the same exact door with the three window panes staggered across the front haphazardly, but it had been painted. He remembered it being a dark green that was almost black, but now it was a cheerful turquoise; in fact, the whole place looked more cheerful. Four storeys high including the basement and three rooms to a floor; when he had lived there it was a dirty-looking building covered in shingles, now it was a bright and sunny primrose yellow. There were hanging baskets, the front lawn was well kept and the walls were freshly painted. This was not the memory Dean had, it was like a photo of a run-down building put through some kind of filter to make it look beautiful. Even though it had been a little rough around the edges, he had fond memories of his time here.

He plucked up the courage to buzz on the door. There was a small delay and then it opened. A lady answered;

Dean didn't recognise her, she was too young to have been there at the same time as him. He had to think how to play this.

'Can I help you?' She was wearing a blue tabard with Sunshine Home embroidered on the chest. She obviously worked here.

The words rushed out of him all at once. 'I used to be here.' He cleared his throat, and tried again. 'I mean, I was here as a child, as a resident.'

'Oh! How lovely! How long ago were you here?' Her face lit up.

'A long time ago now, I was wondering if you know any of the old staff that worked here?'

'I'm afraid not, I've been here around five years now and when I got here none of the staff had been here that long.'

'I see. What about the social workers? Did you happen to meet a woman called Mary Simms? Her husband David Simms also worked here, as a caretaker sometimes.'

'Yes, they have both taken early retirement now though. You knew them?'

'Oh yes, I knew them. They were very good to me.' He wasn't lying. Mary Simms would send her husband around to fix things in the house, he remembered him building a makeshift basketball hoop for the boys in the yard. This was before Dean was dubbed a trouble-maker. Dean had stayed in this house for a little while before getting into trouble and being moved on. In the years after, when he was in the home where he was molested, he wished he could run back to them, he wanted them to save him and Jess, the girl he came to think of as a sister. They had kept them together because Jess could be a handful without him around. He had looked the Simms up several times over the years, but they weren't anywhere he could find them. Maybe this woman would know where they went. 'Do you have an address for them?'

'I don't know if I should. I don't know who you are.'

'Maybe a phone number then?'

'I guess that would be OK.' She pulled a phone out of her pocket and started to scroll through the numbers. 'Do you have a pen?'

'I'll just put it straight in my phone.'

She showed him the phone and he copied the number into his own. 'I hope that's OK for you. I just wouldn't feel right telling you their address.'

'I completely understand. I just came here to see the place and it reminded me of them, I didn't expect it to still be a home.'

'It's one of a handful that have lasted this long. I think it helps that we have the neighbours on board, they give the kids odd jobs and make them feel like part of the community. I know some of the other places I have worked have had nothing but opposition from surrounding houses. The same people who probably donate to kids' charities every month – they don't actually want the problems on their doorstep. They're happy to be seen to be helping kids, as long as they are somewhere else. That's why the work people like the Carters do is so important to the community.'

'Well, thank you so much for your help. I can't wait to catch up with Mary and see if she remembers me.'

'You're welcome.' The young woman paused. 'Can I ask you a question?'

'Of course,'

'Were you happy here?'

'Yes. I honestly was.' He smiled. He wasn't lying, it was strange to see the place again because it reminded him of a version of himself he had long since forgotten, innocent and carefree, a child who was nurtured and allowed to grow.

Dean walked away and copied the number into a reverse phone number search engine – it was much easier with a landline. The search came back with a Mary Simms and her address. The internet was a scary place; if you knew how to look for things, you could probably find them. Before he could change his mind, he got in his car and drove to his previous social worker's home.

Mary had a nice house. There was a cat sleeping on the roof of the garage, it was fat and fuzzy; a happy cat. Dean knocked on the door and an elderly woman answered. He stared at her: apart from her age, she looked exactly the same. He was overcome with an unfamiliar feeling of affection towards this woman, she had been an anchor to him during a time in his life when everything he knew was chaotic, where home was not always a happy place. It was as though he were visiting an old relation. She looked at him quizzically and then her eyes travelled to the pendant.

'I always wondered what happened to you, Dean Kinkaid.' She reached for the pendant and gently rubbed her finger across the surface. 'I think about you sometimes, you were such an angry little boy.'

'I was?'

'Underneath it all, yes you were. I could tell you were a deep thinker.'

'What else do you remember about me?' He had always felt so invisible; he was surprised anyone had even given him a second thought back then. He hadn't even considered that she would remember him.

'You and your sister were inseparable. I heard what happened to her. She was a dear little thing. So sad.'

'She wasn't really my sister.'

'Yes, she was, in all the ways that matter.'

'I wondered if you could remember the name of the place we went to just before you left?' Dean asked, reminded of the task at hand with the mention of Jess. He couldn't talk about her, it hurt too much. As much as he was enjoying this walk down memory lane, it wasn't why he was here. He needed to find the next piece of the puzzle. Mary Simms had no part in the events that followed when he moved to a different home.

'Keeping you two together was always my main concern, I don't think you would have survived half as well as you did without each other. When I heard that she had passed on, I tried to find out what happened to you.'

'You did?'

'They told me you were sent to the young offenders place for killing that horrible man; I tried to visit but it wasn't allowed.'

'No one told me that.'

'I hope you found some peace. You still look a little angry but it's good to know you got through it.'

He wondered if she would feel the same if she knew how he got through it.

'Do you know where it was? The second home we were sent?'

Mary nodded. 'Yes, it was Ford Park House, in Plymouth. That one was shut down as well.'

'Thank you.'

'You're welcome, Dean.' She smiled and he was flooded with memories of her: her acts of kindness, her bringing him little gifts, books, sweets and sometimes marbles to play with Jess. It annoyed him sometimes that only the bad memories fought their way to the surface and pushed out all the good. He touched the marble pendant she had bought him; it was a shell trapped in glass resin, he had given it to Jessica and it had been her most treasured possession. They'd found it in her pocket when they discovered her body. He wore the tiny marble around his neck so he would never forget Jess. So that he would remember to survive at all costs, for her.

Chapter 42

Since DS Imogen Grey's visit, Gabriel had found himself counting shadows, watching his fellow prisoners' every move. God forbid anyone had recognised the detective and seen Gabriel talking to her. The last thing he needed now was a reputation as a grass – he had heard stories from Sol about what happened to people who spoke to the authorities about anything that went on inside. But he knew that's what they banked on, that you would be so afraid of the repercussions for speaking out that you'd put up with as much shit as they could throw at you. They being the manipulators, rapists, blackmailers, thieves and other scum that occupied the system. These people had made a career out of it, they relished the years they had on the new men, able to see the ones who were too weak to endure. Sometimes they were wrong and their victims didn't endure, they ripped off a strip of sheeting and wrapped it around their necks until the oxygen was completely cut off, only to be discovered with their eyes bulging out of their heads and dried spit at the corners of their mouths. The cell would be cleaned and then refurnished with a new person, possibly a new victim. There weren't winners and losers in prison; it was a sliding scale. There were dominants in every relationship, Gabriel thought: if you were lucky you were on the winning side. Then there were people like Sol who were considered neutral. Gabriel often wondered what Sol had done to warrant that role. He was left alone for the most part and was neither threatening nor weak. That was who Gabriel wanted to be but it was too late; Asher had already seen through him to what was going on inside.

Gabriel lay on the bed with his eyes closed. He felt Bailey's presence as he hovered in the doorway, obviously hoping to speak. Internally, Gabriel sighed as the guilt got to him. He hated the idea that Bailey might be in any way intimidated by him; it didn't make him feel powerful, it made him feel like a bastard. He glanced over as Bailey walked into their pad, holding a wet cloth over the side of his face.

'What's going on?' Gabriel swung his legs off the bed, his guilt even stronger now. 'Show me your face.'

Hesitantly, Bailey pulled the wet cloth away and Gabriel saw that his left eye was swollen shut. There was blood coming from his eyebrow.

'It's nothing,' Bailey lisped. Gabriel saw the chip in his front tooth.

'Who did this to you?'

'I fell over.' Bailey wouldn't look at him.

'Did Asher tell you to say that?'

Bailey crawled into his bed-space just as Gabriel jumped down.

'I'm fine.'

'Let me look at your eyes, you can't go to sleep if you're concussed. Where did you fall over?'

'Out by the ping-pong tables, I just wasn't looking where I was going. It was my fault.'

'Look at me, Bailey, and tell me it wasn't Asher!'

Bailey turned to Gabriel, his eyes turned downwards, like a dog who'd just jumped on the table and eaten the roast dinner while no one was watching.

'I promised I wouldn't say anything, he said you would be mad.'

'I'm not mad at you though, mate. I'm mad at this stupid place.' He inspected Bailey's pupils; thankfully, they seemed to be perfectly fine.

'Don't go after him though, you'll get put in Seg again,' Bailey pleaded.

'I won't go after him, don't worry,' Gabriel lied.

Chapter 43

Dean had texted Imogen to tell her he would meet her at her place after receiving an angry voicemail from her. Apparently, she and Adrian had visited the foster home shortly after he'd left and found out he'd already been.

He was in the kitchen when he heard the key in the lock followed by a slammed door. Imogen appeared and looked at him sitting at the dining table, nursing a beer.

'You can't keep doing this, Dean, I can't just let you go around doing whatever the hell you want.' She pulled her coat off and hung it on the door.

'Hell? Do you know what hell is, Imogen? Hell is here, for a lot of people. Hell is today, and tomorrow, and every day for the foreseeable future. Hell is the moment after you wake up, you know the moment I mean? Not the one that's full of possibility but the one just after, when you're properly awake and you realise who you are and what your day ahead entails. Hell is having no one to turn to and say: help me! Hell is being afraid of going to bed, being afraid that you won't wake up, being afraid that you don't deserve to. You know what it's like to have someone's hands on you without your permission. Imagine living in a house with that person for years, being dependent on them for food and shelter!'

The words poured out of him; he tried to stay calm but he couldn't. He felt vulnerable, the more he spoke the harder it was to shut up. He didn't want to say anything he regretted, he didn't want her to be scared of him.

'OK. I understand. I'm sorry.'

'Do you? Do you understand how that feels? You might think you do but you can't. You just can't. This is a truth about the life facing a lot of children, the life that I lived through. I have a right to investigate those so-called care homes.'

'Then let me help you, Dean!'

'You can't,' he said. 'It's too late for me, but there could be others. There almost definitely are. I stuffed my pain down, I used it to fuel me. But I can't ignore it anymore, I need to help the rest of them.'

'It's not your fault. None of this is your fault.' She reached out to him, but he pulled away.

'I know that. But I walked away. I pussied out and walked away. I should have done more. Those kids in that Wallis video, those horrible things they did – don't you see? I understand that. I understand being so completely disconnected from emotion that you would be able to do something like that.'

'But you wouldn't do that. I know you wouldn't.'

'Only because I got lucky, I found someone who looked out for me, who made sure I wasn't completely lost.' He was talking about Elias, the man that had made him realise that not everyone who helped you wanted something from you in return. Her estranged father. He took her by the shoulders and pulled her in for an embrace, it was a diversion to stop him from talking, to stop her from probing him anymore.

'What can I do?' Imogen asked, her face pressed into his shirt.

'Nothing, just don't get in my way.'

He kissed her on the forehead and left.

How could she ever understand? It wasn't something that could be explained or shared. It was a solitary experience. Even if you weren't alone in the room when those things happened, it was your own thoughts you were trapped with for the rest of your life. Pain took you to the very heart of yourself. It wasn't Imogen's fault of course, and he was glad that she didn't understand how it felt, because to really understand was to stare into an abyss of frailty. It wasn't as if he even remembered much; it wasn't about memories. It wasn't even about the facts of what happened. It was about being ruined, feeling ruined.

He had been removed from himself – he had ceased to exist all in one moment. That first moment when the switch had been flipped, when his world had been turned upside down. The sudden realisation that you were helpless and the person who was supposed to take care of you had other ideas, when your vulnerability was exploited. The man who put his hands on Dean knew he had no one to turn to. When forced to make the choice between fighting or fleeing he'd frozen. He'd paused inside himself and never resumed. He remembered hands and lips and whispers but it wasn't about that either. It was about the choices. It wasn't until he had the distance of many years that he realised they had all been just that; children. That was something they never told you about growing up; your mind went with you. The same thoughts and feelings follow you through life, and eventually you forget how old you were when you first thought them because they have been with you for so long.

There wasn't much Dean could do about Imogen. He didn't want to tell her about the abuse, at least not the details of it. He didn't want to change her opinion of him. Even now, even with the limited information he'd given her, she had a fleeting look of pity. He had no time for pity. Pity made him feel weak and weakness wasn't an option. He had made a promise to himself a long time ago never to be vulnerable again and he had proved over and over that he wasn't. It was true that he had set fire to the care worker back then, and he would do the same thing again. He wasn't the only man Dean had killed.

He hadn't told Imogen about the other man, the other man Dean didn't speak about, the other man he had killed without regret. Every night in the Young Offender Institution, Dean would dream of him, dream of finishing him. When he came out at eighteen he had nothing but the man's first name: Graham. Dean's memories had convoluted over time, names and places had blurred into one, but he would never forget his face. It took time and patience, but eventually he found him. The man that had undone him. The man who visited Dean in the dead of night in his third children's home, hand over mouth and foul breath in his ear. Graham's was the face of Dean's nightmares but when he found him again at age twenty, he was smaller than Dean remembered, less frightening. But Dean knew what was inside him. Dean had seen the monster.

Across a crowded bar, half a lifetime ago, Dean had spotted him and pulled up a stool. It had taken a few seconds but the monster's face had shrivelled in recognition – they had shared something, something secret and depraved, as much as Dean wished otherwise their souls were tied together forever. Dean knew that he had the power now; he was no longer prey, no longer afraid. He had sat with Graham and drank, giving him those few hours of fear, letting him wonder what was going to happen as soon as he stepped outside. Familiarising him with that feeling of wondering what horrors the end of the day would bring. That was when Dean realised that murder would be easy. Not like when he had set fire to the other man in anger, an impulsive move. This was cold-blooded murder. Dean had followed Graham until he was sure they were alone and put his hands around his throat. The closeness was all too familiar, except this time it was Dean who was in control, Dean's hands on his body, on his neck. Dean stared into Graham's fearful eyes until the light was extinguished.

With Graham's murder, Dean's nightmares had faded into the background without even a second thought.

Now, with the viral video from the thirteenth of July and the case that Imogen was working on, he was reminded of the other brothers and sisters he'd had as a child, the good and the bad, the ones that had turned into abusers themselves just to escape being victims. He thought of the men and women in the house, who used these kids for entertainment, and he knew he couldn't leave it. He couldn't just walk away anymore. Maybe this was Imogen's influence, but he wanted to find the perpetrators and remove them from society altogether.

Chapter 44

On the way back from dinner, Gabriel saw Johnson standing alone at the guards' station. Hyde was dealing with a minor altercation outside the showers. Gabriel looked around for Asher but he couldn't see him. He took the opportunity to speak to Johnson alone.

'What's Asher got over you?' Gabriel asked.

'What?' Johnson was shocked at Gabriel's directness.

'I've got eyes, Johnson; I know he's got something over you. Tell me what it is.'

'Just leave it. Don't push this or you're going to get in trouble.' He looked around anxiously.

'With who?'

'Asher is protected in here.'

'By you?'

Johnson glanced around them to check that no one was listening. 'Yes.'

Gabriel couldn't understand; from what he had seen of Asher and Johnson's relationship, the guard didn't even like Asher. There had to be some reason why he was letting himself be manipulated.

'You hate him, why do you protect him? Is he threatening someone on the outside?'

'What do you know?' Johnson asked suspiciously.

'My girlfriend's had a visit from his brother. He needs to be stopped.'

'Yeah well, I've got a wife and kids. You don't know what you're messing with.'

'I don't care either. I'm not going to play his game.'

'They all say that. You're not the first person who has tried to stop him,' Johnson warned Gabriel.

'He's a runt, he's nothing!'

'He's got power on the outside, Gabriel. I don't know how, but he does.'

'So, what is it you do for him?'

'Nothing gross. Nothing . . . sexual.'

'Right, but he makes you do something. What is it?'

Gabriel looked around to make sure no one was watching him talk to Johnson; he knew it would get back to Asher if they did, but everyone seemed to be preoccupied with their own things.

'What does everyone want in prison? Power. How do you get power?'

'I don't know.'

Johnson looked around once more before leaning closer to Gabriel. 'Drugs.'

'So, you bring drugs in for him?'

'I don't have a choice. He threatened my wife, my kids. I got photos in the post of my wife at the supermarket, of my kids at school.'

'Why didn't you go to the police?'

'Because before they did anything, one of my kids would've been dead. He's got connections on the outside, bad ones.'

Gabriel saw Sol leaving his room and walking towards his cell. Quickly, he moved away from Johnson but kept within speaking distance. 'Well I'm going to do something about him. I'm not letting him get away with this shit any longer. You can either help or stay out of my way.'

'I'll tell him. You can't.'

'It's happening, Johnson, so you'd better get on board. If you say anything to him, I'll tell him it was your idea.'

'So, you're threatening me too now? How does that make you any better than him?'

'I don't have the luxury of being better than him. That's not my concern right now.'

Gabriel stepped back into his cell ready for bang-up. Johnson wouldn't even look him in the eye as he pulled the cell door closed. Gabriel wasn't sure if he had just made the situation better or a whole lot worse.

'What was all that about?' Bailey asked.

Gabriel ignored him and jumped onto the bunk. He needed to think. There had to be a way out of this.

Chapter 45

Adrian and Imogen sat patiently in DCI Kapoor's office waiting for her to come and bollock them both for not following protocol, for not following orders. From what Adrian could tell about Kapoor so far, she was firm but fair.

'Do you think she's hot?' Imogen finally said.

'Excuse me?'

'The DCI – do you think she's hot?'

'I never really thought about her like that.'

Imogen raised her eyebrow at him, of course he had thought about it, they both knew it. 'Don't be bloody ridiculous.'

'She has that strong woman thing going on.'

'Just answer the question, this isn't some kind of feminist trap.'

'All right, yes, she's hot. If I was attracted to women who scare the shit out of me then yeah, she would definitely be on the list.'

‘Am I on the list?’

‘What?’

‘Do you think I’m hot?’ She fluttered her eyelashes at him.

‘Now that’s definitely a trap. I’m not answering you, Grey.’

At that moment, DCI Kapoor burst into the office. Imogen and Adrian both stood up. She waved at them to sit down as she started shuffling through paperwork on her desk before looking up.

‘Where are we on the case?’

‘Which case?’ Adrian asked, not meaning to sound glib but aware of how irritating his question was. He didn’t want to tell her yet that he thought the two cases were connected, they needed more than suspicion before they could move forward with that one. He also didn’t want to mention the charity angle; as a PR person first and foremost, he figured the DCI would be grateful to be kept in the dark for now. Plausible deniability.

‘The murder, DS Miles, the double homicide from the thirteenth of July, the Wallis murders.’

‘We’re going to take a closer look at the son, Richard Wallis,’ Adrian said. ‘There’s something off about him, I think. His reaction to the murders wasn’t quite right.’

‘Ignore the killers for now,’ the DCI told them. ‘There’s nothing to go on there so far; I want you to look at the vics again. There has to be a reason those two old people were killed.’

‘We’ll find it.’

‘Go over every aspect of their son’s life, too. I didn’t like the look of him when he was on TV. Crocodile tears I think.' Adrian knew what she meant, his distress had seemed rehearsed, copied. The truth was that in most murder cases, you looked at the family first. It was rare for someone to go out and murder an old couple for no reason. There was always a motivation, either some sexual gratification or monetary gain. Sexual motivation certainly didn't seem to figure here, so it had to be money. It wasn't money in the Wallis house though; that had all been left behind, so it had to be somewhere else. Something they hadn't seen yet. Something they hadn't noticed.

Chapter 46

'Do you have any leads on my parents' killers yet?' Richard Wallis asked with a clipped precision that bordered on gloating. They'd called him into the station for further questioning, and he didn't seem pleased.

No, Imogen didn't like him at all. He knew they had nothing, and he was happy about that; it was written all over his face.

'You can't think of anyone who might have it in for your parents?' Adrian asked.

'We've been through all this before, Detective, I don't know what to tell you. Should you really be spending your time questioning me when whoever did this is still out there?'

'We are pursuing several leads at the moment,' Imogen said.

'What about the video of the killing? There's nothing there? Can't you trace it back or get a reflection or something?'

'No: unfortunately, it's been very hard to find anything out about the video upload. Our forensic computer analyst has been working on it.'

'Well I don't know what you people do all day but I actually have to work for a living.' Richard Wallis stood up. 'You can't keep me here.'

'OK fine, but we might be in touch again. Thanks for your help.' Imogen was certain now; Richard was being helpful on the surface, but not really helping them at all. She'd lay money on the fact that he had a hand in his parents' murder.

'I don't know why the son sets me on edge like that,' Imogen said to Adrian as they watched Richard Wallis leave.

'I feel the same; he knows something.'

'So how do we find out what it is he knows?' Imogen said as they sat down at their desks.

'We look at his money. Whatever happened, if he did have a hand in it, he must have paid someone. His parents were insured, all money's going to him and he gets the house when they die. He gets about half a million quid from this; if that's not motive I don't know what is.'

'We know his business isn't doing that well, he's paying his bills a little later than he used to, but he still donates money to charities and stuff so he can't be that hard up. Tax write-off?'

'So cynical for someone so young.' Adrian smiled.

'Which charities are they?'

'Some animal charity, thirty quid a month. Cancer research for about fifty quid a month. A few one-offs as well.' Imogen shuffled through their copies of his bank statements while they waited for Gary to provide a more detailed analysis.

'You think we're wrong about him?'

'No, I think he's definitely hiding something. Maybe he's a Brony or something?'

'What's a Brony, or don't I want to know?' Adrian asked.

'You probably don't want to know. Something to do with My Little Ponies and grown men.'

Adrian screwed his face up. 'Is it a sex thing?'

'Hang on a minute.' Imogen turned serious.

'What is it?'

'There's three big donations here.' She ran her finger down the page of numbers.

'How much?'

'Twenty grand in total. Almost cleared him out, too. There's charity and then there's stupidity. Why would he do that?' Imogen said.

'Which charity?'

'A local one, KIDSMART. They operate throughout Devon and Cornwall. The foundation that runs them is invested in all sorts of local projects.'

'I wonder why them? People usually pick charities that affect them in some way, either directly or indirectly. Something they can empathise with, especially a large donation like that.' Adrian paused. 'Just wondering if that's the case here, especially if, as you say, it almost cleaned him out.'

'Doesn't everyone empathise with kids' charities?'

'Well yeah, but not everyone gives to them. For

instance I usually give to a drug rehabilitation charity, and I suspect you give to mental health charities. Things that mean something to us. Am I wrong?'

There was a pause. 'So what, Miley, you're saying we're all selfish?'

'It's slightly more complex than that. But yeah I guess, in a manner of speaking.'

'You've already heard of the charity KIDSMART before, then?' Imogen said.

'Yeah, haven't you? The KIDSMART charity is run by the Carters, they're the couple that started it back in the eighties and they've grown it from there. They deal with kids in care mostly, right up until they turn eighteen. You must have seen some of those heart-warming stories on the TV – the adverts late at night, showing how Billy's life is miraculously amazing thanks to KIDSMART.'

'That's them?'

'It is.'

'You sound as though you don't like them, Miley.'

'I met the Carters a while back; they were very smooth, polished, hobnobbing with big businesses and stuff. He – Mr Carter – is always lobbying for more money so they can build more centres for kids.'

'Where did you meet them then?'

'At Dom and Andrea's house.' He paused, staring into space.

'You've got that look, Miley, what's going on?'

'Dominic, yet again, all roads lead to Dominic.' He smiled and shook his head.

'Are you sure this isn't just some kind of belated

jealousy? Paranoia? Or do you actually think Dominic being friends with the Carters puts them in the frame for something?'

'That is absolutely what I think. Is there any way these donations to charity could be a front for something else?'

'What? You mean have they groomed a bunch of assassins?' Imogen said flippantly, but Adrian didn't seem to share her amusement. He had a look of deep concentration on his face.

'Why wouldn't we have noticed something before?'

'Maybe something's changed that we don't know about?'

'Well, their financial information is a matter of public record, maybe we could ask Gary to put it through that program of his, to see if there is any connection to Dominic?'

'I hope we're wrong.'

'When are we ever wrong?' He winked at her, and they both slumped back in their chairs. Imogen knew what he was thinking. A kids' charity as a front for something more sinister? Now they really had seen everything. There was one thing she knew for sure though; once they got that sinking feeling about something, the pieces often began slotting into place. It was making more sense than anything else they had so far, and not only was that depressing, the DCI wasn't going to like it one bit.

Chapter 47

Adrian sat on the rickety iron chair outside the tea shop and checked his watch for the hundredth time. From across the green Lucy appeared, flustered and windswept by her own speed. Their relationship had changed from a casual drink after work over the last week to an actual lunch date. He felt his heart catch in his throat the way it used to when he was a lust-filled teen. The sight of Lucy with her look of constant concentration. Adrian didn't think he had ever met anyone who thought as loudly as she did. Sometimes he watched her and saw the thoughts appear and be summarily dismissed at an alarming rate.

As she drew closer, her face softened on seeing him, her cobalt blue eyes squinting as she smiled. Her long chocolate curls bounced against her shoulders with every footstep as she thumped towards him; she always walked with purpose. Her speed increased as she neared and he felt a little victory inside.

He stood up and kissed her on the cheek, although he was sure she wanted more. He wasn't pushing it though; he wasn't going to mess this up again. As they both sat down, her soft hair brushed against him and he suppressed the urge to take in a deep breath.

'Sorry I'm late.'

'I haven't been here long,' he lied.

'I'm sorry, I can't stay long but I'll come to yours later too if that's OK?'

'What exactly are you busy doing now then?' He was disappointed, he had been waiting to see her, in fact whenever he wasn't with her he was waiting to see her. It was a feeling he wasn't used to.

'You show me yours and I'll show you mine.'

'I don't have anything to show.'

'Better luck next time then.' She winked at him.

'Nothing on the body in the signal box then?' he asked.

'Maybe, I've been wondering if we're looking at it the wrong way.'

'How should we look at it?' He smiled, loving her enthusiasm.

'It really is almost as if that Gabriel kid is being set up.'

'Imogen thinks the same.'

'I was speaking to a friend of mine who used to be an arson investigator.' She rummaged in her bag and pulled out one of the photos, placing it on the table.

'The rat shit again?' Adrian grimaced.

'Those things that look like rat droppings are – as we suspected – not in fact rat droppings.'

'Yeah? What are they?'

'My friend thinks they could be cat litter.'

'Cat litter? Why would that be in a signal box?' Adrian asked.

'He saw it once in an old arson case, not round here. Basically, cat litter absorbs fluids and masks the odour somewhat, so maybe someone doused them in petrol and put them in there to get the fire started.'

'So they were trying to get rid of the body?'

'I know it's a crazy theory.'

'I've heard much crazier.'

'Shit.' She glanced at her watch. 'I'll meet you later?' She kissed him on the lips and was gone before he had a chance to protest. So much for lunch.

Back at the station, Adrian walked in to see Imogen going through local foster home records. He pulled up a chair and sat next to her, close enough for her to look at him suspiciously.

'I just spoke to Lucy.'

She raised her eyebrows. 'OK?'

'We need to get the remains from the signal box looked at again, see if there is any way the injuries John Doe sustained were administered before death. Also, to see if he died before the fire actually started.'

'In which case, Gabriel Webb wouldn't have killed whoever was in there?'

'Right. Assuming this is linked to the Wallis murder, there must be some kind of paper trail, or money trail.'

'Assuming Chris Locke is the one in the signal box, and knowing that he spends time with Trey Wilson, it's possible they were the ones in the video,' Imogen said, realising that it was a big leap.

'So, what's the connection between the Wallis murders and Chris Locke?'

'KIDSMART? Chris Locke and his brother both spent time in a KIDSMART home when they were younger, and Richard Wallis would benefit from his parents' death.'

'And he made a sizeable donation to the charity. A charity run by the Carters, close friends of Dominic. Still think I'm paranoid?'

'Admittedly, Miley, that's a few more coincidences than I'm comfortable with.'

'But what has this got to do with Theodore Ramsey, aka Bricks? And if the body doesn't belong to him, then where is he? And who does the body belong to? And if he didn't die on the twenty-sixth of June then when did he die?'

'God knows.'

'Do we speak to the DCI yet?' Adrian asked, still unsure who to trust. He suspected everyone of being corrupt.

'We're still in the speculation phase of the operation. Let's get some evidence.'

'Did you find anything else on the foster home of the Locke brothers?'

'Not yet, but we're close to something, Miley. I can feel it.'

Chapter 48

Ford Park cemetery in Plymouth was a beautiful, large green space set among some trees at the end of the avenue where Dean had spent two years of his life. He had entered his third care home aged eleven, the third in as many years. Dean's memory of his friends back then was sketchy to say the least. He could see the faces of the other children in the homes, but he couldn't remember their names. Sometimes a first name came to him, but even then, he was never sure if he was right. As soon as his former social worker Mary Simms had told him the name of the house, he'd remembered one of the streets he used to live on, purely because of what was at the end of it; a cemetery. He had lived here before anyone needed actual qualifications to run an establishment like this. By the time he'd arrived here as an eleven-year-old, Dean had changed into someone unpredictable and violent – with not many people giving him the benefit of the doubt.

Dean stood outside the former care home. The building's shape was the same but the home itself was gone. It was a small supermarket-cum-off-licence now. The place was much smaller than he remembered it too. In his mind, the homes had all been intimidating; he spent most of his days wondering what horrors awaited him. This had been one of the better ones, or maybe because he had hardened himself to it all he just hadn't noticed the abuses of the people around him. He remembered the physical feeling of choosing not to remember something as it was actually happening.

'Can I help you?' An elderly woman was standing at the gate of the house next door.

Dean cleared his throat. 'I was looking for the foster home that used to be here. I lived there for a while.'

'I thought as much. Could tell by the expression on your face. Come in, dear.' She walked back into her house, leaving the door wide open for Dean to come inside. Surprised, he stepped inside the gate, then walked into the house and closed the door behind him. Inside, it had clearly not been decorated for a considerable amount of time; an overriding brown and orange colour scheme dominated, faded and worn. He heard the clatter of crockery come from the kitchen and walked through the long dark hallway to the back of the house.

'Were you here when it was still a home?' he said.

'Oh yes.' The woman poured hot water into the tea pot and then moved it onto the table. 'Terrible place it was, I used to go around and do the laundry and ironing once a week, sometimes a bit of cooking, but I stopped after a couple of years. I can't tell you how happy everyone was when they shut it down.'

'I don't really remember much about it.'

'They never do.' She put her hand on his, briefly squeezing his fingers; he felt the tissue-thin skin, cold but comforting. She sat down and put a cup of tea in front of him.

'When did it shut?'

'Around ten years ago.' She leaned across and dragged a biscuit tin across the table, a Christmas variety tin of shortbread. She opened it to reveal a little pile of photographs, yellowing slightly with age. 'I still have some of the pictures from then. I never had children of my own, you see, and some of you children were so funny. I kept the photos to remember that it was a happy place sometimes.'

It was rare that Dean ever got to see photos from his childhood; he leaned forward, curious, then remembered that he hadn't even introduced himself yet.

'My name's Dean, by the way.'

'I'm Ruth.' She smiled.

'Do you get many people come back here then?'

'Oh yes, and they've all got that same look in their eyes, like the one you have. Trying to forget and remember all in the same moment.' She grabbed a handful of photographs and laid them out on the table. Immediately Dean saw a familiar face.

'Bilbo!' He pointed. 'Billy something but we called him Bilbo, I can't remember why.' The boy in the picture was squinting at the sun and the camera, washing a car with a sponge and bucket. Dean remembered some of the men on the street would give a pound for a car wash or clearing rubbish, little chores to give the kids some purpose. From what Dean remembered of Bilbo, the boy was a couple of years older than him and he had eventually been arrested for violence, like so many of the others.

'You boys were always getting into mischief for jumping over into the cemetery. Some people around here were just determined to get you all into trouble.'

'I suspect we deserved it,' Dean said as he looked through the pictures, nothing else familiar except the road itself. It had been a hard place, but even the good ones were hard. Dean knew other kids who had had it a lot tougher than him.

'I could hear some of the things that went on in there. One of my biggest regrets in life is that I didn't do something about it. But you didn't back then, did you? Thank God times have changed.'

Dean paused at a photograph of a street fair, the image scratching at his memory. Something there was familiar to him, someone.

'Are there any more of these?' He held the photo out to her; she picked her glasses off the table and inspected the image. Putting the picture down, she grabbed a handful more photos from the tin, deftly searching through the dog-eared images as she so obviously had done many times in the past.

'Here.' She handed him five more photographs. He could feel the tension in his shoulders and neck as he took them from her. He wasn't sure if he was hoping to recognise something or not. People forget things for a reason.

'Thank you.'

The first photograph was of the street, obviously taken from the gate outside the woman's house. There was a fire engine parked outside along with an ice-cream truck, bunting between the lamp posts and some stalls selling jumble and other things he couldn't make out. He was flooded with a memory of the day, of being carefree and running, of the permission to be a child for possibly the last time.

He turned to the next photograph and there he was. There was a lump in Dean's throat as he noted the size of himself, small and slight, a big smile plastered across his face and an ice cream in his hand. He had never seen a picture of himself at this age, in his mind he was still the same person but looking at the picture he realised just how young he was. He remembered those photographs, the photographs where you had to look happy, you had to look grateful because you were having fun, and fun was a privilege. There was nothing on his face to indicate the hell he was feeling inside, nothing at all. For all outward appearances he was loving it. Inside though there was confusion, constant and unresolved, until eventually it mutated into anger. He remembered the worst feeling; the feeling that this was what he deserved, that he wasn't worthy of family or love, that he wasn't worthy of receiving affection without conditions. He had forced himself to have fun and be grateful for it so that no one could get angry with him, no one could hurt him for showing how he really felt. He could never let anyone see his true feelings. He thought that would protect him, but he was wrong.

'Are you all right, dear?' Ruth broke his train of thought.

He swallowed, trying to keep down his feelings. They were feelings he had learned to suppress. 'Yes, thanks. That's me, look.' He showed her the photograph.

'You look like one of the happy ones. I wish I could say I remembered you but there were just so many of you kids coming and going.'

'I don't remember you either. This is very helpful, though.' He looked at the next photo, more generic pictures of the streets and faces he didn't recognise. As he pushed that photo to the back of the pile, he saw what was coming next. The man who ran the foster home. He was shirtless, leaning against the wall of the home with a cigarette. Dean frowned. With the photo not being as sharp as they are now, it was grainy and hard to see the man's features well. He was younger than Dean remembered, possibly even younger than Dean was now. Dean remembered the chain around his neck, a cheap gold chain with a cross dangling on the end of it. It was when he took over running the home that they went on their field trips.

'Ah, that's Sid, do you remember him?' Ruth was smiling a little, obviously remembering something about Sid, something that made her blush. 'He was such a charmer. Lives about three streets over now, at the other end of the cemetery.'

'Really? Do you have his address?' Dean asked. 'I'd love to catch up with him.'

'Yes, of course.' She stood up and went to her telephone, a notepad and pen next to it. She scribbled something down for Dean and handed it to him. 'I see him sometimes but I don't get out that much these days.'

Dean stood up and wrote his own number down on her notepad. 'That's my number, if you need anything please call me, I'm pretty handy with a hammer.' He smiled at her.

'That's very kind of you, dear.' She picked up the small stack of photos from in front of where Dean had been sitting. 'You keep these.'

Outside, he looked at the address before stuffing it in his pocket and opening the boot of the car. He grabbed the holdall full of tools. He hadn't been lying to Ruth; he was pretty handy with a hammer.

Chapter 49

Adrian traced his fingers across Lucy's shoulders, pushing her hair to the side as he slid his hand under it and cradled her neck. She nuzzled into the pillow some more and turned away from him as she slept. Her hair fell onto the pillow and he smoothed it back, away from her ears to reveal tiny gold sleeper earrings. Her ears were as small and delicate as everything else about her when she was asleep. It was hard to see these things when she was awake because everything about her manner was a distraction to Adrian. He moved his body closer to hers and kissed her on the shoulder; her skin was cold against his lips. He pulled the duvet up and over her before slipping his hand around her waist. She instinctively backed into him, the rest of her cold, too. The feeling of her skin against his finger-tips made him want to wake her up with his lips, but at the same time he didn't want her to move, he just wanted her here, with him. The blinds in his bedroom were glowing a cold orange, the sun was coming up. There was nothing he could do to stop time moving forward. He would have to get up in an hour, he would have to go to work, and she would probably move at a million miles an hour before he even had a chance to kiss her.

'You're thinking about something. What are you thinking?' she said, eyes still closed.

'You're awake?'

He kissed her on the lips. She went to sit up but he pulled her in close and put his arms around her for a moment.

'Spill then, I could hear the gears turning.'

'Just thinking how lucky I am. Wondering what I've done to deserve this . . . to deserve you.'

She kissed his arm and shuffled in closer; he knew she was just appeasing him before she had to pull away. 'What time do you have to go in?'

'Soon, unfortunately,' he said. 'We have to investigate some foster homes, see if we can find out more about the kids in there, see if it leads back to the fire.' Adrian felt a heaviness when he thought about those kids in foster care. Especially when he thought they might be being manipulated. Groomed and used. No one to look out for them.

'Adrian? Where did you go? Just then. What was that?' Lucy was staring at him, at the way his eyes had glazed over.

'Just thinking about family and how, even when its fucked up, it's still family.'

'You've never talked about your family. Was it hard,

with your dad? Did you ever wish you were in foster care?'

'No, I don't know if it works like that. I wanted him to get better – be better. When that was obviously not going to happen, I wanted my mum to stop putting up with him, stop taking him back.'

'Why do you think he was the way he was?'

'He was haunted by something, I think. I do remember him before the drugs. He always seemed to be on a path of self-destruction. It scares me sometimes. I wonder if it's hereditary.'

'I think you've proved it isn't.'

'Sometimes though, I understand him. Sometimes I just want to stop trying.'

'But you don't stop trying.' She smiled. 'Do you have any brothers or sisters?'

'No. Not that I know of anyway,' he said with a half-hearted laugh. It wasn't out of the question. He could well have a sibling out there. God only knows what his father had got up to. He knew he was never faithful to his mother. When he was younger, he'd seen him coming out of the White Hart hotel several times, always with a different woman. That was before he started getting high and stopped caring about anything but the fix.

Lucy put her lips on his.

He pulled her in, partly because she had kissed him and he wanted more, but also to stop the talking. Never an easy conversation, his dad, it always made his chest tighten and his breath shorten. He didn't want to feel like that with her. He kept his lips on hers and slid his hand down beneath the covers. They mirrored each other's movements, touching each other's stomachs, moving their hands downwards, teasing each other.

'Dad?'

Tom's voice came from downstairs.

'Shit!' Adrian whispered under his breath. 'Wait here.'

He jumped out of bed, grabbed his trousers and shot out of the bedroom and down the stairs.

'Hey Dad.' Tom was standing next to the toaster, waiting for some bread to pop.

'What's up? Why are you here so early?' Adrian looked over to the table where he had left the paperwork on Dominic. He had been working on it when Lucy had turned up with a bottle of wine the night before and forgotten to put it away.

'Mum and Dom have booked a holiday away starting Friday, well, Dom booked it late last night. Mum was going to call you today.'

'How long for?'

'Well, school breaks up soon, so we're going to America for five weeks. Mum wants you to go and sign the forms to say I can go.'

'Five weeks? But you didn't come and stay with me last weekend either because of some trip your mum had booked, and that trip to London a few weeks ago.'

'Those were Dominic's idea, too.'

Adrian knew this game; Dominic was trying to keep Tom away from him, he had said he would. He suspected Andrea had no idea what the real reason behind all of this was, she wouldn't do this out of spite, not now that things were finally good between all of them. She also wouldn't pass up a trip abroad. No doubt Dominic was pretending this was all for their little family and she was buying it.

'OK well, I'm going to have to speak to your mum about this, I'm not really OK with not seeing you properly for over a month.'

'Well, that's why I stopped by this morning. I missed you.' Tom squeezed a half piece of toast into his mouth. Butter dripped from the corners of his lips.

'Who's this then?' Lucy walked into the kitchen, her hair was tied on top of her head in a loose bun, but other than that she was immaculately dressed again. She pulled her coat from the back of the dining chair.

'Hello.' Tom mumbled through his mouthful, almost choking with surprise.

'Hi, I'm Lucy.' She held her hand out. He wiped his buttery palm on his trousers and shook her hand.

'This is Tom, my son.'

'Poor thing. You look just like your father.' She winked at Tom

'Do you want some breakfast?' Adrian offered.

'Who?' Lucy asked

'Anyone, both of you.'

'OK, I can fit more in,' Tom said.

'I'm afraid I need to get going.' Lucy took a half-piece of toast from Tom's plate. 'Nice to meet you, Tom.'

'Nice to meet you, too.' Tom smiled and raised his eyebrows at Adrian.

Lucy planted a big kiss on Adrian's cheek and he felt his face warming, he didn't like for Tom to meet anyone he might be going out with usually, but for some reason he didn't mind with Lucy, he kind of even wanted her to stick around for breakfast. Adrian was a compartmentaliser and so this was a strange feeling for him.

He heard the door slam and turned back to Tom.

'Bacon sarnie OK?'

Chapter 50

Sidney Brood opened the door with a cigarette hanging out of his mouth and Dean's mind flashed back to an almost identical image from his memory. The man's mannerisms had not changed, but then he supposed that mannerisms didn't. He forgot how entirely familiar Sidney was, a man who was a fleeting, albeit memorable, part of his life. The way he held his arms, the way his back curved to the right, the way even the smallest of clothes looked baggy on his gaunt body. The main difference was his hair, once slicked back with a pomade, now his head was smooth with close clipped grey tufts at the side.

'Can I help you?'

'Hi Sid.'

'Do I know you?'

'I was one of the foster kids when you had the place around the corner. My name is Dean Kinkaid; I don't know if you remember me?'

‘I remember you.’ Sid shifted nervously.

‘Can I come in?’

It wasn’t really a question and Sid knew it.

‘I’m a bit busy at the moment.’ He backed slowly into the house.

‘It won’t take long.’ Dean gently pushed Sid inside and closed the door behind him.

Sid obviously lived alone these days. Which was the best thing for everyone. Considering how much money he had probably made out of the kids over the years, his house was that of a person who had never had much. Dean always assumed Sid was in it for the money; if it wasn’t about money then what the hell was it about? Sid wasn’t one of the worst, as far as he knew he was just a bully, and back then getting a smack around the head was perfectly acceptable. The real problem kids were often put with Sid and he would whip them into shape, sometimes literally. His one weakness was money though; Dean remembered him as a man who was easily bribed. Dean’s bag clinked as he dropped it on the ground – the various tools jarring against each other.

‘What is it you want? I haven’t got any money, if that’s what you’re after.’ Sid tugged nervously at his sleeves, balling the excess fabric in his fists. It was another jab at Dean’s memory.

‘I can see that. I don’t need your money. I just want some information.’

‘I don’t know anything.’

‘Well the speed with which you said that leads me to believe you know exactly why I am here.’

'I'm not sure how I can help you, Dean.'

Even the way he said his name gave Dean a jolt of familiarity.

'I want to know about the house.'

'It's a shop now.'

'Not that house.' Dean opened the holdall and pulled out a hammer.

'Hey come on now, there's no need for that.'

'You drove us out to a house a couple of times, do you remember it?'

'I can't talk about that.'

'You say that like you have a choice.' Dean cradled the hammer in his hands.

'I needed the money.' Sid crossed his arms over his chest. Something struck Dean about the movement, something that hadn't occurred to him before this moment. He had never seen Sid in a short-sleeved shirt; even in the height of summer he always wore long sleeves. He should have guessed he was an addict before now, another piece of the puzzle. The money was a means to an end, a way to keep a habit; that explained why he didn't have much now. It had all gone into his veins.

'Where is it?'

'They'll kill me! Probably kill you as well.'

Dean stepped forward. '*I'll* kill you – we both know I'm capable of it.'

'I heard what happened to you. I heard you went to young offenders for setting fire to that bloke.'

'He deserved it.'

'We probably all did back then. Most of us anyway.'

He looked genuinely remorseful, as though he had given up any hope of forgiveness.

'I just want to know about that place, I'm not interested in anything else.'

Sid looked uncomfortable. 'They stopped all of that years ago, I only went a few times because the money was good, but after you left something happened that stopped them from doing it anymore, I don't know what it was.'

'Who? Who owned the house?' Dean hissed through clenched teeth, his patience wearing thin, too close to give up now. 'Weren't you all worried about getting caught?'

'We were all in the same boat, us for bringing you lot, them for setting it up and paying for it. No one was going to grass anyone else up. I don't think anyone really thought about what would happen five or ten years down the line.'

There was something pathetic about Sid that made Dean think twice about hurting him. He was weak and Dean had known enough heroin addicts both inside and outside of prison to know that they didn't think about much beyond where their next hit was coming from. If anything, Dean was almost impressed at the fact that Sid had tried to keep his addiction hidden, not to the neighbours but to the kids in the house; when the doors were closed to the outside world. Dean had been in other places before this one where there was no compunction about shooting up in front of a child. This was what a functioning heroin addict looked like, not quite high functioning but with some semblance of a life at least.

Dean put the hammer back in the bag and pulled his wallet out. This man was not the enemy here, he had at the very least accepted the fact that he was a monster and who was Dean to judge? The fact that unlike so many of the other homes he was a part of, there was no sexual abuse involved at Sid's was something that Dean took into account, even though Sid was the one who had taken them to that house. The horror house. It wasn't as though Sid had ever taken part in any of it, even if he had been complicit. Dean wasn't after Sid; Sid was a pawn in a much bigger game and he needed to find out who the puppet masters were. He put some notes on the table and saw Sid relax a little. He obviously hadn't taken anything in a long time.

'I'm going to need a name,' Dean said.

Sid looked at the money on the table and then at Dean.

'Stefan and Felicity Carter.'

There was that name again, Carter. Sid's face was ashen, he looked scared. It had taken a lot for him to say those names but there was a resignation about the way he told Dean, as though he had been waiting for this for a long time, as though he was relieved to finally get it out of him.

Chapter 51

Lucy had seen the piece of paper on Adrian's table at breakfast this morning and taken it. A bank statement with a list of payments. The name of one of the payees had jumped out at her. Guardian Angel. She hadn't told him she recognised the name of the establishment and she hadn't told him where from. She wanted to help him though. Whatever he was working on was obviously troubling him if he was bringing it home with him and she had always had a problem keeping her nose out of other people's business. Especially people she cared about.

She pulled up outside the Guardian Angel secure private hospital and walked up to the door. She pressed the buzzer and was let inside just as it started to rain, the sky darkening as the battleship grey cloud hovered overhead. She hoped that no one would recognise her; it was unlikely as she hadn't been there in years, not since her father had been alive. The smell of the place instantly reminded her of the days she had spent playing in the waiting room, waiting, ironically, for her father to finish his shift as the hospital maintenance man.

The home was a place for people with incurable conditions, mental conditions. It was very expensive and exclusive; only the richest people could afford to be housed here. There were only ever twenty people staying at any one time. Now, Lucy just had to figure out which one was important to her, to Adrian's case.

The truth was, she had really liked Adrian the very first time they'd met. They'd gone home together and the sex had been better than most one-night stands, not that she had had many. He had never promised her anything, never made her believe that it was going anywhere other than where it did. She guessed her issue was with the fact that she liked him, and when he'd said goodbye in the morning she'd found herself hoping that he would call, but he didn't. She was irritated that she hadn't been able to captivate him. There was something intriguing about Adrian that had made her want to know more at the time, but the way he'd just walked away had made her feel so ordinary and disposable.

She had grown up a lot since then and realised that no matter what anyone tells you, the world doesn't revolve around sex. Whatever had been going on with Adrian that day, it wasn't a slight on her; the fact that he had woken up the next morning and walked away just meant that he had other things on his mind. She could see now that Adrian had demons, big nasty ones. Sometimes in the night these days she would hear him grind his teeth, his jaw clenched rigid and a look on his face so intense, she feared it might kill him. He never spoke about it when he awoke and they would just carry on as if nothing had happened. Who was she to interfere?

She knew this was important though, if there was a link to this place she would find it for him, she would show him that she was there for him. It felt different this time around, he felt different. It seemed as though she wasn't the only one who had grown up a lot since their last encounter.

She told the lady at the front desk she was a health and safety inspector here to perform a risk assessment and waited patiently for her to go and find someone with authority so she could look at the files. When she finally got behind the counter, she accessed the computer system, quickly going through each resident, looking for something that would jog her memory, something she would recognise. Nothing. She hit print on each patient sheet, not knowing what she was looking for, or even what she was looking at.

She heard footsteps quickening towards her, she grabbed the sheets of paper and looked up. There was a red light flashing; she had tripped some kind of alarm. Fortunately, Lucy had played enough hide and seek in this place as a child to get out unscathed.

She ran into room six, knowing full well that the French doors opened onto the patio. The patient inside stared at her blankly and Lucy smiled back before unlocking and opening the doors onto the front lawn, the sodden grass saturating the hem of her trousers. She rushed back to her car as the sky rumbled ominously and the rain got heavier. Pulling out her phone, she texted Adrian that she was heading home and asked him to meet her there; she had something for him. She chucked the phone on the passenger seat and looked at the papers; they would mean something to Adrian, she was sure of it. She opened the manual for her car and sandwiched the papers in the receipt holder at the back before closing it and slotting it back under the steering column.

Lucy started the car and pulled out, taking it slowly so as not to arouse any kind of suspicion. As she approached the corner she saw a man running out from the hospital and standing in the centre of the road, he stared straight at the car and pulled a phone out of his pocket but made no effort to give chase. The rain pelted against her windshield and she turned her wipers on, only to be reminded that the rubber was on its way out. As she made her way through the streets, she pulled out her phone to see if Adrian had replied. She couldn't wait to give him the papers; she wanted to impress him, to keep him in awe of her. She knew by the way he looked at her that she had him on a hook and she liked it that way. She kept her eye on the road as she checked her phone, then chucked it on the seat next to her when she noticed a car behind her increasing in speed.

Visibility was poor but she had a feeling the car behind was following her. She started to panic and kept her eyes in the rear-view to see what they were doing. *Were* they following her? They were gaining on her; she had to decide now whether to put her foot down or not. Instead of flooring it, she took an unexpected right turn, and the car mirrored her movement. She followed the road as it turned into more of a country lane; there were no houses and she felt sick, she didn't recognise where she was. Of all the roads to turn down she'd picked a deserted track with no drainage; the rain was beginning to pool, whole sections of the road ahead already completely immersed.

Lucy saw a small railway arch up ahead followed by an overpass. The M5 ran directly across the top of the road she was on. If she could drive up there she could disappear into the traffic. The thunder ripped through the air and her throat tightened as she went under the arch. She glanced in the mirror in time to see that the car behind her was accelerating. If she went any faster she wouldn't have to worry about them catching up to her because she would lose control of the steering; the road conditions and the grass verges made it impossible for her to take that chance. She could already hear the water hitting against the underneath of her chassis. She made it to the underpass when she felt a sharp shunt. Her neck hurt from where the seatbelt kept her from hitting her head on the steering column. The car revved again and shunted her harder. She clutched the steering wheel as she skidded on the mud, struggling to keep the car from mounting the verge. One final smack and she lost control, hitting her head on the window. The car juddered and came to a halt.

Lucy felt disoriented, her head rattled and her eyes blurred but she could see someone approaching the car in the rain. As the panic rose inside her she gulped for air. She was dizzy and her hands seemed so far away.

She touched her forehead which had started to throb and felt the blood as it trickled down. She flicked the doors locked and went to grab her phone off the passenger seat but it must have fallen into the footwell. She unbuckled herself and reached for the phone again. It was lodged between the passenger seat and the door. She was leaning across the seat when she heard the glass break and felt the shattered wet shards fall into her lap. Someone grabbed her arm and pulled at her before she got her hands on the phone, but it was too late. A blow landed directly on her temple, making her feel even more dizzy, then her hair was being grabbed and she knew what was going to happen next, she knew he was going to whack her head against the steering wheel. She felt his fist tighten around her hair, pulling it taut so that her temple ached. Then she was propelled forward and everything went black.

Chapter 52

Adrian and Imogen waited patiently for Gary Tunney; he had asked them to meet him in one of the conference rooms, saying it was something important.

'So, what's going on with you, Grey?' Adrian asked.

'In what way?'

'You've been quiet. Distracted.'

Imogen sighed. 'It's Dean, I don't know what's going on with him.'

'Because of this case?'

'He's definitely struggling with things he's not talking to me about. I want him to trust me.'

'How was it ever going to be any different? I'm not saying that to make you feel bad, I'm just asking because – well – you seem to think it may change. If you can't change, then why do you think that he can?'

'Because he can't carry on like this, he'll end up in prison – again.'

'But we see it all the time, people who make the same

mistakes over and over again. Maybe it's just who they are, maybe this is just who he is.'

'I don't accept that,' Imogen said.

'Why does the way you want to live trump the way he wants to live?'

'Because I'm operating within the law. What kind of question is that?'

'In his world, the law fucked him over when he was a kid, so why would he trust the law to take care of him?'

'You aren't helping.' She glowered at him.

'I'm just saying that maybe this is the way it is and you probably need to start thinking about whether you can live with that or not. Maybe he is right.'

'You don't really think that?'

'I think a person should trust themselves. I know myself, I know I'm not a bad person. In the end, I can only trust myself to look after me.'

'Have you been watching Dr Phil or something?' Imogen said, rolling her eyes.

'I'm just saying, if you love him, why is it him that has to change?'

'Have I hit a nerve or something?'

'No. I'm just saying that you shouldn't wait for something that's never going to happen.'

She filled her cheeks with air and turned away from Adrian; he could tell he had upset her. As a friend, he wanted to make sure she confronted what she was actually dealing with, she would do the same for him. He couldn't just tell her everything would be all right. She was counting to ten, either to stop herself from crying or to stop herself from punching him – he hoped it was the latter.

Gary walked in, red and flustered, wearing an orange sweatshirt that accentuated the red in his facial hair and his freckles. He made sure the door was closed behind him and put his laptop on the table next to Adrian. He opened it and Adrian saw that he had about fifty tabs open, making him wish he had a drink. Computer jargon confused him when it was regular mainstream jargon; Tunney always managed to kick it up a notch to the point where Adrian wasn't even sure he was speaking English anymore.

'What did you find?'

'I hope you're ready for this. I've put an envelope with all the main pointers and supporting documentation in your drawer. I suggest you keep this quiet until you have a chance to get some actual physical evidence.'

'Why is that then?'

'Because some very important people are going to try and keep this quiet.'

'Oh good. It's another one of those.'

Chapter 53

The breakdown of Richard Wallis' accounts showed that he had lost a lot of money in the last few years; not enough to lose his house, but from the looks of it, it seemed as though he was getting dangerously close to laying people off, people he needed for his firm to function. Looking through these documents was sending Adrian to sleep, but they had only just begun according to Gary, who had opened another spreadsheet for them to look at.

'What's this one?' Adrian asked.

'Charitable donations over the last few years.'

'We know about the big donation, the one to KIDSMART,' Adrian said.

'Right. It's not the first time either.'

'He's donated big money like that before?'

'Yes, but he only donates that kind of money to KIDSMART. Every other donation is much smaller. The three donations to KIDSMART add up to twenty grand.'

'Do we know why he might particularly be interested in that charity? Grey and I have a theory but that's all it is, we need more evidence.'

'He was never in care and doesn't seem to have any personal or professional links with it,' Gary said.

'Right, so there is no emotional reason for him to have donated that much to them? So why then?'

'That's what I couldn't figure out. I did notice something though.'

'What?'

'Well as you know I have been going through those files Tom copied, Dominic's accounts.'

'Right?' Adrian knew there was a connection to Dominic.

'Well, something was niggling at me while I was looking through this guy's accounts.'

'And what was that? Spit it out!'

'So here, look, I put some of the transactions side by side.' He laid out more papers and ran his finger down the type. 'This is one of Dominic's smaller companies, apparently, they provide garden landscaping and general gardening services. It's one of the companies where Andrea is named as the company director, even though she doesn't appear anywhere else but the set-up forms. So, every time a big payment to KIDSMART is made, exactly four days later, a payment for a third of what has been donated is paid into this company by a maintenance company.'

'Right, so?' Adrian said.

'Well, it's the timing that bothered me. So I went through the Charity Commission and got hold of the public accounts for KIDSMART and, aside from being a bit of a mess, there were several big donations, where exactly a third of the donation value is paid into a smaller company – one is a bus hire company, there's this general maintenance company and there are a couple of other generic companies where it would make sense for them to be in business with KIDSMART – they have buildings and care homes all over and they need maintenance and upkeep.'

'So, what has this got to do with Richard Wallis or these payments to Dominic?' Adrian asked.

'It's the dates and the amounts, they're always four days apart and always for exactly a third; not just from Richard Wallis but from other people too. I flagged up all the large donations to KIDSMART and saw that almost every time, Dominic gets a third of that value four days later. Not to mention there seems to be a pricing structure.'

Adrian nodded, frowning. 'While that's a strange coincidence, what does it prove?'

'OK, so I looked at the people making the donations for the bigger figures like Richard Wallis, and there's something funny about each one of them.'

'Such as?' Imogen asked, frustrated with Gary's love of dramatically dripping out information.

'Brian and Georgia Hiller?' Adrian read the name out.

'I recognise the names, don't know where from though,' Imogen said.

'Probably because it was out of our area. There was a big accident at a warehouse they owned, a fire, the floor manager was killed. It was ruled as arson. I sent a request for the photos for you, you know, in case it helps,' Gary said.

'So, these figures are a payment for services?' Adrian had hoped they were wrong.

'That's exactly what I'm suggesting, yes. There are a couple of other cases too. Similar thing.'

'You think the death was deliberate. That maybe the Hillers paid to have the floor manager killed?' Imogen asked.

'There was a dispute going on between them, they couldn't fire him. He had been fired before and he won a case for unfair dismissal and got reinstated. If there was something dodgy going on in that warehouse maybe they needed to silence him? He might have been blackmailing them or something.'

'There's that imagination of yours again, Gary,' Adrian said.

'I'm just giving you possible reasons. Look at this other one.' He pulled up a news story from another tab. 'This bloke was killed in a car accident.'

'I remember that,' Imogen said.

Adrian remembered it too, the man had driven at great speed into a tree, he'd had heroin in his system and his official cause of death had been drugs, even though he was mangled around the tree. Apparently, the paramedics had gotten him out just in time to see him fade away. The story had resonated with Adrian, made him give up drinking for three whole weeks, reminded of his father's addictions and afflictions. The man himself wasn't a known user and seemed to have no history of substance abuse, there were no suspicious needle marks on his body either.

'So, this charity is a front for a bunch of assassins?' Imogen said with a screwed-up face, obviously unable to get her head around the idea.

'I don't know, but I should say it bears some closer scrutiny.'

'Yes, it definitely does,' Adrian said, looking more closely at the screen.

'There's one problem,' Gary said.

'What's that?' Adrian asked.

'Everyone loves KIDSMART. We need to be careful here. Especially considering what we think they're doing.'

'Are you suggesting we shouldn't look at them?' Imogen asked.

'I'm suggesting we tread carefully. As soon as we make any kind of formal enquiry into the charity we don't know what alarm bells will start ringing.'

'Fair enough.'

'Did you find anything else on Dominic?' Adrian turned to Gary who was busy tapping away.

'I found that he pays a regular payment to a trust that I have not been able to get any information on at all. I will keep digging though. There was a letter from the trust to him in with the paperwork you have, but it was oddly cryptic.'

'You'll figure it out,' Adrian said.

'I guess we need to work out what hand to play next?' Imogen said.

'I will have a look at the charity in more detail and

see if that throws anything up, but as far as Richard Wallis goes, I would put money on it, and I hate gambling,' Gary said.

'What about Dominic?' Adrian said.

'I suspect he is not only involved but in charge somehow of this too, but until I get some more pieces of the puzzle it's unlikely that I'll be able to know for sure. I did include some newspaper articles where Dominic is mentioned in relation to the Carters. I suspect there's more, though,' Gary said.

'I guess we go and see the Carters then,' Imogen said to Adrian.

'Without telling the DCI? They're pretty high-profile,' he said cautiously.

'Better to seek forgiveness than ask permission.' She smiled.

Chapter 54

The Carters' address was easy enough to find, a quick internet search provided the location. Imogen leaned out of the car window and pressed the buzzer on the gate.

'DS Imogen Grey and DS Adrian Miles to see you,' she called into the intercom before sitting back down.

'Just a moment.'

They sat staring at the gate for a few minutes.

'Are they going to bloody open it?'

Adrian watched Imogen as she clenched and unclenched her jaw, drummed her fingers on the side of the car door and scratched her head in agitation.

The gate started to move slowly; it was a thick gate and as it pulled back, the grounds were in full view, a large front garden with all manner of sculpted topiary and a rounded driveway like something out of an American movie. There was a dark blue Bentley parked at the edge of the house, just off the driveway. The house itself was covered in ivy, an old double-fronted stone house with columns and small-paned arched windows. There was something castle-like about it.

As they got out of the car and made their way to the front door, the gravel crunched under their feet. It was a large wooden door with an iron knocker; Adrian grabbed it and pounded hard.

Felicity Carter pulled the door open, a forced grin plastered on her face. She did not look happy to see them. She looked as Adrian remembered her: golden. She wore a cream linen suit with a gold silk blouse, and the parts of her skin that were showing had a bronze glitter to them. Her almost flawless look was only marred by her eye make-up, it was smudged and blurred on the edges. She looked as though she'd been crying.

'Please come in.' She waved them inside.

It was all very open on the inside, with mirrors reflecting what little light came in from the windows, and an opulent Turkish rug in the centre. Through the open double doors at the end of the hall, Adrian could see a large lounge with a wall of windows looking out over the gardens, the myriad colours of the roses clashing with the golds, greys and creams of the lounge itself. Adrian didn't want to sit down. Imogen of course took the opportunity straight away to make herself at ease.

'Sorry to bother you, Mrs Carter,' Adrian began.

'We've met before, haven't we, Detective?'

'Yes, at my son's birthday party. I believe you're friends with his stepfather, Dominic Shaw?' There was no use beating about the bush.

'He has been very generous with our charity.'

'Oh, I bet he has been. Especially when you're paying him off for something.' Adrian had never been very good at treading carefully.

'Excuse me?'

'We know that you and your husband have been paying Dominic Shaw for something, is it protection? Silence? Wages? What?'

'I think you should leave, actually.' Felicity Carter folded her arms defiantly.

'Either you don't know, in which case you're stupid, which I don't think you are,' Adrian said, 'or you know exactly what is going on and you're going to tell us all about it at the station.'

Felicity rolled her eyes. 'He lent us some money, personal money – my husband had some debts and Dominic gave us the money to get straight. It was a loan, that's all. Our lifestyle isn't cheap and we needed money to live on. We were going to lose this house and we've been here together since we got married, when I was twenty.'

'You're a good liar.' Imogen smiled, putting her feet on the coffee table.

'If you had any proof of this there would be a warrant and a search team with you.' Felicity pulled her jacket around her and clutched her stomach; Imogen could tell she was nervous although you wouldn't know it by her face.

'We could call them right now? Hang about until they get it together?' Imogen offered.

'I'll be speaking to Dominic about this, detective,'

she said to Adrian. She had a slightly manic look in her eye. It was probably best if they disappeared now.

'Well I just wanted to give you the heads-up. Give you a chance to come clean.' Adrian smiled.

'I will give you the number of the accountant and he can clear up any financial inquiries you may or may not have. Next time you come to my door you will need a warrant.'

'Just don't leave the country.' Imogen dragged her feet off the table with a thump on the parquet floor. She grunted as she stood up. 'Thank you, Mrs Carter.'

'Just go.'

They both hovered for a moment, looking around the room. Felicity was clearly desperate to get rid of them; her facade seemed to crack even further with every second they stayed. Adrian felt Imogen's hand on his arm, he looked at her and saw that she too had noticed the strained atmosphere.

'Where is your husband, Mrs Carter?' Adrian asked.

'We had a small argument and he went for a drive.'

'Wasn't that his car in the driveway?'

'We have more than one car,' she scoffed.

Imogen walked slowly across the room, her ears pricked. Adrian watched Felicity, looking for something suspicious. It was hard to explain that gut instinct feeling that he had, the feeling that came over him whenever he knew something was off. It was impossible to quantify it in any way.

'I'm going to press charges against you unless you leave my property immediately.'

'Fine,' Adrian said. Imogen followed him to the door.

'I'll open the gate for you.' She pushed the button for the gate and they saw that the entrance was monitored by a camera. He wondered where else there were cameras.

Outside, they got back in the car and Imogen turned the ignition.

'That was weird.'

'What do we do now?'

'We need to do some research on the Carters, I think. Newspapers, history, the lot. See if there is any other way to tie them to this. We also need to go to the foster home they run in the city, maybe their staff can give us some insight. There was one interesting thing though.'

'What's that?'

'She used Dominic's name to threaten you, she was trying to scare you.' Imogen watched Adrian for a moment, trying to see if he really was worried. If he was, there was no indication of it.

'Which means she knows what he's capable of.'

'Which probably means she's a part of this, whatever this is.'

Chapter 55

Dean watched out of the window and waited for the gate to close behind Adrian and Imogen, ignoring the feeling in the pit of his stomach. He didn't have time to think about Imogen now, he was just relieved that she hadn't found him there. He hated lying to her.

Stefan Carter lay on the floor of the bedroom, clutching at the side of his head, blood drying on his hands as he held onto his ear, trying to stop the bleeding. Felicity Carter re-entered the room and rushed to her husband.

'I got rid of them, now leave us alone!'

'Well done,' Dean said.

'They will be back, they said they would.'

'I'm curious as to why you didn't tell them I was here,' Dean said. 'If you had nothing to hide, you could have signalled them or something. You don't think they could have taken me out?'

'How do you know I didn't signal them?'

He knew because he knew Imogen; she wouldn't have left like that; if she'd known Dean was there, she would have done something. When he was satisfied that the gate was fully closed, Dean left the window and pulled Stefan Carter up and onto the bed.

'You had better tell me what I want to know quickly then. Before they come back, before I tell them everything I know,' Dean said.

'You have no idea how many people will be hurt if you do that,' Felicity Carter pleaded with him.

'Is it more than the people you have hurt already? I fucking see you, you uptight bitch, I know who you are! You're not worried about anyone getting hurt! You're probably not even worried about this sack of shit here. You're worried about yourself.'

'Please . . .' Stefan groaned on the bed. Dean pulled out his holdall full of tools from behind the bed and put them next to Stefan.

'How about this then? If you 'fess up now, I make it quick, and I make it look like an accident.'

'Or what?' Stefan Carter said through bloodied lips.

'Or we take our time about this. At the very least we have an hour before the police come back. Do you think you can last an hour?'

'Please, just leave him alone,' Felicity said desperately.

'Then tell me what I need to know. Tell me about this gang of kids.' Dean turned to Felicity, who seemed more likely to spill the beans at this point.

'They are nothing to do with us.'

'But when you saw the video you must have suspected it was something to do with you? That symbol . . . as soon as I saw it I knew it was about this. About the things you did.'

'That symbol is common!'

'The home I was in, that was one of yours.'

'You don't understand . . .'

Dean pulled the hammer out of his holdall, placed the butt of it on Stefan Carter's knee and turned back to Felicity.

'What do you know about that old couple, the couple who died?'

'I don't know anything! I swear!' Felicity shrieked.

Dean lifted the hammer up and brought it down with a swift movement, before Felicity even had time to cry out. As the hammer connected with Stefan's kneecap, a dull crack ripped through the air. Stefan let out an unearthly moan through bloodied teeth and slumped forward, almost toppling off the bed. Dean grabbed his collar and Stefan hissed as he pulled him back.

'When I'm done with him, you're next.' Dean looked at Felicity pointedly

'The killings are nothing to do with us. You have to believe me!' She had a look on her face that wasn't concern for her husband, it was a different kind of concern altogether. She was trying to think her way out of the situation, not for her husband, but for herself.

'But you know something about them?' He searched around in the bag and pulled out a screwdriver. He held it over Stefan Carter's other knee.

'God, no!' Stefan gurgled, his eyes rolling around in his head, the pain already unbearable.

He brought the screwdriver down and Stefan screamed before passing out.

Dean turned to Felicity and she started to back away.

'It was all Stefan, I swear, I didn't want to do it. I didn't want any of it.'

'Who else is involved?'

'He has a book, in the safe, it has a list of names, I can get it for you.'

'Well he's not going anywhere, so I can come with you.' Dean left Stefan Carter on the bed and grabbed hold of Felicity's arm – he knew enough to know that she was the brains of the operation, anyone could see it. He also knew that most people are more afraid of loved ones getting hurt and would gladly take the pain on themselves, but this wasn't what was happening here. She was more concerned with when the torture of her husband ended, because she knew it meant Dean would turn his attention to her.

She wasn't going to get away with it that easily.

Chapter 56

Gabriel was waiting to get Asher alone, without his ridiculous pad-mate who somehow gave him permission to behave with such bravado. He was different when he was alone – still an absolute shit, but somehow less dramatic about the whole thing. Maybe there was some kind of arrangement they could come to, maybe if Gabriel tried to appeal to his humanity he might have some success. Was it worth a shot?

He woke up about an hour before the cell doors opened and started working on his crunches and press-ups. He worked out more now than he had in the last nineteen years of his life, and he felt good, he felt strong. Gabriel grabbed his towel and waited for the door to open.

Roll call.

Asher was standing opposite Gabriel's cell when he stepped outside; he knew he was there before he even saw him. He felt the bile rising in his throat. He made sure Asher saw the towel and walked down to the showers, knowing it wouldn't be long before Asher was there too. He just couldn't resist the opportunity to intimidate Gabriel. He didn't know that Gabriel was an old hand at being emotionally blackmailed and manipulated. For the first time, he was grateful for his father; God knows what would have happened to him in here if he hadn't learnt to tough it out at home.

In the showers, Gabriel washed as fast as he could. The only good thing about Asher at this point was that he had obviously laid claim to Gabriel, meaning that Gabriel was no longer scared of the other prisoners as well. Gabriel knew that if he did get attacked, he would know exactly where it was coming from. As expected, Asher walked in with his towel and stripped off next to Gabriel, who rinsed quickly and wrapped the towel around himself. He moved to the side to get dressed.

Asher smiled at him. 'Where's your little dog? Your mate that follows you around like a lost puppy.'

'Bailey's at breakfast.' The thought of appealing to Asher's humanity was getting harder by the second.

Asher pressed the button for the shower. The water dribbled and he rubbed it all over himself. He carried on talking as he lathered up, eyes on Gabriel, who let him think he was in control of this situation, let him think he was winning. He knew now that this was the only way to beat Asher; he had to play to his ego.

'He's a lot of fun you know, your Bailey. Next time you're in the shower I might pay him a visit. Watch him stuttering around while I piss all over him. Although I do like seeing you in the shower all wet and naked, so maybe I'll get my baby brother to pay that hot little girlfriend of yours a visit. She must be lonely without you. My brother's the looker in the family. I bet she'd love a bit of attention from him. If not, he's pretty persuasive with the drugs, how long before she's promising anything just to get a fix? I could even have a word with Johnson, make sure she gets caught with something when she next comes to visit you. If she's lucky the worst that will happen is a slap on the wrist. But whatever happens, she will never be allowed to visit you again.'

Gabriel could see the excitement on Asher's face as he talked about Emma, and no matter what happened, Gabriel wouldn't let anything happen to her – he couldn't.

'If you want me to . . . cooperate with you, then you need to leave them both alone.' Gabriel said the words so quietly that they were barely audible, sick at what was coming out of his mouth, at the thought of what he was offering to do.

'I told you, there's only one way that's happening.' Asher winked.

'Why me?'

'You should be flattered, I've got quite a crush on you. At night when it's all hot and I'm alone I think about you in your cell, it's a shame you ain't alone anymore or I might see if I could arrange a visit. Not that I think that gimp you have in there would even notice. What the fuck's wrong with him?'

'A lot less than is wrong with you.'

'So, what are you going to do for me then? It's visiting

time in a couple of days; I need to know what I'm telling Johnson.'

'I'll do it as long as no one else finds out.'

Asher was visibly taken aback; if Gabriel didn't know better he would think he was almost disappointed. He wasn't expecting Gabriel to give in this early. Was it because Gabriel didn't seem distressed enough? Because he hadn't cried and begged for mercy?

'You'll do what?'

'I'll do whatever you want me to do.'

Gabriel pulled his black shirt over his head and wandered off, trying to look unruffled, wondering what he had done. The situation was untenable as it was. He wasn't scared of what Asher would do to him anymore. He was scared what might happen to someone else. Would they stop at Emma? What if they hurt his parents? He would rather the decision was his, he would rather be in control and have no one else know.

Gabriel waited by his door for Sol to turn up, which he did not long after, ushering him inside. Bailey was sitting in the chair, the purple bruise around his eye turning yellow.

'We missed you at breakfast.'

'I wasn't hungry.' Gabriel looked up and down the gallery outside to see if he could see Asher; he couldn't and almost everyone else was eating. His head was spinning. What had he done? He couldn't go through with it, could he?

'What's going on?' Sol asked.

'I have to stop Asher. He won't give up on this until he gets what he wants. Who knows who he's going to hurt next? Who knows what he's going to do if Sparks ever gets out of the infirmary? I think I've bought myself some time for now, but I'm going to have to do something,' Gabriel said almost frantically, the words pouring out at speed.

He had a short window of opportunity here. He had already promised himself to Asher, but he hoped it wouldn't come to that; there had to be another way.

'Are you mental? He's too powerful in here,' Sol whispered loudly. 'You'll get put in Seg, or worse.'

'I don't think he's as powerful as he thinks he is.'

'So, what do you propose?'

'I'll think of something, but when the time comes I need you guys to create a distraction.'

Chapter 57

Adrian had a text message from Lucy. That was unusual; ordinarily she loved to keep him hanging and he loved her for it. After a day of staring at paperwork and waiting for something to jump out at him, Adrian had needed a breath of fresh air so had walked over to her house. She had been fine the last time he had seen her, but her text message wasn't playful. Had she found something out? Over at her place, her car was gone and the lights were out. He felt awkward being there when she wasn't, as though he wasn't invited, as though he was being pushy – and that was the last thing he wanted. He checked his phone again but it had been a couple of hours since she'd sent the text.

He walked around the back of her house, but there was still no sign of her. Sighing, he started back home again, keeping one eye on the road in case her car went past him. He looked at the message again to see if there was a clue as to where she might be. He really wanted to see her; it was getting harder to spend time apart.

He got home to a dark, empty house. He missed the mess of other people; when he was alone even being at home was a predictable affair. His weekends with Tom were a break from the monotony of living alone but recently they had been fewer and farther between. If he dropped his clothes on the floor at night they would still be there in the morning. Since he had been spending more time with Lucy he had awoken sometimes to the smell of peppermint tea or just that warm, misty air from when someone had just showered. She wore essential oils and not perfume, something bohemian and musky that reminded him of hot summer nights. He was thrown back to a time when he and Andrea had lived together, of course he'd been much younger, barely qualified for the police and things were different; he was naive, immature. It's hard to look back on a former version of yourself that you're less than impressed with. Adrian had promised himself that he wouldn't give himself any more reasons to hate himself though, and to chalk those mistakes he'd made when he was younger up to the fact that he had no guidance whatsoever. For as long as he could remember, his father had been steeped in his own self-loathing, some mistake he had made plaguing him into addiction. Adrian's mother had always insisted that he wasn't always like that, that he had been a very different man once, that something terrible had happened and he just couldn't forgive himself. She had forgiven him a million times and she had forgiven that, too. How terrible could it be?

He got in the shower and washed, placing his phone on the sink where he could see it in case Lucy phoned. She must have just got held up but he hoped the late hour wouldn't stop her from contacting him. He dried himself off and slipped on some jogging bottoms. Still nothing on his phone. He had a strange feeling, a kind of anxiety, something he would normally stifle with alcohol. He turned the TV on and flicked channels until he found a movie.

He awoke to the sound of knocking on the door. The TV was replaying the news and the dawn was breaking; he must have slept for hours. He got up and opened it to find Imogen on the doorstep, but she wasn't alone. DCI Kapoor walked in behind her.

Suddenly, Adrian felt very underdressed in his jogging bottoms. He grabbed a zip up hoodie from the back of the dining chair and slipped it on.

'What's going on?' Adrian looked at Imogen who was wide-eyed and ghost-faced.

'Is this yours?' DCI Kapoor lifted up an evidence bag with a belt in it. The buckle was a rectangle with a geometric pattern engraved into the surface. He saw the bag had traces of blood smeared against the inside.

'No hello for me?'

'Just answer the question please, DS Miles.'

'I can't be sure,' he lied. It was his.

'Adrian, we found it in Lucy Hannigan's car,' Imogen said quietly, her eyes still fixed on him.

'What?' His tongue stuck to the roof of his mouth as he spoke, the blood draining from his face. 'Hang on. Why were you looking in her car?'

'Do you mind if we take a look around?' DCI Kapoor said.

'Kind of, yeah.' He was having trouble understanding why they were there. 'Where's Lucy?'

'We don't know,' Imogen said before the DCI had a chance to.

'What exactly are you looking for?'

'Nothing in particular,' Imogen said. Something about her was off, he could tell she desperately wanted to speak to him alone.

'Well go for it, then. What the hell has this got to do with Lucy's car?'

DCI Kapoor disappeared through the house into the hallway and up the stairs.

Imogen turned towards him. 'Sorry Adrian, she called me and asked me to come with her, to keep you calm.'

'Calm? I'm pretty fucking far from calm right now. What's going on?'

'I wish I knew, I know as much as you.'

'A heads-up would have been nice!' Adrian was angry; she could have phoned ahead.

'She's been with me since I found out.'

'Found out? Found out what?'

'Lucy's car . . . There was blood in it. I couldn't call you. I think we should tell her what we know.'

Anger flared in him. 'Keeping in with the boss? Going for a promotion, are you? Is Lucy OK? Where is she?' he was asking the questions but he didn't want answers, he wanted reassurance. *Where the hell are you?*

'We have to trust her at some point,' Imogen said, her eyes darting up as they heard the floor creak overhead.

'Lucy's blood?' Adrian asked, struggling to swallow or breathe.

'We don't know, the techs are doing their stuff on it right now.'

'Jesus Christ,' he muttered. 'Where was the car?'

'Langaton Lane.'

DCI Kapoor came back in with her phone open.

'We need to speak to you about the investigation, now,' Adrian said to her quickly. If Lucy had been caught up in this KIDSMART investigation, it was important for the DCI to be brought up to speed with everything, speculation or not. Adrian couldn't even begin to allow himself to wonder where Lucy was.

'What about it?'

'There are some things we haven't told you,' Imogen said.

'Well there's no time like the present.' She pulled out a dining chair and turned to Adrian. 'Black with two sugars please.'

Chapter 58

Imogen had to do this by the book now, she had to confide in DCI Kapoor. She also had to reconcile herself with the fact that she had chosen a career as a police officer, which meant there were rules she was duty-bound to follow. They couldn't keep making things up as they went along – that's how things got messy. She took a deep breath and tried to think of the best place to start. Adrian came in with two coffees and sat with them both. He looked agitated. Ready to go. She knew he desperately wanted to get outside and look for Lucy.

'I know we probably haven't got off to the best start,' Imogen began, searching for the right words.

'What's on your mind?'

'First, I believe all of this ties in to the current case, and potentially goes back even further than that,' she said.

'What do you mean by all of this?'

'Can I start with a little backstory? Just so you understand a bit more about the situation.'

‘OK. Go.’ Mira Kapoor folded her arms in front of her, leaning back in the chair.

‘Someone gave Adrian some paperwork relating to his son’s stepfather, Dominic Shaw, some financial files and other business documents that had come into their possession. Adrian then looked at these documents and found some interesting irregularities.’

‘Such as?’

‘Lots of money being moved around, it seemed to be money laundering of some kind. There’s no record of this being logged into any kind of evidence. It might have been nothing, so we wanted to investigate it further. That’s the first thing you need to know. We found a connection between the fire in the signal box, the Wallis murders and the paperwork on Dominic Shaw. It also links back to the KIDSMART charity and the Carters, who we believe were also involved.’

The DCI’s jaw was clenching and unclenching. Imogen could tell she was trying to be patient.

‘Lucy Hannigan was investigating the fire in the signal box, too. Some of my papers are missing and I’m worried she took them and went off on her own, looking for something,’ Adrian said, anxiously biting the inside of his cheek.

‘You think these people are dangerous and you didn’t tell me?’ she snapped, unable to stay silent any longer.

‘We have very little evidence of that. All we have are a lot of coincidences. It will need a thorough forensic analysis of all the accounts involved. We have been working from photocopied documents and public domain information,’ Imogen said.

'The thing is, DCI, we don't know you, and we've been burned before,' Adrian said. Imogen wanted to comfort him but now wasn't the time. She could only imagine what he was thinking.

The DCI looked at them both. 'I've cut you a lot of slack because of the recent history of the department, but keeping things from me really isn't wise. Is there anything else I need to know?'

'Nothing concrete,' Adrian said.

'So, you think Lucy found something in the documents?'

'I received a text from her earlier, she said she wanted to see me at hers tonight, said she had something to show me. I went over but she wasn't there.'

'And you think this man, this Dominic Shaw, is behind all of this? Is he wealthy?'

'He has several businesses, but there is something fishy about his accounts. Without a proper warrant then there is no way we will know exactly what, but we do know he is connected to the Wallis murder somehow.'

'Explain that to me.' DCI Kapoor sat forward.

'Richard Wallis donated large sums of money to the charity KIDSMART. Well, it's all very convoluted, and Gary can explain it better than I can, but basically a specific portion of that money found its way into Dominic Shaw's account.'

The DCI shook her head in disbelief. 'So, Gary is working on it too? Am I literally the last person to know?'

'Sorry, there isn't anyone else, just us three. Four with Lucy. We were investigating further before we came to you with it but there is a historical connection with Wallis and Shaw; we think Dominic Shaw is a facilitator.'

'For what?'

'We think he is basically taking payments through the charity, and putting people in touch with the charity which is' – he took a deep breath – 'a front for something more sinister.'

'You think the charity had something to do with the death of Richard Wallis' parents?'

'I think the charity provides the kids, yes. We think they recruit young people to commit crimes, arson, body disposal, murder, God only knows what else. Dominic connects the clients with the charity and they tell the kids what to do.'

'That's a leap, isn't it?'

'It would be, but Gary looked through the public accounts of the charity and found other big donations. A few days after each one, money goes into Shaw's account through a shell company and then a little while after that the person who makes the donation suffers a loss – loses either a friend, colleague or family member in an accident. They always lose someone whose death will benefit them financially.'

'If this is true, this is massive.' DCI Kapoor blew out her breath.

'We believe Shaw had friends in the department before, which is why none of this was ever put together. It's why I didn't come to you before, we had to be sure you weren't part of it,' Imogen said.

'And are you sure I'm not?'

'No. But what choice do we have now?'

'So you think Dominic Shaw has something to do with Lucy disappearing?'

Imogen seemed to be getting through to the DCI and she felt the burden lifting as she spoke. It felt good not to be sneaking around anymore.

'Lucy was obviously snooping around and getting close to finding out something that Shaw didn't particularly want found out for whatever reason. And we went to see Stefan and Felicity Carter, so they know we are getting close as well. They run the charity. They mentioned Shaw, too.'

'How did Lucy Hannigan get hold of those papers you had, DS Miles?'

'We were seeing each other; she took them from my home.'

DCI Mira Kapoor let out a big sigh as she tried to process the information she had been given.

'It looks like Adrian is being set up!' Imogen said. 'The belt in Lucy's car . . .'

'How would someone get hold of your things?'

'Dominic would be able to get in here; my son has a key. Aside from that, I usually leave my back door unlocked, someone could have climbed the wall and got in.'

'This is all hugely speculative, although if what you say is true then it definitely merits further investigation. I can't just ignore all the rules you have broken, although I can't say I wasn't warned about you both beforehand.'

'If you don't want me to be part of the case then I understand,' Adrian said.

The DCI paused. 'I think the first task is to get a warrant for the charity, if you say there are links to crimes. Then we need to list them, pull up the files – copy and print whatever you need and we will take it to a judge. From now on, no more sneaking around, unless I tell you to. I'll fill Fraser in. What were you and DS Grey planning on doing next?'

'We were going to go and check out one of the KIDSMART residential children's homes in town. We believe a couple of former residents may be implicated in this case, the Wallis case,' Adrian said.

'Stick with that, your instincts seem to have been paying off so far. After I've spoken to Fraser he can come with you. Somewhere in all this information you have the key to finding Lucy Hannigan.'

'Thank you for listening to us,' Imogen said.

'Well, to be honest I did wonder what you two were doing, I thought you were sitting around with your thumbs up your bums.' She gave a half smile at them. 'It's good to know you were actually trying to solve the case. And I promise you, I'm not the enemy here. Let's keep most of the details of this to ourselves for now. The Carters have a lot of friends around here, so we need to tread carefully. Everyone has been one step ahead of us so far. As soon as Gary gets something concrete on Richard Wallis we'll arrest and charge him, as well as the other people. I'll get some officers on the CCTV and traffic cams to see if there are any leads on Lucy, we'll track her phone, we'll do whatever we can to find her.'

DCI Kapoor's phone rang, she looked at the screen

and held her finger up. She then got up and went outside with it, out of Adrian and Imogen's earshot.

Imogen saw something out of the corner of her eye, on the floor by one of Adrian's shelving units full of collectable toys. It was a set of keys.

'I thought you'd lost your car keys?'

She went over and picked them up, handing them to Adrian.

'I did . . . and I looked there!'

He looked at them in his hand, his face knotted in confusion. After a second, he shook it off and put them in his pocket.

'Maybe you need to go and lie down. You don't look so good,' Imogen said quietly. 'You've had a lot to deal with.'

'Assuming this is Dominic, and that's what I am assuming, why would he take Lucy? It doesn't make any sense. He must know that's just going to make me come after him even harder.'

'Are you sure he even knew about you two?'

'I expect he knew, he seems to know most things.'

Adrian's head was spinning. What was worse was that Imogen wouldn't stop staring at him; she had a wrinkle in the centre of her forehead that was annoying him no end. He hated it when she was sympathetic, it was a very un-Grey thing to be. He could see the silhouette of the DCI pacing outside his lounge window. He picked up his phone again and dialled Lucy's number, it rang for a few seconds then went to answerphone.

A groan of worry escaped him. 'Where is she?' He

desperately wanted to leave and find her, but he knew that he was in a precarious situation.

'We'll find her, Miley.' Imogen put her hand on his knee.

'If she was on Langaton Lane, she wasn't going home. That's the other side of town completely.'

He looked at his phone for the hundredth time, reconnecting the wireless in case it had been disconnected and then checking his emails, phone messages, any other apps he had where she might be able to contact him. There was nothing. He dialled the number again and put it on speaker phone. It rang a few times and then went to answerphone once more.

'You don't know what was on the papers she took?' Imogen asked as he switched the phone screen off.

'I don't. It was just some bank statements, I think.'

DCI Kapoor stuck her head round the door again and ushered them both outside. Instinctively Adrian touched his phone screen to check for messages again, of course, there was still nothing. He stepped outside and saw the DCI standing next to his car.

'Would you mind telling me if anything looks out of place with your car, DS Miles?'

'Nope, its fine.'

'Nothing strange about it?'

'Nothing.'

She seemed to be studying Adrian's face for a reaction.

'Would you call Lucy Hannigan for me?'

Adrian pulled out his phone and unlocked it. That's when he realised what Kapoor must have been alluding to. His hand began to tremble as his thumb hovered over the icon for Lucy's number. He pressed the number and closed his eyes. The muffled sound of a ringtone came loud and clear and Adrian found himself unable to swallow, unable to think. Not just because he knew beforehand that it would ring from inside the boot of his car, but to stop himself from staring at the pool of blood just underneath his tyres. Lucy was in there.

'Could you open the boot for me, DS Miles,' DCI Kapoor said solemnly. It was not a request but an order.

'I don't understand.' He looked straight at his partner, whose face was full of emotion. Seeing Imogen's look of concern for him cracked his composure and he felt the tears springing out.

'Open the boot,' DCI Kapoor said, her voice cracking, quiet.

'No . . .' He started to back away.

None of them wanted to see what was in the boot.

'Give me the keys then? She could still be alive!' Imogen said frantically.

Imogen held her hand out for the keys but Adrian sprang into action with the suggestion that Lucy might still be alive. He unlocked the boot and it clicked open a little. Adrian's hand rested on the back of the car, almost willing it to stay closed, not wanting to know what was inside. Imogen put her hand on his shoulder and he moved back.

Lucy Hannigan's throat had been at least partially severed. She was saturated in blood; there was no way she was alive. Imogen reached in anyway and pressed her fingers against her throat as Adrian watched, unable to tear his eyes away.

The DCI lowered the boot, leaving it open an inch but hiding Lucy's body from view. Not that it mattered because the sight was burned into Adrian's mind: her curls stuck to her face, a startled look in her eyes and her neck enveloped in so much blood it looked almost like a cowl.

'We're going to have to call this in. I'm going to have to arrest you, DS Miles, and with your track record I absolutely won't be able to go easy on you.' The DCI turned to Adrian, who was still staring at the car boot.

'I didn't do this.' Adrian was shaking, he felt Imogen's hand on his shoulder, an attempt to calm him, to steady him.

'You said earlier your keys went missing?' DCI Kapoor asked.

'Yes. I ordered a new set, Grey has been driving me in.'

'And the belt, when was the last time you saw it?'

'A week ago, maybe?'

'A week?'

'I don't know, I'm not sure.' He could feel his emotions swinging between sadness and anger, panic setting in.

'Breathe, Detective, I know this is hard. I'm just trying to get to grips with the facts here.'

'OK.' Adrian heard the words but nothing much was making any sense at the moment. She was dead, he would never see her again. He suppressed a noise. He would wait until he was alone to grieve.

'Your car, is this where you parked it?'

'Yes. I always park it here.'

'Do you think your neighbours are likely to have seen anything?'

'Everyone keeps themselves to themselves here, I don't know. Ask them!'

'OK, I'm about to call this in. Is there anything else you can think of, DS Miles?'

'I can't think at all.' Adrian needed to sit down, he was feeling light-headed. What the hell was going on? *Oh God, Lucy.*

'I'm going to have to take you in and question you properly about this.'

'This is exactly what Shaw wants,' Imogen said to the DCI desperately.

Chapter 59

The sirens whizzed past the intersection at the end of the road, just past the intricate roundabout system between the main town and St Thomas, the area Adrian lived in. He didn't want to get trapped in that side of town, although he knew it well; it was open and easy for cars to move around in. *Don't think about Lucy.* When the coast was clear, Adrian came out of the doorway he had slipped into and continued to run up the hill towards the town centre. He felt his phone ringing in his pocket, he pulled it out and slipped into another doorway, his thighs grateful for the respite.

'Where are you going to go?' Imogen asked, no time for hellos.

'I don't know. I didn't do it, you know that, right?'

'I would hope that if you did you wouldn't be as stupid as to leave her in your boot parked outside your house.'

'This is Dominic, it has to be. He must have taken

my keys and then put them back. I searched the entire house, they were not in that room.'

Adrian stepped onto the high street which was largely pedestrianised. Getting lost in a crowd was better than running out into the middle of nowhere and being completely exposed.

'Why would he hurt Lucy?'

'He clearly just really fucking hates me and wants to destroy me, who knows?'

'We need to find out what she was looking at.'

'You need to get Gary to have a look at her phone. There might be something on there.'

'Talking of phones, we can probably see if her GPS was activated and if there's a log of where she has been,' Imogen said, enunciating her words; Adrian realised she was warning him to get rid of his phone.

'OK, I have to go.'

'Adrian, I'm sorry about Lucy. I'm going to find out what happened.'

He hung up. He couldn't think where to go. His mind was succumbing to the idea of Lucy not being alive anymore. His temples throbbed with an intensity he hadn't experienced since he had been told he wouldn't be allowed to see his son, when Tom was a small child and Dominic had come into their lives. But why Lucy? Was this just to punish him? To frame him? Did she find something out? Was Andrea safe? Was Tom? These questions settled the question in his mind as to where he should go next. It had been twenty minutes since he had seen Lucy lying there in his car boot.

He was close to the department store where Andrea

worked; he had to go in and see her. He had to hope his instincts would be right. If this was Domenic's doing, then Andrea and Tom weren't safe.

Walking quickly into the make-up department, Adrian looked for Andrea's signature black loose side bun that she usually wore to work; he couldn't remember the exact counter she worked on. He spotted her and went over, aware that he was dressed like even more of a scruff than usual, something Andrea would be sure to notice.

As suspected, she did a double-take when she saw him before looking him carefully up and down. She rang up the sale of a lipstick for the woman she was dealing with. Adrian blinked. Thirty-two pounds for a lipstick?

'Adrian?' Andrea looked confused. He'd never visited her at work, not even when they were together.

'Is there somewhere we can talk?'

'Is everything OK? You've been crying.'

He wiped his hand across his face and felt the wetness; he hadn't even noticed, hadn't allowed himself to notice. He shook his head at her and had to hold his breath to prevent himself from breaking down completely. He didn't have time to fall apart right now. Andrea whispered something to one of the other make-up counter staff and took him gently by the arm, leading him into the staff room at the back of the store.

'What the hell is going on? You look terrible.'

'You need to get Tom and go somewhere. Somewhere no one can find you.'

'What are you talking about?'

'You aren't safe, I didn't realise how unsafe you were until now.'

'You aren't making any sense. What's happened?'

'I've been seeing someone.'

Andrea nodded. 'Lucy. Tom said. He said she's nice.'

'She's dead.'

'What?'

'She's dead and I think Dominic killed her.'

'Dominic? My Dominic?'

He could hear the disbelief in her voice. 'I should have told you, I know I should have but I thought you would just think I was trying to get you and Tom back or something, I'm not, it's not about that. When Tom was doing work experience for Dominic he brought me some paperwork to look into, some of Dominic's bank statements.'

'What the hell?' Andrea's face was a picture of confusion and anger.

'Some things just didn't add up. He thought Dominic was cheating on you, because he was away so much. He was just looking out for you.'

'And you didn't tell me any of this?' she snapped.

'It gets worse.'

'I fail to see how. You encouraged our son to lie to me!' She raised her hands in the air in a gesture of frustration. 'This is what I worry about, Adrian, your moral code is all over the place – you think you're above everyone, like you know things no one else does. You think what you want matters more than what's right.'

'He's not a good man, Andrea, he as much as told me that himself.'

'He told you? Utter nonsense.' Despite her words, Adrian could tell from her expression that this wasn't the first time she had suspected Dominic of something, but it may have been the first time she had admitted it to herself.

'He said he could take whatever he wanted from me and there wouldn't be anything I could do about it. Look at me and tell me I am lying to you. You've never wondered where he goes? What he does? Where he gets his money?'

'Why do you think he killed your girlfriend?' Andrea whispered. Adrian wondered why she wasn't answering any of his questions. Did she just not know the answers?

'I think Lucy found something out about him and I think he's so hell-bent on destroying me that you and Tom may be in danger.'

Andrea paused and thought for a moment, clearly weighing up what he was saying. 'So, what am I supposed to do now?' she said sincerely, her anger dissipating almost completely; she had obviously decided he might be telling the truth.

'You need to disappear until it's safe. Do you have any money in your bank account?'

She nodded. 'Yes, I have some savings.'

'Go to the bank and take out as much cash as you can. Do you have any money on you now?'

'About a hundred pounds.'

'From now on you can only use cash, once they figure out I've spoken to you they will be looking for you and bank cards will be the first thing they check.'

'Who is they?'

'I don't know, his people. And don't tell anyone here that you're going. If there's someone you really trust you could get them to cover for you, but don't tell them why.'

'I'll get some money over the counter then get rid of my cards. I'm with two banks. I have an account Dominic doesn't know about.'

'Give me the cash you have and I'll go and get you a new mobile phone while you go to the bank.'

She went to her locker and tapped in the code, pulling out her handbag and then her purse. She had almost a hundred and thirty pounds.

'I'll meet you at the back door of this place in about ten minutes. Don't contact Dominic, especially not on your new phone. Contact Tom's school right now, go and get him immediately after I give you the phone, get a cab if you have to.'

'OK.' She was taking him seriously at least, she even looked worried.

'If you can change your appearance at all that would help, too. Maybe get rid of your make-up and wear a hat or something.'

'OK.'

'Is there a jacket here I can borrow?' He couldn't run the risk of Dominic or his men finding him before he got to the truth.

'Come with me.' She took him into a room next to the staff room. It was a storeroom full of piles of clothing. 'These are all damaged or have to go back for whatever reason. Just take what you need.'

'OK, thanks, I'll see you in ten minutes.'

He stared at the mountain of clothing and tried to find something in his size, something that looked a little less him. He picked up an oversized sweatshirt and some chinos, and threw them on before grabbing a cap and going to get Andrea a new phone. He hoped this would be enough to keep them safe.

Chapter 60

Adrian took the phones out of the packet and set them up; luckily these days they started out with a little battery so you could use them straight away. He remembered the days when you had to charge them from sixteen hours beforehand; that must have been infuriating for the criminals. He programmed his new number into the phone he'd bought for Andrea and put twenty pounds' top-up on there too so that she'd have enough credit. He hoped she believed how serious this was. He hoped she didn't contact Dominic. He hoped she trusted him.

When Andrea returned, she was wearing jeans and a sweatshirt, items which he didn't think he'd ever seen her in before. When they were together, she had always dressed like she was going to a business meeting; that should have been his first clue that she wouldn't stay with him forever. Now, her hair was down and she wore big white bug shades and an Alice band. He had to admit, he wouldn't recognise her in the street, but he would look at her – she still looked great. She was holding a vinyl messenger bag.

'What are you going to do now?' she asked him.

'I have to stop him. You and Tom aren't safe now. I have to get conclusive proof once and for all. I have to figure out what all this is about.'

She opened her bag, pulled out a bundle of twenties and handed it to Adrian.

'Are you sure?'

'It's only money,' she said, spoken like someone who had money and no concerns about it.

'Have you got enough left?'

'I have eight grand left.'

He handed her the phone. 'Did you contact Tom's school?'

'Yes, from work, I'm meeting him at the bus stop, he's going to come into town. I figured it was safer that way. I told him he needed to be careful. I told him what you said about Dominic.'

'You did a great job.' He put his hand on the back of her head and then kissed her on the forehead. 'You had better go.'

'What about you, Adrian, are you in trouble?'

'No, its fine, I promise I'm not in any trouble. I'm just laying low for a bit,' he assured her. 'Give me your old phone.'

She fumbled around in her bag and pulled her phone out. 'I have photos on there.'

He made sure all the photos had been moved to the external memory, then disassembled it and took the memory card out, handing her the micro SD. He tossed the rest of the phone in the bin.

'Be safe,' Adrian said.

Adrian stuffed his own phone in his pocket and then made his way across town, trying to stay calm. No one knew him, he had a hat and sunglasses on as well as a denim jacket and beige chinos, stuff he wouldn't ordinarily wear. He could only assume that if Dominic did have anyone inside the police, they would know he was AWOL and they would be looking for him by now.

Although food was the last thing he felt like, Adrian went into a supermarket and bought some supplies: food and drink, enough for a couple of days. There was one place he knew would be empty, and although unorthodox, he knew his options were limited, he had to stay free long enough to find out what had happened to Lucy.

Lucy. As his thoughts wandered over her name he caught his breath. He pushed her to the back of his mind, thinking about her now would only slow him down. He walked to the cathedral square. He stood at the very edge of the square and watched from behind a lamp post, waiting for the shops to close, trying not to look suspicious in any way. Most people's faces were buried in their phones if they weren't engaged in conversation with someone else. As the last shopkeeper locked up and left, he put his book back in the supermarket carrier bag and walked casually to the door of the apartment he knew to be empty. He pulled the box of paperclips he had bought at the supermarket out of his bag. One good thing about having a less than moral father was that he would try to impress Adrian by teaching him how to pick locks with everyday objects. Adrian's father had always said there were few things more useful in the world than knowing how to pick a lock. It occurred to Adrian that this was the first time he had listened to any of the advice he had ever been given by his father. It warmed him to think of his father right now, he rarely remembered anything good about him, but this tiny thought made him feel a little less alone. He moved the paperclips in the lock until they clicked and he felt the resistance disappear.

He opened the door, looking before he stepped inside, but no one was paying attention to him. The last time he had been in this flat it was an active crime scene. The family had never sold the flat on and so it sat here empty. It was different to how he remembered it, but it was still furnished. The dust was thick on the surfaces and Adrian daren't go into the bedroom where the body had been found. He pulled the dust sheet off the sofa and lay down on it, facing the window. Taking a deep breath, he pulled the phone out of his pocket and dialled Andrea.

'Hello?' She answered on the first ring.

'It's me. Do you have Tom, are you both OK?'

'Yes, I've got him and we're fine, we got a bus and a train and we're on our way to Torquay.'

'Remember not to tell anyone who or where you are. Use fake names. Don't contact Dominic. No matter what happens. That's really important.'

'I really don't think he would hurt me,' she said, her voice rising at the end, marking her uncertainty.

'Well I know for a fact that he has a gun, so best not take any chances. Can I speak to Tom?'

He heard a rustling on the other end of the phone.

'Dad?'

'Hi boy, are you OK?' Adrian's voice cracked on hearing Tom's voice; knowing he couldn't be there protecting him was almost too much to bear after what happened to Lucy.

'I'm OK, but what's going on? Is this to do with Dominic?'

'Yes. You need to make sure your mother doesn't contact him. Did you get rid of your mobile?'

'Yes.'

'Good, now stay inside as much as possible, you mustn't tell anyone where you are, not even your closest friends.'

'It's OK, Dad, I get it.' Tom paused for a moment. 'I love you.'

'I love you too.' Adrian paused, suppressing the lump that was forming in his throat and composing himself before he spoke again. 'Let me speak to your mother.'

'Adrian?'

'Only use this phone to call me. Promise me, Andrea?'

'I promise.'

'I have to go now. Look after each other.'

'Adrian?'

'Yes.'

'Thank you. I know coming to see me was dangerous for you. I know it's because you wanted Tom to be safe, but you didn't have to be honest with me. I'm glad we're friends again and I really truly am sorry about your – your friend.'

'Bye, Andrea,' he managed to say before putting the phone down, his voice giving way, everything giving way.

This was all his fault. Lucy wouldn't be dead if it wasn't for him. A memory of the blood under his car flashed through his mind, hitting him like a punch to the face. The last memory he had of her alive was as she was leaving his house in a hurry, grappling with her handbag, toast between her teeth, keys in one hand and trying to pull her boot on with the other. She hadn't turned around when she'd said goodbye, in fact all she had said was that she would call him later. He remembered the back of her as she left his house, curls bouncing as usual, door slamming behind her. Desperately he tried to keep hold of that image and not the image of her in the boot of his car. He knew, he knew that memory would replay over and over in his mind. He still had flashes sometimes of the last time he saw his father, disappearing as Adrian had left him, crying at a bus shelter outside a church. For months, he had been left with the feeling that he could still go back to that shelter and his father would be there, frozen in time, crying and begging for forgiveness, begging for another chance, begging for money just to see him through a few days.

His body wanted to shut down for a minute, to avoid the stress of thinking about what had happened, to think about Lucy instead. He wanted to dream about her. If he couldn't have her in life, he wanted her any other way he could find. He turned onto his side and let himself fall asleep.

Chapter 61

Imogen paced while Gary laid out papers on the floor of her living room. The coffee table was strewn with empty beer bottles and screwed-up crisp packets.

'Adrian said it was probably something from this lot?' She had given Gary the bag of papers from Adrian's house. Gary had a duplicate set that he had kept.

She rubbed her chin nervously; they had to figure out where Lucy had been. They matched all the papers to Gary's copy until there was one lone sheet of paper left without a partner. That must have been the piece that Lucy had taken.

'OK, look at this. I remember this one.' Gary handed Imogen a piece of paper then grabbed his laptop. 'That place is the only place I haven't been able to identify.' Gary had highlighted something called GUARDIAN.

'Is there any reference to the Carters, or maybe Theodore Ramsey?'

'Not directly. Everything else as far as I can tell is

kind of circular, but this place has nothing to do with Dominic, the money just goes into there.'

'What does that mean?'

'Well at first I thought it was like a newspaper subscription or something until I saw what he was paying.' He showed Imogen the statement figure with wide eyes. 'He pays over a hundred grand a year to that place!'

'That seems like something a journalist might investigate.'

'Well, I couldn't find anything out about it at all, but I looked into Miss Hannigan, and a couple of years ago, she wrote an article about institutions and private hospitals in the area. She was quite an activist about mental health issues as they related to care and homelessness. It almost seemed personal.'

'It usually is.'

'Well anyway, she mentions a secure hospital called Guardian Angel, it's in the area. I looked it up online.'

'What did you find out about it?'

'The website is pretty basic, expensive and shiny but no real information there.'

'Can you find out if she went there or not? Maybe check her phone and see if there are any GPS logs?' Imogen asked.

'It's possible,' Gary said.

Imogen looked at the statement again. Why would Dominic be paying over a hundred grand a year for a secure hospital? She had only met him once, but he seemed too old to have parents still kicking about. A brother maybe? A secret wife? Her best guess was that

Lucy had recognised the place somehow and gone there to investigate. Whatever she had found out had led to her being killed, mercilessly and brutally. When they'd opened the boot and she'd seen Lucy's mangled body, Imogen had felt like she had been punched. What had been worse was the fact that Adrian was standing next to her. The idea of seeing Dean like this had crossed her mind more than once and she couldn't bear it. She just hoped that Adrian would be able to cope with this. There was no getting over seeing someone you loved like that. Lucy's throat had been cut from ear to ear. Imogen was determined to find out who had done this. For Adrian.

Chapter 62

Gabriel was working out harder than ever. He wanted to stay in his cell and never come out. Maybe he should deliberately get put in Seg again? Maybe that was the answer, as at least he wouldn't have to deal with Asher for a little while if he was in there. Maybe it would give him time to think. Or maybe, he just needed to get this over with. Was stalling going to get him anywhere? What was that likely to achieve? He was just delaying the inevitable. But then there was the future to consider. Gabriel could be in here a long time; was he willing to resign himself just yet? Maybe he could renegotiate?

One thing he did know was that he had run out of time. Asher had alluded to today being the day, that he wouldn't wait any longer.

The familiar sound of the bolt scraping in the lock turned Gabriel's stomach. It was visiting day and Asher was expecting his brother to come. Emma would be there too and he had already threatened to plant something on her. He just had to get through today and then he would think of something, he would stop Asher. Within moments of the door opening, Bailey woke up.

'My mum's coming to see me today.'

'That's nice,' Gabriel said.

'She's made me a new jumper, I told her it was cold here. But I'm going to give it to you.'

'We're not the same size, mate.'

Gabriel kept his eye on the door across the way, no one had gone in, no one had come out. It was only a matter of time though. Did Asher know he was watching? He felt as though Asher knew everything.

'I told her to make it nice and baggy, with longer arms so I could really snuggle into it.'

'You don't have to give me anything.'

'I know, but . . . You're my best friend.'

Gabriel smiled at Bailey, his constant talking had been helping combat the loneliness to the point where he was grateful for it. He was a sweet man. Since coming to prison Gabriel had met some people he suspected he would be friends with forever; he couldn't imagine otherwise. They shared something. They were good people who just did stupid things. Lots of people do stupid things, and in Gabriel's mind, that was no reason to write them off. He had genuine affection for Bailey. Even when he thought of Emma and his relationship with her, it felt false somehow compared to this. There was something so real about the friendships he had formed in here. They all shared the excitement of visiting day, or the crushing disappointment of not having anyone come. They usually shared the mixed feelings around the food, the excitement of dinner time followed by the dissatisfaction with the taste of almost every meal, almost every day. And they all shared the fear of Seg, the fear of being alone with their own thoughts.

When Gabriel looked up, Asher was standing across the corridor, in his doorway, and the feeling of camaraderie he had for his new-found friends disappeared instantly and was replaced with a feeling of hopelessness.

'Go and get a shower and some brekkie. I'll be around in a bit,' Gabriel said to Bailey, trying to remain calm.

Bailey pulled his clothes on and grabbed his bowl. Gabriel walked to the door with him and watched him leave. Across the way, Asher smiled at him and turned and walked inside his cell; Gabriel got the impression he was expected to follow. He looked around, making sure none of his friends could see him, and then walked across and into Asher's cell.

'Welcome.' Asher sat down on the edge of the lower bunk. His pad-mate was nowhere in sight.

'Where's your friend?' Gabriel asked.

'Well, I managed to pull some strings and now I'm all alone. So, you can visit me whenever you want. Or whenever I want.' Asher patted the bed next to him. 'Sit down.'

Asher was smack in the middle of the bed and so the furthest away Gabriel could be was around a foot. Well within arm's reach. Knowing it was visiting day today made Gabriel feel like he had no choice but to comply; the stakes felt more real than ever. He sat down. He could hardly breathe being this close to Asher and when he did he could smell his body odour.

'I said I would meet the guys at breakfast.' Gabriel tried to speed this meeting up.

'Of course.' Asher smiled at him. 'But before you go, I'm going to need a show of good faith.'

'What do you mean?'

'I mean I need to know we're on the same page.'

Asher put his hand on Gabriel's leg, and Gabriel tensed every part of him, trying his best not to react the way he wanted to. Trying his hardest not to punch Asher in the face again. Asher slowly moved his hand upwards. Gabriel daren't look at his face; he didn't want to see the look of desire, lust. He wanted to pretend there was still a way out of this, but as Asher's hand travelled up Gabriel's thigh it became more difficult to hold onto that. His fingers travelled up and brushed against the skin of Gabriel's stomach, stroking the hair beneath his navel. He slid his hand inside Gabriel's trousers and caressed the bone of his hip, his hand moving down towards his groin. Gabriel braced himself, but suddenly Asher removed his hand altogether, standing up and slapping both of his thighs.

'We can save the rest for next time. I'm not in the mood today.' Asher smiled. 'Get out.'

Gabriel stood up and left. He guessed this was the next part of Asher's game, now that Gabriel had acquiesced he would make him wonder when it was coming, trying to get the maximum satisfaction out of watching Gabriel squirm. He had obviously passed the test for today though, which meant with any luck he would be getting a visit after all.

Chapter 63

The room was grey when Adrian woke up. It was the light from outside; he could feel it had been raining overnight. He shivered slightly before sitting up. He didn't remember straight away, it took him a couple of moments before the weight of his situation came back to him. He looked at the phone to see what the time was. It was 7 a.m., he had no missed calls, which he assumed meant that Andrea and Tom were safe. He would call them later in the morning but first he had to think about what to do next. It wasn't until this moment that Adrian realised how few friends he had, how all his friends were in the police. Imogen and Gary were probably going through all of the information they had so far. He was confident that no one at the station would think he had murdered his girlfriend. Had Dominic just done this to slow him down? Then there was DCI Kapoor; her whole reputation was based on weeding corruption out of various divisions, it was a solid reputation. There was only one person he could think of to ask for help from without getting them into trouble.

Dean Kinkaid.

Adrian remembered phone numbers, he had a knack for it which probably came from his inherent distrust of computers and the digital age. He still remembered the phone number of the house he grew up in; sometimes he even dialled it when he was on autopilot but was always met with a slow, steady beep. He remembered Dean's number now.

The line connected. 'Hello?'

'Dean?'

'Adrian, what's going on? Is Imogen OK?'

'You haven't spoken to her then?'

'No, is she in trouble?' Dean asked.

'Imogen's fine. It's me, I'm in trouble. I didn't know who else to call. There is no one.'

There really wasn't.

'What's happened?' Dean said, no hesitation in his voice, ready to help.

'I've been set up. They made it look like I killed someone, they found . . .' Adrian stopped. *Don't think about Lucy.*

'What?'

'In the boot of my car, they found the journalist Lucy Hannigan.'

'Weren't you and her . . .?'

'Yes.' He couldn't talk about her right now 'Do you remember a while ago I asked you if you'd heard of Dominic Shaw?'

'I remember. You think he did it?'

'We linked the Wallis murders back to a charity called KIDSMART – have you heard of it?'

'I have,' Dean said.

'I met the Carter couple once at Dominic Shaw's house. Somehow, he is behind everything. I know this is all tied into that.'

'Where are you? Are you in danger?'

'Safe, for now, but I don't know how much longer I can stay hidden from him.'

'Do you know where this Dominic guy is now?'

Adrian detected a note of urgency in Dean's voice; there was at least something uncharacteristically sharp about it. Imogen had mentioned to Adrian how on edge Dean had been lately, and he could really hear it in his voice now. Maybe calling him had been a mistake.

'Looking for me, I expect,' he said. 'I think the plan was that I get arrested to give him enough time to get out of town or something.'

'Where do you think he would go?'

'That's what I'm trying to figure out.'

'Does Imogen know where you are?'

Something about Dean's questions was setting him on edge, as though he was fishing, as though maybe he would come and find Adrian. If there was one thing Dean Kinkaid wasn't though, it was a grass, but Adrian knew something wasn't quite right. 'No one does. Look, I have to go.' He hung up the phone.

He looked out of the window at the people walking through the cathedral, no one was looking up, they were all just facing straight forward. Out on the green,

Adrian found himself remembering the first time he had seen Lucy there and then later in this same spot for lunch. He felt close to her here; he didn't have to face reality just yet.

Unsure of the neighbours, he put the television on so quietly that he needed subtitles and waited for the news, wondering how far DCI Mira Kapoor was going to take this.

His chest was tight as he lay on the sofa, the local news searing through his head with an update on the murder of the tenacious young reporter with her whole life ahead of her. He couldn't breathe and so he closed his eyes, focussing on blocking out the pain, blocking out the memory of Lucy. This was his fault; he had been responsible for her death and that was something he was struggling to deal with. Dominic wanted to hurt him and so she paid the ultimate price. She would have still been alive if she had never met him.

Chapter 64

Imogen and DI Fraser were en route to the The Elms children's residential home which was listed as a place both of the Locke brothers had stayed in. The tension between them was palpable. He was such a straight arrow guy but he was obviously dying to ask her some questions about Adrian; she could feel the curiosity coming off him. So far, Imogen, Gary and the DCI were the only people who knew what had really happened. Fraser knew more than most, but still DCI Kapoor had made the decision that the less people who knew all the facts the better. Imogen kept her eyes on the road and braced herself for a conversation.

'You know I'm really fond of you and DS Miles, don't you?'

'Thank you, Fraser. I like you too.'

'This is what happens when you don't stick to procedure though. What's happening to Adrian right now. All the secret conversations that you don't think I see, they leave you vulnerable to things like this. One day it's going to come down to someone else's word against yours and you won't have a leg to stand on.'

'I know you don't always approve of the way we do things.'

'I know you guys colour outside the lines sometimes, which is OK as long as you remember where the lines are. It's a slippery slope.'

'I know, Fraser. I'm well aware of the lines.'

'Are you?' He paused and took a deep breath that sounded more like a sigh. 'I know you're in a relationship with a former suspect, one with an impressive reputation and record.'

'You know that?' She was surprised, she thought she had been careful.

'And I'm not about to tell you what to do but . . .'

'There's always a but.'

'The but is – how well do you know this guy? I mean really? How do you know he isn't just going to drag you down with him?'

'He's a good man. He's just had a hard life and he's had to adjust accordingly,' she said with more confidence than she felt. Imogen still hadn't heard from him, she hoped he wouldn't prove her wrong.

'Plenty of people who have had a hard life go on to do something great with it, to help others, to use their knowledge for the good of other people.'

'We aren't that serious,' she lied, hoping to put an end to the conversation.

'I hope not, for your sake, Imogen. You are a real asset to us; I would hate for you to ruin that.'

'I get it.'

'I don't think you do.'

'Have you told the DCI about my relationship?'

'No, I wanted to speak to you about it first, I wanted to try and get through to you.'

'Well thank you for that at least, but there really is no need.'

'I disagree,' Fraser said. He looked at Imogen. 'I haven't told anyone this, but I'm considering moving up north. There's going to be a DI spot opening up here and I think you should go for it.'

She was shocked. 'Me?'

'Yes, you.'

'But Adrian's been here longer.'

'Are you going to hold back just for his sake? Are you going to let your loyalty dictate how you live your life?'

'Is that such a bad thing?'

'I'm just surprised, that's all. You know Adrian would be happy for you.'

'Well it might not even matter if we can't close this case, so frankly, this conversation can wait.' She pulled the handbrake on after pulling into the parking space on the forecourt of the foster home.

'Fine. But think about what I've said!' His words echoed after her as she got out of the car.

Imogen walked across the car park and knocked on the door of The Elms residential children's home. Getting a warrant to enter the Guardian Angel secure private hospital was proving a little more complicated than they had anticipated so the DCI had asked them to chase down this lead instead. Imogen could see that it was once a nice building although all the windows had been replaced with UPVC windows that only opened a short way, presumably to stop any escapes or suicide attempts, which she'd heard were becoming increasingly common. The building itself was quite dirty and unkempt on the outside, with the bin area itself littered with rubbish.

'Does anyone monitor this?' Fraser asked, obviously noticing the same things Imogen had.

'Probably not.'

The door opened a crack and a man's face peeked out from a slither behind a chain.

'Can I help you?'

Imogen and Fraser both held up their warrant cards. He closed the door and they heard him slide the chain in the lock. The door opened again and he stood in the doorway, protectively shielding whatever was behind him. She wasn't sure, but she thought she saw a slight flinch on the man's face. There was something familiar about him.

'Are you in charge here?' she asked.

'I'm the registered manager of this home. My name is Henry Armstrong.'

'We'd like to speak to you, if that's at all possible,' Fraser said.

'Of course, come in.'

He led them through to the kitchen area; it was cleaner than the outside of the house, but very stark and white, not particularly homely or comfortable. The dining table was essentially a school cafeteria trestle table and the seats were black plastic school chairs. All the worktops were clear and there were sliding doors facing out onto the garden where two boys were kicking a football to each other.

'I'm DI Fraser and this is my colleague DS Grey,' Fraser said. 'We would like to have a few words about some former residents of yours.'

'OK, tell me who and I'll see if I can help at all.'

'Chris and Asher Locke,' Imogen offered. She knew far more about this case than Fraser who had been briefed all of twenty minutes ago, and she wasn't about to let him mess up the questioning. 'How long have you been here?'

'This home opened in 1998, and I've been here for the last twelve years.'

'Do you remember the boys in question?'

'I do. I don't know if you know much about this home but we deal with particularly difficult children who can't settle in with foster families for whatever reason.'

'So, you're saying they were difficult?'

'Yes, but no more difficult than any of the other children we have had.'

'When was the last time you had contact with either of them?' Imogen said.

'Oh, it's been a long time. Not since they left.'

'And when was that?'

'I would have to look through my records. We get a lot of children in and out of here, as I mentioned before.'

'How many children do you have in here at a time?'

'Up to eight; the boys we have here are usually quite a handful so our numbers are limited.'

'And do you have any information on the children that were here at the same time as the Locke brothers?'

'Nice try, but I'm pretty sure you need a warrant for that information. These children are extremely vulnerable, most from volatile families. You have to understand I'm just looking out for them. I'm just doing my job.'

'OK then, why don't you tell us a little bit about KIDSMART and how they play a part in all of this?' Imogen decided to change tactics.

Henry Armstrong nodded. 'They assess and refer the children to whichever home they feel best suits the child. For instance, this is a single sex facility and so only troubled boys come here. KIDSMART then monitor the child until they leave the system. Each child has a mentor assigned by KIDSMART to monitor their mental wellbeing. We try and accommodate the child's emotional, psychological and educational needs here.'

'So KIDSMART just allocate children to the relevant homes and a mentor oversees their development? I don't suppose you can tell us who was assigned to the Locke brothers?'

'You are correct, I can't tell you that. KIDSMART also pay for the upkeep of this place too, all the equipment and furniture, they assist with educational trips as well.'

'It's a bit of a mess out the front there,' Fraser said.

'I'm afraid our maintenance man retired and we are currently in the process of hiring someone new.'

'How many staff does this place have?'

'We have twelve professionals that service this facility, most of them on a part-time or temporary basis.'

'Is there any other staff here that might remember the Locke brothers?'

'No. This job can be very hard-going and a lot of people don't last long in it. Bit like banging your head against a wall,' he said. Something about him was bothering Imogen. She didn't know what it was or even if it was anything. Not trusting your own judgment was a pain in the neck.

'Where are the children today?'

'Excuse me?'

'The children, where are they?'

'School, of course.' He held her gaze.

'Well, thanks for your help. May we have a look around?' Imogen walked forward into the house without waiting for an answer, poking her head through the doorways. They passed a music room, a television room and a room with some of the most amazing drawings she had ever seen. She stopped and looked.

'This stuff is pretty amazing. Is it your work?'

Henry had followed them. 'It is – mine and the kids. Art therapy is a big thing. A lot of these kids don't want to talk about their experiences but are quite happy to express them in art form. It's a way for them to connect with a part of themselves that they don't normally allow themselves to access. We try and put on an art show once a year at a local old people's home. They all can get quite into it.'

It was the first thing Henry had said that had made her believe he genuinely cared about what happened to these kids. Everything else seemed a little robotic. Rehearsed.

Imogen didn't wish to intrude any longer, now that she was satisfied that maybe he did care after all. Still, there was something bothering her. What was it? She would have to go and look Henry Armstrong up, she wasn't going to ignore her instinct, no matter how much it felt like she was paranoid.

Chapter 65

At the station, Imogen sat down at her monitor while Fraser disappeared into the DCI's office, no doubt to report back on their encounter at the children's home.

Gary appeared at her side and she jumped.

'Jesus Christ!'

'Nope, just me. It's lunchtime, I thought you might want to grab a sarnie or something?'

'Are you joking? I don't have time to go and grab anything.'

'I'm hungry and, no offence, but you look like you could use some nutrition yourself.'

She pulled open her desk drawer aggressively and pulled out a party bag of miniature chocolate bars. She rooted around inside it until she got hold of a mini Twix and then opened it and shoved it in her mouth. Gary was right, she was hungry and hadn't eaten properly in over twenty-four hours, but anything normal and functional like eating and sleeping felt like a luxury as long as Adrian was God knows where, doing God knows what.

'Have one if you want!' she said. 'I have to keep working. If I'm wrong, then I'll take you to dinner and buy you a chimichanga later on.'

'Let me help at least – watching you on a computer is like watching a fish swimming in treacle.' He leaned over and started tapping the keys over her shoulder. She wasn't about to argue; he could do it in about half the time she could.

'I'm not as bad as Miley.'

'There is that. Right. Shoot, tell me what you want.'

'Henry Armstrong, manager of a children's residential home. Do we have anything on him?'

Gary hit the keys at a speed which Imogen would have thought he was faking if she didn't know better.

'Nothing on the NPC or NDAND. He's never had any police trouble as far as I can see. I'll look in local news, then stretch out to a generic internet search. That's a pretty common-sounding name, so if we go too wide too fast we'll just get bombarded with useless stuff.'

Imogen grabbed the bag of chocolate bars and rolled her chair out of the way so that Gary could sit down; he pulled a chair up and started tapping hard and fast. The sugar rush was quite welcome at this point as she was feeling low after her discussion about Dean with Fraser in the car. She basically had to choose between her job and the man she loved. Something she had always known was on the horizon. At this point in time though she didn't even know where Dean was and so there was no point even thinking about it until he came back. If he came back. She might not have to choose at all. Gary was pulling up articles with the name Henry Armstrong but they were all other Henry Armstrongs. Completely unrelated to this case. Imogen was four chocolate bars into the bag of twenty and feeling decidedly more alert when a picture of the residential children's home whizzed past on the screen.

'Stop! Go back!'

'This one?' Gary went back to the previous article. There was a picture of the local carnival but in the byline was a tiny picture of the house they had visited earlier today.

'Yes. Can you make that picture big?' Imogen pointed to the picture of the house with the group of people standing in front of it. There was Henry Armstrong with his arms around two boys. Three other boys were kneeling in front of him, all smiling at the camera. The article was about a carnival float the boys had worked on, they'd made it look like a Japanese temple from fibreglass and plywood with the classic upturned roof corners. The article said that Henry had a workshop in the care home for creating elaborate artistic costumes to help to focus the kids, and apparently, even the ones who weren't artistically inclined enjoyed the more technical aspects of the work. The kids and the authorities were praising Henry Armstrong's art therapy techniques and he had also done workshops with local charities, focussing on projects that would help the community. Gary tapped away at the computer for a few moments and brought up a larger image.

'Don't tell me it's blurred, Grey,' he interrupted before she had a chance to speak.

'Well, it is. I can't see anything on there!'

'I'm going to use fractal interpolation to compensate for each enlarged pixel, so that it matches the properties of its nearest pixel.'

'As much as I love it when you talk nerdy . . . I have no idea what you just said.'

Gary sighed. 'I'm going to make it less blurry.'

A few moments later he pulled up another image. Imogen stood up, the bag of chocolate falling to the floor.

'What is it?'

'That's not who we interviewed today . . . Me and Fraser. It was someone completely different. I mean, they look alike, really alike, same hair and everything, similar shaped head and physique. At a first glance, then yeah.'

'So, who is this then?'

'That's got to be the real Henry Armstrong, so who the hell did we speak to earlier?' She turned and waved to get Fraser's attention; he was still debriefing DCI Kapoor in her office. Both Kapoor and Fraser looked over and saw her. They came out and headed her way.

'What is it?' Their voices came in unison.

'Fraser, this is an article on Henry Armstrong, I don't know who we spoke to today but it wasn't this guy. We need to go back there.'

'What do you mean?' Kapoor asked.

'This is the home we went to today, but this is not

the man we spoke to earlier. Same name though,' Fraser said excitedly, looking intently at the image on the screen.

'You should go and pick him up then,' DCI Kapoor said.

'I know him from somewhere. I know his face. I just can't place it,' Imogen said.

'Go! I'll send back-up.' Kapoor urged but they had both already reached the door.

Chapter 66

When they pulled up outside the children's home for the second time, there were two boys sweeping the front and putting the rubbish into bin bags. Fraser's remark had obviously left an impression.

Imogen knew they had to move fast before the siren cars alerted Fake Henry to the reason for their return. He opened the door before they had even knocked. There was a resigned smile on his face as he stepped outside.

'That was quick, Detectives.'

'I'm going to have to ask you to come with us,' Fraser said.

'I'll talk, I'll tell you whatever you want and I'll do the time, but if you want me to give you any other names you'll have to make it worth my while. See, I've just been offered a whole lot of money to keep my mouth shut, and as far as I know the sentence for identity theft is nothing compared to what I know. What I know is worth a lot more.'

Fraser took him by the arm and Imogen ran inside. The rooms at the front of the house were empty and so Imogen continued on into the kitchen; on the stove was a mobile phone boiling in water. She ran the cold tap and rinsed it off until it was cool enough to touch. She was pretty sure it was irrevocably damaged but she put it in an evidence bag anyway as she heard the back-up cars pull to a halt outside. If she was going to get the moisture out of the phone she needed to act fast; the seconds counted if there was any chance of retrieving information from it. She opened a couple of the kitchen cupboards until she found a bag of rice and emptied it into the evidence bag.

Through the sliding French doors into the garden, Imogen could see a metal bin incinerator, smoke billowing from the chimney shoot at the top, the fire inside it coming to an end. From the moment they had met him earlier on Fake Henry must have been settling his accounts, burning paperwork and destroying technology. He knew they would be onto him.

When Imogen returned to the front of the house, Fake Henry had been bundled into the back of a police car and the officers were asking the boys to go back inside the house and gather together. There didn't seem to be any other staff members present.

Fake Henry had a perfectly content look on his face, he clearly wasn't concerned about what was coming his way, which suggested that he was used to the police and possibly even accustomed to being arrested. It gave Imogen hope that as soon as he was processed, they would get a hit on his identity.

'I just spoke to the DCI,' Fraser said, following Imogen back into the house. 'Because of who the Carters are, and because of the history of our nick, she doesn't want any search carried out until a warrant has been issued.'

'I don't think that's going to make much difference now anyway, looks like he got rid of everything. I put his phone in a bag of rice though, it was boiling on the stove. I'm not sure it will make much difference.'

'Don't touch anything else.'

'I'd rather get back to the station and question him anyway.' She sighed. 'I'm just going to take a look around – without touching anything – in case it helps us with the questioning at all.'

'Fine, I'll meet you by the car.' He bounded back outside as enthusiastically as ever.

As she looked around, Imogen realised this place would now be closed. She assumed Fake Henry had phoned the Carters to tell them what was happening. Either he was going to take the fall for whatever crimes had been committed, or he was going to tell them everything about the operation, everything he knew anyway. Either way this place wouldn't stay open. If they did get a link to the Carters she wondered how many other residential children's homes would be shut down because of this.

She found what she assumed was his bedroom. It was neat and orderly, not many possessions at all. Imogen didn't touch anything though. She wanted to speak to Adrian, to tell him what she knew now, to ask for his counsel and bounce ideas off him. It killed her that she couldn't help him, didn't know how to. She wondered where he was, what he was doing, if he was OK or if he was in danger. She wanted to tell him that their instinct had been right, that the Carters were in neck deep. In what? She didn't know. How did it connect to Dominic? What did this have to do with Lucy? Was it even all connected at all? She needed to see the list of names for the Guardian Angel care home, and then she needed to speak to Adrian. Would she be able to slip away from Fraser? She checked around her and pulled her phone out of her pocket. She rolled her eyes and stared at the contact she'd brought up on the screen. The only person who could help her right now.

'Imogen?'

'Dean, have you heard about Adrian?'

There was a pause on the other end of the line.

'I have. Is that why you phoned?'

'I'll call you later.' She heard so many things in his voice, but mostly she heard that he was desperate for her to tell him that she would forgive him. She hung up before he had a chance to tell her anything that might put her in a difficult position or make her feel guilty. She knew she wasn't about to give up her job for him, and the guilt of that was crushing her.

Chapter 67

Fake Henry wasn't making things easy for them. He had all but burned his fingertips off. Who does that? Imogen asked herself, but she already knew the answer: someone who doesn't want to be identified, someone with a past, someone who has too much to hide. Fraser sat back with his arms folded, trying his best to look intimidating. He had given Imogen the reins on the interview.

'I told you, I want full immunity.' Fake Henry had folded his arms.

'For what?'

'I'll tell you once you grant me immunity.'

'Will it lead to any arrests?'

'I should fucking hope so.'

'Why don't you give us a clue?'

'Well I can tell you who killed that old couple in the video for a start.' He grinned confidently. 'Oh yeah, and a few others. Things you probably don't even know you're looking for yet.'

'In the Wallis murder, they painted a symbol on the wall, what's all that about?'

'Dreadful painting that was. I mean, it was terrible what they did, but the artwork was pretty bad too, don't you think?'

'No. It honestly hadn't crossed my mind.'

'I know about another murder too.'

She stared at his face, the familiarity gnawing at her, trying to let her know that this wasn't paranoia. *You know something. You know something.*

'We don't have any other open murders now,' Imogen said slowly.

'I never said it was open. You want the same person for it as you want for the Wallis killings. Real little machine, he is.'

'What murder are you talking about?' Fraser finally interrupted.

'You've already got someone banged up for it anyway.'

Imogen kept looking at him; his eyes were calm, self-assured, as if he thought they had no chance of figuring out who he was. She racked her brains for other names and faces involved in the case but nothing was coming to her. Until there was something, but she needed to check she was right. She stood up and nodded towards the tape.

'Interview suspended at sixteen oh seven,' Fraser said just before turning the recording off.

'I'll be right back.'

Imogen ran to her desk which was a hair's breadth away from being a rubbish dump. She pushed and pulled the folders around until she got the one she wanted then hurried back to the interview room and sat down, a huge smile on her face. Fake Henry looked at the file.

'Let the record show that DS Grey has re-entered the room. Interview resumed at sixteen ten,' Fraser said.

'What's that?' Fake Henry feigned ignorance.

'I knew I had seen you before,' Imogen said triumphantly, 'I just couldn't place you.'

She opened the file and put it on the desk. She didn't need a lie detector to see that the mere appearance of any kind of file made him nervous.

'We've been looking for you, Theodore Ramsey,' she grinned. The reason Fake Henry was so familiar to Imogen was that she had spent days staring at his files. 'Or should I say, Bricks.'

He stiffened and clenched his jaw. She could tell he was trying to think of a way out of it by the way his eyes were darting around, but he didn't seem to be a quick thinker. Eventually, he sighed and relaxed his shoulders.

'I heard from some of my friends that you'd been looking for me, so when you turned up I kind of knew I was in trouble.'

'So, where's the real Henry Armstrong?'

'It'll come to you.'

Imogen smiled at him, they had knocked some of the wind out of his sails by discovering his real identity so his attempts to annoy her were almost amusing. He was trying to claw back some power because he was losing any leverage he had. She thought back to when they had been looking for him, before the murders, before anything.

'Was Henry Armstrong the body in the signal box?'

He winked. 'I want immunity.'

Chapter 68

Gabriel had been left alone for the time being; there had been a few passing remarks from Asher on how tonight would be the night but then nothing. He was trying to make him crazy, trying to break him. There was a certain element of secondary school bullying to the whole scenario, and the question now was how to deal with the bully. Gabriel was well used to bullies and he knew that, ordinarily, a swift kick to the bollocks and the facade would disappear. With every passing moment, Gabriel was feeling more and more defiant, unable to reconcile with what he had agreed to do. Maybe it was time someone stood up to Asher.

There was a prisoner on the block called Craig who had a history of starting fires; he also had a history of touching blokes up in the showers. Gabriel had instructed Bailey on what to do and Bailey was more than eager to play a part in the game. He wanted Asher dealt with as much as Gabriel, although for different reasons. Being Gabriel's pad-mate put Bailey at more risk than most.

Kenzie was due out of D-wing tomorrow, he wasn't safe as long as Asher was around. Sparks still had a long way to go before he was let back onto the wing, his lung had been punctured during the altercation and he was still on the mend. But he'd testified that Kenzie was not the person who attacked him and threatened to make an official allegation against a guard unless Kenzie was cleared of the charge and moved back onto B-wing.

When the cells opened for association, Gabriel marched straight over to Asher's cell opposite and walked in. His irritating friend left immediately. Gabriel remained close to the door. For a brief moment, Gabriel was sure Asher was surprised to see him. He tried not to relish the feeling of pride that evoked.

'To what do I owe the pleasure?'

'I need some assurances.'

'That's not really how this works.'

'Well I need you to promise me that Kenzie and Sparks will be safe in here.'

'They will be safe from me – I can't speak for anyone else.'

'Well, that's enough for now.'

'And what else?'

'You tell your brother to back off, Emma is off limits too.'

'You do realise this is an ongoing arrangement? As long as I'm getting what I want, your slutty little girlfriend is safe.'

'Fine.'

Gabriel left and walked back to his cell with the same confidence with which he had strolled into Asher's. As soon as he was inside though, he rushed over to the toilet and threw up. He couldn't fuck this up, he had to make sure he wasn't in any actual danger when he was alone with Asher. If everyone did what they were supposed to then he would be safe. He just needed to follow the plan.

Chapter 69

The immunity deal that was offered to Theodore Ramsey was subject to a few conditions, the first being that his information led to the arrest and conviction of the gang responsible for the murder of Patricia and Alfred Wallis that took place on the thirteenth of July, including the whereabouts of Chris Locke who had been as elusive as quicksilver. The second condition was for information on the whereabouts of the real Henry Armstrong; and the final condition was that his immunity did not cover murder.

'So, tell us, Theodore, what do you know?' Imogen began.

'I'm better with direct questions.'

'Fine. What happened to Henry Armstrong?'

'They killed him, because he didn't want to play along anymore. Maybe he grew a conscience, giving the kids dodgy jobs from the Carters was beneath him all of a sudden. Bit late if you ask me, he had been doing their dirty work for over ten years.'

'Who is they?'

'The Carters.'

'How did you end up being Henry Armstrong? Whose idea was it?'

'There was some charity do, a while back, for the homeless people, and we all got free food and stuff. Anyway, someone said that me and Henry could pass for brothers. It was an off-the-cuff remark, but it got us thinking.'

'So, you knew Henry?'

'He came and did some of his art therapy stuff with us at the church. It was great.'

'So, who did the Carters hire to take care of Henry?'

'That Locke boy and his mates.'

'Do you know which friends?'

'One of them was called Troy or something.'

'Trey?'

Theodore nodded. 'That's him, tattoo on his neck. Right little twat.'

'And you said it's because Henry didn't want to play along anymore. Play along doing what?'

'Recruiting new ones – why do you think they want the troublemakers in The Elms? Kids like that are starving for attention and affection, they're desperate to prove themselves. If you don't patronise them then it's pretty easy to get them onside.'

'And you were OK with that?' Imogen asked.

'Why not? Because I'm a homeless guy? Not anymore. I got sick of being patronised, too. I wanted to be useful again, not just pitied and given handouts. I was given an opportunity and I took it.'

'The opportunity to become Henry Armstrong? How did that come about?'

'When I was in prison – I met a guy in there who connected me with the Carters, told me I looked just like Henry Armstrong and I might be able to make some money. They offered me his position.'

'And you just replaced him without anyone noticing?'

'Easy to make someone no one gives a shit about disappear. Not so easy to get rid of someone like Henry Armstrong. People were asking questions, they just needed someone in there to be him to divert suspicion.'

'No one figured it out?'

'I got left alone mostly, apart from the other staff who are all on the Carter payroll as well. A couple of visiting officials inspecting the health and safety on the property. As for the boys, it wasn't difficult for me to get them on board, they know how things work around here.'

'What about Dominic Shaw? What do you know about him?'

'I have no idea who you're talking about.'

Imogen watched his face; there seemed to be no reaction at all to Dominic's name.

'You said you got introduced by someone in prison. Who was that?'

'Locke's brother. We kind of hit it off in there. He oversaw their little gang before.'

'Why did you agree to this?'

'I was sick of the disrespect. Do you have any idea the amount of times people would try and film me when I was on the street?'

'What do you mean?'

'Like I must be desperate just because I slept in a park. Some man would come and give me his coat while his mate photographed it and put it on the internet with some headline about how people treat the homeless – and – oh look what happens when someone is nice to him – look how happy he is. Nothing is private, nothing is sacred – people don't take photos anymore, they take selfies, they take pictures of their coffee or their lunch, they truss their kids up and whore them for likes. People don't own their own faces anymore.'

Theodore had started to get animated, upset. Imogen suspected he had an agenda of his own. He reminded her of her mother briefly, when she was having a manic episode: talking fast, connecting things that weren't necessarily connected. Maybe she needed to push him further, he was being forthcoming but it was all a little too calculated. She wanted him to let go.

'That bothers you?'

'Everyone wants to be an internet sensation; people are dead inside these days. Everything is fake. You can't believe anything you see anymore. The world is a massive marketing machine designed to make you feel a certain way so you buy into certain things.' He spat the words out.

Suddenly Imogen wondered whether she had the missing piece of the puzzle.

'So, was the Wallis video your idea?' Imogen asked.

'It's all very well doing things for money but some things are worth more than that. I thought the gang deserved to be recognised for what they did. I may have asked how far we could push it before people stopped watching. The answer is – it doesn't matter – we are spectators and spectacles. We're not people anymore. We had a conversation and I expressed some opinions, then after I was told who the next target was I may have suggested a social media experiment of my own. It was overly theatrical and the Carters were not very impressed but I thought it was a bit genius. It got people's attention.'

'And you received a payment from the Carters?'

'Yep, and from what they gave me, I gave half to the boys.' He seemed proud.

'And "the boys" who killed the Wallis couple also killed Henry?'

'Correct. But I was only brought on board after Henry was killed. I took his place but I didn't have anything to do with his murder.' He looked down, almost smirking. 'But I did suggest how to get rid of the body.'

'What do you know about the masks?'

'Henry made them in one of his art classes with the kids for fun, they were just in the cupboard in the workshop. The kids used them in one of their little shows years ago but they came in pretty handy for the video. He was an incredible artist.'

'Was Henry going to talk to the police?'

'I think the idea was to stop him before he had a chance to, but you should ask the Carters about that.'

'Do you know anything about the murder of Lucy Hannigan?'

'No, never heard of her, but if it's connected to the Carters I bet you ten to one that Chris Locke did it.'

'What about Dominic Shaw?' Imogen tried again.

'I'm afraid I don't know who that is. As I said.'

'We haven't finished this line of questioning yet Mr Ramsey, but we need to corroborate some of the things you have been saying before we can continue.'

Imogen left the room, her head spinning. Even though she knew she couldn't have put all of this together before this, she was annoyed at herself and all the time that had been wasted. She was annoyed that she hadn't recognised Bricks as soon as she saw him. She wondered what would be next. She still wasn't sure how Dominic connected to all of this, and Henry genuinely hadn't registered any recognition when she mentioned his name. Dominic would see that his plans for Adrian hadn't worked; the DCI wasn't going after him the way Dominic had planned. So, what next? This did seem to be more than just a grudge that Dominic had against Adrian, there had to be a reason behind it. As far as she could see, Dominic had been coming for Adrian for a long time. They just needed to find out why.

Chapter 70

Gabriel waited for the door to open for morning association. His life was spent waiting for doors to open, only to be trapped in bigger rooms with more doors; he felt like the smallest of the matryoshka dolls. Bailey sat on the bed wringing his hands. Gabriel felt an overwhelming sense of protectiveness over him and he couldn't think why. Maybe it was because Bailey let him. One thing was for sure though, he was grateful for his pad-mate. He had given him something to be strong for, something to focus on. He was someone to protect other that himself. He had given Gabriel some control back.

'You need to relax.'

'Sorry, Gabe. I'm really sorry.'

'Look, it's going to be fine, I promise. After today, everything is going to be fine.'

'Sparks is back on B-wing today. I hope he's OK.'

'Apparently, his eye is all fucked up so he has to wear

a patch for a little while but it will get better. We should look out for him though. I don't trust Asher. Thank God Sparks didn't die.'

Gabriel walked over to the door and balled his fists. He looked across the parapet, but for a change Asher wasn't loitering in the window of the cell door waiting for Gabriel to look out. It occurred to him that Asher spent an awfully long time thinking about him and that fact alone actually gave Gabriel a form of power over Asher. As long as Asher knew where Gabriel was going, then he would turn up eventually. Asher always made sure there was no one else around, always made sure it was as intimidating as possible for Gabriel. Well, Gabriel would do the hard work for him by making absolutely sure they were alone today. The door opened and moments later a stony-faced Sol turned up and handed a bundle of something to Gabriel. It was a tea towel.

'Are you sure about this?' Sol asked.

'I'm sure.'

Gabriel grabbed his bath towel and put the tea towel inside it. He stepped out of his cell and walked slowly towards the showers. He had to make sure Asher saw him going there. Out of the corner of his eye, he saw Asher coming back from the canteen with his breakfast. Gabriel nodded to him and showed him the towel, in case it was unclear where he was going. He turned to see Sol and Bailey looking out of his cell, he nodded at them too.

When he reached the showers, there was one person there. He had seen the guy around before but he had nothing to do with him; Gabriel hoped he wouldn't hang around. Gabriel started to undress and before he was done the other guy had gone. He took a deep breath. This was it. He had to keep his nerve, he absolutely had to.

Gabriel had to accept living in prison, but he knew he couldn't tolerate another moment with Asher breathing down his neck. He was pushing Gabriel too far without understanding the beast that he was unleashing. Gabriel had spent years under the influence of a pusher, someone who prodded and prodded; he had spent years with it, learning how to push back, knowing the more you give, the more they push and so it was best not to give an inch. He had to get Asher off his case once and for all. He wasn't afraid of what Asher would do to him anymore, he was more afraid of what he would do to the people around him.

He felt his presence before he saw him. Gabriel looked at the clock on the wall just outside the showers; just past it stood Hyde and Johnson, watching the queue for breakfast and making sure there were none of the usual morning squabbles. In the corner of his eye he saw Asher getting undressed. Gabriel wet the tea towel that was in his hand and wrapped it tightly around his knuckles. He kept his back to Asher, his skin crawling at the thought of what Asher wanted. He felt a hand on his shoulder, moving up his neck and grabbing fistfuls of his hair. Asher tilted Gabriel's head backwards and kissed him. The taste of Asher's mouth on his. It was all Gabriel could do to stop himself from throwing up.

Suddenly, shouting came from outside the showers and Gabriel opened his eyes. The men in the breakfast queue were whooping and shouting at something going on. Panicked, Hyde and Johnson ran from their spot further into the wing. Asher put his hand on Gabriel's shoulder again and turned him around, licking his bottom lip and slowly moving his eyes down Gabriel's body. Before he had a chance to look anywhere past his stomach, Gabriel had swung his fabric-clad fist at Asher's jaw and he was propelled back against the half wall that protected their modesty from the general populous while they were in the showers.

'What the fuck?' Asher wiped his lip that still held the glimmer of a smirk, stunned at the sight of his own blood on his fingers.

Gabriel punched him again before he had time to steady himself. Asher looked around, but there were no guards in sight. The commotion in the servery was still going on – it didn't look like the guards would be back anytime soon. Gabriel's fist came down on him again and he fell, the sound of either his elbow cracking or the tile beneath it echoing in the showers. Asher's blood mingled with the water on the floor and followed the pathways between the tiles to the drains as he struggled to move. Gabriel got down on one knee, aware of but ignoring his own nudity, and brought his fist down again and again on Asher, whose eye was now swelling shut. He let out a guttural scream and Gabriel punched him again, this time dislodging his teeth from the gums. Asher spat onto the ground next to him, his head lolling as he tried to get some traction to stand up.

'You are never going to hurt anyone else, you prick,' Gabriel hissed at Asher.

'You won't get away with this.' Asher's voice was weakening.

'Maybe not, but it feels good. You don't have any power over me.'

'Are you sure about that?' Asher laboured for breath and spat onto the tile. 'You want to know why I own you?'

'Why?'

'Because I'm the reason you're in here.'

'What?'

'I killed that man in the signal box, he was dead long before you even went in there.'

'What the hell are you talking about? You were in here when I got here!' He looked down on Asher.

'I got picked up for assault three days after his death.'

'When?' Gabriel hissed.

'Back at the beginning of June. A couple of weeks later, you turn up.' He grinned

Unable to process what he was hearing and unsure if Asher was even telling the truth, Gabriel felt the adrenaline surge through him, anger taking him over completely. He grabbed Asher by the hair and pulled him over to where the water from the shower head fell.

Gabriel thumped the button and the water started running onto Asher's bloody face. Gabriel got beside him and wrapped the wet tea towel across his face, stretching it across his mouth and letting the water pound against it. Asher flailed and kicked, scratching at Gabriel's arms. He could feel his hands tighten and his arms stiffen as Asher thrashed around, his movements increasingly jerkier as he struggled for oxygen.

'What the hell are you doing?' Johnson was standing in the doorway.

The water stopped and Gabriel released the towel. Asher's body relaxed for a second before he coughed uncontrollably; he saw Johnson and reached his hand out to him. Johnson stared at them, dumbfounded.

'I had to do something. He was never going to stop,' Gabriel said. If Johnson put him in Seg again then it was over, Gabriel would never get this chance again, he had failed. It couldn't end like this. He looked at Johnson, waiting with bated breath for him to detain him and put the wing on lockdown.

'Fucking pussy,' Asher spluttered, coughing up blood. 'It doesn't even matter, you're going to spend years in prison because of me. Whatever happens here, I win. I killed the man that you're doing time for, I smashed his skull in. When my brother hears about this he's going to do the same to your girlfriend.' He sputtered and turned to Johnson. 'And your wife.'

'Well – what are you waiting for?' Johnson looked at Gabriel.

'What?'

'Fucking finish him! If he gets out of this then he'll make your life twice as fucking unbearable. You can forget about him asking you nicely as well, he'll get all his big skinhead friends to hold you down and take turns on you.'

'No.' Asher coughed as he said it, eyes bulging with fear, the reality of his situation finally hitting home. His voice was almost gone, the water had damaged his throat, he couldn't scream .

'I'll make sure no one knows it was you,' Johnson said quietly to Gabriel before looking over his shoulder to check no one else was around.

Gabriel knew Johnson was right, as soon as Asher had the upper hand again he would take it. It wasn't enough to scare him, he would probably look back on this encounter as a win, as the time he broke Gabriel and made him a monster. Gabriel grabbed the tea towel again.

'If you fuck me over on this, Johnson, I'm taking you down with me,' Gabriel said.

He folded the towel on the diagonal to make it longer and wrapped it around Asher's neck, pulling it tight and tying it into a double knot as hard as he could. Asher thrashed and tried to get free but he couldn't get any traction. Gabriel pulled Asher towards the corner of the cubicle and then turned the water on again, washing any remaining blood off his own hands and feet as Asher clawed at the knot around his neck to no avail. The wetness of the tea towel had made it immovable, rigid, even Gabriel couldn't have undone it in time. He walked out of the shower stall, leaving Asher kicking against the tiles.

Johnson stood at the door, watching out onto the wing. Gabriel put his clothes back on and glanced back at Asher, Asher's eyes were still open but unconnected to anything. He was dead. Gabriel rushed out of the showers. There was a fight at the end of the wing, Johnson nodded to Gabriel and dashed to help out. It would be better if someone else found the body anyway. Bailey had walked into one of the unmanned cells and set fire to one of the mattresses to create a distraction. It must have only been a small fire, which was put out almost immediately but Bailey had obviously been seen doing it and so the owner of the cell had come back and tried smacking Bailey around, which is when the guards had interjected for a second time.

Back in his cell, the commotion died down outside quickly after the man who attacked Bailey was carted off to Seg, the guards not willing to believe that Bailey would start a fire. Bailey wasn't a known troublemaker and he certainly wasn't known for starting shit with other prisoners. Gabriel had deliberately picked the cell of a gobshite, someone who would kick off and cause a commotion, hoping that Bailey would come out of it unscathed.

The call for lockdown happened about ten minutes later. Gabriel had spent that ten minutes furiously rubbing his hair with a towel, trying to get it as dry as possible. If there was an investigation into Asher's death that would be the most common sense thing to look for: someone wet. The weapon was a generic blue check tea towel, of which the prison had hundreds. Hopefully the water had washed away the bulk of the evidence, plus a prison shower would have no shortage of random DNA lurking around. He just had to wait now and hope for the best; at least now he knew he was where he belonged. Gabriel had felt sick thinking about Asher's words. He had spent so long feeling guilty over the death of the man in the signal box and it wasn't even him. Knowing that Asher had had that over him the whole time, that the only man that could get him out of prison was now dead: the thought made him want to vomit. At least now he couldn't deny he deserved to be here.

Chapter 71

They had finally got hold of Chris Locke. After keeping eyes on his house proved to be an exercise in futility, he was eventually picked up for acting suspiciously around the Princesshay shopping centre. Chris Locke was an entirely different story to Theodore Ramsey. He was agitated, uncomfortable and nervous. He bit at the skin around his nails and kept his eyes on the floor. Imogen watched him shifting around in his seat in the interview room. He reminded her of her childhood friend's pet rabbit, an otherwise sweet and friendly animal who became quite hostile when poked repeatedly with a stick.

'Bricks has told us everything, Mr Locke. He told us you killed both Henry Armstrong and the Wallis couple.'

'He paid me to do it.'

'In exchange for his testimony he has been granted immunity from prosecution.'

'Well I want immunity or I ain't talking.'

'We'll have to see what we can do,' Imogen said. 'You can have a lawyer here, you know?'

'Fuck lawyers, let's just get this over with.'

'The judge may consider leniency if you tell him anything that we can use against the Carters.'

'I don't know who they are.' He looked down at his hands, avoiding eye contact.

'The people who run the residential children's home you lived in with your brother, The Elms,' Imogen said. She knew he was lying.

He went silent.

'Tell us about Henry Armstrong then?' Fraser said.

'I was told he would be easy, he was sick. He couldn't run or nothing. We chased him through the park and then we killed him with a cricket bat.'

'So, he was dead when you put him in the signal box?' Imogen asked.

'Well dead, yeah.'

'Were you with Trey at that time?'

'Who?'

'Trey Wilson. Ramsey already told us about him so you won't be grassing anyone up.'

'Yeah, Trey was there.' Chris shrugged.

'Do you have any proof that Henry Armstrong was dead when you put him in the signal box?' Imogen was hopeful that he would say yes; this would change things for Gabriel Webb, she hadn't forgotten her promise to help him. Putting Gabriel inside had never felt right, he was a good kid at heart. It looked like she might get a chance to put that right.

'We put him somewhere else and then we had to

move him. Bricks suggested the signal box, said he knew how to get in and how to make sure no one else could. Told us he knew how to avoid the station cameras. We moved the body there about three weeks before the fire. The place usually gets filled up with people burning up or just sleeping rough. We thought it wouldn't be long before it caught fire.'

'Because you covered the place in accelerant?'

'Yeah. But no one came, so Trey said he would sort it.'

'So, setting Gabriel Webb up was no accident then?'

'It wasn't about him; it was about getting rid of the body.'

'Is that why you took Gabriel and Emma there that night?'

'That was Leanne's idea, she wanted to look badass in front of them.'

'Did she know about the body?'

'No.'

'Your brother, Asher – why is he threatening Gabriel Webb?'

'Because he's bored, and in prison, fuck knows – he's more messed up than me. He asked me to drop in on Emma and tell her that her boyfriend needed to do something for him. So I did. He's made me threaten some other people, too.'

'Who?' Imogen said, surprised that Chris Locke would give up his brother so quickly.

'One of the guards' family, I had to take pictures and he's been getting the guard to smuggle drugs in for him.'

'Anyone else?'

'Not that I can think of, not now.'

'What about Lucy Hannigan. Did you kill her?'

Chris shook his head. 'No, I don't know who she is.'

Considering how forthright this man-child had been so far, Imogen was inclined to believe him, it was time for a change of tack.

'Let's talk about the symbol for a minute.'

Chris shifted in his seat. 'What about it?'

'Why did you draw it?'

'Just thought it would make it more scary.'

'Why that symbol particularly?'

'No reason, just one I knew I could draw.' He fidgeted, picking at the skin around his thumb anxiously.

'Where do you know it from?'

'Nowhere, it's just a symbol.' He was becoming agitated.

'You don't know it from a place you may have been to? Did you see it somewhere else maybe?'

'Like where?' he said suspiciously.

'You can tell us.'

'Why? So you can fit me up for even more stuff?'

'What do you mean?'

He started chewing on the skin around his thumbs again and looked at Imogen who was doing her best not to look too hard; she got the impression that wasn't the way to handle this man. He took a deep breath and folded his arms. His next words all came out in a rush.

'I swear I didn't kill them, they were dead when I arrived! I got my mate to give me a lift over there so I could ask them to get me out of the country or something – help me hide – and I would keep quiet about them. After you chased me with the other guy I knew it was only a matter of time before I got banged up again.'

Imogen frowned, confused. 'Who are you talking about?'

'Them! The Carters! I went over, the gate to the drive was open, so I went up to the house, and when I looked in the window I could see they were dead.'

Imogen glanced over to the two-way mirror, she imagined the frenzy behind the glass. They had no idea the Carters were dead, no idea that was even a possibility. DCI Kapoor had ordered them to stay away under pain of disciplinary action since their visit four days ago, until they had been through the financials and got enough to apply for a search warrant. She composed herself, not wanting Chris Locke to know they were caught off guard.

'What's that got to do with the symbol?' she said.

'It was on their floor, like those roman pictures. A mosaic.'

That was the house Dean remembered, the house he had been taken to as a child and used as entertainment. Had Dean found them? Imogen cast her mind back to the time when she visited the house with Adrian, she would have noticed the symbol, wouldn't she? Then she remembered the striking rug they had in the entrance, it must have been under that. Had Dean done this? She pushed the intrusive thought away for now, she would think about it later.

'So, it was the Carters that the symbol related to? Why did you use it in the Wallis video?'

'It just came into my mind. The Carters had a few parties at the house that we used to go to,' he said in a tone that sent chills up Imogen's spine. She remembered what Dean had said about the parties.

'Tell me about those parties.'

Chris looked very uncomfortable. 'They filmed them. The videos are probably in that house somewhere. I'm not going to talk about it.' He stared at his hands.

'Why did they keep these films, do you know?'

'I was told that if I didn't do what I was supposed to then people would see them. We all were. They gave us money, but it wasn't about the money. We had no choice but to do what they told us. I didn't want anyone to see any of those films with me in.' He sucked in a deep breath and rubbed his eyes. When he looked up they were red and wet.

'And what were the films of?' Imogen asked, hating herself for it. She could see how difficult it was for him to tell her this.

'Things that I wouldn't want anyone to see. The people who went to those parties . . . liked kids. They would do stuff to me and Ash. He had it bad, he was never the same after. He went mental at the thought of anyone finding out what they did to us.' He paused. 'There's something else.'

'What?'

'I went to the house a few days ago – the day I found them dead – to get some money off them. There was another bloke there, he was shouting at them so I left. He looked a bit mental. When I came back they were dead and he was gone.'

'Who was the man?' Imogen's heart thumped as she asked.

Chris shook his head. 'I didn't know him, but he knew his way around the place, so I'm guessing he knew the Carters. He had a hammer in his hand.'

'What did he look like?' Imogen asked. There was a sinking feeling in her stomach.

'Tall guy with short, browny-blond hair. He was pretty built.'

'White?'

'Yeah, but quite tanned skin.'

It might not have been Dean, there were lots of other people who would fit that same description. That's what she was telling herself anyway. She took a deep breath.

'So, you only committed the murders because you were blackmailed into them?' Even though she had seen the video of what they had done to that poor Wallis couple, she couldn't help feeling some compassion for this man, who behaved like a young teen, angry and volatile.

'Does it make any difference?'

Imogen thought about Dean, how he'd had someone looking out for him, how that had helped him. Maybe that was the difference Chris Locke needed in order to be able to stop, maybe he just needed someone to give a shit. But then if Dean did kill the Carters, then maybe none of it made any difference at all.

'I think if you had a lawyer they might help you to get the right sentence, Mr Locke.'

'I want a lawyer then.'

'I'll get someone to make a call for you.' She stood

up. The interview was over for now, and that's how she wanted it; the poor kid had incriminated himself enough but it was obvious that he had been groomed and manipulated into doing what he'd done. She felt her phone vibrate in her pocket. It was Dean.

Chapter 72

Imogen walked into the Dolphin pub; it was one of a chain that constantly had two-for-one offers on meals and drinks so it was always busy. The football was showing on the screen in the corner and most people's eyes were directed towards that. Making her way through the bar, Imogen looked around until she saw him.

Adrian was sitting in the corner, in a quieter booth near the toilets. He was sporting more stubble than usual and a baseball cap too, but she knew it was him. He stood up as she approached and she put her arms around him. Admittedly hugging was not something they ever really did but anything else would have felt strange at this point. She was very happy to see him. They held on for a little longer than was comfortable and reluctantly pulled away. It wasn't until Imogen tried to speak that she realised she was crying.

'It's so good to see you.' She kissed him on the cheek and then sat down. 'I'm so sorry, Adrian.'

'Do you know anything yet? Do you know what happened to Lucy?'

'Not yet, but we are in the process of getting Gabriel Webb released. The man in the signal box was already dead when the fire was started. We haven't told Gabriel yet though, we need some concrete evidence. I don't want to get his hopes up.'

'That's brilliant news.'

'The people we've questioned don't seem to know anything about what happened to Lucy, and they are talking, so I don't know what's going on there yet.'

Adrian sighed. 'As much as I'm trying not to think about it, this has to be something to do with Dominic.'

'We think Lucy went to a secure hospital for people with extreme disabilities just before she died. I took a copy of some paperwork they found hidden in her car – here it is.' Imogen pulled it out of her pocket and handed it to him. 'By all accounts the hospital is like Fort Knox. They're heavily protected by an army of lawyers, we're trying to get a warrant to go inside. There's nothing we can do at this point, but if she was there then that could be why she was killed. It must have happened immediately after; CCTV in the surrounding area of the hospital seems to support that and it would explain why she was on Langaton Road.'

Adrian frowned as he looked down the list, his finger coming to rest on a name.

'Who the hell is James Shaw? Same surname as Dominic, but I don't recognise the first name at all.' Imogen could see Adrian's mind ticking over. 'People with extreme disabilities? And a Shaw? It must be a family member, it can't be his father, so maybe a brother? But why keep it hidden?' Adrian had spent all of his time going over everything he knew about Dominic already. He hadn't come across anything that suggested a family beyond Andrea and Tom.

'I don't know, Miley, I really don't.'

'Where exactly is the place?'

'I'm not going to tell you that. If you go there and do something stupid you will get caught.'

'I need to know what happened. I need to know why they killed Lucy.'

'You think maybe she got too close to something?'

'I have to think that, because if she was just used as a pawn to set me up for murder – how do I live with that?'

'You can't control what other people do, Miley. Whatever the reason is for killing her it won't ever be your fault. You can't take that on yourself.'

'Tell me where it is, I promise I'll be careful.'

Imogen didn't want to add any fuel to Adrian's fire, just like with Dean, she couldn't save Adrian from himself – she could just be there for him when it all went wrong.

'Just let the DCI handle it. She's got your back. There's proof you reported your car keys missing, and Gary has been going over everything you two have found together. If you do something silly and get arrested, it'll ruin your career. Kapoor hasn't officially named you as a suspect either; she has a lot of pull, Miley, and so far, no one is giving her shit over it.'

'Are you sure?'

'I like her, I've decided to trust her.'

'I hope you're right. But I need you to trust me, too. Tell me where this place is?'

He looked sad but he seemed calm enough. Keeping secrets from Adrian felt completely wrong; she hoped she didn't regret this. 'It's called the Guardian Angel. It's a secure private hospital. It's in the Mount Pleasant area. Peel Road. Please don't do anything stupid.'

'To quote the hardest fucking person I know: I can look after myself.'

'You know I always get hurt really badly after I say that, right?'

'I had noticed.'

'Look, there's something you need to know. We were right about the Carters, we were right about all of that shit. We think Dominic gets paid to introduce these people, the people who have an issue that needs solving, and they pay the charity to sort out a problem for them, whatever that problem is. The charity then gets in touch with the homes, and the job is passed down until it gets to the kids, then the kids carry out whatever they're told to. They get paid for it but they are also blackmailed. It's not just about money.'

'Blackmailed how?'

'The kids were taken to paid parties at the Carter house. They were filmed doing all kinds of unspeakable things at these get togethers then told the footage would go public if they stepped out of line.'

'Did you bring the Carters in yet?'

'They're dead. Shot with a 9mm in their homes.'

Adrian's shock was obvious. 'Do you know who did it?'

'From what we know already, there is no shortage of suspects. There may be a recording from their gate camera. And we have picked up Chris Locke who told us there are hidden cameras all over the house – the tech guys are up there now pulling the place apart, trying to find any recordings.'

'Any suspects?'

Imogen nodded, not meeting his eyes. 'We're about to make an arrest.'

There was a roar from the football supporters in the bar around them. Adrian glanced around. 'OK. Look, Grey, you'd better get moving. If I need to speak to you I'll contact Dean.'

'That might not be possible.'

'Why?'

'He's the person we are about to arrest on suspicion of the Carter murders.'

'Fuck. I'm sorry, Grey. Are you OK?'

Imogen avoided his question, blinked hard to stop the tears that threatened to come to the surface. 'Adrian, I miss you. Please don't do anything stupid.'

He nodded. 'I'll be back soon enough.'

Imogen walked out, wondering when she would next see her partner again.

Chapter 73

Dean sat in the interview room waiting patiently. Imogen had asked him to come in and answer some questions. He'd heard the distance in her voice when she'd rung; he knew she was pulling away from him, he had felt it recently. He was pushing and she was letting him, there really was no hope for them. He wondered if she would be the one to interview him. They had sat across from each other in a room like this one before, but that was before they knew each other, before they had fallen in love. She had warned him numerous times, she had told him that she would have to do her job if it came down to it. What she didn't understand about Dean was that he had to do what he had to do, too.

Imogen walked in with DI Fraser and a uniformed officer. She looked angry. DI Fraser set up the tape and Imogen just looked at her hands. Even with a sulk on, she looked beautiful; in fact it brought out the fire in her eyes.

'What's going on?' Dean asked.

'Did you not think we would see the surveillance tapes from the gate at the Carters' house?' Imogen snapped. Her voice was full of disappointment; he wasn't sure if it was him or her she was most disappointed in though.

'Ah.'

'Is that all you have to say? Were you in there when myself and DS Miles came to the house on the twenty-eighth of July?'

'I was upstairs.'

'And you made Felicity Carter get rid of us?'

'I told her if she didn't I would kill her husband.'

Imogen darted a look at the tape. He had promised to always be honest with her but she didn't want him to spend his life in prison because of it.

'Why would you do that?' Imogen asked.

'Because they had something that belonged to me.'

'Belonged to you?'

'Yes.' He sat back and folded his arms.

He could see the veins protruding around his wrists and up to his elbows as he clenched and unclenched his fists.

'What would they have that belonged to you?'

'Pictures, videos.'

'What kind of pictures?' She was pushing him.

'It's kind of annoying that I can't smoke in here. I miss the nineties.' He forced a smile.

'Did you find the pictures?'

'I did.'

He watched as Imogen's eyes took on a glassy sheen, saw her compose herself before speaking again.

'Were the pictures of any criminal acts that may help us in our investigations or lead us to any persons of interest?'

'They were.'

'Could you explain the nature of the criminal acts in the photographs for the tape, please.' She spoke quietly, her voice on the verge of cracking.

'They were images of teenagers and children . . .' He couldn't finish, the words stuck in his throat.

'Are you saying they were pornographic?'

'Yes, that is what I'm saying.'

'Why do these pictures belong to you?'

'I was looking for particular pictures that I knew had been taken. I am in some of those pictures.' He tried not to lose his temper, staying calm would be the best way through this, even though this was the one thing that made him completely irrational. The knowledge that these pictures had been taken.

'You removed the pictures from the Carter residence then?' she said, her voice calm and professional but he saw a tear hovering at the corner of her eye.

'Of course I did.'

'Why would you do that when you knew the police would need them to investigate the Carter family?'

'I knew you were eventually going to get onto them and I wanted to get hold of the images before you did.'

'For what purpose?'

'To destroy them, of course. What other reason would I have than to get rid of that sick shit?'

'I don't know.' She took a deep breath and looked

down. 'There can be a lot of money in the distribution of child pornography.'

Dean felt an anger burn in him at the suggestion she had just made. He flexed his jaw to stop himself from speaking. Did she really think him capable of such things? He felt his stomach turn over at the thought of the images that he'd recovered from the Carter house. Their eyes met across the table and he could see she was sorry, there was a fear in there that reassured him.

'That's not why I removed the pictures.'

'Maybe there are no pictures, maybe you really broke into the Carter house to kill them?'

'So, they're dead?' He smiled, this was the best news he had had all day.

'You're claiming you didn't know?'

'I didn't know, no, but I'm not going to cry about it.'

'Had you met the Carters before?'

'Apparently, although it was a long time ago.'

'Could you describe the nature of your acquaintance with the Carters?'

'I grew up in foster care. When I was younger I was taken to their house, twice. It was full of adults who had either paid for sex with us or to watch us fight. Some other kids went a lot more often; I guess I was lucky.' His voice was sarcastic.

'Were the photos taken at these parties?'

'Apparently, there were hidden cameras in each room. The Carters were inclined to blackmail some of their guests.'

'Did you look through the photos?'

'Only to ascertain they were the ones I was after, I didn't look through them properly, no.'

'You realise that by destroying the pictures you are effectively protecting the people who are committing the indecent acts.'

'It wasn't them I was trying to protect.'

'Yourself?'

'Not just me no, I was trying to protect the kids. Imagine being at the lowest moment in your life, scared out of your mind and forced into situations that no one should ever have to endure. Now imagine someone filmed or photographed it and could watch you in that moment, that hideous moment, whenever they wanted. Imagine someone getting excited watching that, watching your vulnerability and fear and getting off on it. Frozen forever in time.'

'You destroyed the evidence?' DI Fraser asked.

'That was the plan.' Dean had forgotten he was there, his focus had been on Imogen.

'So you haven't yet?' Imogen said.

'I did consider that the police may want the images. I've put them somewhere safe for now. I need to think about it a bit longer.'

'That's withholding evidence and would be a violation of the conditions of your probation,' Imogen said.

'It's something I have no problem going to prison for.'

'If the police can investigate—'

Dean interrupted her. 'Random strangers, even if they are police, are not much better than perverts.'

'I'm trying to be understanding here, Dean.'

'Going to prison is a more appealing thought than having you – or anyone else – see the images.'

'How many images are we talking about?'

'I recovered around twelve memory sticks. Stefan Carter assured me that there were no hard copies available. They had all been scanned in. I have no idea how many images were on those memory sticks but there were almost fifty-six thousand on the one I looked at.'

'How do you know Stefan Carter was telling the truth when he said there were no hard copies?'

Dean smiled. 'Because I know how to make sure people are telling the truth.'

'So, you admit to torturing him?'

'He was quite receptive to threats actually, there wasn't much need for real physical violence.'

'And then you killed them?' DI Fraser chipped in.

'There is no evidence that they were alive after you left. No evidence because the cameras inside the house were disabled as soon as you got there, but I guess you didn't know about the one on the gate?' Imogen clarified.

'As I said, I didn't kill them. And as for the camera on the gate, I just assumed it would run to the same storage device, I turned it off and wiped the hour before I arrived, or at least I thought I did.'

'Where is the bag you took to the house? Was there a gun in it?'

'I don't use guns.'

'We're going to have to hold you until we can verify anything you have said at all.'

'Look, people like the Carters – well let's just say lots of people had a reason to want them dead. Not just the people they hurt, not just the kids they exploited and humiliated, but also the others they blackmailed for money.'

'Interview suspended.' Imogen stormed out of the room.

Dean felt nauseous, lines had been crossed. He had always maintained he would be honest with her if she asked him anything directly and he had been. The hardest thing for him was knowing that she didn't believe him, knowing these things would always be between them. He was going back to prison now anyway, he would have to serve the remaining few months on his sentence for the attack on Stefan Carter that he'd admitted to. Unless of course they never found out what actually happened to the Carters. He hadn't lied about that; he didn't kill them – he hadn't lied about anything. The fear of not being believed was something that Dean feared more than anything, it was the reason he told the truth. He might be evasive and cryptic but he didn't lie.

Chapter 74

It was a few hours until nightfall and so Adrian decided that rather than going back to the flat he would kill time some other way, until he was ready to get on with his plan. With no real inclination to go to the museum or any art galleries, he settled for the cinema. He could barely remember the last time he had seen a movie there; it must have been one of the Batman films with Tom, this time he opted for a sci-fi thriller.

An hour and a half later, film finished, he left the cinema, pulled out his phone and walked towards the football ground in St James Park.

'Andrea?'

'Adrian, what's happening?'

'Are you both OK?'

'A little stir crazy maybe, but we're fine.'

'You haven't contacted anyone, have you?'

'No. I promise I haven't.'

'It will all be over soon. Is Tom there?'

'Dad?' Tom's voice came on the line.

'You guys OK?'

'We're OK, I wish we were back home though.'

'Soon. I'm doing my best. I have to go now, I love you.'

'Love you too Dad, be careful.'

He hung up the phone. At least Tom was safe; as hard as this was, and as bad as he felt about Lucy and what had happened to her, there was a voice in the back of his head that kept reminding him it could be worse. Dominic could have set Adrian up for the murder of his own son, it could have been his child in the boot of that car.

The local football match had just kicked out, so Adrian had plenty of cover as he walked up past St James Park and on to Peel Road in Mount Pleasant. He found the location of the Guardian Angel facility with ease; it was a big house, nicely kept and tucked away. There weren't a whole heap of places for Adrian to hide but he managed to slip into the courtyard and down a passageway to the side of the building. There was a gate through to the garden but it was closed.

Adrian pulled out his phone and texted Imogen: *I'm going inside.*

Quietly Adrian pulled one of the bins over and climbed on top of it, then scaled the rest of the fenced wall with a little more difficulty than he would have liked. He clung to the top of the wall as he tried to control his descent. The wood cut into his hands and he let go, landing on the side of his foot. Ignoring the throbbing, he stood up and moved forward. There was no one in the garden, but when he tried the side door, it opened easily.

Adrian was in a utility room. Even from inside this room, Adrian could feel the calm of the building. He opened the door a crack and peeked outside. There was a large, empty hall with two security guards talking in a whisper at the far end. It was more like a hotel than a hospital, the overall feel of the place was lavish. There were plants and greenery everywhere, and the rich hand-printed wallpaper was also adorned with layers of green ferns. The floor was a dark wood parquet and the furniture coordinated perfectly with both the walls and the paper. It was like the set of a movie, everything perfectly polished and every single detail important. The lamps in the hall were all set to a dim glow, adding to the feeling of tranquillity. He could see the front desk, also dark wood with a plant on the corner. There was a woman at the front desk tapping away on a computer. He watched for a moment and she stood up and walked past the security guards with a notepad tucked under her arm. The security guards were engrossed in their conversation; from their demeanour he guessed they were most likely talking about football, they had that intense, angry focus men get when discussing sports. Adrian stepped out of the utility room and crouched, carefully walking across to a door that led to a staircase, sticking well within the shadows. There was a lift next to the stairs, but at this moment in time, he opted for not being trapped in a steel box.

Having climbed the stairs and checking for any sign of security guards, Adrian discovered the first floor was much the same as the lobby, complete with the wallpaper and plants. So far, there was nothing sinister or disturbing about this place other than the apparent emptiness of it. He noticed there were numbered rooms. Each room had a wooden unit on the wall next to it with a green leather folder poking out of the top. Adrian checked around himself before pulling one out and looking inside. It was the name of the patient in the room along with a constant stream of notes, detailing each visit, each action taken and any communication between staff in the event of shift change.

Adrian checked the other two names on this floor – neither of them was James Shaw. He went to venture down another of the corridors but saw a security guard sitting with a coffee at a desk at the far end. He made his way back to the stairs when he heard some light, quiet laughing, mumbled whispering and then a couple of doors closing before silence descended again. He imagined living or working in a place like this might make him a little crazy. He had never been good with silence.

There were a few more rooms off the central hallway on this floor and a corridor leading to another door. Adrian knew he should check the solitary door first. Just a hunch. He looked at the name inside the green folder and he was right: James Shaw was behind this door. He took a deep breath and opened the door a crack.

'What took you so long?' Dominic said.

Chapter 75

The man Adrian assumed was James Shaw sat in his wheelchair in front of the window. He looked as though he was in his late twenties at the youngest. Glancing around, Adrian saw that the room was decorated as though it belonged to a child, with football posters, a bookcase full of animated DVDs and books aimed at primary school children; clearly, the boy was developmentally delayed. Dominic was sitting and feeding him cereal from a bowl. Adrian watched as James laboured with each mouthful and Dominic wiped the milk as it dribbled down his chin. There was a tenderness about Dominic's actions that Adrian had never seen before.

'What's going on?'

'I knew you would find me, I've been here a while, just waiting. You did a pretty good job of going to ground. I was a little disappointed that you didn't get arrested though, I must admit. The trouble is I know how badly you want to take me down, so waiting was always my plan.'

'Who is this?'

Dominic looked at him. 'This is my son, Jamie.'

'Andrea never mentioned . . .'

'She didn't know.'

Anger sparked inside Adrian. 'Have you lied to her about absolutely everything?'

'She makes it so easy. I didn't realise she was really that stupid.'

'How can you talk about her like that?'

'She never mattered to me, Adrian. Never.'

'So why the hell are you with her?'

'Because you wanted her, Adrian, and I had to stop that.'

'I didn't even know you back then!'

'No, but I knew you. I've known you your whole life.'

'What the hell are you talking about?'

'You've met my son Jamie before, too.'

'I haven't!'

'It's been fun watching you for years, you know. Waiting and hoping for you to fuck things up; after all, we know that genetically speaking you are predisposed to it. You're just so damn resilient, Adrian. Doesn't matter how many times I try and destroy you, you always make it back on top.'

'I don't understand!'

'Your dad, Adrian. I knew him, we used to be neighbours. A long, long time ago. He's the one who did this. He did this to Jamie.' Dominic spoke in a soft, gentle voice as though he were trying to get a child to sleep.

'You knew my dad?'

'He was fucking my wife while you and my son lay asleep in the bed upstairs, except Jamie wasn't sleeping, Adrian, he was suffocating.' Dominic smiled at Jamie as he spooned another mouthful in. The boy seemed oblivious to their conversation, his focus occupied by the cereal.

'What?'

'When they finally got him to hospital they found he had brain damage. They said he might improve with time, but he never did.'

'So, this whole time . . . You and Andrea?'

'You were so easy, the way you pined over her when she ditched you . . . I knew how easy it would be. She was too good for you anyway. You didn't deserve her. I had money by then and she's incredibly shallow. She didn't want to stop you from seeing Tom, but I convinced her it was the right thing to do.'

'To get back at me? For what?'

'Look at you. My perfect son is ruined and you get to swan around doing whatever you like. It should have been you and not him. You should be the one in here.'

Adrian stared at him, his mind racing. 'You can't honestly blame me for that? I was a baby!'

'I thought destroying your father would be enough for me, but Charlie was so weak; you really do have more about you than him.'

'He was an addict.'

'Not when I knew him. Sure, he liked a drink or

two but nothing stronger. The guilt of what happened to Jamie really did a number on him though. Your mother just let him ruin her along with him. I tried to get her to cheat on him, but she wouldn't do it, not even after I told her what he had done. Why my Jamie was like this. She forgave him, just like that. But I lost my wife, she took her own life. Not that I would have ever forgiven her. Charlie was miserable and drinking all the time but it wasn't enough for me, I wanted him to suffer, I wanted him to lose everything, and so I made sure he was in a position to do that. I made sure he became an addict.'

'This is insane, you are insane!'

'Watching you grow up was torture. You miraculously made it through school, even despite your useless parents, then meeting Andrea, having Tom. Tom was the decider; and I knew what I had to do. I would go into the department store where Andrea works, and spend lots of money on make-up for my imaginary mother, the most expensive stuff she had. Her head was easily turned.'

'What do you mean, turned?'

'It took a long time, to her credit. One day my poor fake mother died and I asked Andrea if she would accompany me to lunch at the best restaurant in town. I suggested she meet me each week for lunch on the day I would normally dine with mum. At the beginning, she did it because she felt sorry for me but after a while I think she saw that the life you were going to give her would never amount to much. Money softened her heart.'

'You mean you were seeing her when we were still together?'

Dominic smiled. 'I'm the reason she left you. I'm the reason you had to work late all those nights and left her in the lurch. I knew people in the police even back then. I made sure you neglected her. That was the end of your relationship. She detached herself completely from you and then it was so easy to unravel what was left. She felt so guilty but I made her realise it was you, you were the problem.'

Adrian clenched his fists. 'What about Lucy? Why did you kill her?'

'She was here, she found Jamie. The walls were closing in. I wasn't quite ready to let go of you just yet. Lucy was a new way to hurt you, two birds with one stone. I made sure I told her it was purely because of you just before I sliced her throat, that she had picked the wrong person to align herself with.'

'You didn't have to kill her,' Adrian said through gritted teeth. 'There's no way you'll get away with that.'

'Don't you see? It's not about me, it's all about you, what you've taken from Jamie. Jamie's condition is getting worse and I'm not getting any younger. I couldn't have you being happy again. I just couldn't. If he doesn't get to have a life, then you don't either.' He brushed Jamie's hair back. Jamie's face remained unmoved.

'I should kill you.'

'Then I win, your life will be over. Either way I win.' He smirked. 'I know you like to skate on the thin ice, Adrian, that's why you're here. That's why, rather predictably – you ran when they discovered Lucy's body.

You're all alone. All I have to do is call to the police and they'll come and arrest you for Lucy's murder. Game over.'

'Were the Carters part of your payback plan? What were you thinking there?'

'They were always weak, they were going to try and cut a deal. They had already handed a load of evidence over to that Kinkaid character. They tried to book a private plane from the airfield, but I know a man there, he told me and I put the rest together myself. When I got to their house, Stefan was a bloody mess and Felicity was her usual scheming self. So I shot them.'

'Their operation will be shut down completely,' Adrian said. 'All those people who were presumably involved with you will be looking to make deals. You're never getting out of prison. The police have recovered all of their files.' He was lying now, making things up. 'Once the investigation into you is in full swing there will be nowhere to hide.'

'I only do business with people I can blackmail.' Dominic clutched at his side, he seemed to be in discomfort.

'There's one thing you were wrong about though, Dominic. I didn't run.'

Adrian pulled his phone out of his pocket and showed it to Dominic. The line was open. Just before entering the room, he had called his boss DCI Mira Kapoor, knowing full well she would get Gary to trace the call.

Dominic's face was impossible to read. 'How did you know I would tell you anything?'

'Because you're an egomaniac. You jumped at the

chance to tell me things last time as well. You think you're so fucking clever and that's your weakness. You just needed a chance to gloat.'

Adrian heard the sirens, the sound of voices and footsteps, all the while watching as Dominic wheeled his son over to the bed and lifted him inside. He pulled the blanket over him and stroked his forehead. He sang a lullaby in a low whisper and then stood up as the voices got closer. It was a moving scene. Adrian couldn't imagine how he would feel if Jamie were his son, knowing what his quality of life was – trapped inside this room, trapped inside his own body.

'You're too late anyway, Adrian,' he said. 'As usual, you really aren't very clever.'

'Too late?' Adrian didn't understand. 'What do you mean?'

Dominic picked up a pill bottle and tossed it to Adrian, the movement causing him to wince. It was morphine.

'I crushed half of them up and put them in Jamie's cereal, the rest I took myself.'

'You slippery fucker.' Adrian should have known that Dominic couldn't stand to lose, in his mind this was still a win, and maybe he was right. He was robbing Adrian of the chance for retribution. He rushed over to the bed and smashed his hand against the red button repeatedly, maybe the nurses could save them in time. 'You're not going out like this!'

'You're too late!' Dominic smiled.

The door opened, DCI Kapoor and DI Fraser came in. Fraser immediately grabbed Adrian's arm, leading him out of the room. Adrian's first instinct was to struggle; he wanted to see Dominic go down, but Fraser gripped him tightly, only releasing him once they were in the hall. Adrian was breathing heavily.

'You OK?' Fraser asked.

Adrian looked down the corridor, trying to find his partner. If anyone could calm him down, it was her.

'Where's Grey?'

'Back at the station, trying to sort this mess out. Gary is going through everything with her. The DCI says you aren't allowed near it.'

Paramedics rushed past them, into Jamie's room. Adrian's every instinct was telling him to go back inside, but he forced himself to stay put, knowing it would make things worse.

As though reading his thoughts, DCI Kapoor came out into the corridor. Her face was flushed.

'We'll deal with him now. You go get your family and go home and rest. We can debrief in the morning.'

Adrian could hardly believe it was over. He had been so tense for so long.

'That's an order, Miles. Go home.' The DCI paused for a second. 'I'm sorry about Lucy,' she said, more softly, then turned her back on him and re-entered Jamie's room, closing the door behind her.

Lucy. The mention of her name was like a bullet to his chest. He felt the burn of grief trying to make its way to the surface. *Not yet*, he thought, *just let me get home first*.

Chapter 76

Imogen had her arms crossed and was staring at Gary, who had two phones laid out in front of him. One belonged to Dominic Shaw; the other to Chris Locke.

'So, what did you find?' Imogen asked. She could see that he was full of information, he always had a funny look about him when he had found out 'new stuff'.

'First off: Chris Locke's phone.'

'Yep?'

'He had some deleted files that I managed to retrieve. Including the murder of the real Henry Armstrong. It's brutal. He's with a person we have identified as Trey Wilson and his brother Asher Locke. The video was taken at the beginning of June, a few weeks before the fire. We also found the original footage of the Wallis murder, but there doesn't seem to be any indication of who the third person in the Wallis murder is. As Asher Locke was already in jail at this point, we're kind of stumped. We'll need to keep investigating this.'

'Is it time-stamped?'

'Yes. And it pre-dates the twenty-sixth of June, the night of the fire. This is the only positive thing about camera phones as far as I'm concerned. People record anything that's interesting, even if it could get them in trouble.'

'Yeah well, people are stupid.'

'I mean, even if you delete things, they're usually still somewhere. Most people don't even know if they have a cloud account attached to their devices or not. Chris Locke certainly wasn't the sharpest tool in the box. He barely even deleted things, he just moved them into a different folder.'

'Now what about Adrian?'

'The confession on the recording we have from Adrian's phone is good, it's more than likely enough. But add to that the fact that we have the contacts in his phone and so many of them match up with names from the Carter files . . .'

'You have the Carter files? Dean gave them up?' She had to admit that she was glad Dominic had confessed to the murder at the Carter house, Dean's story was completely corroborated. Although Dean went outside the law and could have killed them, he held back when it mattered. Part of her wondered if that was because of her.

'He did.'

'Where are they?'

'One of his stipulations was that you not be allowed to see them.'

'What?'

'Don't ask me, take it up with the DCI!'

'Right.' She wanted to see Dean in that moment and make sure he was all right, but given how the interview had gone she wondered if she had the right to do that anymore.

'The DCI has promised that only a small handful of police officers will be granted access at this time, and Dean has offered to help identify people in the pictures where he can.'

'In exchange for what?'

'Seeing as Dominic confessed to killing the Carters, charging Dean for assault against Stefan Carter seems kind of pointless, especially when he can help in the enquiries.'

'So, he's free?'

'They let him go a little while ago.'

'OK.' She couldn't think about that right now. 'Adrian?'

'He's gone with Fraser to go get Andrea and Tom.'

'And Dominic?'

'Chained to a bed at the hospital, the doc said he won't last the night. Tomorrow is going to be a bureaucratic nightmare. The DCI wants you to meet her at the prison, she's in a meeting with someone from the Innocence Project right now. She doesn't want Gabriel Webb to spend another night in there. They are just getting him out now. If you hurry you might make it.'

She left the security of Gary's office lab and went to her desk to pick up her things. Her head was spinning. Tomorrow, she would be back at work and everything would be back to normal. What *was* normal, anyway?

Chapter 77

Everything had changed since Asher was gone – since Gabriel had disposed of him. Gabriel wasn't sure if it was his imagination but there was a definite sense of calm about the prison that hadn't been there before. Johnson and Hyde had been the ones to discover Asher's body, at least that's what they told the warden. The other guards had all banded together and supported Johnson's version of events, the version that said he was with them, dealing with the fire. Asher's death was ruled a suicide by asphyxiation, his bruises ignored. The truth was, most people were happy to see the back of Asher, especially the people running the place. For a little while at least, there would a bit more order on the wing.

After the hubbub of everyone returning to their cells following roll call, Gabriel pulled on the jumper that Bailey's mother had knitted. Bailey had made her promise that it would be completely black, knowing that Gabriel was more likely to wear it if it were. It was a great comfort to him, even though he was rarely cold; it made him feel safe. Sol and Bailey were the only people aside from Johnson who knew what Gabriel had done and none of them would speak against him.

'Webb?' Barratt's voice was outside the door. 'Get your things.'

'Excuse me?' Gabriel slowed his breathing down and swallowed hard. Had they figured out what he'd done to Asher?

'You're being released. The charges against you have been dropped.'

'That's amazing!' Bailey shouted, jumping up and hugging Gabriel who still couldn't believe what he had heard.

'A judge commuted your sentence this morning. It's official, you're innocent.'

'How?'

Gabriel's head was spinning. He had resigned himself to staying here. It didn't feel right to leave now, not after everything that had happened.

'I don't know, that is literally all of the information I have.' Barratt shrugged.

Gabriel was stunned. 'Can I say goodbye first?'

Barratt handed Gabriel a carrier bag and he started to fill it. Why had no one warned him this might happen? He was completely taken off guard. Suddenly, the world was opening up again and it was terrifying. He held a black T-shirt in his hands that had an ace of spades on it; he knew that Bailey liked it and so he held it out to him.

'I can't take that.'

'It's only fair, in return for the jumper. You can keep my books and stuff too if you want, or trade them for something better. Keep the radio, as well.'

Gabriel threw his arms around Bailey and hugged him hard. It was the first time he had allowed himself to be emotional in any way. He would miss Bailey.

'Bye Gabe.'

'Bye Bailey, put me on your visitors list, I will come and visit you as soon as I can. And say goodbye to the boys for me.'

'I will.'

'Come on now, let's get going,' Barratt said.

Gabriel followed Barratt out of the cell holding all his possessions in an ironically titled Bag for Life and traced his way through the wing until they reached the door Gabriel had come in through what felt like a lifetime ago. He was someone else now. Did his parents know he had been proven innocent? Did they even care? He wasn't sure where he would go, he didn't feel as though he had a home to go back to. Maybe a friend would put him up for the night – but he wasn't even sure who his friends were anymore.

As he went through the series of locked doors that he hadn't thought he would ever go through again, he feared what lay on the other side. As lock after lock opened and closed, Gabriel couldn't tell whether he was afraid or excited. Before he knew it, he was standing outside, the prison door closed behind him, with a carrier bag full of stuff he no longer wanted and his inhaler. He looked up ahead and saw DS Imogen Grey standing with her arms folded.

'Can I give you a lift anywhere?' She smiled at him.

'Imogen,' he said, squinting and tucking his hair behind his ears. 'I'm good thanks. I might walk.'

'Have you got money?'

'They gave me some cash.'

'Here, wait.' She grabbed her bag and rummaged for some money, thirty pounds.

'I can't take your money.'

'Please, you will be doing me a favour, I feel bad for what you had to go through.'

'It's not your fault.'

'Look after yourself, Gabriel.'

'Thanks for looking out for me. It meant a lot.' He smiled at her, feeling guilty that he had let her down even though she had no idea what he had done.

'You were worth looking out for.'

'Well, no offence but, I hope I never see you again.'

'The feeling is mutual.' She smiled again and got into her car. He watched as she pulled away. He walked down the ramp and onto the road where it all started, he was equidistant between the signal box and the prison now. He wouldn't look though. That part of his life was over. He would never colour outside the lines again. Within the space of a couple of hours the world had opened to him again, and he wouldn't mess it up this time.

Chapter 78

Imogen walked along the embankment, trying to clear her head. She sometimes came running down here but she wasn't in the mood to run right now, she was exhausted. The case was over, and her relationship was most likely over too, after what she had said to Dean. At least she had Adrian, he had been cleared from any involvement after Dominic's confession. She was grateful that she had never doubted him at least. She was angry at herself for the way she had spoken to Dean, angry that she had abused his trust like that. Who was she? She walked back to her car to find Dean leaning against the bonnet.

'How did you find me?'

'Disappointed to see me?'

She unlocked the car. 'Get in.'

They drove for a while in silence but Imogen couldn't keep her mouth closed. It just wasn't in her nature.

'What do we do now?'

'You can drop me at the train station if you want.'

'If I want?' she said, a little louder than she had intended.

Silence fell in the car again; she could hear Dean preparing to speak and then stopping himself. Maybe the damage was too much. Maybe she had ruined everything.

'It's hard to know where I stand,' Dean said.

'You stand where you have always stood. In between me and my job.'

'That's not fair, Imogen.'

'I feel like we've crossed a line. I genuinely don't know what to do.'

'What do you want to do?'

'I want to keep my job, but I don't know how to do that and be with you.'

'Why don't you ask me?'

Imogen frowned. 'Ask you what?'

'How many people I've killed. That's what you want to know, isn't it?'

She kept her eyes on the road.

'I've killed three people. That's it.'

She snapped at him, sarcastic. 'Oh, is that all? Why would you tell me that?'

'You already think I distribute child pornography.'

'I never said that.'

'That's exactly what you said. Is killing people better or worse than that do you think?'

The car swerved slightly and she straightened her hands on the wheel.

'Why don't you ask me why I killed them?'

'Because I don't want to know any more about it,'

she said. Knowing about crimes he had been punished for was one thing, she could pretend to herself that he was just misunderstood, that his reputation was exaggerated. But this? This was too much.

'I killed the first one for killing Jess. I killed the second one for raping me and I killed the third one for hurting you.'

'Me?' she said, his words cutting through her.

'Yes, you.'

He pulled a memory stick out of his pocket and held it in his hand.

'What's that?'

'That day when we were in my house, when we were attacked, when that animal put his hands on you and made me watch. I had cameras set up, they recorded everything that happened. This is the only recording of what took place in that room, of what he did to you. The only evidence of what happened is on this thumb drive. Would you want me to give it to the police?'

Imogen's heart was racing, she took her eyes off the road for a second and stared at the drive in his hand. *Vasos. The reason she'd ended up in hospital on their last case.* The memory of the attack made her feel sick. 'No.'

'Even if it meant the man who did it to you might get away with it?'

'Even then.'

'Then what do I do with that man? Do I just let him continue, knowing that he's touched you against your will? Knowing that he wouldn't hesitate before doing it to someone else?'

'You can't kill everyone who wrongs you, Dean. Or who wrongs me.'

'No, and I want to do better, which is why I gave the police the files from the Carter house. Even though it kills me, the idea of you seeing those pictures of me kills me even more.'

'But Dean, you saw me get hurt, you were there. We've both seen each other in terrible situations. What that man did to you wasn't your fault. I would never hold it against you. Do you think badly of me for what happened to me?'

'No. But sometimes I don't sleep because of it.'

Imogen stared straight ahead and tried to calm her thoughts. She couldn't take much more of this, not because she hated him for it but because she understood, and worse, she thought he might be right. She knew that not everything could be solved by a stint in a prison cell. Some people were unfixable; some people were evil. Maybe Dean was the solution for all that. Maybe she just needed to sleep.

'So, what happens now? Are we done? Have I confirmed everything you thought about me?'

She took a deep breath. 'Dean, what happened to you when you were a child must have been . . .'

He held up a hand. 'Don't. Don't blame what happened to me. I'm an adult. I made my choices.'

'And I make mine.' She felt her stomach twist. 'And, God help me, I really don't care what you've done.'

'But you do,' he argued.

She shook her head. 'Meeting you has made me realise something about my job, and that's that sometimes, hurting people is justified. What I care about is the fact that you're changing me. I'm scared to be the person that I am with you. I'm scared of losing myself.'

'Then don't be with me.'

'I can't just stop feeling. Can you?'

He looked down at his lap. 'Probably, yes. I'm pretty well-trained in blocking things out.'

'I don't want you to.' She started to cry, the weight of the situation finally hitting her. She wanted someone to be there for her; from the moment she had met Dean he'd been the one she turned to and now she might have ruined that. He made her feel so vulnerable and she didn't know why – was it because she had always looked after herself and been so strong that the idea of him as a saviour was so appealing? Maybe that was just too much to ask of him. She wiped her nose on her sleeve and tried to focus on the road, scared that her blurry eyes would cause an accident. 'I'm sorry. It's been a long week.'

'You're telling me.'

She put her hand on the gearstick and he placed his hand on top of hers, stroking her reassuringly with his thumb. She didn't know what to do now. She was afraid to speak, afraid of the next thing to come out of her mouth. She drove straight past the train station and back towards her place. Dean must have noticed because his hand travelled up her forearm, gently gliding up again to her shoulders and then the nape of her neck, playfully wrapping her hair around his fingers. She parked the car and leant over to kiss him, tasting her own salty tears on his lips as he kissed her.

Inside, they took off their coats and she buried her face in his chest as he embraced her. She couldn't make this decision tonight, tonight she wanted to be held and to feel safe. She hoped that they would be able to find their way back from this. With any luck, he wanted the same.

Tomorrow, when she had to get up for work again she would consider all the options. It really was down to Dean or the job, and right now she wasn't sure which one she loved more. Maybe it was because he was forbidden fruit, maybe that's what was making this so impossible to let go. She was drawn to relationships that she wasn't allowed to pursue. Self-sabotage, falling in love with a killer. Wonderful. Great job, Imogen.

Chapter 79

Adrian was at home. The last time he had seen Lucy alive she had been leaving his house, he felt her presence here weighing down on him. He hadn't changed the sheets since she had slept in them and all he wanted to do was climb in bed and fall asleep to the trace scent of her shampoo on his pillow. It felt strange to be there as the place was still a mess from when the police had searched it. Still, the search must have been somewhat restrained because all his limited-edition toy boxes were still intact; he had forgotten about them in all the chaos. He didn't really care about anything in his house anymore. They had impounded his car and to be honest he didn't want it back, he couldn't imagine ever driving it again. For now, they had let him use one of the pool cars. The DCI had been very accommodating so far, letting him take the time to help Tom and Andrea, letting him find Dominic rather than immediately bringing him in over Lucy's murder. He would be forever grateful for her lenience. Maybe it was for his benefit, or maybe it was because she was trying to limit the bad press, either way, it seemed as though he was off the hook for now. Adrian's phone rang. It was Imogen.

'Hey.'

'Hey. Where are you?'

'I'm sitting outside the cathedral.'

'At this time in the morning?'

'It's almost six a.m., Grandad.' He could almost hear her smiling down the phone.

'I heard about Gabriel Webb,' he said. 'How are you doing?'

'I don't know yet. How are Andrea and Tom?'

'Upstairs, asleep.'

'Both of them?'

'Yep, Andrea didn't want to go back to her place. She's got Tom's bed and he's on the floor. We got the call that Dominic died about an hour ago. She's still reeling. So am I.' He wasn't lying, he had been fuelled by his investigation into Dominic for months, using every spare moment to try and figure him out but now it was really over and he was bereft, it was done. Adrian sat on the sofa and plumped up the cushions. Leaning back and relaxing for the first time in what felt like months.

'I don't blame her.'

'Dean?'

'He's at my place, waiting on me I think. Or he might've left by now, I really don't know. We brought him in for questioning and I was pretty tough on him.'

'I heard.'

'Gary?'

'Yep.'

They fell into silence, he could hear her smoking on the other end of the line, inhaling deeply with a tiny sigh in each breath, as though she were casting her worries out.

'I'm sorry about Lucy. I know I said it before, but I mean it. You mustn't blame yourself, Adrian.'

He couldn't respond, his voice wouldn't come as his body worked overtime to make sure he didn't cry, his throat constricted with the restraint. It was too late though, he felt the tears sliding down his cheeks onto the back of the sofa. He let out a frustrated grunt and stood up, wiping the wetness from his cheeks and ears. Pulling himself together.

'I don't much fancy being alone right now. Can I come and hang out with you, Grey?'

'I'd like that.'

'I'll be there in ten minutes.'

Adrian went upstairs and gently opened the door to Tom's room. Andrea and Tom were both sleeping soundly and so he closed the door again. He put a note on the table for when they woke up. As he put the keys in the pool car door, he noticed the dark spot on the road. They had tried to clean it but Lucy's blood had left a stain. He had to get away from this place and be with his partner. They would get through this; they had got through enough before.

He made his way to the cathedral just so he wouldn't feel alone. Or at the very least, so that they could feel alone together. He walked over to the segment of wall where Imogen was sitting and sat next to her; funny that she should pick this place, the place that reminded him of Lucy the most. They huddled close together in the cold morning air. She held her hand out and he intertwined his fingers with hers as they sat in silence looking up at the cathedral framed against the black sky, waiting for the night to pass, waiting to see what tomorrow would bring.

Acknowledgements

I would like to thank Avon for their continued support and overall loveliness. A special thanks to Phoebe Morgan for being a kickass editor.

Thanks as well to my agents Diane Banks and Kate Burke and all at Diane Banks Associates for looking after me so well.

A super huge thanks to all the amazing people online who have been supportive and encouraging, especially the book bloggers who are invaluable. I love to get tweets and messages from people who have enjoyed the stories and I try to respond to everyone.

A special thanks to Jeremy Fewster for his role as consigliere.

Thanks to everyone who leaves Amazon reviews, I really do read all of them. It's really important to leave reviews for authors as it helps with the magical mystical algorithms that I don't understand.

Over the last year I have met a lot of writers and I

can honestly say you will never meet a bunch of nicer people than crime writers, I have been well and truly welcomed into the fold. So generous with support and help, a very magnanimous lot. You know who you are.

I would like to thank my friend Rebekah Sunshine, one day we will make the Sunshine & Diamond Detective Agency a reality. We will need a moped with a sidecar for me (as that is how sidekicks travel). Also, sorry for forgetting to acknowledge you exist before.

Thanks as well to Anna Caravan for organising me and accepting a dishwasher as payment.

Thank you to all my other friends who have bought my books or just listened to me complain a lot.

Thank you to my enormous family, both near and far. And finally thank you to my husband and children for not being alarmed when they find one of my hand-scrawled notes on how to kill people and get away with it.

Everything you *think* you know is a lie . . .

The Queen of Crime returns in her second Miles and Grey novel.

Looking for your next obsession?
Look no further . . .

A shocking psychological thriller where love affairs turn deadly.

You can only run from the past for so long . . .

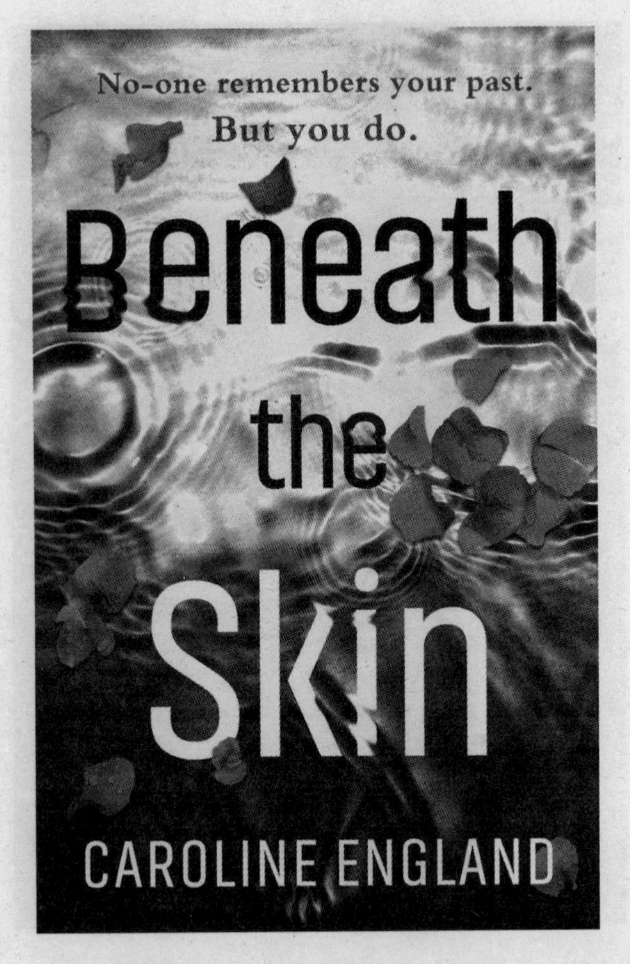

It will always catch up to you.